PENGUIN BOOKS

Angel in the Shadows

Walter Lucius is the pseudonym of screenwriter, director and producer Walter Goverde. Walter used to be a stage director, and has produced dramas, documentaries and various television series as well. He has also founded Odyssee Producties, an audio-visual company with which he has carried out several projects for a number of Dutch government ministries.

Angel in the Shadows is the second instalment of the Heartland trilogy, following *Butterfly on the Storm*. Walter lives in Amsterdam where he is currently completing the final book in the series.

Angel in the Shadows

The Heartland Trilogy

Part 2

WALTER LUCIUS

Translated from the Dutch by
Lorraine T. Miller and Laura Vroomen

PENGUIN BOOKS

PENGUIN BOOKS

UK | USA | Canada | Ireland | Australia
India | New Zealand | South Africa

Penguin Books is part of the Penguin Random House group of companies
whose addresses can be found at global.penguinrandomhouse.com.

Penguin
Random House
UK

First published in the Netherlands as *Schaduwvechters* by Luitingh Sijthoff, 2016
First published in Great Britain by Michael Joseph, 2018
Published in Penguin Books 2018

001

Copyright © Walter Lucius, 2016

The moral right of the author has been asserted

Typeset by Jouve (UK), Milton Keynes
Printed and bound in Great Britain by Clays Ltd, Elcograf S.p.A.

A CIP catalogue record for this book is available from the British Library

ISBN: 978–1–405–92143–5

For Anny – everything at the end of the rainbow

Every act of enlightenment
– all ambitions to save souls,
all the basic impulses – is so dogged
by the weight of what follows it,
the shadows, the violence that has
accompanied the Enlightenment.

– William Kentridge

If men were angels, no government
would be necessary.

– James Madison, *The Federalist*, Feb. 6, 1788

PART ONE
Attack

I

She could see her reflection in the lens of the digital camcorder. Standing behind it was the bald man with the vulture eyes who looked like a condor. He'd flung her into the boot of the armoured Falcon four-wheel drive and driven into central Moscow. Once there, he dragged her down long, empty corridors, like a hunk of meat. The few words he bothered to utter were in English, with that thick Slavic accent so typical of Russians. He spoke gruffly, barking commands. His movements were hurried and stiff, mirroring the cold-blooded expression on his face. The only sign of weakness was his panting. Every so often he sucked on an inhaler.

In a tiled room with blacked-out windows, he'd tied her to a chair in front of the camcorder. A man dressed in camouflage gear entered. He was holding a Kalashnikov and wearing two ammunition belts as well as a holster containing a powerful gun. From the way he talked to the condor, she figured the two must know each other well.

A woman in a black robe and a headscarf was filming everything on her mobile. With her pale skin and blue eyes, she looked quite striking. The man in the fatigues barked something at her, after which she disappeared and reappeared again seconds later, shoving a girl of barely twenty ahead of her. He took the girl and forced her to kneel down beside the condor, who switched the camcorder on and, without looking at the girl, casually pressed the barrel of his Zastava against her temple.

The girl begged for her life. Her mutterings in Russian

sounded like a whispered prayer. The condor took no notice of her. He had eyes only for the woman handcuffed to the chair opposite him. His tattooed finger pointed to the lens.

'Look at this!'

Farah Hafez raised her head and stared into the camcorder's reflective black hole.

'Now say what I want you to say, bitch. And do it convincingly. You can save this girl's life.'

'What do you want me to say?' Farah murmured.

'Repeat after me.' Farah listened to the words he'd prepared for her, words that were not hers, words that would never even occur to her. She moved her lips in an effort to repeat them. The girl mustn't die.

Her vocal cords barely vibrated, and the lines came out as little more than a sigh. The condor cocked his Zastava. The camcorder's red light flickered. The girl flinched.

That's when the words came. Unexpected and forceful. Like vomit.

'I, Farah Hafez, support the jihad against President Potanin's criminal regime.'

The condor smiled coldly and pulled the trigger anyway.

The Zastava's dry click betrayed an absent bullet. When the girl fainted, the pungent stench of urine filled the air.

Farah swore at the man, yelled at him in Dari that his mother was worse than a whore – she'd done it with dogs and *he* was the spawn of that coupling.

The condor charged at her like he'd lost control. Despite being tied up, she kicked him as hard as she could in the shins. When she tried to avoid his next charge, she fell over, chair and all. Undeterred, he grabbed her by the hair and dragged her, still bound to the chair, out of the room and down a corridor to an auditorium, where a large group of

4

young men and women had been herded together and were being held at gunpoint by a woman in black.

She was still handcuffed to the chair, and now he stuffed a piece of cloth into her mouth and taped her lips shut – she could hardly breathe. Then he picked up a small, flat, metallic box, connected to a laptop with wires, and strapped it to her chest.

He stood before her, sweating profusely and sucking hard on his inhaler.

'You're going to go out with a bang, you bitch.' Somehow he reminded her of a giant bubble about to burst. He marched away.

2

The red-hot ash rain and thick, grimy smoke drifting across the road from the woods prevented the armoured Falcon from speeding ahead, allowing journalist Paul Chapelle and his Russian colleague Anya Kozlova to shadow it in their Škoda. They drove in the direction of the Seven Sisters, their destination the Moscow State University's Mass Media Centre, where hundreds of students were being held hostage by Chechen rebels. A few hundred metres from the besieged building a ring of Russian Army tanks and trucks had hermetically sealed off the complex.

Paul and Anya were amazed that the Falcon, after a brief stop, was allowed on to the grounds.

The crisis centre was in complete chaos. No one could tell them what had happened, how many people were involved or what was going on inside.

Outside, next to a waiting ambulance, Anya spoke in hushed tones for a few minutes with two paramedics. Paul watched from a distance. Her persuasive body language was all too familiar: in the end, she got the men to hand over two white doctors' coats and a handful of medical supplies. Paul saw her slip them a few rouble notes.

Dressed in medical garb and claiming some of the hostages needed immediate medical attention, they were allowed through the line of infantry surrounding the building where Anya herself had once studied and later taught. They had no problems entering the premises through a basement door, where they quickly dumped their white coats. Anya pulled out her press card and shoved the Nikon into Paul's hands.

'*Zhurnalisty!*' she called as they made their way down a dark corridor. Within seconds they were surrounded by three women wearing black headscarves and brandishing Kalashnikovs.

'Anya Kozlova, *Moskva Gazeta*. I'm here for Chalim Barchayev. He knows me. I've interviewed him before.'

The women planted the barrels of their rifles in Paul's and Anya's backs and led them to the canteen. It had been transformed into a command centre.

Barchayev's brooding presence, Paul thought, made him look like Che Guevara reborn. He hugged Anya as if she were one of his girls. She was bluffing. He could hear it in her voice. But that didn't stop her from chatting to him like an old friend. She wanted to report on the hostage-taking: to tell the world his side of the story. She asked if it was okay for her photographer to take some pictures.

In the auditorium, facing a large black flag inscribed with an Arabic text, Paul saw her. She was handcuffed to a rickety chair, sweating and trembling all over, a wide piece of tape across her mouth. A green metallic-looking box with the words FRONT TOWARDS ENEMY was strapped to her chest. Paul recognized the military explosive. It was filled with hundreds of steel balls designed to make just as many bloody wounds in the young bodies of the hostages. Two wires were connected to a laptop that showed a digital clock counting down.

It was as if he could feel her breathing, hear her heart pounding, faster and faster, just like his.

One of the black widows kept a close watch on him through the sight of her Kalashnikov. He tried to avoid any indication that he recognized her.

He brought the camera to his eye and slowly clicked . . . click, click.

Farah opened her eyes wide. It looked like she was out of her mind with fear.

Fear.

That was the last word that crossed Paul's mind before a bash to the back of his head stopped time and snuffed out the light.

3

The heat was oppressive, and Farah was trembling all over. She'd stopped smelling the stench of urine, shit and cold sweat, and her limbs had become numb.

For a moment, she thought she was hallucinating.

Paul was standing before her: his tall frame; his longish, dark-blond hair more unkempt than ever; the distinctive square jaw that made him the spitting image of his father; those ice-blue eyes staring at her.

But she wasn't imagining things.

The fear in his unshaven face, which was covered with scars, stitches and plasters, was very real. He was holding a camera, pretending not to know her. And, although her head felt like it was filled with blood-soaked cotton-wool, she got it.

They weren't *supposed* to know each other.

Then she saw what was happening behind him. She opened her eyes wide, as wide as possible. It was the only way she could warn him. Although the gag in her mouth stopped her from producing a sound, inside she was screaming.

Turn around, turn around!

But he didn't get it and came closer, snapping away with his camera.

The butt of a Kalashnikov slammed the back of his head and he crumpled to the floor.

The condor looked almost winded as he regarded his latest victim, sucked up some more oxygen and then dragged Paul out of the room by his legs.

Not long after, a dull explosion could be heard from another part of the building. Shouting. A flare was shot into the auditorium and commandos charged in. Russian special forces commandos: the Alpha Spetsnaz. Muffled shots rang out, sounding like a series of champagne bottles being uncorked, as all the women in black received a bullet to the head.

Seeing this, Farah lost consciousness.

Paul's voice brought her to again. But he was standing behind her, so she couldn't see him. She was still tied to the chair. When he removed the piece of tape and pulled the gag out of her mouth, she retched. All this time, she could hear his voice – snippets of sentences that would stay with her forever.

Do you know how that feels? Listen to me, it feels brilliant. It feels amazingly brilliant! We're going to be okay, you hear me, you and I.

She felt his breath as he leaned over her, and drops of blood as thick as melting wax dripped on to her shoulder. He'd tell her later that it was blood mixed with bits of skin – the condor's, to be precise. While he was talking to her, three commandos were trying to defuse the explosive attached to her body. Behind them, the man in fatigues came into view. He emerged from a cloud of dust, wailing like a wounded animal, his Kalashnikov aimed at the commandos. Bullets from the machine gun of an Alpha Spetsnaz commando riddled his body.

Farah looked into the solemn eyes of the commando leader who'd carried on defusing the bomb strapped against her chest.

'Front towards enemy,' he said in broken English, pointing to the text on the metallic box. 'You no enemy.' He smiled. 'You free.' With that, he removed the box, no longer wired up to the laptop.

She rose unsteadily to her feet and wrapped her arms around his neck, kissing him on the cheeks and thanking him. He gave her a hug and laughed in her ear – a resonant, masculine laugh.

She floated back down the same long corridors towards the exit.

A tiny, fragile bird in Paul's arms.

Outside, she was blinded by floodlights. Male voices were asking questions in Russian that were answered by a woman. Anya – the name came back to her now. She was the *Moskva Gazeta* journalist.

Then she heard Paul's voice again, talking to her calmly. 'You're safe. I'm with you.'

Those were the same words she'd spoken to the boy injured in the hit-and-run in Amsterdam barely two weeks ago. Now she realized that talking like this to someone in shock actually helped. She was lifted into an ambulance.

'Where are we going?'

'A hospital. I want to be sure you're okay.'

Inside the Casualty Department of Hospital Number 5, the paint at the bottom of the walls and doors was peeling and the gurney's squeaky wheels scraped across grimy linoleum. Farah saw Anya handing the doctor a bunch of rouble notes while whispering to him.

'He hasn't actually done anything yet,' Farah muttered.

'This is a way of thanking him in advance,' Anya assured her.

Farah's lungs were checked by a skinny doctor with a long nose and a face as drab and blotchy as his soiled white coat. It was like being examined by the spectre of death. Number 5 was known as one of the better hospitals in Moscow. But, however decent it was, it was always better to stay clear of any hospital at all when in Russia. There were more humane ways of kicking the bucket.

When the room began to spin, she asked Paul to take her hand. As he did so, she felt a needle enter her arm. Doctor Death explained that everything was fine. The injection had merely been to calm her nerves.

All went quiet inside and darkness descended around her.

4

After leaving the hospital, they navigated through what, to Paul, remained an impenetrable web of streets and made their way towards Zamoskvorechye, the old commercial district south of the River Moskva. Sirens could be heard in the distance: police cars, ambulances, fire engines. There were helicopters in the sweltering night sky. The entire city was wrought with chaos.

Given the possibility of checkpoints, Anya avoided the busier streets. Finally, she parked the Škoda beside a sparsely lit stretch of river bank, right by the entrance to an old block of flats. The hazy conditions provided some cover. They got Farah out of the car, hoisted her in between them to make it look like she'd had a few too many, and carried her into the lobby.

Paul thought there was a risk the ancient lift would get stuck halfway, so he carried Farah up eight flights of stairs, all the way to the old building's rafters, where Anya's attic apartment was located. They lay her down on the bed, closed the curtains, which felt thick enough to stop bullets, and let her sleep.

'Her breathing's irregular,' Anya said.

She and Paul sat down to eat borscht and dark rye bread, washed down with wine, and switched on the television. Channel-hopping between the likes of Rossiya, NTV and Channel One, they saw on-the-scene reporters and news-readers behind their studio desks, all giving them the latest updates about the hostage-taking in the university's media centre. The message was that Russia was not only besieged by foreign enemies, such as NATO and the CIA, but also by Muslim terrorists from Chechnya.

At a special press conference, President Potanin praised the commandos of the Alpha Spetsnaz anti-terror unit, who'd not only managed to free the hostages unharmed, but also eliminated all the terrorists, including their leader, Chalim Barchayev. There was to be a comprehensive security review. 'Chechen terrorists now have the capability to penetrate the heart of Moscow and threaten the lives of innocent Russian citizens. We will hunt them down, track them to every last hiding place in Chechnya and eradicate them.'

Anya wanted to crawl inside the television and beat the shit out of him. 'He's using the hostage-taking as an excuse to start a new war against Chechnya!'

Potanin had immediately asked the Dutch government to clarify the role of their journalist who'd been involved in the hostage-taking and was now on the run.

At that point, Farah appeared on screen, and they got to see her on-air statement for the first time.

Paul had never seen her so fired up as on that screen, so out of control.

'I, Farah Hafez, support the jihad against President Potanin's criminal regime.'

The image froze. An emergency phone number appeared on screen. The rich male voice issued an urgent appeal to all Muscovites: anyone who spotted this 'fugitive terrorist' — whose Afghan background had made her sympathetic to the Chechen cause — should call immediately.

Paul heard a shriek.

Farah was standing in the doorway, white as a ghost, staring at her terrorist self on television.

She felt like she'd slept the sleep of the dead. And, when she woke, she had the weird sensation that she'd never be able to sleep again. Her whole body was rigid with tension. Her head was teeming with images of recent events. Panic racked her body. She remembered the hospital and the needle going into her arm.

She didn't know where she was. It was far too dark. She broke out in a cold sweat and crawled out of bed. Floorboards creaked beneath her feet. By groping around, she managed to locate a door. On the other side of it was a corridor, and at the end of that a crack admitting a flickering light.

Steadying herself against the wall, she teetered towards the light, to the muffled sound of agitated voices. The corridor was no more than five metres long, she estimated, but navigating it felt like running a half-marathon. By the time she reached the door, she was out of breath. As she peered through the crack, she saw two figures, staring wide-eyed into the glare of a television.

She pushed the door open and heard herself speak. The words didn't come from her own mouth, but from her likeness on the screen. From the terrorist she now was to the outside world.

'I, Farah Hafez . . .'

Then her knees gave way and she slowly crumpled to the floor. The voices receded, and the light was swallowed by darkness.

She opened her eyes again when Anya covered her with a soft blanket and asked, 'Do you know where you are?'

She didn't know the answer.

'You're at my place,' Anya said. 'And you'd better forget this as quickly as possible.'

Anya vanished through a brightly coloured beaded curtain. As Paul placed an extra cushion under her head and smoothed her hair, she tried to smile at him. He asked her what she remembered.

'Everything,' she said. 'I remember everything.'

'That's good.'

'No, it's not. I wish I could forget it all.'

'No way. We want to know every last detail.'

She let her head fall back against the cushions. All she wanted was sleep. The sweet sleep of oblivion. But her eyes remained wide open, and the shadows cast by the television crept along the walls and up to the ceiling.

Anya came back in with a big bowl of soup in her hands. 'I made a large panful,' she said. 'You need to get your strength back.'

Pieces of potato, beetroot and red pepper floated in the hot beef broth. No sooner had Farah eaten her first spoonful than she realized just how hungry she was. In no time at all, she emptied the bowl and held it up like a trophy. When Anya returned to the kitchen, Paul asked, 'Why did we do this again? It was a crazy plan.'

'It wasn't even a plan,' said Anya, re-emerging from behind the beaded curtain with a second steaming bowl. 'It was just insane.'

With her eyes closed, Farah slurped up the second bowl of soup and thought back to how it had all started: to the night she'd seen Sekandar in the Emergency Department, a child made up to look like a woman, wearing cheap jewellery with little bells around his arms and legs. His injured body was covered in rags that might have passed for exotic and seductive earlier that evening, but that were by then smeared with mud and blood. She'd known it at once: he was *Bacha Bazi*, a 'boy to be played with', the way rich Afghan men had been doing for centuries in her native country. He'd been left for dead somewhere along a deserted woodland road, just outside Amsterdam, and she intended – no, she was determined – to find out who was responsible for it. After ten years with the *Algemeen Nederlands Dagblad*, she'd finally begun to make something of a national name for herself with articles about the way the Dutch government treated Afghan refugees. And now, through the hit-and-run, she'd discovered a shady connection between the Dutch Finance Minister, Ewald Lombard, and the CEO of the Russian energy conglomerate AtlasNet, Valentin Lavrov.

Lavrov was known the world over as an art collector who made extravagant purchases. The idea that her Editor-in-Chief, Edward Vallent, had come up with was ingenious and naive in equal measure: securing Lavrov as the guest editor of a special *AND* art supplement would be a quick and efficient way of getting close to the fire.

Lavrov agreed to take on the role and Farah joined him in Moscow.

And now here she was: clutching a bowl of soup with trembling hands in an unfamiliar Moscow apartment, caught up in a network of elusive figures that operated in the shadows, and wanted as an accomplice in the hostage-taking of innocent students.

She, an inexperienced journalist with a hidden agenda, had approached a Russian oligarch, who'd obviously carried out a thorough background check on her. It brought to mind the warning words of the Editor-in-Chief of *Moskva Gazeta*, Roman Jankovski, when they first met: 'When dealing with Lavrov, you could hope for the best, but you'd better be prepared for the worst.'

Paul held the digital screen of the Nikon up to her eyes. She saw herself standing beside Valentin Lavrov on the large patio of a glass house on the edge of a lake.

'We followed you,' Paul said.

She gasped and relived the moment she looked into Lavrov's grey-green eyes, set in his chiselled face with its broad jaw and narrow lips. She could smell his aromatic scent again – a combination of mint, lavender and bergamot.

Agonizingly slowly, Lavrov's words came back to her. She heard him say, 'Come and work for me,' while holding out a glass of champagne. 'Better than writing phony art supplements about naughty oligarchs, right?' And then that complete composure with which he issued his threat while staring out across the lake, 'I'm throwing you a lifeline, Farah, do you understand?'

She looked at Paul.

'He knew,' she said. 'He knew . . . right from the start.'

6

The forests surrounding Moscow had been on fire for almost a week now. A thick layer of smoke crept through the suburbs, deeper and deeper into the city. The concentration of toxins in the air was seven times higher than levels considered safe by the authorities. Yet that didn't stop thousands of illegal Azerbaijanis, Armenians, Kyrgyzs, Uzbeks and Kazakhs, crammed into dilapidated vans, from making the trip to the north-east of Moscow, as they did every day. They sold their contraband to the equally illegal stall-holders of Cherkizovsky Market, which was spread across an area three times the size of the Kremlin. In spite of the heat and smog today, hundreds of thousands of Muscovites and tourists would come to buy Caspian salmon, black caviar, spices, carpets and electronics of dubious quality, as always.

It was six o'clock in the morning. Besides the normal nervous energy of setting up the market stalls, another sort of tension hung in the air – caused by the whirr of rotor blades. As a military helicopter circled menacingly above, Paul and Anya made their way through the maze of thousands of stands to reach the heart of the market as quickly as they could.

They'd managed to hide Farah in such an obvious place that the authorities wouldn't ever begin by looking there: Anya's apartment. Still, Farah couldn't stay for very long. Where would she actually be safe? Not in Russia, given she was still accused of being a terrorist by the media. Not in the Netherlands, which was now closely cooperating with Russia because of Farah's alleged role in the hostage-taking and because there were Dutch students among the victims.

Thanks to Interpol, nowhere in Europe was safe.

She had to get much further away; needed a new look, a new identity.

That's why Anya and Paul had come to this autonomous enclave with its wheeling and dealing, even its own infra-structure: security, hotels and brothels, and an entire underground industry for false travel documents. This trade had already helped hundreds of thousands of Chinese, South-East Asians and other illegals to escape to the West via Russia and the Baltic States.

Right here, in Cherkizovsky Market, lay Farah's best chance of disappearing without a trace.

But time was running out.

Arriving at a bastion of steel-plated containers, they were stopped by two men, their dark Ray-Bans tightly hugging their tanned Caucasian heads, their Nagant revolvers visible in the holsters under their black leather jackets.

'Mr Dadashov is expecting us,' Anya said.

'Not today.'

The helicopter made a low flyover. They instinctively ducked.

'It's important,' Anya insisted. 'He knows me. It won't take long.'

The men quietly consulted. One of them walked away. Only then did Paul notice they were being watched from several vantage points by men in the same leather gear. All members of the private security force of the man who ruled over Cherkizovsky Market from a network of containers, like an emperor ruling over his realm from a throne. The son of a poor cobbler from Azerbaijan, Azim Dadashov had run a sophisticated smuggling operation for years, building his rogue empire into what it was today: a thriving hotbed of mainly illegals from Central Asia. But his days were numbered. The Russian President had recently enacted a law restricting the right to operate stalls in the market to Russian citizens only. A major purge hung in the air, and it had the whirring sound of helicopter blades.

Anya was afraid they were too late. She saw it in the men lugging heavy boxes and computers from the containers to a large waiting van. She saw it in the eyes of the surly bodyguard when he returned.

'You've got five minutes,' he said, much to her surprise.

After checking their IDs and thoroughly patting them down, he led them into an inner ring of containers. Via an antechamber, they entered an air-conditioned space, strewn with Persian rugs. One wall was covered in monitors. They were in the security control room. Three men kept watch over the shadowy contours of the Mi-24 combat helicopter, which was being observed via security cameras positioned at different vantage points in the market. The man in the middle turned around. His large, gleaming, bald head seemed to sit straight on the shoulders of his gigantic body, which was stiff with tension. In his shiny suit and red silk waistcoat he looked like a wrestler posing as the Maharaja of Jaipur. The moment Azim Dadashov made eye contact with Anya, a quizzical smile appeared on his troubled face.

She never stopped amazing Paul. Just a few days ago, she'd embraced a Chechen terrorist leader. And now it was the turn of a mafia boss from the Caucasus. But the two men had something in common. Both hated Potanin's guts.

'It's the final countdown, my dove,' Dadashov whispered to Anya after he'd given Paul a crushing handshake. 'That helicopter is a sign that a major raid is about to take place. The National Guard is already on its way. They'll surround the market. So I don't have as much time as I usually do for you. Unless you care to run away with me?'

'Perhaps another time, Azim.'

'I'll keep hoping, sugar-pie. What can I do for you?'

'I need a passport, Azim. And an exit visa.'

'Sorry, you'll have to go elsewhere. Our entire operation is being dismantled as we speak.'

'If it wasn't a matter of life and death, I wouldn't be here, Azim. You're the only one who can help us. A friend of ours is in trouble. Serious trouble. She's a journalist. If you've followed the news about the hostage-taking, you'll have seen her message on TV. She walked into a trap. The recording is a fake. They forced her.'

'They?'

'The whole hostage-taking was probably bogus. Potanin is looking for an excuse to invade Chechnya again. We're fighting the same enemy, Azim. The man everybody is afraid of. Except you and me.'

'Wait,' Dadashov said resolutely. He turned around, briefly consulted with two other men and motioned for Paul and Anya to follow him.

'Does she know where she wants to go, our heroine? Scandinavia, England, America?'

'The other direction,' Paul said. 'Indonesia.'

He thought back to that moment when Farah had come up with the idea.

They'd seen Valentin Lavrov on the television. He was giving a press conference in the Russian Embassy's grand hall in Jakarta. Amid the flashes of the intrusive photographers, he announced that in the foreseeable future AtlasNet would sign a 'historic deal' with the Indonesian government: the construction of twenty-seven floating nuclear power stations in the Indonesian archipelago. Admittedly the plan still needed the approval of the 560 members of the People's Consultative Assembly, but Lavrov smiled into the camera as if he'd already sealed the deal.

'*Saya pergi ke Jakarta*,' Farah had said. 'I'm going to Jakarta.'

She'd been to Indonesia. Years before. She'd taken part in an intensive Pencak Silat training session in Bandung. She'd learned enough Bahasa to understand basic phrases and have a simple conversation. Jakarta was a city of millions. The perfect anonymous arena in which to find out how Lavrov had managed to get such a project off the ground. She'd suggested they each investigate the activities of AtlasNet from a different part of the world: Anya from Moscow, Paul from Amsterdam and she from Jakarta.

It was an insane plan. 'But,' he said to her, 'the most courageous thing you could have come up with. Like three horsemen of the Apocalypse, we'll bring down Lavrov's empire.'

Paul and Anya followed Dadashov through a passageway that ended inside another container: a workstation, lit by glaring fluorescent tubes, in the process of being dismantled. Computer screens were turned off, documents hastily packed. Stacks of passports, undoubtedly false, disappeared into boxes. Dadashov shouted to a little man with an Asian appearance, snapped some orders and pushed him in Paul and Anya's direction.

'Tell him what you need and he'll do it. But make it fast, very fast.'

'I have everything with me,' Anya said. She stroked Dadashov's fleshy cheek. 'Thank you, Azim.'

'Anything for you, tough cookie,' he said. The smile on his face was gone before he'd left the room.

The Asian sat down behind a computer screen and motioned, almost frenetically, for Anya to hand over the necessary info.

She was well prepared. She'd hacked the Myspace account of a Russian woman who resembled Farah in age and appearance. The details, combined with the MRZ information, were fed into the data system. Everything happened very quickly. The printer spat out pages of a special, thick paper displaying a watermark. The Asian ran to a workbench, where he cut, stapled and placed the pages in a cover. Anya handed over the photograph of Farah, which she'd taken the evening before. The Asian added fake stamps and pasted in phony visas. The hectic activity in the container increased. The security guards in their black jackets shouted for everyone to evacuate the premises. The Asian shoved the passport into Anya's hands, grabbed the laptop and quickly disappeared. They heard an explosion. The container shook. They ran in the direction of Lokomotiv Stadium, about two hundred metres away, to the nearest metro station.

They heard the cracking sound of breaking wood. Behind them bulldozers rammed stalls still filled with goods into a heap of wreckage. Desperate stall-holders tried to escape with their most valuable wares. Whoever was run down in the chaos fell prey to the security forces, who were beating people indiscriminately with rubber batons.

In the mêlée of collapsing stalls and fleeing people, Paul and Anya were able to reach the station, where they ran into the entryway and then descended on the long escalator. There they blended into the mob of people on the overcrowded platform.

It was well over thirty degrees in the metro. No air-con here. A uniformed man rolled around the car on a wooden board, holding out his hand. A Chechen veteran who'd lost his legs during the war. Anya gave him a clap on the shoulder and handed him some rouble notes. They sped under the centre of Moscow in possession of a new identity for Farah.

7

With Moscow's dismal suburbs flashing past, Farah closed the curtains on the sliding doors of her compartment and pulled down the outside window screen.

She stared at the passport that featured her new likeness and the false name Valentina Nikolayeva. It would take some getting used to.

Moments earlier, under the glass roof of Platform 10 at Moskva Kiyevskaya Station, she'd stood opposite Paul. Without makeup, but with cropped chestnut-brown hair and dark lenses to mask her bright blue eyes, she was barely recognizable. She was wearing a faded pair of cords with a dark-grey T-shirt, and her small rucksack was filled with some underwear, a supply of nuts and dried fruit, a well-thumbed book called *Bahasa for Beginners*, a handful of roubles, her false passport and her laptop. On Anya's instructions, she'd wrapped up her real passport and left it in a locker at the station, along with Raylan Chappelle's letters to her mother.

In spite of everything, she had to laugh at the fact that, even in this heat, Paul was still wearing his leather jacket. With his Jimi Hendrix T-shirt, his loose-fitting, faded jeans and grimy cowboy boots, he looked like he was busy with a DIY project that would never see completion.

'Are you sure you want this?' he'd asked.

'Positive.'

She'd pushed the visor of his baseball cap aside, given him a quick peck on the cheek and then boarded the train without looking back.

As she reached for her laptop and opened it, she could feel her heart racing. Her head wasn't nearly clear enough to retain all the instructions Anya had given her last night. She was afraid she'd already forgotten most of it.

Her memory was like a sieve.

She raised her right wrist and turned it a few times this way and that to look at the charm bracelet Anya had given her as a parting gift. The charms included an orange-red heart, a butterfly, a flower and two small, book-shaped rectangles – one black, the other white. She gripped the white book between her thumb and index finger, the way she'd practised the previous evening. She squeezed and pulled a mini USB stick from its white case and inserted it into her laptop.

As she watched a seemingly endless sequence of code flash past on the black screen, she thought about what Anya had impressed upon her.

'Even in Jakarta, disappearing in the masses will be difficult. The moment you phone me or Paul, use a search engine on your laptop or send one of us an email, you'll be leaving traces. If we're going to exchange sensitive data across large distances without being detected, and communicate without leaving a digital trail, we need to take strict precautions.'

The mini USB stick was one of those precautions.

It featured a Linux operating system that Anya had put together herself, which was now communicating with the hardware of Farah's laptop. All the regular software she'd ever used had been removed by Anya, who claimed it contained built-in back doors. It allowed security services such as the FSB, as well as the FBI and the NSA, to gain easy access and scan her hard drive. Throughout her undercover operation, Farah must never save anything on that drive. The USB stick was protected: the file system was 'read only' and the stick formatted as such – no hacker would be able to change anything on it; it was like hardened cement.

Farah opened the folder Anya had installed for her. It contained the most important data on AtlasNet and the nuclear-energy project the company was hoping to realize in Indonesia.

Since the hostage-taking, she hadn't so much as glanced at a newspaper, looked at a book or read a word. Normally, she could read an entire novel in a single evening. She was able to decipher and analyse all the stuff released by the international press agencies faster than any other *AND* editor. But now the sentences inched past slowly and without meaning, her head refusing to let in the information she needed to do her work.

'You were teetering on the edge,' Paul had said to her. 'You had a narrow escape. Now you need to get up and learn to walk again – in every respect.'

He was right. She could tell by the way she'd floundered when she tried to tell Paul and Anya what had happened to her in the Seven Sisters. Several times she forgot halfway through a sentence what it was she wanted to say. Her memories were all in a muddle, lacking either a beginning or an end. She was trying to put the puzzle together, but kept getting lost in a jumble of fragmented details.

Feverish with fatigue and overcome by the heat, she swayed back and forth to the monotonous cadence of the hurtling train, without realizing that her eyes were falling shut.

She had no idea how long she'd been unconscious. Nor did she have the time to linger on the question. A male voice boomed in her ear. Forceful fingers curled around her upper arm. She felt the grip of a hand roughly shaking her awake.

She reached for the laptop, which was still open. She looked into a pair of bloodshot eyes. Framed by dark circles, they were set deep in the pale, sunken face of a man wearing a faded green uniform with Army-style epaulettes, which looked like it had never been washed. His Russian sounded irritable and insistent. She couldn't understand a word of it, until she heard the phrase that instantly put her into panic mode.

Passport.

'*Minutuchku!*' she said. 'One moment, please.'

With Anya's help, she'd learned a few Russian sentences by heart. According to her passport, she was a Russian national. At immigration counters, you usually just hand over your passport without saying anything, but Anya reckoned it might be more convincing if Farah produced the occasional simple sentence.

As she rummaged around for her passport, a second man entered the compartment. He compensated for his skinny colleague's sickly pale complexion with fleshy, bright pink skin, which was beaded with excessive sweat. Farah made a half-hearted attempt at a smile.

'*Tak žiarko segodnja,*' she said – 'Gosh, it's hot today' – and handed him the passport with a small stack of rouble notes between its pages. The man with the bloodshot eyes looked at them disdainfully and casually threw them back at her. The notes whirled down on to her lap.

He spent a long time scrutinizing her passport and then asked her something she didn't understand.

On the off-chance, she uttered her three fictitious names and her equally fictitious date of birth.

Both men looked at her as if she'd just told them a bad joke.

'*Izvinite, ya vas ne ponimayu, ya ne znayu,*' she stammered as sincerely as possible. 'Excuse me. I don't understand, I don't know.'

The look in their eyes confirmed her worst fears. Before she'd even reached Kiev, before she even realized it, she'd been found out.

The wiry man slipped the passport into his breast pocket and ordered her to hand over the laptop.

Reflexively, she slammed the laptop shut and quickly set it down beside her.

As she did so, he leaned over to grab it.

The side of her hand shot out and hit the artery in his neck, hard enough to stop the blood flowing to his head for a few seconds; and long enough for Farah to weave the fingers of both hands together, link her arms and sharply ram her right elbow into her assailant's left temple.

As he fell over, she stretched out her arm and landed the knuckles of her fist against the back of his head.

From the corner of her eye, she saw the other man reach for his gun. In the split second it took for him to look down to undo the safety catch, she grabbed his head with both hands and brought it down towards her knee as it shot up.

She heard the cracking of his nasal bone and gave him the finishing blow against the back of his head with her elbow.

Then she grabbed the revolver, which had dropped to the floor. She'd never held a gun in her hands before. Unsure what to do with it, she tossed it on the seat and found a set of handcuffs dangling from the second man's belt. She clicked them open, grabbed the men's wrists and slapped on the cuffs.

Panting, she reached for her laptop and pulled the USB stick out. *Always take that USB stick with you.* Anya's orders. She reinserted the stick into the casing on her charm bracelet, slipped the laptop into her rucksack, which she hoisted on to her shoulders, and carefully slid open the door.

To her right, some ten metres away, an elderly man was

smoking in the aisle. His head was sticking out of the lowered window.

As she watched him, all kinds of questions flashed through her mind. How much longer would they be under way? How many officials were on board? Were those two the only ones?

Either way, she had to get as far away from this compartment as possible. It was the front carriage she wanted to get to. Kiev was a terminus station. It meant that when they arrived, she'd be able to get off close to the main concourse. Farah closed the doors behind her and walked into the aisle, quickly glancing over her shoulder at the smoking man. He was fully concentrated on Kiev's passing suburbs.

In the aisle of the third carriage, she saw two other men in uniform heading her way. She turned around and sought refuge in a toilet. It might be another fifteen minutes to the station, twenty at most. She could lock herself in and wait until everybody had left the train. But the officials would undoubtedly spot the red 'occupied' sign, knock on the door, and ask her to come out and show her ticket, maybe even her passport.

Her passport.

She'd forgotten her passport.

She made her way back to her compartment as quickly as she could. The smoking man in the aisle had gone. As she slid the doors open, the man on top stirred ever so slightly. She pushed him aside. The thin man lay motionless on the floor. Worried that he might be dead, she pressed her fingers against his carotid artery and was relieved to feel it beating.

With a great deal of difficulty, she managed to turn him over so she could retrieve her passport from his jacket pocket. She heard footsteps in the aisle. Two men walked past, talking loudly. She listened carefully and heard them disappear. She put her passport into her rucksack and checked for sounds in the aisle; only when it was completely quiet did she find the courage to slide open the doors.

This time, she walked all the way to the back of the train, straight into the restaurant car. There she spotted the same officials she'd seen earlier in the front part of the train. They were the men who'd passed her compartment while she retrieved her passport from the pocket of their unconscious colleague. She recognized them by their loud voices.

Keep moving now. Don't turn around. If she turned around, she'd attract attention.

The younger of the two winked at her as she walked past and shouted something at her for ignoring him. She kept going, but, realizing it might be a mistake not react to him, treated him to a cheery smile before disappearing through the connecting doors and into the next carriage.

How much longer before they'd arrive in Kiev? How much longer before the two men in her compartment were discovered?

She stopped in the vestibule of the next-to-last carriage and looked outside. They were entering the centre of Kiev now. Passengers with hand luggage, suitcases and backpacks emerged from the various compartments. They thronged around her. It felt uncomfortable in the heat, but at least they also provided some protection.

A couple of minutes later, the train entered the station. The platform slipped past. She tried the door handle. It wouldn't budge. She had no choice but to wait until the train came to a complete standstill and the doors centrally unlocked.

Farah was the first to get out. She looked towards the front, but was unable to see the end of the platform because it had a gentle curve. She started walking, trying to stop herself from breaking into a run. When she saw the customs officials get out, she slowed down and mingled with the men and women pulling their noisy rolling suitcases so as to draw as little attention to herself as possible. Cleaners in blue overalls entered the empty carriages with brooms and rubbish bags. When she passed the one that contained her compartment she noticed the screen was still down.

At the sound of animated voices from a walkie-talkie, she stiffened. She kept staring straight ahead and quickened her pace. Two station guards came towards her and walked past at a trot.

By now the men must have been discovered. They'd be able to give a very accurate description of her. Not long now before the alarm would be raised.

Don't run. Whatever you do, don't run.

Once she reached the top of the platform, she entered the main concourse and headed straight for the escalators leading to the metro line that ran in the direction of Boryspil Airport. Where she could, she mingled with groups, constantly scanning her surroundings for unexpected movements. In the metro carriage she stood next to a small band of backpackers as she waited for it to pull away. From where she was standing, she could see something of a commotion at the bottom of the escalators. A man extricated himself from the crowd and ran towards the train at full tilt. He was young, wore a dark suit and carried something black in his hand. He ran in her direction. When he squeezed in through the closing doors, she was relieved to see the logo of an airline company on his lapels.

The train started moving and ten minutes later it arrived just below the international departures hall for Terminal D. She took the escalator up and looked around. Perhaps it was the calming voice of the female announcer, the soft echo of the many footsteps and luggage carts, and the muffled voices of the passengers, but it all seemed quiet – too much so for her liking. It was as if something were hiding behind that layer of stillness.

She walked over to the Qatar Airways check-in desk and handed the ground stewardess a printout of her reservation and her passport. A few seconds after checking Farah's data on her computer, the stewardess asked her to wait a moment. With a hint of nervousness, the woman checked something on another screen.

That's when Farah realized that she might have walked into a trap.

They'd want to pick her up without a disturbance. Given the large numbers of passengers in the hall, there was a realistic chance of chaos breaking out. Instead they'd escort her to a quieter place. She'd have nowhere to turn.

She looked around. To her right, some twenty metres away, she saw two armed police officers lurking unobtrusively behind a group of tourists. It was the same story to her left: two more with automatic weapons trying to keep a low profile. At the main entrance to the hall she saw another two carrying rifles.

For a moment, she was unable to breathe, think or move. She was completely and utterly panic-stricken.

'Madam?'

She turned to face the stewardess.

'We're able to offer you a free upgrade to business class, if you like.'

So that was the plan. Business-class passengers were always allowed to board first. They'd be waiting for her in the jet bridge, or perhaps even on the plane itself. With nobody else around, they'd be able to detain her discreetly. She wouldn't stand a chance.

She heard a voice inside her head – her father's voice. She could picture him too, towering above her. She was still a little girl. *Never take a step back*, he said sternly. *As soon as you yield for your opponent, you'll have lost the fight. There is only one way to victory, and that is forward.*

'Fine,' she said to the stewardess.

After receiving her ticket, along with the necessary information, she made her way to the gate. Fifteen minutes to go until boarding.

At immigration, the official checked her passport, the way he must have done hundreds of times that day, and wished her a pleasant journey.

This is what it must feel like, she thought to herself, as she walked through the still empty passenger bridge on to the plane. This is how people headed for the scaffold or a firing squad feel. You know it's over, yet you hope for a miracle that will never come.

A steward had been stationed by the entrance to the plane. Everything seemed normal. His uniform fitted perfectly and she couldn't detect a weapon anywhere. When she showed him her boarding pass, he escorted her inside, where she took her place in one of the luxury business-class seats.

Passengers started trickling in, finding their seats and stowing their luggage in the overhead bins. The plane was still only half full when the doors were locked. Even now, she couldn't believe everything was fine.

They taxied to the runway. The roar of the starter engines sounded like cheering rising up from deep within the plane.

When they took off, she knew for certain that she'd chosen the only path she could have taken.

Her way now was that of the attack, and it lay before her, wide open and welcoming.

PART TWO
Ritual

I

Radjen Tomasoa listened to the wind doing its best to yank loose the clay roof tiles. He lay on his back; it'd become something of a habit. Something he did when he couldn't sleep. This storm, which seemed to be announcing the early arrival of autumn, reminded him of the past, of days long gone. Lost to him forever.

He was in his early twenties then, lying on his back in a tent on the shores of Lake Trasimeno. A hefty thunderstorm burst loose directly above him. Pelting rain drummed on the canvas. He imagined himself floating in the eye of the storm, unreachable by anything that might harm him. He wasn't the least bit afraid he'd be hit by lightning or that the wind would blow him, tent and all, into the lake. He shut out the chaos; his thoughts were crystal clear. He felt in complete control of life. *His* life. There, in the eye of the storm, he was powerful enough to accomplish everything he set his sights on.

Everything.

He stared at the crack in the ceiling. Like a river with narrow tributaries, it ran diagonally to both corners of the bedroom – it had been there for more than thirty years. By now he could draw every millimetre, much like he could sketch the years of his marriage. There was no more energy left to repair cracks like these. And, even if he were inclined to do so, it would then be etched in his memory as a tedious and rather unpleasant time in his life.

The question of who was at fault for the loss of what was

once young love wasn't even the issue. He'd decided it was nobody's fault. Anyway, marriage was primarily meant to camouflage the fact that the love between two people seldom lasts a lifetime. What was the alternative? The lonely life he'd undoubtedly lead after a divorce in his mid fifties seemed unbearable. For him, divorce was the equivalent of admitting that little or nothing was left of everything he'd dreamed about in his twenties.

But that was not the reason Radjen was still awake. Voices echoed in his head. The voices of the men who'd led the internal investigation of his detective team. In a room at headquarters, made especially available for the occasion, they'd sat to his left and right on either side of a camera. Each had one leg crossed over the other. A perfectly symmetrical set-up. They carefully formulated their questions. And, who knows, perhaps they'd orchestrated the long, painful silences even more carefully. Silences in which Radjen could hear the blood coursing through his veins, feel his temples throbbing. Silences in which his heart irregularly skipped the occasional beat like a clock ticking out of control.

So you were not aware of the duplicitous role Detective Diba played in your department?

Detective Marouan Diba, who'd once achieved nationwide fame because of his discovery of 600 kilos of cocaine in the belly of a plane, who'd caused a stir as one of the first minority detectives in the police corps, who was young and bursting with ambition, but who, as he got older, was weighed down not only by his BMI but by life itself. Yes, he, Radjen Tomasoa, Chief Inspector of the Amsterdam Police Force, had tried pumping new life into his demoralized detective. A year earlier, he'd appointed the young up-and-coming investigator Joshua Calvino as Diba's partner. The combination had ultimately ended in disaster.

No, I was not aware of the kind of contacts Detective Diba had outside his unit. How could I have been?

Is that a question, Chief Inspector?

Rhetorical.

So, not a question.

Again silence. Radjen's blood boiled, his temples pounded, his heart felt like a time bomb attached to a tightly wound clock run amok.

What do you think happened in that interrogation room?

Arseholes! How should he know? Control yourself, breathe, breathe deeply, take a sip of water, pick your words carefully, describe what happened that evening as objectively as possible. That fatal evening.

Again, I was not present at that interrogation. I can only deduce what might have happened from the facts.

We'd appreciate you sharing those facts with us.

And that's what he did. Thoughtfully, in guarded terms. They wouldn't get him on a slip of the tongue, a show of weakness or even a hint of uncertainty.

During the first interview, it became clear the suspect had more information than he was willing to share upfront. He was prepared to release that information only in exchange for witness protection. That was the reason why Detective Calvino left the room, to consult with me.

The silence. Scratchy throat. The urge to stand up and shout: get the hell out of my face! Detectives investigating other detectives. Backstabbers dressed in better weekday suits than he wore on Sundays and holidays. Besides, he had better things to do than rat out his own men. He still had to deal with that Afghan boy. The one who was found dressed as a girl, involved in the hit-and-run. Sort out matters that had led him to a Dutch minister's inner sanctum, where he'd seized a computer. A computer with sickening images of children; photos that made his stomach turn. But these bastards in their everyday Hugo

Boss monkey suits weren't interested in that. No, they were more concerned with some Russian lowlife who was found in a puddle of blood with a gaping hole in his head just minutes after Detective Calvino had left the interrogation room.

Were you aware that the suspect was alone in the company of Detective Diba? The man with whom — according to phone records we found — he'd had regular contact for many years.

No, I wasn't aware of it. I was told that one of my sergeants had temporarily taken Calvino's place. But apparently he was dismissed by Detective Diba.

And you weren't aware that the suspect was handcuffed during the interrogation?

No.

He felt like they wanted to drive him into a corner, make him complicit in the matter, trap him, if need be, with a misplaced word, so they could accuse him of giving inconsistent answers. Push him up against the ropes, make him sweat, let him feel who had the upper hand here, let him know how badly he'd actually botched it, by looking the other way for years. Something a capable chief inspector would never've tolerated. He mustn't give them the chance.

You mentioned the suspect was pushing to be placed in witness protection. Do you really believe that such a person commits suicide by beating his head against a table?

I'm not in a position to judge. You're the ones conducting the investigation into all of this.

Touché, you motherfucking morons.

He'd seen the Russian. Up close and personal. In handcuffs — his cracked skull lying on the table. A sergeant had supposedly sent out for coffee. Coffee for whom? Not for the Russian, who later joined the spirit world in the ambulance en route to hospital. Certainly not for Detective Diba, who disappeared without a trace, only to throw himself off the Rembrandttoren a few hours later. Thirty-six storeys high. His body hit the glass entranceway canopy with such force that he was impaled on its steel points. They needed a crane to lift him off. Diba, who was not buried with police honours, but swept under the rug like a nobody. And Calvino missed out on the promotion he deserved. Radjen chastised himself for not making the slightest effort to check in on Calvino – officially, because he didn't want to appear partial. But the real story, of course, was that he was too chicken. If he'd had to face his most talented detective, in whom he recognized his own passion, he wouldn't have known what to say.

The essence of the story – the case of the 'hit-and-run kid' – was becoming too much of a strain. A Russian suspect who'd indicated that the Russian energy conglomerate Atlas-Net had something to do with it all had been killed by a detective during interrogation. One of the main suspects in the case was a Dutch minister who, thanks to the protection of the Public Prosecutor's office, could keep working as though nothing had happened.

Chief Inspector Tomasoa, you've indicated you were not aware of the unwarranted activities of Detective Diba nor those of Detective Calvino. You've also indicated you have no knowledge of what actually took place during the fatal interrogation that night.

Correct.

Are you actually aware of anything going on under your command?

It felt like he'd forgotten how to breathe. His blood ran cold; his heart seemed to stop. He'd managed to hide his feelings, stared at them coldly. The men didn't say anything else, made some more notes or pretended to, and turned off the camcorder. He'd shaken hands, fastened the middle button of his blazer and left the room. He was determined to prove he was right, solve this mystery, unravel the whole tangled mess and severely punish the guilty parties.

If forced to resign, he would do so with his head held high.

He threw off the blanket and felt the chilly dampness in the room. He heard his sleeping wife heave a deep sigh. Her life, their life, one long-drawn-out sigh.

On his back, with his eyes closed, he was once again under the tent canvas, which was fiercely flapping in the gale-force winds whistling between the hilly slopes of Trasimeno. With every gust, every distant sound of thunder, he again had that feeling of being in complete control, like before, in control of the future, no matter how little there was left of it.

He made a decision. He would take control of time.

He'd organize it according to how he saw fit, as he'd done in his twenties, as he'd done for years, as he perhaps still did in the eyes of his trusted colleagues and those who served directly under him.

Through the echoing thunder came a soft, urgent hum. He involuntarily glanced at the bedside table. His mobile phone was luminous and vibrating. With that he became acutely aware of his own breathing, the rain clattering against the window, the soft sighs of his wife in her sleep.

He turned on his side, reached for his phone, picked it up and heard a woman's voice – one he recognized. He hadn't heard it in weeks; he'd missed it. But what that voice had to say hit him hard.

The way lightning could strike a solitary tent pitched on the shores of a lake.

2

Anya Kozlova sped through Moscow with the fanaticism of Formula 1 drivers who race the streets of Monaco during the annual Grand Prix. Curves were taken almost perpendicularly – preferably on two wheels – merging was tantamount to cutting off other cars and braking seemed to be a capital offence. All of it irrelevant if you were driving a Hummer, but this was a Škoda Felicia from the 1990s.

Paul recalled something Farah had once said: 'Better to do something bordering on insanity than go insane doing nothing.' The immediate consequence of this was that he was now sitting speechless, sweating bullets, beside Kamikaze Anya in her battered Škoda.

The term 'suicide mission' popped into his head.

Appropriately, because they were on their way to the place where – as one of *Moskva Gazeta*'s editors had discovered – the executed black widows from the Seven Sisters had been taken. Police headquarters at 38 Ulitsa Petrovka had given orders to agents on duty at the bureau in the nearby Tverskoy district the night of the hostage-taking. They'd followed the Alpha Spetsnaz anti-terror commandos into the Seven Sisters building. After seizing all the explosives and the dead rebels' personal belongings, they'd transported the bodies directly to the Potemkin Hospital morgue.

Farah had repeatedly tried to tell Paul and Anya about what had happened to her in the Seven Sisters. She had to wrap her head around so many confusing details, put them together like pieces of a puzzle.

In the process, she remembered the woman who'd started filming her the moment the condor sat her down in front of the camera. Her striking blue eyes, her white skin, the diagonal scar that ran across her right cheek – visible because she didn't wear her black headscarf like the other women, with only their eyes showing. She had her scarf tightly wrapped around her head, so you could see her entire face.

With the help of Farah's description, Anya feverishly scoured through old files on her laptop. She thought she'd seen the woman before.

And her hunch was right, because she located the photo she had in mind. There she stood, somewhere in Alkhan-Kala, a wintery village south-west of Grozny: a young woman in her late twenties in khaki fatigues, who wouldn't look out of place at boot camp. Blue eyes. Her blonde hair sticking out from under her military cap. A rifle slung over her shoulder. With that scar running diagonally across her right cheek.

She wasn't Russian, but nor was she Chechen. She'd asked Anya who she worked for: without a hint of emotion, almost casually, yet at the same time commanding authority. Anya told her she was a journalist from the *Moskva Gazeta*. 'Anti-Potanin,' the woman responded in a friendly tone. 'Then, as far as I'm concerned, feel free to do whatever you want.' She spoke Russian with a Baltic accent. Anya thought she came from Estonia. Later she heard about female snipers who were active in that area. Women who could shoot off a Russian officer's balls from a few hundred metres away. Mercenaries. Super Snipers. According to unverified reports, they were all women from the Baltic region.

The woman was as much a Muslim as Farah was a terrorist. She must have been the one who'd filmed Farah with her mobile after she was dragged into the Seven Sisters.

What was her exact role during the hostage drama? With whom had this woman been in contact? The answers might lead Paul and Anya to the reasons behind the hostage-taking, even shed some light on Valentin Lavrov's possible involvement.

Three days had passed since the crisis had ended. Two things were noteworthy. First, no official Chechen resistance group had claimed the attack, just as nobody had claimed responsibility for the Russian apartment bombings earlier. And second, no images of the terrorists were circulating in the media.

The Potemkin Hospital loomed large in the soot-filled mist. Because of the smog, caused by the forest fires and the scorching sun, the poplars had hardly any foliage. Spotted brown-black leaves were strewn across the hospital lawn, which had a cinder hue of its own.

Ambulances sped away and returned: the number of heatwave victims increased daily. To avoid panicking the Muscovites, the state media reported much lower numbers of deaths than those officially recorded.

The second they passed through the massive revolving glass door into the hospital's entrance lobby, Paul was ready to turn on his heels. A soul-crushing sense of hopelessness grabbed him by the throat. Decay, he thought. Disease and decay. The worst thing you can ever experience as a human being.

'The Prime Minister visited here a few weeks ago,' Anya said without a trace of emotion. She shoved the Nikon into his hands. 'The hospital corridors he was scheduled to visit were renewed with plastic panelling and the floors re-covered with linoleum. But the second he left, the panelling and lino-leum were pulled out and sold off.'

Anya announced their arrival at the front desk. To get

full access to the hospital morgue as quickly as possible, she'd called Potemkin's press office to say the *Moskva Gazeta* wanted to do an article about the cuts the Russian government was planning for the healthcare sector. Thirty hospitals, including Potemkin, were threatened with closure. Three thousand medical personnel would end up on the street. The hospital board agreed that in exchange for this article Paul and Anya would get unlimited access to the entire hospital, so that they could take some photos.

A plump woman in her mid fifties, with bleached-blonde hair and an unusually friendly smile for a Russian, introduced herself as Olga. She worked in the Communications Department and apologized for the bluish haze hanging everywhere in the building.

'The air-conditioning system is on its last legs and refuses to work in this heat.'

Anya got straight to the point. 'What happens to heatwave victims who die?'

'They all end up in the morgue, which has been chock-full for days.'

'A morgue packed to capacity with no air-conditioning. A perfect metaphor for the effect of the cuts. Let's start there.'

Olga's eyes frantically darted back and forth between Anya and Paul. 'It has to be a hard-hitting article, Olga,' Paul said. 'Hard-hitting. So people wake up.'

After Olga had given them masks soaked in cologne, she hesitantly pushed opened two large swinging doors that gave them access to a dimly lit antechamber, three by three metres in size. The place smelled like all the hospital's garbage had been dumped there.

Paul pressed the mask closer to his face, inhaled through his nose and realized it didn't help much. He felt himself getting dizzy, but pushed on.

The next swinging door led them into a large tiled room, badly lit by old-fashioned fluorescents. Then they entered other tiled areas. Around seven. Without asking permission, they opened the doors of large metal cabinets and pulled out half-rusted shelves holding strangers, some in body bags. Paul shot photos.

The flash was like lightning striking. Each new dead face an unanswered question.

Due to lack of space, the dead were also laid out on tables, on rickety stretchers, even on the ground. They had young faces, old faces, their mouths were often open. They had glassy eyes, as if they still couldn't believe they'd never see the light of day again.

In the fifth room they found them.

The black widows, stark naked, each with a dark-red hole in the middle of her forehead.

Olga's voice was flat and uncertain. 'I'm not sure we're allowed to be here.'

Paul and Anya simply ignored her. In the light thrown by Anya's mobile, they gazed at their faces. Faces of young women from the North Caucasus. Women who'd lost their husbands and often their children in Chechnya's struggle for independence. Women who'd finally felt so trapped they saw no other way out besides blowing themselves up in markets, metro and train stations for money. Women with Kalashnikovs who'd held students hostage. Women who hadn't gone to hell, but ended up somewhere even worse. Here in this basement.

With each new woman she saw, Anya shook her head.

Once again, they could hear Olga's agitated voice: 'We really have to go.'

Anya was now hanging right above one face. The last woman staring back at her with blank eyes.

'Photo,' she whispered unemotionally. 'Photo.'

Paul positioned the lens above the face. Despite the fact it was as white as marble and the eyes as lifeless as stone, he recognized their colour and that scar running diagonally across her right cheek.

3

After Farah cleared immigration and entered the arrivals hall, Jakarta hit her like a hot, wet flannel. Before she knew it she was besieged by a bunch of pushy guys and several older men with terrible breath, all trying to outbid each other. *'Taxi, taxi! Hotel, good hotel! I take you lady, I take you!'* They were all smiles even as they were manhandling her. At one point she thought she'd lost her rucksack in the mêlée; the next moment someone slipped a fake Rolex around her wrist.

She hotfooted it to one of the waiting buses indicating STASIUN KOTA as its destination. She'd heard about Kota, the original city centre. Apparently it was full of Dutch colonial buildings. There was a seat free in the back of the vehicle, close to an open window. The bus drove off, and, from the vantage point of the elevated motorway outside the airport, she watched the intricate labyrinth of the Indonesian capital unfold before her. The national monument towered above everything like a white-hot needle.

Downtown, the bus got held up. Thousands of people with banners and flags came pouring on to the street from all directions. They were wearing swimming goggles and face masks, probably as a precaution against tear gas, and shouting slogans. *'Kami sudah cukup dengan korupsi,'* an elderly man yelled. 'We're sick of corruption.' The bus passengers leaned out of the windows to egg him on. To her surprise, she didn't see any police or soldiers. After the procession finally disappeared in a cloud of dust, soot and exhaust fumes, the traffic got going again in fits and starts.

The evening sky was practically purple by the time the bus reached its destination. Farah got off at Fatahillah Square, where a large number of colonial buildings were in a state of serious disrepair, and walked in the direction of a run-down suspension bridge, the old-fashioned type you saw these days only in Dutch villages. Soon, she found herself on the quay of the old port. Hundreds of wooden boats were moored here. Short, wiry men with heavy sacks scurried across the narrow gangplanks. Most of them were grey from the dust wafting from the sacks. Elsewhere, men balancing long beams of hardwood on their shoulders walked across another gangplank on to the quay.

Boys stopping gullible tourists in an attempt to sell them ships in a bottle paid her no attention whatsoever. The men in the small boats offering tours of the harbour for a handful of rupiahs didn't shout to her either. With her flip-flops, faded jeans, grey T-shirt and makeup-free face – and her Eastern features of course – she was apparently of no interest to them. It reassured her. Here she could do what she intended to do: disappear among the masses.

At the nearby market, swarms of flies hovered above scraps of that day's salted fish. Emaciated cats scavenged for waste underneath the stalls. The place stank of putrefaction and decay. She ended up in a maze of narrow streets full of half-empty fish stalls, lit-up food carts and small shops selling everything you'd need on a small fishing boat, from life jackets, nets and ropes to compasses, helms and anchors.

In a tiny shop illuminated by strip lighting and crammed with sacks of rice, tins of food and Chinese waving cats, Farah found what she was looking for: an unlocked smartphone, a RedBerry, for the equivalent of less than twenty euro. Both its price and name betrayed its origins: Chinese imitation. She also bought an Indonesian prepaid SIM card and seven euros' worth of credit. After receiving a confirmation text, she immediately sent a sign of life to Paul, as agreed.

She saw the phone trying to connect with the international network and the short message doing its best to be sent. Even the fastest method of communication couldn't dispel the notion that she was more than twelve thousand kilometres away from Paul – and with little if any help available for the time being. The enthusiasm with which she had conceived her impulsive plan to travel to Jakarta was gone. All she was interested in at this moment was finding an affordable place to sleep.

She kept walking and then, among the shacks of corrugated iron, concrete and musty wood, she discovered a dirty white art-deco building on the quay. There was a crowded restaurant on the ground floor where perspiring waitresses walked around with large, overloaded trays on their shoulders. The place was full of blaring television screens and ceiling fans that whirred like helicopter propellers.

The handwritten sign dangling from the building's first floor indicated a hotel. After climbing the worn teak staircase, Farah stood panting at the counter, where a bored receptionist, not a day over eighteen, was filing her nails. 'That's fifteen thousand,' she barked in English without looking up. About one and a half euros. With her last bit of energy, Farah tried to arrange for bottles of water, fruit and some food to be delivered to her room. 'No room service,' the girl replied.

Farah got the key to the room with 'special view', locked the door behind her, stripped the clammy clothes off her body and didn't even bother to lift the mattress to check for dirt or vermin.

She threw herself on to the bed, face down, and slipped into a deep, deep sleep.

4

According to the weather report Radjen Tomasoa was listening to as he drove through the deserted streets of Amsterdam towards Olympiaplein, it was an early-autumn storm. A low-pressure area was causing masses of cumulus clouds to blanket the country, with gusts of wind here and there up to 110 kilometres per hour. He drove along Apollolaan and, after the bridge over the Noorder Amstelkanaal, and the East Indies Monument, took a left past the local team's football pitches. In the distance, to the right of the square, an ambulance and a police car had pulled up alongside the wide pavement. Once he'd parked, he saw her: smoking in the doorway.

Esther van Noordt, a straight-talking brunette.

As a single woman in her thirties, she led an independent existence and in the police corps was valued for her meticulousness, her commitment and loyalty. She had the rough-and-tough look of a rock chick. In her spare time, she was an avid rower and played bass in a heavy-metal band called Elysium Cop.

As he approached her, she quickly took a last drag of her cigarette and stamped it out. She shook his hand and forcefully blew out the smoke in a long stream.

'The forensics guys are still busy, Chief,' she said, handing Radjen an extra-large white overall. 'The wife called it in. An ambulance and patrol car were first on the scene. Initially they didn't see any reason to notify the Murder Investigation team. It didn't look like a murder, just a normal suicide.'

'To the extent that you can call any suicide normal,'

Radjen replied, struggling to pull the white suit over his huge body. He looked at her apologetically.

'We're not in a rush.'

'When did they realize who he was?'

'While waiting for the medical examiner. Like the forensics team, I thought it was advisable to wake you up. Given your involvement in the whole case and all.'

'Thanks for the heads up.'

To complete his metamorphosis, Radjen slipped on white plastic shoe covers.

Esther pushed open the front door and accompanied him into the living room. He saw a plate holding a half-eaten sandwich and a cup of milk beside the computer and looked at Esther questioningly.

'He was checking out rental properties on the Ghanaian coast.'

Radjen Tomasoa gazed at the computer screen and saw the distorted reflection of a large, bald man in tightly fitting forensics garb. He looked around the room. Not a trace of violence anywhere. Each piece of furniture neatly in place, where it had probably stood for years. His gaze lingered on the wedding photo, in an ornate, gold-leaf frame, on the mantelpiece. The victim, young, with a shy expression, in his wedding tux, beside his young African bride. Radjen observed the man with the narrow, unremarkable face whom he'd recently met at the police station. Despite the festive occasion, the man's smile was reserved, overshadowed by serious eyes behind oversized glasses.

'The best day of your life.' She was right behind him, looking over his shoulder at the picture.

'No plans of your own, Detective?' Radjen asked.

'Enough plans,' she said, smiling. 'But that . . .' she added, pointing at the wedding photo, 'not going there.'

'After you,' Radjen said, and together they walked across the slate path towards the small green shed in the back garden with a double door and Plexiglas windows with yellow frames. The wind rustled the leaves of the towering sycamores and the mulberries, blowing them loose and scattering them all over the garden.

'Atlantis,' he said aloud, reading a plaque above the shed door. Like the window frames, it was painted yellow and looked like sandstone. Forensics were busy inside, securing whatever evidence they could find.

From the doorway, Radjen stared at the man he'd just seen as a shy groom in the photo. He was wearing grey silk loungewear. With his head in a noose and his tongue between his teeth, he dangled about thirty centimetres above the ground in the neon-blue light cast by a total of seven aquariums.

'How long has he been up there?'

'Hard to know,' Esther said. 'Rigor mortis usually sets in within an hour or two of death: starts at the jaw and then spreads to the rest of the body. Within eight hours he'd be quite stiff.'

She carefully lifted up his silk jacket, pressed a spot on his abdomen that was getting dark and examined the slight change in colour. Patting the jacket back in place, she then ran her hand along the slanted zip pocket. 'Given that the bruises are still responding to touch, it means he's been hanging here for less than six hours.' She grabbed the man by his waist, turned him towards Radjen and shone a torch on his face. 'Look at the skin around his mouth.'

Radjen Tomasoa reluctantly took a step forward as she demonstratively ran a finger of her gloved hand over the purplish skin around his lips.

'Abrasions,' she said.

'From what?'

'Tape, I suspect.'

'Could it be from anything else, maybe something earlier?'

'These are recent, Chief. Something damaged the skin around his mouth. After death you see it quickly, because it discolours.'

She looked at Radjen with the impatient look of a seasoned professional who'd already drawn her conclusions and was now awaiting the agreement of her superior.

Clearly, she was way ahead of Radjen. He looked at the peak of the shed and estimated the distance. Two metres seventy. The man in the noose was around one metre eighty. That meant there were about ninety centimetres of room for a hanging. The rope was stretched; looked like it was made of cotton. There was also no trace of violence here; only the stepladder he'd stood on was out of place.

'I've never seen anything like this before,' Esther said, sounding impatient.

'Like what?'

'With a hanging, the rope always closes off the neck veins and stops blood circulation. And the head always ends up dangling loosely, either to the right or left. But that's not the case with our friend here. His head is hanging down, as if he's contemplating his navel.'

She turned to Radjen, who thought he heard a note of triumph in her voice. 'First suicide case I've come across with a broken neck.' She seemed convinced she was right. 'It's the noose,' she said, pointing to the knot under the man's chin. 'Normally, it's on the other side.'

Radjen's interested look gave her the encouragement to continue. 'Hanging means suffocating yourself. And suffocation is a slow and painful process. People who do themselves in like this wildly kick the air. That's the natural reaction. Our man didn't do that. The moment the stepladder disappeared from under him, his head rolled back so hard that his neck broke from the force of the noose.'

'You typically see this with people put to death,' Radjen said.

'Correct. The executioner fastens the noose around the neck in such a way that when the condemned person falls through the hatch, the C2 cervical vertebra snaps in half like a matchstick. A quick, painless death. I bet we're looking at a hangman's fracture here, Chief.'

Radjen again estimated the distance between the beam and the floor. The length of the fall was important. It had to be far enough to cause the necessary force for a fatal cervical fracture. But neither could the fall be too great. Otherwise the victim would be decapitated by the noose. He looked up at the rope again, at the way it was tied. Nothing here was in line with just plain suicide.

Length of fall, professional knot.

He'd even donned his best PJs for the occasion.

Completely inconsistent with the half-eaten sandwich beside the computer displaying Ghanaian seaside villas.

Esther's voice had the timbre of alcohol and cigarettes. 'This hanging was planned, deliberate. Not a rush job. Why would you walk away from your computer midway through a sandwich while looking at dream locations to take your own life in the shed out back?'

'Let's wait for the pathologist's findings,' Radjen said inattentively. He heard how tired he was in his own voice. Saw it in the way Esther looked at him. She smiled. As if she understood that it wasn't only exhaustion or lack of sleep.

'He was important, right?'

'As important as witnesses get.'

The fish in their blue tanks darted erratically past underwater ruins, making Radjen wonder if they'd been fed since their owner's death. He threw a last glance at the two forensics investigators, who were impatiently waiting to proceed, turned and walked back along the slate path, took a deep breath and silently looked around the garden. He was frequently surprised by how much lush nature was hidden behind the façades of Amsterdam.

'I think you're right.' He said it softly. Softly and slowly.

'I'm sorry,' she said, speaking just as quietly as he had.

'Because you're right?'

'No, that I didn't take into account how important he was for you.'

It was almost 2.30 in the morning. A rattling garden gate distracted Radjen. He walked over to it, took out a handkerchief, wrapped it around his right hand and pushed down on the handle. It led to a long, tiled alleyway that was deserted.

There was moisture in the air. Their breath condensed. He turned towards Esther. 'What do you smoke?' he asked.

'Gauloises Blondes.'

'Not really my brand, but give me one anyway.'

She pulled out a crumpled blue pack. He could taste the cigarette before he brought it to his lips, and he immediately got a whiff of lighter fluid from the Zippo as she flipped it open and the flame appeared.

He inhaled deeply. He hadn't smoked for six months.

'We're in violation, Chief,' she said, grinning, as she also lit a cigarette.

He tipped the ash into his open palm. 'Where's the wife?'

She turned her head and blew the smoke in the direction of the bedroom window on the first floor.

'There's a policewoman with her.'

They entered the hallway via the living room, and went upstairs. On the cramped landing, they wormed their way out of their white overalls.

Esther cautiously opened the door to the bedroom. There she sat. The smiling bride in the photo, now newly widowed, in a state of shock on the edge of the unmade bed. A prisoner of her own despair. A police officer, an appropriate distance away, in the corner of the room.

'Mrs Meijer,' he thoughtfully said and waited until she looked up at him. 'My name is Radjen Tomasoa. I'm the Chief Inspector of Police. I want to express my condolences.'

Her hand was warm and limp. 'That's very kind of you.'

He knelt down and looked directly at her. He saw how red and swollen her eyes were from all the grief and panic.

'This must be a particularly difficult time for you, ma'am. But I still want to ask you some questions. In connection with the investigation.'

Her eyes were now focused on his. Her voice was calm, despite the desperation her entire body exuded.

'You don't have to call me ma'am. My name is Efrya, Efrya Anane Konadu Meijer.'

'Can you tell me, Efrya, in your own words, what happened?'

'Mr Tomasoa . . .'

'Radjen . . .'

'I woke up. From the wind. The door downstairs. It was banging. Sometimes he leaves it open. When he goes to the shed, he often forgets . . . just forgets to shut it behind him . . . I went downstairs. To the living room . . . But . . . he wasn't there. I knew . . . there was something . . .'

She was silent for a moment. Staring straight ahead, as if imagining herself standing in the empty living room again, looking into the garden.

'Efrya?'

When she gazed back at him, her eyes were blurry with tears. 'He went out to the shed just about every night. He could spend hours there. With all the things he'd built himself.'

'The island of Atlantis,' Radjen said softly.

'He believed in it. "One day," he said, "I'm going to take you there. To Atlantis."' She wiped her eyes dry with a tissue.

'You were in the room . . .'

'I went outside. In the shed . . . I found him.'

Efrya closed her eyes. As if returning to the very moment she found him hanging there. Radjen imagined the silent scream she'd let out.

'We were going to do this together, Radjen. When the time was right. Together. We'd promised each other. We'd never leave the other behind.'

She dabbed at her tears with the tissue clutched in her hand. He saw her face change: her taut features relaxed. It was as if she'd turned her eyes inward, trying to find strength in what she now told him in a trusting whisper. 'He'd promised it would stop. It couldn't go on like this.'

She began to sob.

Radjen nodded to Esther, who put her arm around the crying widow.

His body was still half asleep. His muscles stiff. Kneeling was too tiring. He stretched his legs while bending over.

'Efrya, we'd like you to come with us. We're going to police headquarters, where you can tell us more.'

Like an inconsolable, displaced child, Efrya let herself be guided from the room. Radjen stayed behind in the bedroom by himself.

His eyes focused on the bed. Here a woman had slept beside her husband. He imagined them. Entwined. Each with their dreams, their expectations. The man and woman in the photo on the mantelpiece downstairs. The man who woke up. Crept downstairs in the dark. Sat down in front of his computer. Ate a sandwich, drank some milk. Looked at villas on a Ghanaian beach. And then died. In his own fantasy world, Atlantis.

The man who could've helped him unravel a case. A case that had started with a young boy who was a hit-and-run victim on a dark woodland road.

The man who'd been driving was now hanging in a noose.

Radjen went downstairs and outside, where he saw the police van driving off with Efrya Meijer inside. He approached Esther van Noordt.

'We're going to solve this together, Van Noordt. You and me. See you at the station.'

He turned and headed to his car without waiting for her reply. He had enough unanswered questions of his own.

5

Ulitsa Petrovka owed its name to the Vysokopetrovsky Monastery at the top of the hill, but other than that the street had nothing whatsoever to do with religious affairs and all the more with worldly matters. The street was jammed with Porches and Ferraris, which were double-parked in front of high-end department stores such as Petrovka Passazh and TsUM, restaurants and nightclubs. But Paul and Anya were largely oblivious to all this. Their eyes were on the robust nineteenth-century building with the triangular colonnade that housed Moscow's police headquarters: 38 Ulitsa Petrovka.

In the Potemkin Hospital mortuary where the air-con had been out of order for days and Olga of the Communications Department would've liked to usher them out the door as quickly as possible, they stumbled upon more clues that something about the Seven Sisters hostage-taking wasn't quite what it seemed.

A woman who was most likely Estonian was supposed to have passed for a Chechen rebel. And this woman had allegedly shot a video of Farah on her mobile – footage that could prove she hadn't given her recorded statement voluntarily.

Together with the photos Paul had taken, this material could be instrumental in clearing Farah's name. But, in order to get hold of it, they'd have to find a way into the depot, where the confiscated possessions of the hostage-takers had been taken.

The depot at 38 Ulitsa Petrovka.

The bust of Dzerzhinsky, the notorious founder of the Soviet Union's first secret police force, took centre stage in front of the main entrance. The bust reminded Paul and Anya of something they'd known all along: without help, they'd never get past the front door.

Via Petrovsky Bulvar, the street behind Ulitsa Petrovka, they entered a bar that did what bars are supposed to do: give you the feeling it serves the greatest drinks in the world. But the best thing about it was the absence of a shaven-headed, shiny-suited Neanderthal at the door. And so, among smart, Western-looking young Russians of means, expats and a handful of heavily made-up blondes eager to expand their male network, they could meet up with Viktor Antonovich in anonymous luxury. In his thirties, with a crewcut and an inscrutable gaze, he was waiting for them at one of the round tables. According to Anya, he was able to do what they couldn't: smuggle a terrorist's mobile out of police headquarters.

Paul estimated Viktor at over a hundred kilos, much of which was muscle. The emblem of the Moscow division of the paramilitary force OMON, a red bison, graced his right bicep. His face looked as if a hundred-tonne T-42 tank had just rolled across it, and Paul saw the butt of what might be a Makarov pistol sticking out of a holster.

Anya made a beeline for him and shook his hand. Viktor was one of those men who'd let people smash furniture on his back during his Army training, who'd lie down on a bed of glass shards and nails while a mate did a Cossack dance on his bare chest. When a man like that shakes a woman's hand, it always looks vaguely ridiculous.

Anya had met Viktor during one of her trips to Chechnya. His OMON unit had been deployed there for *zachistka*, mopping-up operations in which entire villages were surrounded and door-to-door searches carried out with the aim of locating and eliminating Chechens suspected of terrorist activities. At some point, Viktor himself had been ambushed by Chechen troops, captured and tortured. But, loyal to his unit's motto – 'Special forces show no mercy and never ask for it' – he'd not given an inch. Eventually, more dead than alive, he was exchanged for Chechen prisoners. Anya's article about how he'd narrowly escaped death in captivity made him a hero within OMON's ranks. It was time for him to return the favour.

That, at any rate, was Anya's thinking.

What Viktor thought about this was anyone's guess, but the way he scrutinized Paul didn't bode well. Dogs sometimes looked at you this way when they weren't entirely sure whether to attack or to leave you be.

'I expected you alone,' Viktor said to Anya.

'He's a trusted friend.'

'And an American,' Paul added. 'Would you like something to drink from an American?'

'His blood,' Viktor said.

Friends for life, Paul thought to himself, and beckoned one of the waitresses, who looked like she lived at the gym and slept in a tanning salon.

'It's about a mutual friend and colleague,' Anya said. 'Whatever's on that mobile can prove her innocence.'

'I don't care about any of that,' Viktor replied. 'I promised I'd help you. That's all the reason I need.'

Anya gave him a smile that Paul was only too familiar with. It involved curling the right-hand corner of her mouth, a bit like Elvis Presley did in the early days, when he sang 'Jailhouse Rock'. Once upon a time, she'd reserved that look for Paul. And for him alone. Now she freely gave it to an OMON man, someone he also had to pay eight hundred dollars to. Obviously, Viktor needed these reasons as well.

Eight hundred dollars was a lot of money for a second-hand iPhone – or the comparable dark rectangular model Farah thought the so-called terrorist had held in her hands – especially when you consider that people in Moscow threw away so many used mobile phones these days that the city's sanitation department had set up a special recycling unit. But Paul was prepared to pay tenfold if necessary to retrieve the footage that was supposedly on it. Anything to prove Farah's innocence.

Viktor slowly pulled the envelope with the dollar bills towards him, all the while fixing Paul with a peculiar gaze. Then he downed the Old Boy he'd ordered, a mix of vodka, grapefruit juice and Thai chillies, and stood up.

'When do you expect to be back?' Anya asked. Paul detected a hint of nervousness in her voice.

'No idea. You'd better wait here; this may take a while,' Viktor said, and off he strode out the door.

Anya looked over Paul's shoulder in the direction Viktor had gone. There was scepticism in her eyes.

'Don't worry,' she said to Paul. 'He's a man of his word.'

'He's definitely a man of few words,' said Paul, who noticed how apprehensive she'd become in the space of a few minutes. And, as he observed her, he felt something he'd rarely felt for her: a strange kind of compassion. It was a sentiment that had no place in their relationship, not even now that it was purely professional. In the days when he'd lived with her, there'd been a permanent electric charge between them. The sparks were always flying with Anya. Not only was she a passionate lover, but also a confrontational life partner. She gave herself to him with her heart and soul. And she expected the same in return. Together, they would fight the world's ills.

A fight she was destined to lose.

And now that he was briefly back in Moscow because of

Farah, now that he was sitting opposite Anya in a bar, she revealed an unexpectedly vulnerable side.

'I still miss you,' she said.

The realization of just how unhappy she must have been since he'd swapped Moscow for Johannesburg more than eighteen months ago without so much as a word weighed on him like a concrete block.

He tried to think of something to say, something to alleviate his sense of guilt without compromising his true feelings, but he was denied the chance. A punkish girl ran into the bar screaming, chased by two men from Viktor's unit. Panicked guests fled and she tripped on an overturned table. The OMON men closed in, grabbed hold of the girl, and were about to drag her out when they were set upon by sympathizers who'd followed them inside. Smoke drifted into the bar, probably from a smoke bomb on the street.

Paul and Anya escaped with the other customers, straight into the chaos on Ulitsa Petrovka.

Opposite police headquarters, on a hastily improvised stage constructed of pallets, the heavily made-up lead singer of a punk-rock girl band yelled 'Kiss a pig!' A handful of other girls, with bared breasts and lips painted blood-red, charged at the surprised police officers, flung themselves around the men's necks and tried to kiss them on the mouth.

The hardliners of the 'Kiss a Pig' group, organized in protest against a new police law, used the OMON's prompt arrival on the scene as an excuse for a battle.

'We can't stay here,' Anya shouted.

Paving stones and smoke bombs were flying about. The OMON were making a baton charge in an effort to clear the immediate surroundings of 38 Ulitsa Petrovka.

Paul and Anya ran into a narrow side street. Back on Petrovsky Bulvar, Paul realized he'd not only lost his eight hundred dollars, but that their entire mission was becoming something of a disaster.

The fighting was encroaching on them. Anya couldn't get the car started. A fist pounded on the driver's window. Then the emotionless face of Viktor came into view, his eyes hard as steel.

He stuffed a jute bag through the hurriedly opened window.

'No idea which one it might be,' he said. 'These are all the dark rectangular models.'

With the flat of his hand he slapped the roof of the Škoda and disappeared as quickly as he'd appeared.

6

Farah saw her haunting image again: the girl who'd fainted in Moscow. This time she was sitting at the foot of the rickety teak bed in the clammy hotel room near Jakarta's old port. It was the same girl, except she was no longer begging for her life. She wasn't moving – in fact, she didn't even seem to be breathing – and her eyes were wide with horror.

The young woman was just sitting there, like a frozen memory, while Paul's voice boomed in Farah's left ear.

'Describe to me what she looked like.'

'Do you have any idea what time it is?'

'You're four hours ahead of us here . . . I'm sorry . . . but it's important, otherwise I'd never –'

'It's okay, Paul. Good to hear your voice again.'

'Even though it's four o'clock in the morning?'

She heard him inhaling. 'Are you smoking?'

'Yes, it keeps me awake. Whereabouts are you?'

'In some shabby hotel, not far from the old port.'

'Jakarta?'

She produced an affirmative sound.

'You made it.'

She looked straight ahead, into the eyes of the motionless girl in front of her.

'Do you hear me, Farah? You made it.'

'Blonde . . . medium-length, straight hair . . .'

'What?'

'The girl.'

'Oh, right. What about her eyes?'

'Blue . . . hang on . . . red.'

'There's no such thing as red eyes.'

'I reckon she's a redhead, but she dyes her hair. Her skin's pale, nearly translucent. She's got freckles and a bit of a pout.'

'Sounds like she's from England or Scotland.'

'Eastern European, I'd say. Maybe Russian. She was muttering to herself when she thought she was . . . It sounded Russian, certainly not English.'

'Age?'

Farah saw the girl's perfect skin, the glassy eyes, the outline of her hunched-over shoulders, her cowering body.

'Early twenties at most.'

In the silence that followed, she heard him inhale again.

'What's wrong, Paul?'

A deep sigh followed. She pictured him blowing out the smoke in a long, straight line.

'Paul?'

'I'll get you out of this, Farah, I promise.'

'I believe you, but please tell me what's wrong.'

'We found the woman, the terrorist, or, that's to say, the woman who was supposed to pass for one . . .'

'But?'

'We don't have her phone. We do have other shit, phones that . . .'

'That what?'

'I think we've been taken for a ride. The person who was going to smuggle the phone out of the depot turned up with a whole bagful – about thirty in total. We're taking out the memory cards to read them. We're still working on it, but so far . . . there's nothing there . . . just rubbish. I don't think . . .'

As Paul took a strong drag, she could hear the soft, crackling sound of burning tobacco. When he resumed talking, he sounded different – less heavy.

'All this time we completely overlooked the fact that we have a witness. We may not need those phones after all. You know what, I'm going to find that girl. I'm going to record her side of the story, consolidate it with my own account and the photos we already have, and then you won't have to spend any more time all by yourself in some shabby hotel worrying. I'll call you as soon as I've tracked her down. Hang in there.'

Farah just kept listening to the dialling tone. The morning light crept in through the worn shutters. The girl dissolved in a cloud of whirling dust particles.

You made it.

In Moscow there had been first the numbness and then the relief at having survived being taken hostage. It was only now, now that she'd made it through all the immigration checks, now that she'd escaped the security services, only now in this grubby hotel room on the other side of the world, that the real fear set in.

Hang in there.

Through the chinks in the closed shutters, she could hear the buzz of frenetically honking mopeds, the sputtering of small wooden boats mooring and unmooring, and the hollering of men on the quay.

Exhausted, she shuffled towards the bathroom. Keep moving, she had to keep moving. She had to get a grip on what was happening to her.

It was the only way she could get back to work.

She clutched the shower bar with one hand and turned on the tap with the other. Tepid, rusty water splashed over her head, dripped down her body and splattered on to the green, mildewed stone floor. Leaning her forehead against the tiled wall, she supported herself with both hands.

Hang in there.

With the water gushing over her back, she allowed the tears to flow freely.

She unwrapped a small piece of soap and began to rub her body with it, as if she could scrub away all the misery from her memories.

When the final soap suds had been rinsed off, she cupped her hands and splashed her face with the water. This she repeated, over and over, like the final step of a purification ritual.

She'd stopped crying.

7

The concrete car-park slabs were flooded by the previous night's heavy rainfall. The police headquarters was brokenly reflected in the puddles like loose pieces of a jigsaw puzzle. As always, Radjen Tomasoa manoeuvred into a parking spot at too much of an angle and had to put his car into reverse to straighten it out. He thought of the sigh Elisabeth would have let out if she'd been sitting beside him. A sigh that would have said so much more than the long silences that stretched between them. A sigh that grated on the strapping bald man now staring at him in the rear-view mirror.

He pulled back out of the spot, furiously shifted gears, let the engine roar and the wheels spin, pushed down on the accelerator as hard as he could and spun around on the concrete slabs. Brakes screeching. His headlights illuminated a metre-high spray of water that resembled a fountain lit from underneath. He felt a sense of satisfaction as he deftly slipped the car in between two other police vehicles.

The usual activities were in full swing in his department, despite the early-morning hour. No matter the time of day or night, the station teemed with life: arriving via emergency calls, manifesting itself on the screens of search engines displaying criminal profiles and sending suspects to interrogation rooms, such as the widow of the man who'd supposedly hanged himself in the bluish reflection of his aquariums.

Radjen took the stairs to the third floor and made a pit stop at the king-sized coffee machine, so familiar to him after all these years that their relationship had taken on almost human qualities. A slight kick against the right side, a caressing smack with the flat of his hand top left and a quick press on the next-to-last button gave him what he so desperately needed at this moment: a double espresso. And on the way to his office, as always, he burned his tongue taking the first sip.

He opened his desk drawer and pulled out a file. This case had become even more sinister than it was already because of last night's suicide. He laid the folder on his desk without opening it, sank into his leather swivel chair, took another sip of coffee and closed his eyes.

He imagined the man in his silk garb, atop the kitchen stepladder in between the illuminated tanks, watching the fish listlessly swimming in never-ending circles. A crude kicking movement with his feet. The ladder clatters to the ground. Why didn't anyone hear it? The man falls straight down; the taut rope cracks his neck. His head hangs down lifelessly.

'Normally, I'd knock.'

He looked up and saw Esther van Noordt entering his office holding two steaming mugs of coffee. He tried to force a smile, but his lips were too dry. She approached him, leaned over and placed one of the mugs in front of him on the desk.

Beside the aroma of caffeine emanating from the mugs, he caught a whiff of the sea. As if he wasn't at his desk at all but taking a morning stroll along the beach. He inhaled the scent and realized it was mixed with something else as well. It smelled like holding a Granny Smith apple close to your nose, one that had spent days in a cedar box. It couldn't have been the scent of her shampoo, or her body lotion, because he would have noticed it before. He'd stood right beside her in the shed. Perhaps after installing Efrya Meijer in one of the interrogation rooms, Esther had gone back to her desk and from a small perfume bottle dabbed this scent on her neck and wrists.

And here she was: one of his most talented detectives, who'd been on a three-week holiday because of all the overtime she'd accumulated. It was her first day back. Tanned skin, straight brown hair streaked from the sun, a small ring through her right nostril. Surrounded by the scent of sea and apples.

'So what did you actually do for those three weeks?' he heard himself asking.

'Went to England.'

'England's a big country. Where?'

'The Isles of Scilly.'

'Why there?'

'Gig-racing championships.'

'What's the attraction?'

'Everything – the training, competitions, working together with your crew.'

'Did you win anything?'

'We're just amateurs. We were up against women pretty much born at sea, who had oars shoved into their hands before they could even walk. We were fourteenth in our category.'

'Doesn't matter – it's the glory of the challenge . . .' Radjen raised his espresso in a toast. 'To the challenge!' Clichéd words of wisdom, perfect for a ceramic tile or mug. He removed a photo from the file and slid it towards her. 'Tell me what you see.'

'A girl, seriously injured.'

'I'd take another look if I were you.'

Esther stared closely at the image. 'A boy?'

'Child slave, young whore, plaything for men, whatever you want to call it. Run down by a car on a deserted road in the Amsterdamse Bos. Left for dead. Undoubtedly smuggled into the Netherlands. Forensics found evidence at the scene of the accident that matches a dark-grey Mercedes-Benz E-200 Guard, the vehicle of choice for chauffeuring Dutch ministers.'

Meanwhile, he'd pulled out a second photo and held it up in front of her. 'Do you recognize her?'

'They also have television on the Isles of Scilly, Chief. Isn't that the journalist? Involved in the hostage-taking in Moscow? Farah . . . something or other . . . ?'

'Hafez.'

'What does she have to do with this?'

'Initially, nothing. The traffic police and forensics thought they had the case covered. Until she appeared on the scene. If you ask me, she should have joined the police instead of the press. She was the first to recognize that the type of clothing, the jewellery and the way the boy was made up are a traditional form of child abuse that apparently still takes place in certain parts of Afghanistan. Young boys are kitted out as dancers and forced to perform for men, after which they're sexually abused. *Bacha Bazi*. Literally means "playing with boys". From the moment this Hafez stepped in, everything quickly started to fall into place. She discovered an evidence trail near the site of the accident that led into the woods. She took us straight to a run-down villa, where forensics found shell casings, traces of blood and drag marks. The estate in question is owned by the Dorado Group. Or Armin Lazonder, owner of IRIS TV, Managing Director of *De Nederlander* newspaper and the man behind the New Golden Age Project: a huge development in Amsterdam, with offices, a marina, hotels and all the rest. Lazonder bought the place six months ago because his wife wanted to create some exclusive club there. Those plans never got off the ground.

The villa is still empty; nothing has been done to refurbish it. Lazonder denied having any knowledge of what took place there that night.'

He took a quick sip of his espresso. 'A few kilometres from the villa we also found a vehicle, at least what was left of it after it'd been torched. Identifying the two occupants from the evidence we gathered wasn't possible: no matching DNA in our database. However, the pathologist did find a match between the shell casings left at the villa and the bullets in the bodies of the two fire victims. You do the maths.'

'The two men found in the burnt-out car were both victims of the shooting at the villa.'

'Based on this, we no longer have just a traffic accident, but a double homicide. This means that, besides being the victim of a hit-and-run, the boy may have witnessed what happened there. We arranged a special ambulance and transferred him to a secret location, where he's receiving medical treatment, pending questioning.'

'He hasn't told you anything yet?'

'To this day, hardly an intelligible word has crossed his lips. No doubt due to the trauma he's suffered.'

'Pretty clear-cut,' Esther said. 'How did you track our Atlantis man down?'

Radjen drank the last sip of his espresso and crushed the cup with that familiar cracking sound into a sticky pile of plastic. 'We also owe that one to her,' he said, pointing at Farah's photo. 'Meijer went to her because he needed to get the story off his chest. She convinced him to come in and give a statement.'

'Remarkable for a journalist,' Esther said. 'Usually they're only interested in scoops.'

'Hafez is pretty unique,' Radjen said. In his mind he remembered her walking on to the mat in the Royal Theatre

Carré. He was fascinated by her calm stride and her steadfast gaze, but, above all, by the pride with which she carried herself.

That was only a few weeks ago. He slowly pulled the coffee mug Esther had delivered towards him. Only when he went to take a first sip did he realize she'd been staring at him impatiently the entire time.

'Sorry,' he mumbled, putting the mug back on his desk. 'It was a really tiring night.'

'Why did Meijer leave the scene?'

'Because he was forced to. There was someone else in the car. Finance Minister Ewald Lombard.'

She looked at him intently. 'What was a government minister doing in the Amsterdamse Bos at two o'clock in the morning?'

'They were on their way to the villa. If we can believe what Meijer said, the boy was meant for Lombard.'

With an almost brusque movement Esther bent forward over his desk. 'You didn't get much sleep, Chief, and I've been out of the running for a few weeks, so let me recap this – if you don't mind?'

'Go right ahead.'

'Meijer ran down a young boy in the Amsterdamse Bos at night. Not an ordinary boy, but one dressed up as a girl meant to serve as a sex toy for Minister Lombard. Meijer kept going because Lombard ordered him not to stop. But Meijer's conscience got the better of him, so he went looking for a listening ear. He told his side of the story to a journalist, who then persuaded him to come here to give a statement. Have I got it right so far?'

'So far, so good. Though two days after his first statement, Meijer showed up again, this time accompanied by a lawyer. He wanted to change his statement.'

'Change his statement? As if we do in-store exchanges here.'

She leaned on his desk, her arms and fingers outstretched. She was sitting with her legs wide and there was fire in her eyes.

Radjen tried to sound business-like. 'I made it clear to him that giving a new statement would lead to significant problems with the justice system. Because in one of the two, he would have committed perjury. But that didn't stop him.'

'What did he say the second time around?'

'Only one thing. That Lombard hadn't been in the car with him.'

'For Christ's sake. But whether Meijer was alone in that car or not, he still left the scene of an accident. Seems like a clear case of causing serious injury by dangerous driving. Good enough reason to keep him in custody. So why did you let him go?'

'First of all, Meijer wasn't an immediate danger to himself or a threat to others. And let's not forget he'd been immensely helpful with his first statement. Meanwhile, the prosecutor gave us permission to search Lombard's apartment: the one in The Hague he keeps for work.'

'I see,' Esther said. 'Did you find anything there?'

'Files on his computer . . .'

She leaned back. Each movement accentuated by the creaking of her leather jacket. 'I hear a "but" coming.'

He planted his elbows on his desk, brought his palms together and rested his chin on his fingertips. 'Let's just say that the procedure didn't go as smoothly as it should have . . . I had an expert from the Netherlands Forensic Institute do a preliminary investigation of the place.'

'I assume he made a backup of the hard drive, sealed it and investigated everything on it at the Institute?'

Radjen was silent. Esther looked at him incredulously.

'Chief . . . ?'

Radjen coughed, bit his lip and grimaced.

'Jesus, Chief . . .'

'If a minister is suspected of child abuse . . . of course you need to intervene and as quickly as possible. But I know it's quite questionable, legally speaking, to start investigating a computer on location and I know –'

'Questionable? Anything could have been added to that computer! If it ever goes to court, Lombard's defence is going to make mincemeat of you all.'

He knew she was right, but he couldn't handle her saying it directly to his face, not at this hour, not in this place, after first intoxicating him with the soothing scent of sea and apples.

'We discovered incriminating evidence during the investigation, including a video with the boy.' He lifted his chin. 'And let's just say: he wasn't dancing. His dancing costume was long gone, torn from his body.' Radjen realized he'd raised his voice unnecessarily, and he stopped.

Esther's voice sounded hoarse. 'As far as I know, Lombard hasn't been arrested.'

'True,' he said, but so softly that it almost seemed like a surrender. 'The Netherlands Forensic Institute is still examining the computer files.'

'When will they be finished?'

'Hopefully today.'

'They sure take their sweet time.'

'We're talking about the files belonging to a minister.'

'Even then.'

He could no longer avoid her penetrating stare. 'Okay, Van Noordt, spit it out. Say what you have to say.'

She straightened her back, placed her hands flat on her

thighs, like sumo wrestlers do before a fight, and looked him right in the eye. 'So, has anything happened between the discovery of those files and now? Has any action been taken against Lombard?'

'Of course.'

'Then why isn't he in custody?'

'The day that we found those files, Detective Calvino immediately left for Moscow. Lombard was there with a Dutch trade delegation. Based on the evidence, we thought we had a good chance of getting international legal cooperation – making it possible to arrest him abroad.'

'In Moscow?'

Her tone was starting to irritate him.

'In Moscow, yes, and, even if it'd been Beijing or Timbuktu, we had to do something and we had to do it quickly. Calvino went to Moscow in an attempt to convince the Russian authorities, via the Dutch Embassy, to arrest Minister Lombard before his extensive network got wind of it. The prosecutor hesitated and ultimately didn't issue an international arrest warrant. And, in the end, not only did Calvino look like a fool, but he was seen as a detective who'd overstepped his jurisdiction.'

'I had a feeling this case was fishy,' Esther said. 'But after hearing this story, I know it for sure.'

Perhaps it was only some wild fantasy, or maybe the combination of her perfume, her eyes, her posture and the tone of her words, but all these things relayed the same message: *No matter how badly you've screwed this up, whatever mistakes you've made, I'm one hundred per cent behind you. I want to help you.*

'And you know what I think is worst of all?' she continued. 'That a little boy and an innocent Ghanaian woman are the victims of this.'

'How do you know Efrya Meijer is innocent?'

'Intuition.'

'As a woman or a detective?'

'Both.'

'Well, we'll just have to see how good that intuition of yours is.'

He slid the photos back into the folder, tucked it under his arm and picked up his coffee mug.

Esther looked a bit riled by his comment. 'I put her in Number 3, the least intimidating interrogation room,' she said.

8

Dark acid-jazz beats wafted towards Paul as he walked past one of the enormous arched windows on his way back to the central workshop of the Hammer and Sickle steel factory, somewhere east of downtown Moscow.

Paul barely heard the music. His mind was focused on the girl Farah had just described.

Blue eyes, pale skin, freckles, red hair dyed blonde. Early twenties, Eastern European, possibly Russian.

Inside the workshop, which was crammed full of computer screens in sleep mode, mixing panels and connectors, he made his way to a large desk where Anya had just picked a dark-grey mobile off a pile. It was a YotaPhone. The device looked vaguely similar to an iPhone, but it was a cheap Russian make and, because of its sluggish processor and low-quality camera, it was a phone no trendy Russian would want to be seen dead with.

'Anything new?' she asked without looking up, while dislodging the back of the device.

'Maybe we're lucky this time,' Paul said.

'You reckon?'

With a fingernail she prised open the lid at the back, removed the battery and then carefully pulled out the micro SD card.

Number eighteen.

Another twelve to go.

They were all being read and analysed by a frail-looking, chain-smoking young man who went by the name of Lesha. He had a large bald patch on the right side of his head, the result of being caught in a fire as a child. His maimed ear was pierced and full of little rings. The skin on part of his neck resembled that of a lizard.

He sat motionless behind his laptop. Only his fingers were moving as they unlocked the images, code, documents and videos saved on the SD cards. They'd been at it for hours, but Paul suspected they could have saved themselves the trouble. They'd been given crap. After snatching black mobiles from a bin of confiscated items at police headquarters, cramming them into a jute bag and shoving them through the Škoda's window, that OMON guy was eight hundred dollars richer.

As a journalist, Anya had a sizeable network of contacts, but in having so many it was impossible to vouch for all of them. Not everybody was reliable, far from it, and certainly not those whose services had to be bought. Paul had made up his mind: he was going to search for this witness on his own.

No connections, Trojan horses or inside help. This was his task now. And his alone.

He picked up the printout with the names of all the students who'd registered for the International Summer School. Lesha had hacked Moscow State University's digital archives. However, the problem with the list he'd produced was that it gave only the names, nationalities and ages of the students. Finding photos and addresses to go with those names would be a gargantuan task. But that was another problem Paul intended to solve in his own way.

'Can I have the car keys?' he asked.

Anya was prising open the next device. 'Why?'

He thought of what he'd said to Farah.

I'll get you out of this, I promise.

'I'm going to follow up on another lead.'

*

The International Summer School module that was taught at the Seven Sisters was an initiative of the Peoples' Friendship University of Russia, or Rossiysky Universitet Druzhby Narodov, RUDN for short. The university had been founded during the Cold War with the aim of attracting students from the newly independent Asian and African nations to Moscow and offering them a first-class university education. In this way, the then Soviet government hoped to create a worldwide network of young academics who shared the same Communist ideals.

The programme boasted quite a few illustrious alumni, Paul had discovered. The three most prominent ones were Ilich Ramírez Sánchez, also known as Carlos the Jackal, the man who'd gained global notoriety with his hostage-taking at OPEC headquarters in 1975; Ali Khamenei, the supreme leader of Iran, aka an enemy of the US state; and Mahmoud Abbas, President of the Palestinian Authority – not exactly a paragon of virtue either.

Paul walked through the gate of the university complex, which was so high it made him feel like a dwarf. The outline of the building, erected in the middle of a park, loomed up faintly in the smoky morning fog. The steel structure of a colossal globe was attached to the building's façade. The immense entryway steps made the Colosseum look like a doll's house, and the lobby was so big you could land a plane in it.

The woman at the reception desk peered at him through glasses perched on the tip of her nose. Paul thought there was something provocative about a woman of a certain age peering over her frames in this way. To him it conveyed something like, 'Charm me, or get the hell out of here.' He showed her his press card from the *Citizen*, even though he'd recently been sacked from that South African paper.

He told her he was looking for students who were prepared to talk to him about their experiences during the recent hostage-taking.

She took off her glasses and scrutinized his credentials. 'You're a long way from home, Mr Chapelle.'

'The best stories rarely happen on your doorstep.'

She gestured for him to wait, pressed some keys and donned her headset. Behind him, footsteps echoed in the lobby: students on their way to their first lectures. Although the woman spoke softly, Paul caught a few snippets of what she said to the person on the other end of the line: '. . . journalist from Johannesburg . . . to write about the hostage-taking . . . has the face of a boxer . . .'

Paul leaned towards her. 'It's my Bruce Willis look,' he said with a smile.

She looked at him with her eyebrows raised.

'Bruce Willis, at the end of each *Die Hard* film, smashed to bits . . .'

She was now speaking loudly into her headset without taking her eyes off him. 'His name is Paul Chapelle, thinks he's Bruce Willis and speaks Russian like a cowboy.'

She listened to the response, inaudible to Paul, and frowned in surprise. Then she hung up and pointed to the graphite-coloured sofa behind him. The sofa alone was big enough to give someone agoraphobia.

'Wait there until you're collected.'

'By whom, if you don't mind my asking?'

She looked at him, quasi-annoyed. 'Our Press Director, Sergey Kombromovich.'

'I'll wait here.' He leaned towards her again. 'I enjoy waiting in pleasant company.'

'You can find your company elsewhere, cowboy. You're blocking my view.'

Paul could tell that cheekiness as a charm offensive was still working on her.

Sergey Kombromovich was a balding man with an artistic goatee and brown horn-rimmed glasses, somewhat shabbily dressed in oversized green cords and a brown tweed jacket. A worldly intellectual who'd read all the Russian classics, Paul thought to himself, and probably spent his free time writing experimental poetry.

With the courteousness of a gentleman, Sergey gave him a decidedly firm handshake, while greeting him, much to Paul's surprise, in perfectly accented English.

'Very pleased to meet you, Mr Chapelle.'

Paul wondered what he'd done to deserve this deferential treatment.

'Would you follow me, please?' Sergey made the kind of gesture you often see ministers and presidents make after they've finished posing for the press with an important guest and the moment has arrived for getting down to business at the negotiating table.

'I wasn't expecting such a warm welcome at a state-controlled organization,' Paul said.

'Let me correct you,' Sergey said, as he walked to the lift. 'We're an independent institution.'

'That was rather different in Soviet times.'

'That was then. This is now.'

They stood face to face in the lift.

'You know,' Sergey said, still sounding friendly, 'I thought the latest *Die Hard* was rather disappointing. Again, that stereotypical American idea of Russians who're all addicted to vodka, speak atrocious English, sing patriotic hymns, are criminals and have leaders who don't know what's going on in the world.'

'Sounds pretty realistic for the most part,' Paul replied. 'But Bruce Willis is the last person we can blame for that anyway. He only does what he's told.'

'And you?'

'Luckily I'm not an actor.'

The lift doors slid open. At the end of a long, mahogany-clad corridor, Sergey swung open the door to his office, which must have normally provided an impressive view of the park, but today looked out on nothing but rust-coloured fog.

'What inspires a journalist from Johannesburg to write about a hostage situation in Moscow?' Sergey asked, after graciously inviting Paul to sit down in one of the red-velvet Art Deco armchairs and pouring him the mineral water he'd asked for.

'I used to work in Moscow as a correspondent for the *AND*, a Dutch newspaper. I happened to be visiting friends here and –'

'I'm familiar with the *AND*,' Sergey interrupted him. 'I believe my esteemed friend Edward Vallent is still in charge there, isn't that right? Please give him my warmest regards when you see him next. And forgive my impertinence, Mr Chapelle, but my belief in serendipity is like the faith of an atheist. So let me ask you the bothersome question again. What's the real reason behind your visit?'

Paul sipped his water and pondered the question. 'It's personal, I'm afraid.'

A frown appeared on Sergey's forehead. 'The combination of the terms "personal" and "afraid" is a most remarkable one,' he said. 'I mean, what's there to fear about the personal? The world, Mr Chapelle, isn't comprised of coincidences, and often it's much smaller than we think . . . Am I supposed to fear this meeting because it's a personal one? I don't think so.'

He sprang to his feet and darted to the immense bookcase,

where he ran his fingers along a few spines before pulling out a book.

Paul immediately recognized the cover.

'In 1968, RUDN acquired a fourth academic department,' Sergey said as he returned with the book. 'At that time, one of our guest lecturers was a driven US war correspondent, who was brave enough to seriously question his government's war rhetoric and true intentions.'

He put the book on the table in front of Paul. *Bol'shaya Lozh*, the Russian edition of *The Big Lie*, the book about the Vietnam War by his father, Raylan Chapelle. With the restraint of a classical musician, Sergey turned to the title page, which was signed.

'For my friend Sergey, with warm wishes from Raylan,' Paul read.

'I was a student at the time – hungry for knowledge,' Sergey resumed. 'Your father's lectures and book only made me hungrier. Later on, I ended up reporting on a number of wars. I've spent time in Afghanistan, where I witnessed our own mistakes – the Russians', I mean. The same mistakes the Americans made in Vietnam. After ten years of pointless warfare, I saw General Michailov walk across the bridge over the Amu Darya and back into Russia. He was the last Russian to cross the Afghan border. It was the ultimate humiliation, packaged as a victorious homecoming. Our government also tried to sell lies wrapped up as truths to its citizens. Just like your father at the time, I saw it as my duty to expose those lies. If there's anything I've learned in life, it's what he taught me during his lectures.'

Sergey sat back down in his designer armchair. 'And now I'm sitting opposite his son, right?'

Paul smiled uncomfortably and nodded.

'I'm sure I'm not the first or only one to say this,' Sergey continued, 'but you look just like him, you know that? You're his spitting image.'

'I hear that a lot,' Paul said.

'Think of it as a compliment,' Sergey said. 'Anyway, the fact that I'm now having this conversation with Raylan Chapelle's son makes this meeting all the more personal, don't you agree? So what could you, or I, for that matter, be afraid of? What secret, what mystery or what important information could you possibly want to withhold? So let me repeat my question, Mr Chapelle. What has really brought you to Moscow? What has led you to this university, to this room, effectively to *me*?'

Paul took out the list he'd brought along and unfolded it, which was a fairly pointless exercise, because it didn't add anything to what he was about to say. But at least it gave him some time to process what Sergey Kombromovich had just told him and, above all, what he'd just shown him.

His father's handwriting. The same as his own illegible scrawl.

He'd had many confrontations with this man he'd loved, but whose early death had not only made him an unattainable figure but also one impossible to live up to.

He ran his finger down the list of student names. 'One of these hostages witnessed my colleague being forced to record a video statement,' Paul said.

'And by "colleague", I assume you mean the Afghan journalist who's wanted?'

'You're well informed. But Farah Hafez is a Dutch national.'

'I've spent many years working as a journalist in Afghanistan, Mr Chapelle. Look deep inside the heart of an Afghan and you'll see they love no country other than the land of their birth. Your colleague is as much a Dutchwoman as you're a Dutchman, for that matter.'

Paul wasn't sure if the irritation Sergey Kombromovich provoked in him sprang from the ease and directness with

88

which he spoke or from the way the man kept hitting the nail on the head.

'I watch television too, you know,' Sergey resumed. 'And of course, like the rest of Moscow, I thought I was witnessing the coming out of a fanatical Muslim when I saw Farah proclaim her sympathy for the Chechen cause. It seemed only logical that she should make common cause with the Chechens, after the Russian occupation of Afghanistan.'

'In reality, she was a desperate woman trying to save a student. The girl was going to be shot if Farah refused to say what she was told to.'

'A journalist forced to sell a lie, who ends up saving a girl's life, but at her own expense. Is that an accurate enough summary?'

'I'd like to give her back what's rightfully hers,' Paul said. 'Her life.'

'That's not only a noble objective, which you're right to pursue, but it's your journalistic duty as well, I should think.'

Sergey sat down in front of his computer, typed something and turned the screen towards Paul as he began to scroll down a list with personal data and photos of smiling, sometimes shy but often self-assured-looking young men and women.

There were a great many of them, and, because of their youthfulness, they began to resemble each other, even when they were different ethnicities. But as soon as he saw her, he knew.

Her blue eyes had an inquiring gaze, her smile was timid, her face pale and freckly. He read her name out loud: 'Yelitsa Andreyevna, aged twenty-two, Number 54 Volzhsky Boulevard, Kuzminki, Moskva.'

Over the edge of the computer screen, Sergey peered at him long and hard. 'Are you absolutely sure?'

It was her. It *had* to be her.

Paul nodded.

'In that case it's me who's afraid now.'

Paul looked at him, taken aback.

'I'm afraid it brings this pleasant, but unduly short meeting to an abrupt end. You need to find that young lady asap.'

Paul didn't know what to do except shake Sergey's hand. 'Thank you for your trouble.'

'No,' Sergey replied. 'It's me who ought to thank you.'

'For what?'

'For breathing new life into my memories.'

Sergey accompanied Paul to the lobby. There they stood facing each other, without a word. When they shook hands again, Sergey cited an old Russian proverb. 'Those who fear wolves –'

'Shouldn't enter into the woods?' Paul finished his sentence.

'But you *are* going into the woods,' Sergey said. 'And you're doing it fearlessly, just like your father. If he could see you now, he'd be proud.'

Paul felt at least as awkward now as he had when he and Anya had been in the bar and she'd told him how much she missed him. He didn't know how to respond to people's warmth; it made him uncomfortable. It brought home to him just how ill-equipped he was to meet friendliness with friendliness, warmth with warmth, love with love.

Acutely aware of this, he gave Sergey a comradely slap on the shoulder and was surprised to see the emotion it produced in the man.

While crossing the seemingly endless lobby to the glass sliding doors, Paul felt Sergey's eyes in his back. When he looked over his shoulder, the Russian was still in the same spot, motionless, with one hand in the air — like a tragic figure at the end of Maxim Gorky's *Summerfolk*. A man after his own heart.

Outside, the world greeted Paul with a haze of soot particles and snippets from charred trees a long way away.

9

Without drying herself first, Farah walked straight from the bathroom to the closed shutters of the stuffy hotel room and flung them wide open. The early-morning light poured in, and modern-day Jakarta's tower blocks rose up behind the masts of the wooden schooners in the old port.

It reminded her of standing in front of her window in downtown Amsterdam, the evening before she was due to leave for Moscow. At the time, she'd had the disconcerting feeling it might be the last time she looked out on to the old square.

The view across the port only seemed to reinforce the feeling that she would never see her home again.

From a distant minaret, the sounds of a muezzin came drifting across the quay of the Sunda Kelapa, calling the faithful to morning prayers. She remembered what her mother once told her when she was little.

If you have true faith in God, you'll always be happy.

After all that had happened to her in recent weeks, it had become practically impossible for her to believe in a god. And, while deep down she might long to bow towards Mecca, the way she'd done as a child, to do the prostrations, touch the ground with the palms of her hands, knees, feet and face, and ask Him to free her 'from all the evil the devil whispers into people's hearts', she probably would never be able to bring herself to do it again.

Placing her salvation in the hands of another felt like an empty and pointless thing to do.

She had to keep moving, keep steering her own course.

Never stand still; never take a step back.

She took the laptop from her rucksack, removed the USB stick from her charm bracelet and used the decryption key to unlock Anya's files. To her great relief, she managed to read the documents just as she used to: incredibly fast. Hungry for information, she devoured the sentences, each and every word.

As expected, Anya had done a good job.

The first file revealed the background of the Indonesian government's ambitious nuclear programme, one which they hoped would allow energy supplies to keep pace with the explosive rise in population. New nuclear power stations were to be erected across the entire Malay archipelago. After an international call for tenders, a Chinese firm, a large Japanese company and Russia's AtlasNet had made it through to the final round. An independent commission under the chairmanship of Indonesian Finance Minister Gundono had assessed the plans submitted. Valentin Lavrov's Sharada Innovation Project, which proposed the construction of small floating nuclear power stations off the Indonesian islands, emerged the winner. The decision had been made; now Parliament had to rubberstamp it. And there lay the rub. There was opposition to the project. The most vocal opponent was Baladin Hatta, a prominent member of the Partai Persatuan Pembangunan and the Mayor of South Jakarta.

Anya's second file contained information on the Indonesian magazine *Independen*. The magazine had a long-standing reputation for being controversially critical, having overplayed its hand in a corruption affair surrounding Gundono. He was depicted on the front cover holding a piggy bank, and it was claimed he'd lined his pockets with foreign bribes. Gundono had taken *Independen* to court for slander, and a six-month publication ban was slapped on the magazine. The editorial offices were bombarded with stones and fire bombs – a 'spontaneous street protest', according to the authorities; a revenge attack orchestrated by Minister Gundono, according to Editor-in-Chief Ayu Saputra. Saputra went to the police to report an act of vandalism, blaming Minister Gundono, and in response was thrown into a cell where half a dozen police officers had a heavy-handed 'word' with him. Subsequently, a seriously injured Saputra retracted his allegation and *Independen* was officially disbanded.

Farah could feel her heart racing. It was certainly not unthinkable that Lavrov had clinched his nuclear-energy project in Indonesia by bribing ministers. What if she could somehow find evidence of this? But it didn't take long for Farah to be overcome by her usual doubts. What did she, a woman on the run, with a false passport, hiding in an unfamiliar metropolis on the other side of the world, think she could do against a Russian industrialist who was in cahoots with a powerful Indonesian former general?

Her mother used to warn her all the time. *My child, one of these days your blood's going to boil over. Think before you act!* Back then, Farah's mother, Helai, knew her better than she would ever know herself. Again, she had been ensnared by her own impulsiveness.

She'd managed to convince Anya and Paul with her Jakarta plan. They'd helped her to make her way over to Indonesia. But now that she was actually here . . .

Keep moving.

She packed the few things she'd brought – her passport with the strange name, her laptop with the encrypted files – into the small rucksack, and without so much as a glance over her shoulder left the room where she'd spent barely any time.

The room bill turned out to be three times higher than agreed the previous day. Farah paid the girl behind the desk only the agreed rate and then calmly walked down the stairs, ignoring the threats of having the police sent after her.

Shielding her eyes from the bright sunlight, she walked on to the teeming Sunda Kelapa quay, where she blended in with the crowd.

10

In the stuffy silence of the interrogation room, Radjen Tomasoa sat down at the table opposite Efrya Meijer, leaned forward, looked into her eyes and saw an impenetrable darkness filled with grief.

'I can imagine this is hard for you, Efrya, but we need more information. You were the last one to see Thomas alive; you knew him better than anyone else. Whatever more you can tell us about him would be very helpful for our investigation.'

'He hanged himself, Radjen. What is there to investigate?'

Radjen shifted uncomfortably in his chair. Esther, who was sitting beside him, said in a calm voice, 'Wouldn't you like to know why he did it?' Tears welled in Efrya's eyes as she nodded. 'Same goes for us,' Esther said softly. 'We'd like to know too . . .'

Efrya drank the glass of water, wiped the tears from her face and looked both of them in the eye. From the depths of her sadness, the faintest smile appeared. The fragile smile of a frightened child in need of comfort.

'I saw him for the first time on Good Friday,' she said. 'What a blessed day. For years I'd asked God to send me a good man. Thomas arrived in my life that day.'

'When was that?'

'Just over three years ago.'

'Where did you meet each other?'

'In Axim, where I was born.'

Axim was the place furthest west on the Ghanaian coast that Radjen knew. Dutch settlers had built a fort there once, mainly as a transit point for African slaves from the interior of the country who were being transported to the Caribbean. The fort in Axim was now run-down and the town itself didn't seem to be any better.

'I was teaching at a primary school and there was a nine-year-old girl in my class named Gifty. Her mother died in childbirth and nobody knew who her father was. Her aunts were taking care of her. She got money via a charitable fund. Thomas was involved with that fund. He paid for her schooling from the Netherlands and wrote to her on occasion. He came to Axim because he wanted to meet her.'

Radjen didn't know where all of this was leading, but he saw Efrya relaxing, and he decided go with the flow. 'So Gifty was the reason you met?' he asked.

'She shouted "Daddy, Daddy" and they hugged each other. That night we went to church. Gifty sat in between us. Thomas held one of her hands and I held the other. A moment I will never forget. Through Gifty, I was connected to Thomas in some way.'

Radjen saw a spark of life appear in Efrya's eyes. 'We got married in Accra; our car was covered in ribbons. People danced and sang the whole day. I was so happy . . .'

'The best day of your life,' Esther said; this time without any trace of irony.

'His wife had died two years earlier. Thomas didn't think he'd ever meet a woman again who'd be important to him,' Efrya said.

'Did Thomas have children?'

'He had one son, but they didn't have contact.'

'Did he say why?'

'His son got divorced. Thomas disagreed with his decision. "If you make a promise to someone," he said, "you mustn't break it."'

'He was more than twenty years older than you,' Radjen said. 'Was that ever a problem?'

'Love knows no age,' Efrya said. 'There were problems, but not between us.'

'What kind of problems?'

'It started when Thomas went to the Dutch Embassy in Accra with our marriage certificate to officially register the marriage. An employee asked him, while I was standing beside him, whether he was aware of the risk he'd taken by marrying a Ghanaian woman, and especially one so young. The woman said that most young wives leave their husbands once they arrive in the Netherlands. Our marriage was acknowledged by the embassy, but I couldn't go to the Netherlands with him right away.'

'And why was that?'

'I first had to do something called an integration exam: learn to speak the Dutch language and get to know more about your country's history. Thomas paid for the books and the course, and I took the exam at the Dutch Embassy. I passed. We wanted to bring Gifty with us but first we had to officially adopt her. This was a long and difficult process, so we agreed that Gifty would finish school first while living with her aunts and I would come to the Netherlands. But I missed my family. I missed Gifty too. I did my best, tried to make Thomas happy. I cooked for him, did the housekeeping, attended the compulsory civics course for permanent residency. Classes three days a week at a primary school. I was used to standing in front of the class, not sitting in a classroom.'

'You did everything you could to try to make Thomas happy,' said Esther, who seemed to sense that there was something else going on. 'Did you manage it?'

Efrya nervously dabbed at her nose with a tissue, paused and looked away.

'We're here to help you,' Esther said calmly. 'You said it yourself: you did your very best.' Behind Esther's calm tone, you could hear her pushing for more information.

Efrya looked at her a little shyly. 'Thomas said that I was his wife, so now I had to give him a child. A child who was really ours.'

'And what did you think about that?'

'I told him that he'd promised to always care for Gifty as if she was his own daughter and that she'd brought us together. Without her first coming to live with us, we'd never be a real family.'

Radjen was beginning to lose patience. He forced himself to remain calm.

Efrya's face was now pale.

'Around that time he started having nightmares.'

'When was that?'

'I think, four or five months ago. He saw faces.'

'What kind of faces?'

'Faces of children, dead children.'

'Did he tell you anything more about this?'

'Only that he saw them.'

'Not why they were dead?'

'No.'

Esther took Efrya's hand. 'Tell me,' she said softly, 'just tell me, you'll feel a lot better.'

Efrya opened her mouth. First, there was no sound, as if despair had paralysed her vocal cords. 'I was worried that we would have a dead baby, that his dreams were a prophecy.'

Radjen stared at the young widow with scepticism. Esther kept holding Efrya's hand. She seemed not to notice either of them, as if she were in a trance.

'One night I woke up . . . it was about a month ago. The spot beside me in bed was empty. There was a light on downstairs. He was sitting bent over in a chair. I'd never seen him cry. I often saw in his eyes that he wanted to, but he never did. Now he was sobbing like a baby. He told me that he couldn't keep it in any longer. I was shocked, afraid it was about us. But it was the things he'd seen. A boy he'd hit with his car. But he wasn't the only guilty party, he said.'

'Did he mention who else was involved?'

Efrya shook her head adamantly. 'It was better that I didn't know. For my own safety, he said.'

'What was he afraid of?'

'He said that one of the men involved was very powerful; he could send me back to Ghana. That it was better if I knew as little as possible.'

'Shortly after that, Thomas gave us a statement,' Radjen said. 'He told us that he had indeed hit a child. Indicated the place, time and the name of the man who was in the car. That man, he said, had forced him to keep driving, to just leave the child he'd hit behind on the road.'

Radjen pulled a photo of Lombard from the case file and pushed it towards Efrya. She froze.

'Do you recognize him?'

Efrya nodded. 'He's a minister.'

'Do you know his name?'

'I believe it's Lombard.'

'That's right,' Radjen said. 'A few days after making his statement, Thomas came back in to see us. He wanted to change his statement. He said he'd been mistaken, that on the night of the collision he'd first taken Minister Lombard home. After that, he drove back to Amsterdam and when he hit the boy he was alone in the car. What I wonder, and perhaps you as well, is which version we should believe?'

He looked at her, with the hope that he'd somehow forged a bond with this inconsolable woman opposite him. A bond that made her feel safe enough to tell them what she knew. He heaved a sigh when she continued.

'He wouldn't get jail time if he said he was alone in the car. That's what they promised him . . .'

'Who do you mean by "they"?'

'I don't know. The people involved.'

'Does that include the minister?'

'No, Thomas spoke to someone else. Someone who gave him advice.'

Radjen pulled out another photo. 'Was it this fellow?'

Efrya nodded. 'He came to see us twice.'

'That's Lombard's lawyer. He's not the one who decides about prison sentences. Ultimately it's a judge's decision. Thomas would've known that. Why did he still want to change his statement – what do you think?'

Efrya could barely get out her words. 'It was for Gifty,' she stammered. 'They would arrange for her to come to the Netherlands. That's why he lied the second time. But he also couldn't bear that he'd done that. It made him sick, sick in the head. He didn't dare go to sleep, he was afraid of having the same dream. That the dead children would return. He wanted to get away, far away. He wanted to return to Axim. He said he had a plan.'

'Who else knew that?'

'Nobody.'

Radjen and Esther glanced at each other. They saw that Efrya was exhausted.

'One last question, Efrya. The gate to the garden. Do you use it a lot?'

She shook her head. 'It's always locked.'

'Good,' Radjen said. 'You've helped us enormously, Efrya. Please take care of yourself.'

She looked at him with hollow eyes. 'Is it my fault he's dead?'

'No,' Radjen said, 'you're not responsible for his death.'

Esther leaned towards her. 'You did everything you could. You tried to make him happy.'

'Then why did he want to die?'

Esther looked at Radjen with a raised eyebrow. Radjen got it and nodded to indicate that she didn't have to beat around the bush. She cleared her throat. 'We're not sure yet,' she said as gently as she could, 'but it's possible that Thomas didn't commit suicide.'

All the colour drained from Efrya's face.

'There's a possibility he was murdered,' Esther said.

'My Thomas is dead,' whispered Efrya. 'No matter what you find out, it won't bring him back.'

'You're right. I'm sorry,' Esther said.

'I'd like to leave now.'

'Is there someone you can stay with tonight?'

Efrya shook her head and stood up as if she were now shouldering the weight of the world. The hand she gave Radjen in parting was even clammier now than it had been earlier that morning. Esther escorted her out of the interrogation room.

For a time Radjen stared at the blank wall in front of him. There was a crack in it that was gradually increasing in size, just like the crack in his bedroom ceiling. He had a keen eye for cracks and fissures, and an even greater reluctance to do anything about them.

He rose with some difficulty. As if in a daze, he walked over to the coffee machine and performed his familiar kick-smack-press ritual. With a cappuccino in hand and the file under his arm, he headed down the hall to his office with the same number of paces as always. He kicked his door shut with his heel, placed the cup – with almost mathematical precision – on the dark-brown circular stain left by all the previous coffees and sank into his chair just as he'd done for years.

He closed his eyes, listened to his agitated breathing and the heavy whooshing of his much too rapid circulation. He envisioned himself lying in a tightly zipped tent. From afar he heard an imaginary storm approaching and he felt himself shrinking, growing smaller and smaller, until he, as insignificant as an ant, was small enough in his mind to crawl through an ingenious network of tiny corridors looking for the path that would help him to make sense of these unsolved cases. He inched through cramped spaces where it reeked of rot, moved more deeply into the caverns, where he hoped to find a trace of evidence, a hint of a clue. He crawled through the darkness until his whole body was sweating. And he felt it: that same sensation he once had as a young man lying in his tent. At that moment, as if struck by lightning, he suddenly knew what he had to do.

He opened his eyes and saw Esther standing in the doorway.

'The forensics guys are finished with the house. A female officer's going to drive Efrya home.'

With the same inviting gesture he'd been using for years, he pointed to the seat facing his desk. Esther spun it around and straddled the chair, planting both her heels firmly on the ground. Her brown leather jacket made a squeaky sound as she threw her long hair over her shoulder.

'If Efrya Meijer is telling the truth, and why should we doubt her word,' Radjen said, 'then Meijer changed his first statement under duress. His reward: the half-baked promise of a family reunion.'

'But even if what Efrya is saying is true, it still isn't proof.'

'Right. But it makes it plausible that Lombard was with Meijer in the car at the time of the hit-and-run.'

Radjen looked out of the window. It was gradually getting lighter: the city coming to life.

'Have you ever taken a good look at an anthill, Van Noordt?'

'Can't say I have, Chief.'

'Ants can build an entire underground colony, complete with transit routes connecting different parts with each other. It's amazing how huge and complex these structures are. And' – he turned to her – 'they're basically invisible. All we see are some scattered mounds. That's what we're dealing with here: underground structures all connected to each other, and the only thing we see are tiny heaps of dirt. From the moment of the hit-and-run to the discovery of Meijer in his shed, we've been dealing with matters related to each other. But we don't have any proof. And a few hours ago we lost our key witness. We have only circumstantial evidence. Unless the NFI can confirm what we suspect. Let's get the hell out of here. I'll brief you in the car.'

11

Kuzminki was one of the poorest and perhaps the most colourful of Moscow's working-class districts. A greater contrast with the wealthy, flashy city centre was inconceivable. Even the smog was worse here. In a hazy and deserted park, a blind old man without teeth played his accordion. Amid discarded household goods and ripped rubbish bags, he sang about the lost love of his life.

> This fine evening,
> under a starry sky
> I'm still dreaming
> one day you'll return . . .

A large concrete tower block loomed up against the dark-grey sky.

She was supposed to be in this thirteen-storey tower. The girl Farah had described to him. The girl called Yelitsa Andreyevna who lived in an *obshaga*, a dormitory at Number 54 Volzhsky Boulevard, Kuzminki.

It felt like it was at least forty degrees Celsius in the tower block's neon-lit lobby. Behind a fold-down desk, a surly-looking woman who was well over fifty sat in the air current of a rattling fan. Her thinning grey hair had been dyed black, the wrinkles in her face plastered with foundation, her eyes heavily lined with black kohl and her thin lips painted a dark shade of red. She was the woman with the keys, the concierge, landlady, police officer and mistress of this dormitory.

She was all of these things rolled into one and the look in her eyes indicated 'immune to charm'.

Beside her hung a gigantic wooden board with thirteen rows of small hooks: a row for each floor; a hook for each room key. Most of the hooks were bare.

'I'm looking for Yelitsa Andreyevna,' Paul said.

The woman held out her wrinkled hand. 'Papers.'

Paul gave her his tourist visa, in which he'd enclosed a small stack of rouble notes. She snatched them out and compared the photo with the man standing in front of her.

'American,' she muttered. She could have used the same intonation to say the word 'cockroach'. These kinds of ageing women seemed to suffer from the chronic and incurable ailment known as dourness.

'I'm her guest lecturer.'

'And I'm the first woman on the moon.' She returned his visa and made a bored go-on-up gesture.

'Top floor, room at the back.'

Since the lift was the size of a cupboard and reeked of fast food and urine, Paul decided to give the steps in the dilapidated stairwell a try. Each floor he passed looked more dismal than the previous one. Behind each of the twenty doors were small rooms, closets really, filled with two or three bunk beds, a table, a wardrobe, chairs and a few odds and ends. Each floor, which housed between twenty and forty residents, had only a single shared shower, toilet and kitchen. Since the introduction of the national state exam, which had students flocking to the capital from the surrounding provinces, these dirt-cheap *obshagas* were the only affordable places for pupils who'd moved to Moscow from the surrounding provinces.

By the time he arrived on the thirteenth floor, Paul was

gasping for breath. Hearing female voices, he made his way to the kitchen, where he found three young women around a table surrounded by stacks of dirty dishes. As soon as they spotted him in the doorway, they broke off their agitated conversation.

'I'm looking for Yelitsa,' Paul said.

'And you are?'

He hesitated. 'A journalist.'

'What do you want with her?'

It sounded defensive. He watched their serious faces.

'She's got . . . important information.'

'She doesn't want to talk to anyone – and certainly not to journalists.'

'Maybe she will when she finds out why I've come to see her.'

'And why is that?'

'I don't know if it's wise to share that with you. She may have seen things during the hostage-taking . . . It's probably best for you to know as little as possible.'

One of the young women, the middle one, suddenly stood up. Her face was flushed and she slammed her fist on the table.

'What's with the secrecy? What happened to her? Since that hostage-taking she's become a shadow of herself.'

The other two tried to calm her down, but to no effect.

'We shared a room; I was one of her best friends. But now . . . now I'm afraid to sleep there. She scares me.'

'Has she told you anything?'

'No.'

'Let me talk to her. I'll see what I can do for her.'

It was a promise he probably couldn't deliver on, but the girl who'd jumped to her feet was already coming towards him.

'I'll take you to her.'

*

They walked into a grimy corridor, lit by a few puny bulbs. The ceiling leaked and the exposed electrical cables looked as if they could cause a fire at any moment.

The young woman knocked on the last door. Behind it, Paul could hear grunge rock – distorted guitars, accompanied by drums. When Kurt Cobain's gloomy voice launched into the first verse, he recognized the unmistakable sound of Nirvana.

His companion pushed open the door. Paul peered into the dusky room and his eyes took in the unmade bed, the battered table, the kettle, the mugs, the overflowing ashtrays, the clothes scattered across the floor.

Then he saw her, barely five metres away from him.

She was sitting with her knees drawn up on the sill in front of the open window. Wearing nothing but an olive-green camisole and underwear. Her face was turned away and she clutched a half-burnt cigarette between her fingers. Behind her, the contours of the other tower blocks loomed dark and grim against the dirty brown smog.

Paul slowly walked towards her, unsure if she'd seen or heard him. She didn't react.

Through the small speakers, Kurt Cobain was screaming with despair.

Paul turned down the volume. When he looked up again, she was still in the exact same position. Her cigarette ash had dropped to the floor.

'Yelitsa?'

She inhaled the cigarette smoke. Paul drew closer. He wanted her to know that he meant no harm, that he hadn't come to demand anything, even though there were things he desperately needed to know.

'My name is Paul. I'm a journalist. I'd like to know what you went through, over there in the Seven Sisters.'

Slowly, very slowly, she turned her head towards him. Her face looked blank, drained. The timid smile she'd had on her university ID photo had seemingly been hollowed out by her experience. Her eyes were empty, pale face even paler. She blew out the smoke as if trying to make him disappear.

'I'd like to hear your story,' Paul said.

He produced a printout of Farah's photo.

'Do you recognize this woman?'

She seemed to stare straight through the image, inhaled deeply, stopped breathing for a moment, and then sank even further away into some black hole, a place no one could reach, where she must have found a safe space for herself.

He took another step towards her – she smelled as if she hadn't washed in days.

'Everybody believes this woman to be a terrorist, and that she chose to say what she said. But you and I both know that isn't true. She was forced. Just like they pressed a gun to your head and forced you to kneel down.'

She exhaled, slowly, her gaze miles and miles away.

'She saved your life, Yelitsa. By saying what they wanted her to say, she saved your life. I'd like . . . You could save her life now . . . you can do that . . . You're the only one who can do that. Tell me what they did to you.'

Yelitsa gazed at the almost-finished cigarette between her thumb and index finger for a moment before tossing it out of the window. For a split second, it seemed to be floating weightlessly in the mist, like a firefly, before falling to the ground, thirteen floors below.

Paul could hear noise in the corridor. One of the young women who'd been in the kitchen yelled something in Russian to her friend by the door.

'*Oni za ney prishli.*' 'They're coming for her.'

Paul snatched a sheet of paper from the table and picked

up a pen. Then he wrote down Anya's phone number and gave it to the young woman by the door.

'This is the number of a friend . . . She's Russian. Maybe Yelitsa will consider talking with her if not with me.'

Footsteps could be heard moving rapidly down the corridor, accompanied by fearful shouting from the young women in the kitchen. When Paul left the room, he saw two men approaching. They looked impeccable in their suits, their eyes pointing straight ahead. He could tell from the way they walked that they were armed.

He knew instantly that they hadn't come for the girl by the window. They weren't there for Yelitsa.

They'd come for him.

12

At a food cart right beside a Dutch colonial fortress with a view of the old port, Farah bought some *pecel lele* and sat on the steps to eat the fried catfish, rice, vegetables and chilli sauce, among businessmen in white button-down shirts, guys in sweaty T-shirts and tourists with sun-burnt faces in Bermuda shorts. Each mouthful made her stomach growl and purr with pleasure. With the chatter of people around her, the medley of languages and the sound of the gently murmuring sea, she felt good, almost like her old self again.

When a newspaper boy walked past, Farah bought the English-language edition of the *Jakarta Post* off him.

With screaming headlines and an alarming photo, an article on the front page reported on a leaking nuclear research reactor near the coast of Johor, the southern-most province of Malaysia. The plant had been hermetically sealed off from the outside world, and the Malaysia Nuclear Power Corporation had declared that there were no health risks for Indonesians on the adjacent islands of Sumatra, Borneo and Java. But the genie was out of the bottle. Rumours about acid rain causing burns, hair loss and cancers were rife. Both supporters and adversaries of the new Indonesian nuclear-energy project had seized on the incident at the Malaysian plant to put their arguments forward.

The leading opponent, Baladin Hatta, was quoted as saying, 'The incident with the Malaysian nuclear reactor confirms once more that our part of the world is not suited to nuclear energy. Far too few Indonesians possess the necessary qualities and work experience to operate a nuclear reactor. Corruption among the authorities is such that there are bound to be mistakes. The nuclear-energy programme proposed by our government is potentially lethal to all Indonesian citizens.'

Finance Minister Gundono clearly disagreed with this view. 'Indonesia has no other choice. By 2025, our power consumption will have tripled. We must have the courage to be forward thinking. Nuclear energy is our future.'

Farah folded up the *Jakarta Post*, put it in her rucksack and then descended the fortress steps.

In an internet café on Jalan Kalibaru Barat, she ordered a Coke and thirty minutes of time; then, on the sluggish Toshiba, she googled 'Baladin Hatta'.

The greasy screen displayed a handsome man in his forties dressed in a dark-red polo shirt. He had a determined look in his eyes and a masculine smile; in a word, he came across as charming and confidence-inspiring. Each image depicted Hatta in his comfort zone, be it as a politician in Parliament, a sportsman among sportsmen, an ordinary person among ordinary people. Many faces, many different guises, but always that determined yet charismatic look, a man anyone would buy a car from. Baladin was especially popular among Jakarta's multitude of poor and young people. He was the founder of the Waringin Foundation, a legal-aid organization that provided assistance to members of vulnerable urban communities, but specialized in helping children from the street. Through care programmes, education and sheltered accommodation, Hatta sought to make them fully fledged members of society. He was an idealist after her own heart, this Hatta. In the process, he'd also become the face of the growing anti-nuclear-energy protests in Indonesia. Needless to say, his ideas and activities didn't go down well with the current government, which had labelled him a Communist, an opportunist and an agitator. All good things come in threes.

Having googled the address, she flagged down a *bajaj*, one of the motorized tricycles that crisscrossed the city in their thousands, to take her to his party's headquarters in South Jakarta for two thousand rupiah. Shouting street vendors brandished their wares, mopeds buzzed around the place like cruel wasps, lorries spewed exhaust fumes, and countless cars slalomed through it all. It was the everyday chaos of a city of millions.

The party office was located in a large old building. Small groups of people walked in and out as if there were some kind of non-stop performance going on inside. On either side of the street, traffic police were standing beside their gleaming motorbikes, busily conferring with one another. She entered the hot and crowded lobby of the building and wormed her way through to a woman behind a desk that said PRESS.

'Journalist?'

'No . . . uhm, yes,' she said. That brief hesitation was enough. The woman made a bored gesture, as if she were swatting away flies. That same moment there was a commotion outside. Hearing the shrill noise of traffic whistles in the street, Farah followed the people who hurried out, and in the distance she saw three black SUVs approaching almost without a sound. Bodyguards got out, kept bystanders at bay and opened doors. From one of the cars emerged Hatta, again in his comfort zone and looking even better than he did online, smiling in a relaxed way and shaking hands on his way into the building as if everybody were his best friend. Among the press photographers, Farah spotted a camera team close by. She might be wearing her brown lenses, and her hair was short and dyed, but her face remained the same – she could well be recognized. She ducked behind a shoulder and allowed herself to be swallowed by the crowd while the group made its way into the lobby, in pursuit of Hatta.

She cursed herself for her eternal, uncontrollable impulsiveness.

Hold out a carrot and I'll chase it.

What on earth did she think she could accomplish here, at the party headquarters of a politician she knew only by name, just because he'd produced a few nice quotes that suggested he might be on her side? What was she thinking? *Hello, Mr Hatta, would you like me to give you some more background information on that scoundrel Lavrov? Yeah, sure, let's hear it, Ms Journalist, high on the list of internationally wanted terrorists.*

Disoriented, she looked around. If the city were a body with a network of nerves and blood vessels, she was now standing beside one of its main arteries. This is where the blood of a metropolis bursting at the seams circulated in the form of a stinking stream of motorized traffic tearing right past her.

That's when she felt an arm grab her, and a voice say, '*Kamu sudah mau mati?*' 'Have you got a death wish?'

Startled, she turned around. It was one of the traffic officers. Shaven-headed, macho smile, his eyes invisible behind mirrored shades. She looked at him, unsure what he was after.

'Crossing here equals suicide. And you're too pretty for that.'

In a reflex, she flashed him a smile and apologized. '*Maaf, maaf.*' 'Sorry, sorry'. He let go of her arm. From a distance, his colleagues were watching with big grins on their faces. She muttered '*Terima kasih*' – 'Thank you' – and was about to move on. She was clearly too confused for her own good; she needed to get away from any kind of uniform as quickly as possible.

'Hey!'

His voice again. More forceful this time. Her breath caught in her throat. She turned around and forced a smile as she instinctively reached for her rucksack to open it. She'd have to show the passport with the false name and the false date of birth. He'd leaf through it and stare even longer at the photo and the personal details than the officials in the Moscow-to-Kiev train had done.

Then he'd fix her with the look of someone who wouldn't have the wool pulled over his eyes. He'd bundle her off to his colleagues, with her hands restrained, and they'd put her in the back seat of one of their cars and take her to the police station — for questioning, for maltreatment, or something worse.

'Please be careful. I don't want to lose you yet.'

She could hear the good-natured chuckling of his colleagues. With a smile and a wave in their direction, she hurried on her way.

Her heart was pounding in her throat.

13

Radjen had the nasty habit of throwing plastic bottles and food wrappers behind the driver's seat, leaving toothpicks in the ashtray and shoving crushed coffee cups into the side pockets of the car doors. It had been an eternity since he'd cleaned out the Corolla. In a half-hearted attempt to get rid of the musty smell, he opened the window and then sat up as straight as possible. When he was standing, he could suck in his belly, but behind the wheel it blatantly bulged over his belt. He quickly pulled on his jacket to cover himself, but the damage had been done. From the corner of his eye he saw that Esther had already noticed.

As he looked up at the cobalt-blue morning sky dotted with airplanes and clouds, he realized Esther had been right. The NFI had taken their sweet time in examining Lombard's computer. He wasn't prepared to cut them any more slack. Earlier, he'd seen a key witness hanging in a noose and, with this, they'd lost a vital part in the case against Lombard. Those computer files were now the only evidence. He wanted confirmation, as quickly as possible, that those files hadn't ended up on the minister's computer by accident, but had been downloaded intentionally by Lombard himself. Most likely sent to him by a circle of anonymous fellow users. Maybe they would even manage to find other paedophiles who were accessing the images. Child pornography enthusiasts often comprised a tight-knit, secretive group, a closed network.

At Esther's urgent request, he stopped at a petrol station,

where she scored some hamburgers and large coffees. They parked the Corolla where the lorries stood, clicked open their burger cartons and took a few big bites. A hundred metres in front of them three lanes of traffic had come to a standstill.

'Roadside tourists,' he muttered between bites. 'We've become bloody roadside tourists having a picnic.'

He turned towards her. She just nodded; she was too busy satisfying her hunger. He looked at the traffic again. Why was there always that compulsive need to fill the silences?

'In the past, when motorways were first built, people came with tents and spent the entire day on the side of the road gawking at the traffic.'

Esther didn't respond; just stared ahead. She seemed annoyed, or withdrawn. He took a sip and sighed, but was determined to keep his mouth shut.

His mind was racing.

A boy run down, a minister under suspicion, two charred corpses in a burnt-out car, the abused body of a female doctor riddled with bullets, the attempted abduction of the injured boy, the broken body of one of his detectives, who'd plunged a hundred and fifty metres, only to impale himself on the spiked beams of a glass entrance canopy.

And, as the icing on the cake: the recent hanging of a key witness.

He saw himself as a child again, on the large rug in his parents' living room, with all the different colours, shapes and sizes of Lego scattered around him. He would look at it until he knew exactly what kind of a construction he was going to make. Now, fifty years later, it was a habit of his to look at every aspect of an investigation under his wing in exactly the same way.

Each case was, in fact, a whole bunch of building blocks

you had to analyse one by one, to figure out how the whole structure fitted together. The larger the puzzle, the stronger the incentive to look at the matter from different perspectives, zoom in on details, establish some distance and fill in the small gaps, discover new approaches, to finally construct a scenario in which all the isolated facts connected to each other. Sooner or later the chronology of events did become clear. Then cause and effect, perpetrator and motive, all emerged.

That's how he worked, and he'd always trusted this approach. His method served as confirmation, time and time again, that what he did mattered, that he had control over the world around him. And, above all: a grip on himself, on his own life.

But he'd lost hold of this observational role. The Lego blocks threatened to bury him.

'What I don't understand, Chief . . .'

Her voice startled him. Esther was staring straight ahead, as if she'd seen something in the distance that took her train of thought in a new direction.

'Two years ago they won the election, the Liberal Democrats, and that had everything to do with Lombard. He's not all that young any more – how old . . . mid fifties?'

'Fifty-eight.'

'My God, he got dealt a good set of genes: he looks young but at the same time trustworthy, with that touch of grey at his temples. I mean, when he speaks, I believe what he says.'

We're contemporaries, Lombard and I, Radjen thought. Same generation. Different lives.

Esther rubbed salt into the wound. 'I mean, the man is a walking success story. Makes a big impression on TV. Lots of female voters. Still has the look of an ideal son-in-law, despite his age. And he's doing it with little boys?' She shook her head and took a last bite. 'Hard to believe. I don't get it.'

'You're not the only one,' Radjen sighed. 'We think we know the man, but we only see how he's presented by the media. We believe what they feed us, not what really happens, who people really are.'

He thought about the YouTube clip he'd seen of the 'terrorist' Farah Hafez. She was a totally different woman from the one he'd seen during the Pencak Silat Gala, a woman driven by passion, the woman who'd brought Thomas Meijer in as a key witness.

'It's true,' he said. 'Lombard the jovial politician with the ash-blond curls, always dressed to kill, trustworthy. He could be the neighbour you invite to a barbecue or who helps you wash your car on a Saturday morning. It's hard to believe that a man like this is capable of offences against children. But I've seen the pictures stored in his computer and they tell a different story.'

He looked at her. Her face silhouetted against the morning sky. 'You're not telling me you think he's innocent?'

She licked her fingers and looked at Radjen. He unexpectedly felt the same intimacy he had last night on the landing of Efrya and Thomas Meijer's house when he was removing the white overall. He could see she felt at home in his presence, as if they'd been friends for years. She removed a cigarette from her packet.

'Innocent until proven guilty.'

'Why did you become a detective in the first place?' he asked.

She wiped her mouth with the back of her hand. 'No idea.'

'You wanted to make the world a better place?'

'No. Did you?' She offered him a cigarette. 'Do we still have time?'

'You smoke one for me.'

She took his coffee cup and the fast-food boxes, crawled

out of the Corolla, dumped all of it in a rubbish bin and leaned forward out of the wind to light her cigarette. He watched her from the Corolla the entire time. And he realized that watching her did him a lot of good: it created a pleasant state of turbulence within him.

When she returned and he started the engine, it crossed his mind to drive day and night, to the shores of Lake Trasimeno, to light that missed cigarette tomorrow morning with her, just in time to watch the sun rise from behind the mountains.

The heavily guarded rectangular building of the Netherlands Forensic Institute was close to the motorway, on the edge of a modern suburb. Lustreless black steel strips partly encased the glass structure like a protective shield. A bunker of steel and glass overlooking a sprawling residential neighbourhood, a tangle of motorways and a lush golf course, deserted at this hour.

Radjen reported to reception. Less than a minute later they were heading upstairs on one of the wide escalators, accompanied by a somewhat portly man with three archive folders tucked under his arm.

'Tom Dalsven,' the man had introduced himself. 'I understand it's urgent.'

'True, new developments in the case.'

Radjen estimated that he was in his late fifties. He had no natural charisma, no energy, not even a measure of vitality. A man who exuded some authority only because of his size, thick glasses and a plump, sweaty handshake.

They silently took the lift to the third floor, where Dalsven led them through a high, cube-shaped corridor with all the warmth of an ice rink and, still silent, held the door open for them. They entered a predominantly white space. There was a large work table with round steel legs, a screen and state-of-the-art hardware for copying data.

'We've searched the internet history to establish a digital timeline so we could see what the owner did on his computer. In this way, we hoped to determine whether the suspect was looking for something specific or accidentally came across the images while he was browsing.'

'And?'

'Before I show you what we found, I should tell you that, in addition to looking for files, we also checked which ones, if any, were shared with others. Files with the characteristics of child pornography are usually downloaded in a network. Surprisingly, we didn't find a network. We found the following photos and it's of course up to a judge to determine whether being in possession of these is a punishable offence. I'm not in a position to say.'

Dalsven tapped something on the keyboard, and the screen revealed a stream of data, numbers and symbols.

And then the first photo appeared.

Radjen estimated that the girl suggestively eyeing the lens couldn't have been older than twelve. Her shoulder-length blonde hair was partly covered with a thick layer of soapy foam, as if she were wearing a white woollen cap. Other than that she was naked, in a pose somewhere between standing up and sitting down. Perhaps she was getting out of her bubble bath at that very moment. It was a gaze he wouldn't quickly forget. A child's gaze, but also the look of a woman-in-the-making who knew she was being watched, and who shamelessly let herself be seen, because she had nothing to hide. Not because she wasn't aware of how attractive she was but precisely because she was intensely aware of it. Radjen couldn't explain it any other way. This image was about more than the naked innocence of a child. She was letting herself be watched, and she didn't care about it, which made what he was seeing so confusing. She was aware of her body, that much was clear. The suds on her shoulders that had dripped from her hair, the foamy bubbles on her arms, the reflections on her glistening breasts and belly. He could see all of her body to her thighs, and then he realized it. She exhibited the same audacity as those women who pose for calendars you always see in garages. Calendars not meant for jotting down birthdays or appointments.

'This is not one of the photos I saw before.'

'There are more.'

The next picture was of the same girl. This time leaning against a tree, her knickers and shorts pulled down around her knees. Her upper body was bare, her back to him. She stood against the tree as if trying to push it over, her body tensed all the way down to her stretched toes, but her pinched buttocks, bent head and the stream between her legs flowing to the ground told a different story. Radjen saw that she was demonstratively urinating against the tree. A few metres away two of her friends were laughing in embarrassment.

'No,' he hoarsely said. 'Not that one either.'

The third image was the most bewildering. The same blonde girl, in sensual black and white, hanging backwards on a dark-coloured rope she had tautly clasped between her legs. Her head was tilted seductively; her blonde hair hanging in strands. Her face reflected a languid ecstasy, mouth half open, her hands gripping the rope on which she appeared to be swinging back and forth. Radjen was aware that he was observing her as he would a grown woman, with the same lust. For several moments he stared at her bare belly, the navel, and sensed in himself the shameless need to reach for that belly with his hand, to stroke her there and whisper gentle words to make her feel safe, saying she would never fall, because he'd be there to catch her.

'No,' he said again. 'Not that one either.'

More pictures followed, and all of them portrayed the same summer scenario of a country girl amusing herself with friends.

'It was easy to locate the source of these images,' Dalsven said. 'It's the black-and-white documentary photo series *Ich bin Waldviertel*, about two girls from the countryside between Vienna and the Czech Republic. The photographer followed the daily lives of two sisters in a small rural village.'

As if on automatic pilot, Radjen's hands reached for his temples to massage away the headache he felt coming on. He thought about the thin line between innocence and sin, the difference between light and dark, a line he'd just crossed. The photos were suggestive, but certainly not forbidden.

'These aren't the images I saw, damn it!'

He stopped rubbing his temples and looked up. 'Where's the video?'

'There is no video.'

'I saw it. The detective who was with me saw it as well. As did the forensics expert. What happened to it?'

'You need to ask the external contractor.'

'External?'

'Given the hour of your request, our regular staff were unavailable or couldn't be reached on the night in question. The situation demanded a quick reaction, so we contacted the Nationwide Forensics Bureau. A reliable partner. They always do a good job.'

'What happened to that computer once it left the building in The Hague?'

'What normally happens. It's sealed and delivered back to us the next morning with a detailed report.'

'The next morning? So, in the period between its being confiscated and the return delivery –'

'It was stored by Nationwide Forensics and then brought back to us. We have a track-and-trace policy so from that moment on it's possible to follow the computer.'

'From that moment, yes. But my concern is the hours before that.'

'In these kinds of cases we work with certified companies. No doubt they'll be able to give you an account of how this was handled.'

'I'd expect no less,' Radjen replied. 'We're taking this computer for a second opinion. In the meantime, nobody else gets access to this info.'

He was fuming inside, but determined not to let his feelings get in the way.

'That bureau, Nationwide Forensics. Where is it?'

Dalsven gave him an address in the centre of The Hague, on Paul Krugerplein.

They were given the computer in a sealed box and transported it to the car on a special trolley that they didn't bother to return before they drove off.

'We had him,' Radjen said, slamming the steering wheel with his fist. 'We had that bastard by the balls and now he's slipped through our fingers.'

14

Paul thought of the two men who'd walked towards him in the narrow, dimly lit corridor, the clinical tone with which they'd ordered him to come along, the ruthless force that command had held.

They'd taken him downtown, in a dark-grey vehicle without number plates, via Nikolskaya Ulitsa, which connected Red Square with Lubyanka Square; finally, they'd passed through a gate and entered the courtyard of the Lubyanka, once a prison run by the KGB. Now it was the headquarters of the Federalnaya Sluzhba Bezopasnosti, better known as the FSB, the Russian security services.

As Paul got out of the car, the smog impaired visibility on the square, but the sense of threat was palpable all the same. In the Soviet era, thousands of political prisoners had been executed by firing squad here. Although decades had passed, this was still known as a lawless place from where you could disappear without a trace.

The two men stood on either side of him. There was no need for them to say anything, to waste words on him; they hadn't done so during the twenty-minute drive either. Their body language alone was enough to accomplish what needed to happen. In this case: his walking to the wide entrance, even though it ran counter to all of his instincts, even though the sweat was gushing down his back and his heart rate was unnaturally fast.

In the massive entrance hall, they passed through two electronic security scanners, and then walked down several wide, high-ceilinged corridors, their footsteps echoing almost in sync. When they came to another lobby, he was told to wait.

He looked up at an icon on the wall. Several metres tall, it depicted a tree of all of Russia's rulers, with branches laden with medallions of grand princes and tsars. As he looked at it, he wondered if his feelings were anything like the emotions that go through the head of a condemned man in the final minutes before his sentence is carried out.

At that moment two tall doors opened. A stylish-looking man in his fifties, wearing a dark-blue suit, made straight for Paul and greeted him like one would a guest in a five-star hotel.

Alexander Arlazarov projected an image of a modern Russian. He had a firm handshake and his dark-brown eyes fixed Paul with a penetrating stare. He had the affable half-smile of a man who, as head of the counter-terrorism department, had no trouble managing a staff of several thousand people.

'Mr Chapelle, I'm sorry to have given your day a slightly different turn than you undoubtedly had in mind, but I thought it was time for us to meet. Please follow me?'

Leaving the other two men in the corridor, they entered an austere-looking study in which one wall was covered with shelves full of pale-blue files. Shades of dark grey dominated the rest of the soberly decorated room. On the desk, next to a silver-coloured bust of KGB founder Felix Dzerzhinsky and a pile of papers, stood a large samovar.

'A family heirloom,' Arlazarov said, as he filled one quarter of a glass with a dark liquid from the little teapot on top before adding hot water from the tap on the side.

'Russian or English?' he asked blithely as he handed Paul the glass. 'You're my guest, so it's your choice.'

Paul accepted the glass. 'Why am I here?' he asked in English.

'Besides being a journalist, you're clearly also a mind reader,' Arlazarov said while preparing a glass of tea for himself. 'That was my first question. Why are you here? Here in Moscow, I mean.'

'I happened to be nearby.'

'Nearby?'

'From Amsterdam, it's less than a four-hour flight. After eighteen months away from Moscow, it's a small sacrifice to make for a drink with former colleagues.'

'And by former colleagues you mean –'

'Journalists . . . friends . . .'

'Girlfriends . . . ?'

'Mr Arlazarov, why am I here?' Paul asked again.

While observing a measured silence, Arlazarov took an equally measured sip. 'Please take a seat,' he said, as he sat down at his desk and opened the file in front of him.

The chair Paul was offered forced him to keep straightening his back. Spartan was the term that sprang to mind. This was no ordinary study, no comfortable executive office. This was something halfway between an interrogation chamber and a solitary confinement cell.

Arlazarov took a photo from the file and glanced at it, appeared to change his mind and casually put it aside. 'You know what,' he said, 'let's not talk about your former colleagues here in Moscow, however interesting they may be . . .'

Paul saw the photo that Arlazarov had put next to the file. Anya's face stared at him upside down.

'Let's talk about your current colleagues,' Arlazarov continued, as he pulled a second photo from the file. 'Of course I'm referring to a woman who has produced little if any socially conscious journalism of note in her career. True, there are two recent articles in which she accuses the Dutch government – legitimately, if you ask me – of inhumane treatment of Afghan asylum seekers. But, other than that . . .'

He studied the photo intently.

'Other than that, she's rather beautiful.' He looked at Paul again, this time with a smile. 'And, trust me, from a male perspective, that's not a problem. But this woman, Chapelle, this woman unexpectedly pops up during a hostage situation and boldly declares her solidarity with the Chechen scum bringing death and destruction to Russia. And then, Chapelle, after delivering her video message, she vanishes into thin air. That begs the question: does she have magic powers? Even Houdini couldn't pull that off.'

Alexander Arlazarov regarded Paul for a while without a word.

'And, believe me, Houdini was a master. One of the best.'

'What do you want to know?' Paul asked.

'Your connection with her. And what she was doing there, in the Seven Sisters.'

'I'm a *stringer*, a freelancer working from Johannesburg. I have nothing to do with my colleagues from Amsterdam.'

'So it was a coincidence that the two of you travelled from Amsterdam and arrived here in Moscow practically at the same time?'

'A twist of fate, I'd say. I was here on private business. Hafez was here, I assume, for work.'

'Do you assume this, or do you know this for a fact?'

'As I said, I have nothing to do with my colleagues in Amsterdam.'

'Not even when Hafez has an editor-in-chief who's also your uncle, and with whom you're regularly in contact, even though you work in Johannesburg?'

Arlazarov leafed through the file and paused on a page. 'Edward Vallent – am I pronouncing it correctly?'

Paul silently stared at the file in Arlazarov's hands. There was no doubt that this man had plenty of trump cards to fall back on – information, photos, names and yet more information. Who knows, maybe Paul had been shadowed by Arlazarov's agents from the moment he touched down on Russian soil. How else could they know he'd gone to hear the story of a traumatized girl in a decrepit dormitory room somewhere in Kuzminki?

'You know, I think journalistic integrity is admirable,' Arlazarov said as he pulled a packet of Marlboros from his breast pocket, 'but protecting the lives of Russian citizens is my top priority, I'm sure you understand.'

He tapped a few cigarettes out of the packet, which he then held out to Paul.

'No, thank you.'

'You don't mind?'

Paul didn't bother to respond to a question that wasn't really a question. Arlazarov produced a green flame from a metal lighter sporting an image of a double-headed eagle and lit his cigarette.

'I'd like to impress on you the need to adopt a cooperative attitude.'

'Do you really expect me, a journalist, to share my information with an organization that intimidates my colleagues and tries to make it impossible for them to do their work?'

Arlazarov stood up from his chair and sat down on the edge of his desk, from where he looked down at Paul in a casual yet intimidating manner.

'What's the life of a female Chechen suicide bomber worth, do you think?'

'No idea.'

'Less than a hundred dollars. Her family, or whatever remains of it, can live on that for a year or so. A black widow will blow herself up for a hundred dollars. And for that amount she'll send about forty to fifty innocent Russians to their deaths. From a terrorist viewpoint, a hundred dollars provides an optimum return on your investment.'

Arlazarov took a drag of his cigarette and blew out the smoke through his nostrils.

'The people and the media are supposed to believe that these are desperate individuals who see no other way out than blowing themselves to smithereens. Though in reality there's a complex machinery behind it all, a well-financed organization that manages to persuade these women to translate their despair, frustration and honour into systematic suicide attacks. All for a hundred dollars per black widow. *One hundred dollars.*'

Arlazarov rose to his feet, stubbed out his cigarette and sat back down behind his desk.

'Such an organization doesn't need an unknown journalist to express her sympathy for the cause on the internet. In other words, I believe fuck all about this story, Chapelle. And I believe the same goes for you. Someone's trying to take us for a ride.'

Arlazarov drained his glass and looked Paul straight in the eye.

'C'mon, tell me, man to man, who's trying to pull one over on us? Who is it?'

Arlazarov was using a curious tactic, Paul thought to himself. He was hinting that he knew exactly what Paul was up to, although it could well be a double bluff. At the same time, he was trying to make Paul believe that, although their journalist and FSB Director roles might put them in opposing camps, strangely enough they had some shared interests in this case. However bizarre it was, Paul realized he had to do something to break the impasse. He thought of the girl. They'd seen him emerge from her room. He'd told the woman at the dormitory reception desk he'd come to see her. They'd interrogate her, no doubt about it, and use God knows what methods to make her talk. This seemed to provide an opportunity to meet Arlazarov halfway and hopefully come out of this curious situation relatively unscathed.

'The girl was one of the hostages,' he said.

'There were hundreds of hostages. Why specifically her?'

'I'm prepared to share that information, but only on my terms.'

Arlazarov showed a charming smile. 'Since when are you in a position to dictate terms?'

'I'm doing something I don't normally do. Only because I don't want you to ruin the life of an innocent student by subjecting her to a grilling she's far too traumatized for. She had a gun pressed to her temple. They were going to shoot her in the head unless Farah Hafez said what she said. That's her story.'

'A story that would exonerate your colleague —'

'Farah Hafez is just as innocent as that young woman and all those other students who were held hostage there.'

Arlazarov regarded him gravely. 'There's actually a warm, beating heart underneath that journalistic armour of yours. But, whether you like it or not, Chapelle, I'll have to pick up the girl for questioning. At the very least, we'll have to verify whether she's telling the truth. If we get her to talk, of course.'

'You give me the impression, Mr Arlazarov, that you're a man of your word, that you can be trusted. And that's why I told you about this girl.'

'I'm interested in the man who pointed the gun, Chapelle, and I suspect it will bring me a step closer to the mystery of the missing journalist. Or, as the media insist on saying, "terrorist".'

Arlazarov walked to the door and threw it open with a grand gesture, issued a few curt orders to the two men in the corridor and beckoned Paul.

'As far as I'm concerned, you're free to go.'

He looked hard at Paul, as they shook hands.

'Where is she, Mr Chapelle. Where is Farah Hafez?'

'I've given you the girl. I hope she's in good hands.'

Something inscrutable came over Arlazarov's smile, like he was looking straight through Paul, seeing all his secrets, all the things he'd kept back.

'I promise. All the best, Chapelle.'

They had a code. Back when they were still together, when they worked together, when they did everything together. A code for when one of them was in danger and they couldn't meet each other freely. Anya had used that code twice. Now, after all this time, now that he'd come back, it was his turn.

As the two men escorted him through the long corridors, Paul realized that, while he may have left Arlazarov's room a free man, from now on there would always be someone looking over his shoulder, listening in on his conversations, no matter where he went, no matter who he spoke to. From now on, everybody he met would be at risk, just like the girl from the dormitory.

By the time he'd left the building via the main entrance and walked across Lubyanka Square, with the eyes of the two men in his back, he'd made up his mind. In the process he'd bitten down on his lips so hard that he could still taste the blood as he said the code into his phone. He did it in the middle of car-free Ulitsa Arbat, among the souvenir stands, the cafés and art galleries, the street performers and portrait-painters and the innumerable tourists. Right in one of Moscow's busiest spots.

'Please congratulate Miroslava from me this evening. Her twenty-first, how time flies.'

Despite the noise around him, he felt the silence in his bones – the silence at the other end of the line, a silence that seemed to signify shock.

She responded to the code. 'I'll pass your best wishes on to her.'

Then he broke the connection, walked to Arbatskaya Metro Station, took Line 2 towards Dinamo, changed to Line 13, and spent the next half-hour changing lines to and from the city centre, until, finally, Line 5 brought him to Park Kultury, where Line 1, which ran right across Moscow, intersected with the ring. There he changed, at the last minute, to the train in the opposite direction.

It was 8.45 p.m. by the time he arrived at Kolomenskoye Metro Station. He was positive that he'd shaken off any potential shadows, anyone that might have followed him. Yet he walked faster than usual. He took the side entrance into Kolomenskoye Park, to the left of Ulitsa Novinki, not far from the wooden church and the domes of the seventeenth-century Nikolo-Korelsky Monastery.

They were to meet beside the small watermill by the Zhuzha River, among the ancient oak, birch and linden trees in an old graveyard where few Muscovites or tourists were ever seen. It was where Peter the Great is said to have played as a child. They'd chosen the name of an unknown woman on one of the gravestones – Miroslava – as the code word for their meetings here. The woman's age indicated the time they'd meet.

Each arrived from a different direction, shielded this time by the smog from the forest fires. In the distance, they could hear the low hum of the motorway and the bells of the Church of the Ascension

When she hugged him, he could feel her hands trembling.

'I found the girl,' he said. 'And I led the FSB straight to her. They must have been tailing me – all along.'

'It's not your fault. You did what you thought was necessary.'

'They know we're in this together – you and me. I don't know how, but they do.'

'I've been on their radar for years, Paul. They know about us, about us back then, I mean. So it's not surprising that when you're in Moscow . . . they –'

'Farah was right. Each of us needs to investigate this from a separate location. I'm jeopardizing your safety by being here.' He took a deep breath. 'Did you get anywhere with those memory cards?'

She looked at him for a long time, without responding. She realized what he'd just said, that he was leaving her again, so she needed a moment to pull herself back to the here and now.

'Almost a day's work wasted. We looked at them all, every single SD card, all except one, which was so badly damaged it contained no data.'

'I still think we're on the right track,' Paul said. 'The girl . . . I don't know if she'll talk. I passed your number to one of her friends.'

'How are you planning to reveal everything that we do know?'

'I'll consult with Edward when I get back.'

'The moment you disclose your information and publish the photos of Lavrov, he'll come after you. And then it won't matter whether you're in Amsterdam or in Tokyo. He'll find you.'

'Sure, but he'll find *me*. And me only. You . . . you'll be able to carry on here.'

Without a word, she took his head in her hands. Her eyes changed when she looked at him. He'd never seen her in tears before. This was the first time. She kissed him – not with her former lust, but with vulnerability, with lips that tasted of salt.

'And now it's time for you to get the hell out of here.'

With that, she let go of him, turned around and disappeared in the smog.

15

It was getting dark. It was later than Farah realized, and she was too tired for her own good. She turned into a side street, and then another, and before she knew it she found herself in a labyrinth of mud puddles, sputtering mopeds racing past and countless radios blaring out a mix of saccharine Indonesian ballads, heavy metal and *kroncong* music.

Evening fell the way it does in the tropics. All of a sudden it was pitch-black. Lights popped on, fires were lit, and the aromas of fresh *nasi goreng*, *ketoprak*, *rujak* and *gado-gado* wafted towards her from all possible directions. She smelled the sweet scent of ginger, the citrusy aroma of *galangal* and the rotten stench of *trassi*.

She thought of the promise she'd made.

The promise to the boy who'd been left for dead in the Amsterdamse Bos.

'I'm here. I won't leave you,' she'd said to him.

Instead of fulfilling that promise, she was now wandering aimlessly down muggy alleyways in an Asian metropolis.

For a moment, it didn't seem to matter where she was going, as long as she kept moving. It was something she'd seen the junkies in Amsterdam's Red Light District do; they were always on the move and yet never arriving anywhere. That's how she felt right now. An addict without a goal, a wanderer who thought she could compensate for the lack of any real prospects with motion, by moving ever further away, miles and miles from home.

In messy courtyards full of playing children and crouching

women, fires were lit, meals cooked and food noisily eaten. But she kept walking. As long as she didn't stop, she wouldn't have to think about where she came from and where she was headed. All she had to do was to keep walking.

Keep walking. Where to? With what aim?

Breathe in, breathe out. Think.

Get a handle on the growing panic. Determine your course. Choose your direction.

She could flag down a rickshaw, a *bajaj* or even a taxi, and be grossly overcharged for a trip through the stinking city, but it would be worth it, because she'd be taken to a place that felt safe, or at least offered the illusion of safety. A place where she could consider her next step, where she could consult with Paul and Anya about her strategy.

She was certain about one thing. She wouldn't let her actions be guided by impulse this time.

That's when she saw the man in white.

He was standing in the twilight, less than ten metres away. For a split second, she thought he was a ghost – a ghost with the bearing and appearance of her father.

She heard a jangly melody behind her, a repetitive sequence of cheerful sounds typical of mobile vendors of ice cream, sweets and other food stuffs.

It was a snippet of a memory, and no sooner had it come than it was gone. She wasn't a child in Kabul, standing opposite her father, asking if she'd like a treat. The man facing her was an Indonesian who was waving happily at a young man on a moped pulling up behind her in the alleyway. A small sound system had been attached to the moped's luggage carrier and hooked up to a megaphone on a stick. A slightly hysterical female voice urged everyone to come and join the protest.

Groups of men and women began to emerge from the

alleys, as if they'd been waiting for the young man and his message. Some were carrying torches. They were all tense in a cheerful sort of way, like children going to a big party for the first time in their lives.

Farah thought back to the moment her bus ground to a halt in downtown Jakarta. When was that again? Yesterday? The day before yesterday? It felt like a long time ago. On that occasion, too, the crowd had come from all directions, both men and women, young and old. This time they were all dressed in white.

'Where are you going?' she asked.

'To Merdeka Square. Hatta's due to speak.'

'Baladin Hatta?'

'Do you know any other Hatta?'

This was met by jolly, friendly laughter. Farah accompanied the group to the end of the alleyway, and saw a much bigger stream of people in white march along the wide, car-free street. Banners were unfurled, more torches lit, slogans chanted.

It all seemed to happen spontaneously, like she could just float along, which is exactly what she wanted. It felt safe. She wanted to walk with these singing slogan-shouting men and women in white through Jakarta's streets to the large square. To hear this man who had now crossed her path for the second time.

All around her, fists were raised, and more mantras shouted. She became part of a collective anger that was winding its way through the city's streets like an illuminated snake. For a moment, it felt as if her anger about what Valentin Lavrov had done to her was shared by all of these people and they were expressing their revulsion on her behalf.

At each junction, more people joined in, and the demonstration became not only increasingly large but increasingly chaotic. Farah realized she was completely hemmed in. Sweat started to pour down her body, and her head was throbbing like an anvil being hit by a hammer.

That's when she felt the hand on her upper arm. A young woman held out a plastic bottle of water. Her face was open, like that of a child's, and her smile revealed a row of milky-white teeth. Even her eyes were smiling. Farah put her in her mid twenties, quite a bit younger than herself, and shorter too. Her long, black hair was tied into a ponytail, and she was wearing a white, long-sleeved shirt and linen trousers. She wore trainers on her feet.

'Thank you.' She gulped down some water and handed back the bottle.

'You're not from around here?'

'That's right.'

'On holiday?'

'No, just passing through.'

The young woman held out her hand.

'Aninda.'

'Valentina,' Farah said. 'My name is Valentina.'

For a split second, it felt as if they were floating in a bubble of silence. Then Farah let go of the woman's hand.

'Why's everybody dressed in white?'

'It signifies non-violence. We want a peaceful revolution. White is also the symbol of our hope for a new beginning.'

It wasn't so much what she said or how she said it, but the look in her eyes that made Farah feel happy. This young, unknown woman felt like a long-forgotten friend.

Out of a linen bag, which she carried across her body, Aninda pulled a strip of white fabric.

'You can use this as a bandanna,' she said. 'Would you like that?'

Farah nodded, accepted the strip of fabric and tied it around her head.

'Now you're part of us,' Aninda said with a smile.

Then suddenly her smile vanished. A shockwave swept through the crowd. A Molotov cocktail exploded in the distance, releasing a plume of fire and black smoke. Farah heard muffled shots. Canisters exploded above the heads of the demonstrators, releasing a nebulous substance that floated towards them with a hissing sound.

'Tear gas!' Aninda shouted.

In a panic, people took off in all directions. Some tripped and fell. Those who didn't get up quickly enough got trampled underfoot. Farah faltered and saw everything change through a haze of tears. Her eyes, nose and mouth appeared to be on fire. She began to cough her lungs out. Aninda held on to her. '*Saya berada di sisimu.*' 'I'm with you,' she yelled in Farah's ear. 'I'm with you and I'll get you out of this.'

For a second she was no longer in Jakarta. She was tied to the chair in the auditorium, with a bomb strapped to her body. FRONT TOWARDS ENEMY. The same anxiety, the same accelerated heart rate, but another lifetime. Paul's voice, a distant echo.

'I'm here with you.'

She felt like she was choking. She clapped her hands in front of her eyes. 'My lenses,' she cried. 'I'm wearing lenses!'

All around her she could hear deafening screams and gunshots, while more tear-gas canisters whizzed through the air and exploded. She'd lost all sense of direction and stumbled.

But she didn't fall. Aninda had her arms wrapped tightly around her.

16

Arriving back at the police station in Amsterdam, Esther and Radjen went directly to the digital-investigation unit with Lombard's computer. The room was full of seized computers, mobile phones, navigation equipment, USB sticks and security cameras. Anything electrical that contained data to be examined was awaiting analysis by one of the force's most promising digital detectives, Laurens Kramer.

Laurens was part of a generation who'd never known life without computers. He was fascinated by the huge amount of trace evidence he could gather from a computer, mobile phone or other data carrier in each and every one of the cases he investigated.

He'd attached the original hard drive from Minister Lombard's computer to a data copier, to which he'd coupled an empty hard drive. This allowed him to make an exact forensic copy. Tension hung in the air. Laurens stared at the computer screen. He reminded Radjen of a sniper looking through night-vision goggles at a hidden enemy.

'Data and images, accidentally or deliberately deleted, are often invisible but still present on a data carrier,' Laurens said, self-satisfied.

'Data recovery,' Esther acknowledged.

Suddenly Radjen felt like an old man.

'So even when information is erased and other data saved on the carrier, a trace of the original data is always left behind,' Laurens said.

'That's what I was hoping,' Radjen said. 'How the hell did they get rid of all those files?'

'They used a USB stick, a pre-programmed one to be exact, with software that was launched as soon as this computer was restarted. Whoever wanted to remove those files went to the Basic Input/Output System, where he clicked on his USB as the boot device. Are you still with me?'

'I lost you right after USB stick,' Radjen admitted.

'What you're trying to say is that the computer didn't use its own operating system when it was restarted, but what was on the USB,' Esther said.

'Correct,' Laurens replied. 'And that system is top of the bill, the cream of the digital crop: it automatically goes in search of deleted or altered files like a hunting dog. The system relies on a so-called wipe tool that uses just zeros to go through the files that have to be erased. Zeros, zeros, over and over again. Layer after layer, until the files are no longer detectable. Until there's nothing left to uncover.'

'And these images?' Radjen asked, pointing at the black-and-white photos of the two girls.

'They were copied over it.'

'Where are the original images, then?'

'Untraceable.'

'Even for you?'

'Even for me. But . . .'

Radjen saw the triumph in Laurens' eyes.

'But what the NFI failed to report is the time frame of when these pictures were posted. Sloppy work. It happened at five in the morning. So barely three hours after the confiscation of the computer. In other words, we don't have the original files, but we do have hard evidence that these photos were purposely removed and exchanged for the series we are now seeing.'

Laurens turned to Radjen.

'What's the name of the bureau that examined the computer on behalf of the NFI?'

'Nationwide Forensics,' Radjen said. 'In The Hague.'

'If you want to speak to the arsehole who messed with these files, best you check there,' Kramer said.

Radjen and Esther looked at each other.

'Back to The Hague we go, Chief.'

They drove the roughly sixty-five traffic-free kilometres from Amsterdam to The Hague in record time. In the old Transvaal district stood a recently opened Hindustani temple beside a building site. Two large cranes were moving large concrete slabs that would be used to build new luxury apartments.

'This neighbourhood is known as Little India,' Radjen said, as they passed shops of exotic vegetables, carpets, second-hand furniture, clothing and videos, all housed in nineteenth-century buildings.

It was if they weren't driving through Paul Krugerlaan in The Hague, but through a neighbourhood in Mumbai.

'The Hague is quickly becoming the Indian capital of the world. Nowhere in Europe do you find as many Hindustanis as here.'

The private company Nationwide Forensics was located on Paul Krugerplein. It was impossible for Radjen to find a spot for his car, so he double-parked. When he got out, he was almost hit by a cyclist, a Hindustani boy with a younger girl sitting behind him on the luggage carrier. The bike rode on to an area with market stalls, where residents in saris, burqas, tracksuits and leggings were hauling big shopping bags, and a musician with dreadlocks on a small stage played music that sounded equally devout and hip.

'That's chutney,' Esther said.

'Chutney?'

'A mix of traditional Indian folk music and calypso from Trinidad.'

At that moment he felt the ground shake.

Later he'd remember it happening, how it took only a few seconds. But those shards of memory would always plague him. They would remain embedded in his mind forever.

After the shaking came the storm of glass. Large splinters shooting across the street with immense speed.

He'd remember not the sound, but the vibration, and the explosive force with which not only the glass shattered but also the boy and girl were thrown from their bike at the moment they passed Nationwide Forensics.

After the glass storm came the fire, towering flames lashing out, followed by iron, stone and rubble. Windows burst from the intense heat.

Radjen threw himself on top of Esther in an effort to shield her. He protected her head and felt the rain of glass and debris fall on them, and he saw the glow of the firestorm reflected in her eyes.

For a moment all was quiet.

Then came the huge roar of walls that had lost their support, a ceiling collapsing. Thick clouds of dust spewed from the building. From every direction came the sound of screaming. The crying of children, dogs howling and barking, car alarms going off.

Carefully raising his head, he saw a street that looked like it'd just been struck by a meteorite.

He checked how Esther was. She sat up. She had abrasions on her face and he touched them with trembling fingers, almost as if he were caressing a wax figure. She nodded, stared at him blankly. He supported her, and she grabbed his hand, gave it a squeeze, and then released it, indicating she could handle this on her own.

Dizzy and with intense ringing in his ears, he managed to get to his feet. An extreme example of a situation where feelings are nothing more than useless obstacles. Action was what was needed now. He called Central Dispatch and quickly briefed them on the situation, so it was clear what kind of assistance had to be sent to the scene. The entire façade of Nationwide Forensics had been blown to smithereens. Only a smouldering charcoal hole was left, twisted blackened metal, a fountain of burst pipes.

Radjen stood over the boy who had ridden past with the girl on the back of his bike. They lay motionless on top of each other, ten, twenty metres from where they'd been cycling when the explosion occurred. Both had severe cuts to the head, neck, arms and legs. The boy had a piece of metal sticking out of his right thigh. His face looked battered. The girl was bleeding from her mouth and her ears. Radjen saw she was missing a leg. She opened her eyes and clutched his hand. He stroked her head gently and told her that the ambulance was on its way.

She clung to his gaze, her hand in his.

He knew she could no longer hear him.

He gently shut her eyes.

Every one of his actions after that, from receiving and briefing the police, fire and ambulance personnel to reassuring the neighbourhood, was done on autopilot. Perhaps it was comparable to the way cameramen and photographers do their work in war-torn zones; how they're able to coolly and decisively capture the most horrifying things. But only because the lens is between them and reality. Radjen's immense commitment to the job fulfilled a similar function.

It enabled him to defuse emotions, to act decisively and afterwards to spend hours giving a detailed statement – together with Esther – to the police so they could hand over the whole matter to their colleagues in The Hague.

But now, as Esther drove them back to Amsterdam, it finally struck Radjen just how far he was from any insight that could help him to solve a case he had as much control over as a herd of wild horses.

PART THREE
Flight

I

The glass white board took up nearly the entire wall in the Murder Investigation Team's space at Amsterdam police headquarters. Radjen Tomasoa studied the arrangement of captioned photos, arrows pointing to names and question marks filling the board. He'd just brought the entire team, comprised of investigators, analysts and administrators, up to speed about the recent death of the minister's chauffeur, Thomas Meijer. He'd told them about the child pornography files on Finance Minister Lombard's computer being deleted and replaced by arty images of scantily clad girls. He'd also filled them in about the explosion in The Hague, which had not only killed the owner of Nationwide Forensics but also a staff member and two passers-by.

He turned and looked at Esther van Noordt, who'd stayed behind at his request once everyone else had left the room. She'd flipped the chair around and straddled it. Leaning forward, her elbows resting on the back, she studied the captioned photos without realizing Radjen was quietly observing her.

Some things simply go unnoticed, he thought: clothing that wears thin, a body that ages, a marriage that slowly falls to pieces. Things in his life would never be again what they had been in the past. But occasionally he got a glimpse of the promise his future could hold. Like the first time he'd laid eyes on Esther van Noordt. That must have been five years ago now.

Last night, when he'd seen her at the door of Thomas

Meijer's house, he understood it. You could sweep something under the rug for five years, but eventually it crept out from under. Announced itself. He'd been aware of the feelings he'd had for her for years, and it didn't look like they were letting up. She didn't know. He didn't want her to know how he felt. It could end up being an embarrassment.

He walked over to the glass board, directly into her field of vision, and looked her in the eye.

'Now that you're back from holiday, I'm officially making you a member of the MIT. That means I need to give you the whole picture, tell you a lot more than I did at the initial briefing.'

He pointed to the photo of the Afghan boy with the frightened dark eyes. SEKANDAR, CHILD TRAFFICKING and BACHA BAZI were written above it.

'As I already mentioned to you, Detective Calvino was involved in this case from day one. Of the entire team, he was by far the most committed. He took Meijer's first statement. He convinced me that we needed to go through Lombard's computer while he was away on a trade mission in Russia. It was also Calvino's idea to follow Lombard to Moscow. We were convinced that a quick arrest would throw Lombard off guard and compel him to admit his guilt. Anyway, it was worth a try. Calvino met with the liaison officer at the Dutch Embassy, but the guy wasn't prepared to cooperate until the Netherlands delivered an arrest warrant. That authorization never came, and Calvino was sent packing. The military police were waiting for him at Schiphol Airport when he landed. The end of the story so far is that not Lombard but Calvino was picked up – for violation of diplomatic law. But, of course, the joke was he'd gone to Moscow without his badge. He'd officially taken some time off and paid for his ticket himself. As a private citizen, he could do what he wanted. Legally, they couldn't touch him. Still, they're going to charge him with something else.'

'What?'

'The death of a suspect in custody. I told you Sekandar could be a key witness and that we therefore moved him to a secure place with a special ambulance.'

He directed her attention to a photo of a battered ambulance that was designed specifically for the transport of intensive-care patients.

'The mobile intensive-care unit was hijacked and, during a chase on the motorway, involved in a major accident. The hijacker was captured and taken to the station for questioning.'

Radjen pointed to the photo of a man with a wide jawline and steel-blue eyes under plucked eyebrows. His head was shaved on both sides. His jet-black hair was tightly pulled back in a ponytail on the crown of his head.

'Sasha Kovalev. A Russian who takes care of interiors; a so-called freelancer . . .'

'He doesn't look like the maintenance type,' Esther said.

'I mean he's a stylist . . . Uh . . . there's another name . . .'

'Designer?' Esther said.

'His main client was AtlasNet. Kovalev did up all of their offices worldwide . . . you know what I mean?'

'He did the styling,' Esther said, grinning.

'Kovalev's last "styling" job was renovating the management offices of the former headquarters of the Dutch Trading Company, here in Amsterdam. A branch of AtlasNet is now located there. We suspected that his work was actually a cover for other illegal activities. It quickly became clear during Kovalev's interrogation that he had more information than he initially wanted to share. He was prepared to offer up more in exchange for witness protection. To give us a taste of how important what he had to offer was, he told us he had evidence that a prominent Dutch politician was involved. Guess who?'

'Jesus Christ?'

'He's a prominent figure, true, but he's never been a politician and certainly not a Dutch one. Kovalev said that the villa was used as a location where Lombard could meet the boy. And Kovalev had to coordinate that meeting.'

'What went wrong?'

'From what Kovalev revealed during his interrogation, it seems like he wanted to keep the boy from being abused. He tried to free him. There was a shoot-out with the two men who brought the boy there. The boy fled through the woods, ran in a blind panic and ended up on the road, where he was hit by Minister Lombard's vehicle.'

'But this means,' Esther said as she stood up, 'that Kovalev's a key witness.'

'Was . . .'

Radjen felt a bit dizzy. He searched for the words to describe, as objectively as possible, what happened on the night Detective Joshua Calvino, halfway through Kovalev's interrogation, came to him to discuss the suspect's request for witness protection.

'I still don't know exactly what happened in the interrogation room while I was consulting with Calvino,' Radjen said, 'but when Calvino returned, Kovalev was unconscious; his head bloodied on the table, and Detective Diba was nowhere to be found.'

'Fucking mess,' Esther sighed. 'Then he took a swan dive off the Rembrandttoren, Diba, right?'

Radjen nodded. He felt sick to his stomach, probably as a result of the explosion in The Hague. He threw open a window, leaned out, took a deep breath and soon felt a bit better. He closed the window and walked back to the white board, ignoring Esther's worried look, and pointed to the photo of a tanned woman with serious eyes and short blonde hair.

'Except they weren't only after Sekandar . . . but her as well. Danielle Bernson, the doctor who was caring for the boy. She'd been back in the Netherlands for only a short time; had spent years working in Africa, in war zones. She was totally taken with Sekandar. For her, he was symbolic of the unscrupulous ways human traffickers operate. She sought out the media, and signed her death warrant with that. The way she was murdered was so out of control and cruel, it seemed more like a violent sex crime than a hit-for-hire.'

Esther looked at the photos and cursed. Radjen hated swearing. Except when it came from Esther.

He felt a second wave of nausea and his ears were ringing. The room began to spin. 'I'll be right back,' he said, staggering into the hallway. To keep himself from falling, he imagined a white line on the ground to focus on. The corridor was spinning around him. He tried to grab on to something that was ungraspable: emptiness.

He felt two hands support him from behind. Her hands, her voice. Esther's voice. She pushed open the door to the lavatory and tightly held on to him as he bent over the toilet bowl and vomited in minute-long waves. Then she hoisted him up, accompanied him to a sink, pushed his head under the tap and let him drink some water to wash away the sour taste in his mouth.

He heard the crisp crackling sound of her leather jacket behind him. Her hands gently directing his head as he felt the cold water flowing across his face. She rubbed his head, without saying anything, as if she'd been doing this for years.

He gave in to her, incapable of resisting. He was beyond being embarrassed.

2

As the KLM Boeing 747 took off for Schiphol Airport through a luminous, rust-brown layer of clouds, Moscow gradually faded in the late twilight.

Unsurprisingly, the customs officials at Sheremetyevo International had turned Paul completely inside-out. But, since he'd taken the necessary precautions, they'd come up empty-handed. Once he cleared customs in Amsterdam, Anya would send him all the picture files encrypted.

He closed his eyes and tried to get a handle on the ringing in his ears. That ringing was a constant companion, the only one he couldn't walk out on. It remained with him wherever he went. Everything that had happened to him over the past few weeks, from the moment he got beaten to a pulp in Johannesburg to this moment of take-off, had made the ringing and its associated undercurrent of panic more persistent than ever, especially in situations from which he couldn't escape, like this enclosed aircraft cabin.

He checked his watch. It was nine in the evening.

He'd travelled to Moscow to act as Farah's safety net, to protect her if anything went wrong.

And he was returning alone.

Their very first encounter kept running through his head. The butterfly garden of the presidential palace in Kabul. Her jet-black hair, her bright blue eyes, her caramel-coloured skin. The arm that felt so surprisingly cool when he accidentally brushed against it. She was both brave and beautiful. He'd felt it even then: the desire, no, the *need*, to protect her.

Instead, he'd acted all tough and tried to outdo her when she showed him her Pencak Silat moves. Then, holding his father's hand, he'd walked away through the corridors of the presidential palace. Without looking back.

Thirty years. That's how long they hadn't seen each other. But she'd never left his thoughts.

However big he'd tried to make his world, however far he'd travelled, a twist of fate had made it so small that after all this time he'd found Farah again. And, strangely enough, it felt as if they'd never been apart, as if they remained connected in their innermost souls.

The young girl who'd taught him his first rudimentary fight techniques had become a driven journalist who'd got it into her head to make life difficult for a Russian oligarch. It had only fuelled his desire to protect her. And, in exposing his soft side, a character trait he didn't even know he had, she'd confused him to his very core.

He could have accompanied her to Jakarta to look after her, keep her from harm's way. But instead he'd agreed to her insane plan: work together, but each from a different part of the world, from a different city: Amsterdam, Jakarta, Moscow.

Paul tried to take his mind off things by going through the papers he'd bought at the airport, but he kept being drawn to the articles on the aftermath of the hostage-taking at the Seven Sisters.

Le Figaro cynically asked how thirteen heavily armed terrorists could have struck in the heart of Moscow. The world news page of *The Times* displayed the headline DUTCH JOURNALIST UNMASKED AS AFGHAN TERRORIST. It asked how it was possible for this woman to have disappeared without a trace. The *New York Times* featured a short but striking report on the ending of the hostage-taking, citing the leader of the

Alpha Spetsnaz commandos. Having found Farah Hafez strapped to an explosive device, he'd proceeded to deactivate it. According to him, there'd been an American journalist on the scene who'd identified her as his colleague. Instead of being one of the terrorists, she was actually their victim. A spokesperson for the Russian Ministry of Justice flatly denied this. Farah Hafez, who'd worked for the Dutch daily *AND* for ten years, was of Afghan origin. Hafez's mother country had been occupied by the Russian Army for over nine years. Enough to explain why she'd joined the Chechen cause. After all, the Chechen rebels were fighting against the Russian occupation of their country. Hafez had only recently shown her violent disposition and anti-Russian sentiments by so severely injuring her Russian opponent at a martial arts gala in Amsterdam that the woman had needed hospital treatment.

Under the headline BLACK WIDOW FARAH H. BECOMES ENEMY OF THE RUSSIAN STATE, *De Nederlander* dedicated a full-page article to the search for the 'fugitive Farah H.', which had been launched by the Russian FSB in collaboration with Europol. The article quoted a study saying that in the Netherlands alone more than 30,000 people had been influenced by radical Islamist ideas. According to *De Nederlander*, Farah was now their standard-bearer.

On the domestic news page, a short article caught his eye, 'Driver who hit Afghan boy in Amsterdamse Bos kills himself. Thomas M., a suspect in the case surrounding the hit-and-run of an Afghan boy, has taken his own life. The police declined to provide any further details on the ongoing investigation.'

He was further startled when the aircraft entered an air pocket and listened anxiously to the stewardess's announcement that they were encountering heavy turbulence. He took a few deep breaths before pinching his nose and clearing his ears, again and again. When he felt his heart rate accelerate, he squirted a bit of Rescue Spray on his tongue and drank some water.

The FASTEN YOUR SEATBELT sign flickered on in an alarming shade of red. Lightning flashes lit up the windows. They were flying through the tops of storm clouds, where gusts of wind could reach speeds of up to 150 kilometres per hour.

An hour later the pilot started the descent. Paul felt the aircraft's cowl flaps slide out, the air current being deflected and the aircraft forced down.

Lastly, the landing gear was lowered. Looking through the window, Paul noticed the plane approaching the runway at an angle, as if the pilot had decided to land diagonally. He reminded himself that the pilot had to bank into the wind so he could fly the aircraft straight and managed to get the better of his panic.

The left wheel was the first to touch the runway, followed by the right and then the nose wheel. But the copious rainwater had left an oily film in places and the wheels couldn't seem to grip the tarmac. Paul heard the thrust reversers being activated and the engines began to roar. Instinctively, he pressed his soaked back against the seat, as if by doing this he might be able to provide enough of a counterbalance to avert an imminent crash.

3

The hell Farah'd landed in had become all but invisible. She could hear only the shooting, the screaming and the shrill whining of gas grenades being fired over their heads at the demonstrators behind them.

But gradually all these noises died down. For a moment, she thought she wasn't just going blind but deaf as well, though she could still hear her own breathing and Aninda repeatedly saying, as she steered her away, 'Stay calm, we're nearly there.' She also heard the hurried steps of other people running past them and realized they were slowly leaving the tear gas, the injured and the chaos behind.

Aninda helped her into some place away from the turmoil outside. A wave of cold air struck her face. A rapid exchange of words between Aninda and a man. An iron roll-down shutter being slammed shut. The buzzing of an air-con unit. Aninda's hands gently pushing her forward. She was crying with despair.

Aninda turned on a tap and water splashed into a metal basin. Her hands held Farah's head under the jet of water. She thought of Paul and how he'd done the same for her, in Moscow – just as firmly, just as lovingly – and how she'd cried, back then, and again now. The icy water streamed across her face. She tried to open her eyes, keen to know whether she could still see. When she saw white streaks, her panic increased. She thought she might go insane with fear.

The fear was even worse than the pain.

'Focus on your breathing, and count with me,' Aninda said. '*Satu, dua, tiga.*'

The same numbers. *Satu, dua, tiga.* Over and over. Like a mantra. *Satu, dua, tiga.*

She rested both hands on the counter and listened to Aninda's calming voice. The panic lessened.

'Excellent. Keep counting. I'm going to prepare something for you.'

'My lenses.'

'In a minute. Keep counting now.'

Satu . . . dua . . . tiga.

Consultation in the background, while cupboards were yanked open and closed with brisk movements. *Satu.* A fridge door was opened and slammed shut. *Dua.* Crackling plastic, a strip of tablets, a pestle grinding something. *Tiga.* Something was whisked in a small bowl.

Then the light was switched off. Erratic flames danced on her retina.

'Come with me.'

Gently, Aninda guided Farah to a chair, which she'd placed behind her. 'Lean your head back a bit. Yes, that's it. Open your eyes, as wide as possible.'

Farah did as she was told. Her eyeballs felt electrically charged, with lightning flashing all around her.

'I'm about to drop something into your eyes. It will sting a little, but soon bring relief.'

Mere droplets on a scorching hot plate.

'What is it?'

'Keep counting.'

'*Satu . . . dua . . .* what is it?'

'Lemon juice, milk, water . . .'

'*Tiga . . .* What else?'

'Antacids. Keep counting.'

'*Satu* . . .'

The burning pain subsided.

'Antacids . . . ?'

'Sit still. Keep your eyes open as wide as possible. I'm going to drop sterile water into them and take your lenses out.'

She heard the male voice in the background again. Then a small light was directed at her eyes.

'Don't look into the light. Look straight ahead.'

Farah saw Aninda's finger appear in front of her right eye, move towards the iris and touch the lens. She felt pressure, then the finger disappeared. The same action took place on the left.

'You're lucky, Valentina. They're out.'

She dropped some more fluid into Farah's eyes before covering her face with a damp tea towel. 'Stay seated like this for a while.'

Farah was left alone in the dark with the towel over her face. The flashes of light became less frequent and the pain less searing, until it finally subsided altogether. As she regained her composure and her heart rate steadily slowed, she heard Aninda make a phone call.

The tea towel was lifted from her face.

'How many fingers?' Aninda asked with a smile while making the V-sign.

'Five,' Farah joked. 'But everything is still really blurry.'

'It will get clearer. How about the pain?'

'Much better.'

'Good. All the other women made it home in one piece. That leaves just us.'

She helped Farah up and together they left their place of refuge, a kitchen behind a shop full of sports shoes, T-shirts, tracksuit bottoms and hoodies. A man who looked like he'd never done a day's exercise in his life pulled up the storefront shutter so Farah could walk out, unsteady on her feet, supported by Aninda.

It had grown quiet in the street; eerily quiet. In the distance, Farah saw the night sky glow orange-red above the rooftops.

'There are heavy clashes on Merdeka Square,' Aninda said. 'All the barricades have been set alight. The police are using live ammunition.'

She stopped a *bajaj*, helped Farah into it and asked where she was going.

Farah stared straight ahead, looking confused.

'I don't know.'

'Don't worry,' Aninda said. She got in, wrapped an arm around her and yelled an address, after which the young man behind the wheel set off. Farah rested her head on Aninda's shoulder and closed her eyes. There was no room for suspicion. An unknown woman had stepped in to look after her as if they'd been lifelong friends. Any place she'd take her would be fine.

Two hands stroked her face. She opened her eyes. The *bajaj*'s engine was idling. They'd come to a halt. Aninda was cradling Farah's head. She was so close their noses almost touched. Farah realized she could see her clearly; the blurriness had gone. Aninda curled her lips into a disarming smile.

'Blue. They're incredibly blue.'

Farah looked at her uncomprehendingly.

'Your eyes, I mean.'

Farah coughed hard to clear her throat. Aninda handed her a plastic bottle of water, which she gulped down, then paid the driver and helped Farah out. She found herself standing, still somewhat unsteady on her legs, in front of a large colonial warehouse with a white stucco façade.

'This used to be a storage depot for furniture,' Aninda said, as the *bajaj* drove off. 'It had been empty for years. The foundation bought it.'

'What foundation?'

Aninda tugged at the narrow steel gate, which creaked into motion, and pointed to the text beneath the tree logo attached to the rusty bars. 'Can you read what it says here?'

'WARINGIN RUMAH UNTUK ANAK JALANAN,' Farah read aloud. 'Waringin Shelter for Homeless Children'.

'All credit to the antacids,' Aninda said, laughing, and, with an arm around Farah's waist, ushered her through a long, narrow entranceway. The tiles, which were covered in a thin layer of water, glistened in the moonlight. 'We keep as many children as we can off the streets. Some live here permanently. If we only enable them to go to school here and they return to the streets at the end of the day, they don't retain much of what they've learned and we have no control over where they are or what they do. We don't know whether they'll sniff glue again, or let themselves be lured away by a tourist, or whatever. If we can keep them here, we can offer them a roof over their heads and a good meal.'

Again, she gave Farah that disarming look.

'And if we can give shelter to homeless children, we can certainly do the same for a lost angel, right?'

At the end of the passage, they halted. Surrounded by high, solid walls, away from the noise, chaos and stench of the city, was a large courtyard. Within it several smaller buildings with pagoda-style roofs grouped around a twenty-metre-high gnarled tree with bark that looked like elephant skin.

'A *waringin*, or weeping fig,' Aninda whispered. 'You'll find one in nearly every Indonesian village. The aerial roots reach all the way to the ground. Village elders meet under its branches to discuss important matters. It's a cycle that repeats itself generation after generation.'

Farah barely heard what she was saying. It felt as if she'd travelled back thirty years in time, back to the walled garden in what had once been her parental home in Wazir Akbar Khan, Kabul's well-to-do neighbourhood. As if all she needed to do now was to wait for her father to emerge in his pristine white shirt and linen trousers, so they could do Pencak Silat exercises together while he counted out loud in this language she'd recently started learning from a well-thumbed book, '*Satu, dua, tiga . . .*'

Given the chance, she could have stood there all night, but Aninda led her down the deserted gallery adjacent to the courtyard. 'We have to be quiet. The children are all asleep.'

She stopped in front of the final door.

'Would you mind waiting here a moment?' She kicked off her slippers and went inside.

A bamboo rollerblind was pulled down. A lamp was lit. A fan began to whirr. Farah could hear clattering. A moment later the old door swung open again.

'Welcome,' Aninda said shyly.

Farah took off her trainers. As she brushed past Aninda, she could smell the young woman's body – a combination of perspiration, sandalwood and lime.

An ancient upright fan was working feverishly, but the heat of the day still pervaded the spacious room with its wide, worn, wooden floorboards. It must have been at least thirty-five degrees inside. Hardly any furniture: a stack of cushions, a large wooden table on trestles, a dozen upturned crates serving as bookcases and an old racing bike leaning against a wall covered in children's drawings.

Aninda came and stood close beside her.

'I supervise the children here. They made those drawings

for me after I taught them the song of the little star. It's about how it feels to dance and fly like a star and shine in the sky along with all the other stars.'

Softly and delicately, almost under her breath, she sang the first line, *'Bintang kecil, Di langit yang tinggi, Amat banyak, Menghias angkasa . . .'* Then her voice faltered and she stopped. 'Homeless kids sleep under the stars. They see them every night. Those stars are just as remote to them as the lives of the people who pass them by every day in their air-conditioned cars.'

Silent and numb with fatigue, Farah gazed at the drawings of figures that appeared to be floating in a paper sky. She thought of Sekandar and turned to Aninda.

'Terimah kasih.' 'Thank you,' she said. 'Thank you for looking after me. I'm sorry I made things difficult for you.'

Aninda put her hand on Farah's upper arm. 'I'm not sorry at all. I'm glad I met you.'

Farah looked at the thick mattress. It was lying on top of a pallet, but, thanks to a wide, flared-out mosquito net, it looked as elegant as a four-poster bed.

It was her final conscious image.

Then her mind went blank for a long time.

4

At the junction of De Nieuwe Meer, Radjen exited the A10 motorway and took the A4 in the direction of The Hague. The wind blew in his face. His thoughts were clear. A half-hour ago he'd been hanging over a sink, dizzy, cold water splashing over his head, with Esther right behind him. Now she was sitting beside him in the Corolla.

'Ever heard of *Midnight Ninja*?' he asked.

'Sounds like a tacky Kung Fu film,' Esther laughed.

'A computer game in which ninjas are tasked with freeing a princess or capturing a treasure, going about their business like shadows in the night.'

'Nimble warriors trying to rescue a helpless woman sounds even tackier.' She put two cigarettes in her mouth and lit both.

'You can play the game at higher and higher levels,' Radjen continued. 'And with each new level the risks you take increase. The way it's put together is ingenious.'

Esther inhaled deeply, turned and handed him a lit cigarette.

'Is this your coming out, Chief? You're secretly a computer-game junkie?'

He accepted the cigarette with a grin, enjoyed the smoke filling his lungs and let it out with a long sigh.

'No, just trying to make a comparison.'

'With what?'

'With everything we're now dealing with. We've reached the highest level.'

'Because of the possible involvement of a minister?'

'Exactly. We started at the bottom level. The shooting at the villa; the corpses in the burnt-out car. Flunkies, anonymous pawns. A step higher: we find Thomas Meijer and Sekandar, the driver and the injured boy. Perpetrator and victim. Cogs in a much larger machine.' He turned up the air-con and the cigarette smoke drifted towards the back seat.

'Then we go a step further, arriving at the next level, with the possible involvement of the businessman Armin Lazonder. The night-time shooting happened at a location that belongs to him. Another step further and we have the doctor, who wanted to expose the whole thing to the public. She was the next victim. On all these different levels, a number of individuals involved are connected to Lombard. We've arrived at the ministerial level. That's about as high as it gets.'

The Hague appeared in the distance. Towering ministries with their pillared brick and granite façades loomed over the monumental buildings of the city centre.

'What I'm about to tell you stays between us, okay?'

She nodded.

'I'm convinced we're never going to get to the bottom of this with an official investigation. Big Brother is keeping a close watch on the MIT. We unexpectedly raid the work quarters of a minister, we find child pornography on his computer, and shortly afterwards it seems to have been removed without a trace of foul play. We follow a lead to Nationwide Forensics and before we make contact the place is blown to smithereens.'

'They're always one step ahead of us . . .'

'That's why I want to form a shadow team. A trusted group that can operate quickly and quietly without immediately attracting attention from above.'

'Who did you have in mind?'

He paused and looked at her. 'Just you and me . . .'

He merged left in the direction of Voorburg and Leidschendam, and exited on to Laan van Nieuw Oost-Indië. There he turned on to Bezuidenhoutseweg.

'I've watched you over the years and I'm . . . I have faith in you. I'm convinced that you're ideal for the task at hand.'

They drove passed the Ministry of Economic Affairs but couldn't find a parking space. In one of the streets behind the huge building, Radjen found a spot right in front of a café. They went inside and he ordered himself a double espresso, a glass of water and a club sandwich. Esther ordered the grilled cheese with fries and a sparkling water.

On a small round table on the wide pavement in front of the eatery, they hastily wolfed it all down. They only had fifteen minutes before their appointment with Minister Lombard.

'Well?' asked Radjen after a few big bites.

'Well what?'

'What do you think?'

She pulled out a packet of Gauloises, lit a cigarette and exhaled away from him.

'Something bothers me.'

'Let's hear it.'

'I'm honoured. I mean, it's not every day that I'm promoted to the order of the secret ninja. But, if I agree, does it mean I'm doing something illegal?'

'According to the letter of the law, yes.'

He could see her tense up; her gnawing doubts.

'That's the crux, Chief. I became a detective because I believe in the law.'

She looked at him in silence. Seriously. Without a hint of a smile, neither mocking nor inviting, nothing. He hadn't expected this reaction from her, but respected her more than ever because of her conviction. Esther had a tough exterior, but it didn't mean she could be corrupted. She believed in what she was doing, even more than he'd imagined. And now he'd asked her to do something that would probably never have occurred to her, and that was apparently the opposite of everything she held dear.

'Sometimes the law falls short,' Radjen said. 'Let's not forget we're facing an unknown ring of individuals with a personal stake in Lombard, people who think they're above the law and who see the death of innocent people as nothing more than collateral damage.'

He paused and gulped back his espresso. 'As far as I'm concerned, they crossed a line by killing two innocent bystanders in the Nationwide Forensics bombing. Call it the boundary of what is moral, what is acceptable, call it whatever you like. But what I want while I'm on this case, damn, what I want while I'm serving the people, is no more unnecessary deaths. No innocent casualties. I want . . .'

He faltered as she unexpectedly stood up and restlessly threw her long hair over her shoulder.

'Justice. I get it, Chief. I need some time to think about this, okay?'

She threw her cigarette butt on the pavement and stamped it out with a twisting motion of her right boot heel.

In the glass-domed hall of the Ministry of Economic Affairs, they were not only met by three bronze nude figures on pedestals but also by Minister Lombard's secretary. She was a stocky woman in chunky heels, who had undoubtedly seen everything there was to see at the ministry, and wasn't flustered by anything. Certainly not by a tall detective strutting the halls with his female colleague as if the building belonged to them.

When they reached his office, Lombard greeted them

with what appeared to be a welcoming smile. But Radjen estimated it was actually a smile meant to keep an opponent at arm's length. A smile that weakened any kind of resistance from the other with the first handshake. The kind of smile that was deployed whenever needed, but that said nothing about his real intent, and everything about his cunning nature. His dark-brown eyes were tender, displaying a hint of melancholy. Yet Radjen now also saw something menacing hidden deep within, as if someone else were secretly watching from the shadows, where it smelled like a musty kind of loneliness.

Lombard's office in the ministry had obvious similarities to his pied-à-terre on the fortieth floor of the Kroontoren in The Hague, which Radjen had searched while Lombard was in Moscow. The walls were a crisp shade of white, the blinds looked like stylish draperies, and sleek silver desk lamps and bright red armchairs dominated the room. But, instead of the rather clichéd Cubist art that had adorned Lombard's walls in the Kroontoren, Radjen now saw enlargements of the same black-and-white photos he'd viewed earlier on Lombard's computer with the guy from the NFI. The images depicting the youthful sensuality of half-naked girls that had completely thrown him.

The photos were an obvious provocation, and at the same time evidence of Lombard's superiority. Here was a man who apparently had nothing to hide from the outside world. And that's exactly how he behaved.

'If I were to tell you,' Lombard said, standing too close and encroaching on Radjen's personal space, 'that I receive national and international colleagues here, diplomats and even heads of state, with these photos brazenly displayed on the wall, right beside this distinguished portrait of our Queen, while these very same pictures on my computer have been branded "suspect", well, then you can imagine that I find this rather puzzling, as would the average Dutch citizen.'

'Our focus, sir, is investigation,' Radjen said. 'Not riddles.'

'Good: that increases my confidence in the Dutch police,' Lombard said as he broadly gestured in the direction of three comfortable armchairs positioned in a semicircle around his desk. 'Have a seat.'

Radjen wasn't at all surprised that Lombard's lawyer was present. A man trying to enhance his bloated face and greying hair with stylish horn-rimmed glasses. When he introduced himself as Weisman, Radjen had to laugh: what's in a name, he thought to himself.

'As you know, my client has no direct involvement in the case,' Weisman said. 'Given the nature of his duties, I must request that you keep your questions short and take up as little of his time as possible.'

'I'm expected in Parliament in fifteen minutes,' Lombard added. He was now the only one of the group still standing. Lombard was an overweight man, but he carried it well, given how tall he was: almost two metres, just slightly taller than Radjen.

'Then Parliament will have to wait,' Esther replied. 'As my colleague said, sir, this is an ongoing investigation. As a suspect in this case, of course, you're under no obligation to answer.'

Lombard wasn't fazed by her reply. He even looked amused. 'National interest versus the suicide of a chauffeur. A rather interesting dilemma, young lady.'

'We have good reason to believe that Mr Meijer's death wasn't a suicide,' Radjen said.

Lombard's face tightened.

'In the light of these new developments, we're looking into all aspects of the case again. That means that we're also questioning everyone involved again.'

'The point is,' Lombard said, taking a seat in his large desk chair, 'that the contact between Mr Meijer and myself was strictly limited to business. He was my driver. He took me from *a* to *b*. I find it hard to conceive what more I could add to this.'

'There's a lot more,' Esther replied. 'Even your remark that after years of working with him your relationship with Mr Meijer was strictly business raises questions in my mind.'

'That may be so, young lady, but you're making a serious mistake. Mr Meijer and I did not work together.'

'He was your chauffeur, right?'

'Correct, but Mr Meijer, just like my other drivers, actually worked for the government and, in that capacity, he chauffeured me. That was the extent of it. Like I said: from *a* to *b*.'

Lombard tried to add weight to his 'from *a* to *b*' statement by moving an invisible box through the air with his hands stretched out in front of him. A gesture politicians love to use during a speech or an interview. Someone must have once come up with the notion that such a gesture was the sign of a strong leader. But it was entirely irrelevant in this context. It was now crystal clear to Radjen. Lombard wanted to show them that he, not the two detectives sitting across from him, was in control here. Radjen straightened his back and immediately took the initiative again.

'When did you last have contact with Mr Meijer?' he asked.

Lombard slowly leaned his massive body over his desk towards Radjen. This deliberate, unhurried action had something intimidating about it.

'My last contact with Mr Meijer was on the same night he allegedly ran down that child.'

'What time was that?'

'As I previously indicated to your colleagues, Mr Meijer brought me home around ten thirty that night.'

'Besides you and Mr Meijer, is there anyone else who can corroborate this?'

'My wife.'

'Did your wife see Mr Meijer?'

'No.'

'Where was your wife when you arrived home?'

'She was in the living room.'

'And where was Mr Meijer at that time?'

'Mr Meijer deposited my two heavy briefcases in the hall-way, returned to the car and drove away.'

'Did you notice anything unusual about him?' Esther asked.

'What do you mean?'

'You live in Blaricum, Meijer in Amstelveen. Bit strange, to say the least, that, after leaving Blaricum, Meijer took the route through the Amsterdamse Bos to get home. Why take a detour on a dimly lit forest road, when you can make better time on the motorway? Anyway, less than half an hour after dropping you off, he hits a child at a suspicious location and leaves the scene of the accident.'

'I can't explain it. Like I said –'

'Your relationship was strictly business.'

'Exactly. And I prefer not to waste time repeating myself, young lady.'

'You need to stop that.'

'What?'

'Stop calling me "young lady".'

She said it without raising her voice, without a hint of emotion. Radjen saw the surprise on Lombard's face and wanted to smile. Lombard now turned his entire body towards Esther.

'I am happy to cooperate with your investigation, but I insist you control your tone.'

'You're mistaken, sir,' Esther said. 'I'm not here to have a pleasant conversation. This is an interrogation. I'm a detective. And that's how I want to be addressed.'

There was a pause. Lombard's confident smile, meant to convey the impression that this was all below him, had shrivelled to a grimace, but he quickly recovered.

'All right, *Detective*. We both serve the national good. However, the similarity ends there. Best you remember that you operate on a much different level than I do.'

'What do you mean by "different level"?'

She still sounded confident and calm, but Radjen wondered how far Esther would go in letting someone like Lombard bait her. He was capable of getting her to make statements that would only work against her. Radjen was ready to jump in if necessary.

'What I mean,' said Lombard, 'is that you'll have to explain to your superiors why you made it impossible for a government official to properly execute his duties. While the entire Parliament waits, you've kept me here and wasted my time about a matter that doesn't involve me.'

Radjen noticed how much Lombard's voice riled him. It was the tone of a man who was not used to being contradicted. To his surprise, Radjen caught a look of disdain in Esther's eyes. She seemed impervious to Lombard's authority.

'I get the impression, sir, that you're trying to distract me, but, to be completely clear, you're involved in this case up to your ears. First of all, because in Meijer's original statement given to us, he asserted without a doubt that you were in the car at the time of the hit-and-run.'

Lombard remained stone-faced. Even his voice sounded composed. 'A man who happens to be one of my chauffeurs drives to the Amsterdamse Bos in an official vehicle, for God knows what reason, and runs down a child there. It's a desperate attempt, by this man, this Meijer, to repudiate his own guilt by pointing the finger at me. *Me* of all people!'

That superior, jovial smile reappeared on Lombard's face. 'Question: was I behind the wheel? No. Was I present at that moment? No. So there we have it, Mr and Mrs Detective. It's not my place to tell you how best to do your work, what methods and resources to use. But I would suggest that if you go so far as to implicate a minister as a suspect, and in a case involving a driver from the carpool at that, you'd want to have irrefutable evidence and a substantiated motive.'

Lombard prepared to stand. 'Because all these elements seem to be missing, and, despite my earlier warning, you persist in defaming my character. With your permission, I'd now like to bring this conversation to a close.'

Radjen crossed his legs and calmly stayed in his seat. 'As my colleague said, sir, this is not a conversation, this is an interrogation. And we decide when this is over, not you. Please sit down.'

Lombard was perched in an uncomfortable, almost ridiculous position, somewhere between sitting and standing. In bewilderment he glanced at his lawyer, who nonverbally indicated that it would be better to cooperate. When Lombard took his seat again, he looked furious.

Radjen had waited for this. The moment that would tip the scales. The moment that a man who considered himself untouchable would have to admit that his superiority was based on a lie and there was now the possibility of that lie being exposed.

Radjen leaned back, and kept his voice as low and neutral as possible. 'In his first statement, Thomas Meijer indeed said that at the time of the collision you were in the back seat of the car, and, although he revised his story in a second account, it is up to the courts to determine which of the two is based on truth. New facts, however, have emerged that give us more reason to believe his initial statement.'

Here Radjen intentionally paused. Longer than was necessary. Esther caught his eye, understood and took over from him.

'We have recent information indicating that Mr Meijer was forced into making his second statement,' she said, calmly glancing back at Radjen.

'Thomas Meijer contradicted his first statement so he and his Ghanaian wife could be reunited with their foster child,' continued Radjen, who was enjoying the back and forth with Esther as they cornered Lombard.

'You don't have to respond to this,' said Weisman to Lombard, almost whispering. 'You're not required to answer.'

Lombard seemed to heed his advice. He leaned back in his large leather armchair and thoughtfully rubbed the flat of his hand over his mouth.

Radjen saw Lombard's eyes grow dark. I've hit a nerve, he thought. You're trying to fight back the pain. But I've got more in store for you.

'We also have a statement with far-reaching accusations against you, sir,' Radjen said. 'A suspect we had in custody claimed that on the night of the hit-and-run you'd arranged a meeting between yourself and the boy.' He looked Lombard straight in the eye and continued: 'He gave us your name.'

Ewald Lombard's frown seemed etched into his forehead, but a curious smile appeared on Weisman's face, as if he had tacit agreement to borrow it from Lombard.

'Detective, are you referring to a Russian you had in custody who was allegedly beaten so badly during his interrogation by one of your people that he succumbed to his injuries? I believe this happened on your watch?'

Radjen had not expected this. His triumphant feeling turned to dismay and he felt a migraine coming on.

'The matter is being investigated internally,' he said. 'But the failure of the detective involved has no influence on the status of the witness's testimony.'

'I believe you're mistaken,' Weisman said. 'The testimony of your Russian detainee was ultimately obtained using violence and won't stand up in court. Despite all your bluffing, you've got nothing.'

Being confronted with Weisman's ruthless truth made Radjen feel completely powerless. Sasha Kovalev's testimony was as worthless as yesterday's newspaper. Their key witness, Meijer, who was in the morgue with a broken neck, had revised his statement about Lombard's presence in the chauffeured car right before he died. And the photos and videos of children being abused on Lombard's hard drive, which had been copied by forensics, were now buried under a dense layer of digital zeros.

The immediate effect of all this was inescapable: their trail had hit a dead end. And apparently Radjen wasn't the only one who knew this.

'There is an old Chinese saying,' Lombard lectured them, as he stared at Radjen and Esther in turn. '"Those who know, do not speak. Those who speak, do not know." I have the feeling that the aim of all your talk is to conceal the fact that you don't know very much.'

Radjen slowly rose to his feet. He placed both his hands on the edge of the desk and slightly leaned forward. His voice was calm. 'I've heard and seen enough evidence against you, sir, to send you away for years to a place where they know damn well what to do with child molesters.'

'If that is true, Mr Detective, why don't you arrest me right now?' Seemingly unperturbed, Lombard stood up and pressed the intercom button. 'Mr and Mrs Detective are ready to be shown the door.' Then he went to shake Radjen's hand.

Radjen ignored the gesture and didn't move.

'At this very moment, a boy who was run down by a car and left for dead is fighting for his life, sir.'

Lombard's face turned red and a slight smirk appeared. 'I declare this hearing adjourned. But I have no doubt we'll speak again soon. Then we'll see who has the last word. I can assure you it will be the person who knows the most. Namely me.'

Radjen turned and walked with Esther to the door, where the secretary in chunky heels was waiting for them. Radjen made no effort to react to the threat that Lombard hurled at him as they left the room.

'By the time you're ready to set foot in my office again, Detective, you'll find you're out of a job. That's a promise. Goodbye.'

Five minutes later, Radjen and Esther were on the breezy square in front of the ministry complex, with their foreheads almost touching, as Radjen folded his hands around the cigarette lighter and Esther tried to light two Gauloises. He'd quickly become attached to the casual way she handed him lit cigarettes.

'Do you remember, Chief, that I didn't initially believe he was guilty?' she said, after exhaling her first drag.

'I certainly do.'

She chuckled as she put on her sunglasses. 'Well, I was awfully naive.'

'Naive is not a word I'd use to describe you.'

'Hate to tell you,' she said, turning towards him, 'but throw a red cape over my shoulders, give me a wicker basket filled with goodies and there you'd have it: I'd mistake the big bad wolf for my granny.'

'You were really on your toes just now,' he said.

'We were,' she said. 'Teamwork.'

'Take credit where credit is due?' He gave her a reassuring look and smiled. 'You did great. A damn good job.'

She glanced at him, feeling slightly self-conscious. 'Well, thanks for the compliment, Chief.'

'And it's Radjen, not Chief.'

'Okay, then, Radjen. Let me ask you about something that's been on my mind?'

'Go ahead.'

'What does this plan of yours actually involve?'

He inhaled deeply and glanced up at the bright blue sky, with white cumulus clouds drifting by. 'Well, it isn't exactly a plan. It's something I want to try, an experiment. Whenever we discover something new, we don't immediately share it with the MIT; we keep it to ourselves. Might be for an hour, a day, a week, depending on how quickly and effectively we can move. The idea is to operate under the radar wherever we can.'

'Okay, then.' It sounded almost casual.

'What okay, then?'

'Okay, Radjen, welcome me to the Order of the Secret Ninja.'

She grinned as she exhaled the smoke from her last puff, flicked her burning cigarette in the direction of the ministry building and headed back to their parked car.

Radjen lagged behind, watching her. He couldn't remember ever being so hard-pressed in a case, while at the same time feeling so excited, as if he could take on the world.

5

The Boeing had skidded diagonally on the runway. Nearly forty-five minutes later, Paul boarded the shuttle bus that would take him and his fellow passengers to the terminal. Once inside, after having to join an endless queue for passport control, he informed Anya that he'd landed. Another forty-five minutes later, he finally lifted his bag off the luggage carousel and shuffled past customs into the arrivals hall. To his surprise, he was met by Edward, who was chewing on a liquorice stick in an effort to kick his nicotine addiction once and for all.

'I hope this is a one-off,' he said, giving Paul a hug. 'I'm still struggling to get my head around this turn of events.'

Edward's voice sounded surprisingly steady for someone who'd been rushed to hospital with chest pains barely a week ago after seeing the YouTube clip of Farah giving her jihad statement.

'You look a lot better than I expected,' Paul said.

'It was a mild attack, the doctor said. But what would he know?' Edward placed his arm around Paul's shoulders and together they walked through Schiphol Plaza towards the escalators in the large central hall.

'For sixty-two years I managed to convince myself that I was immortal. Call it naive or foolish, but I got away with it. Other people were dying. I wasn't going to get on that train. And guess what? Suddenly I'm on the platform, ready to board.'

'Thank God you forgot to buy a ticket,' Paul quipped.

They paused in front of a piece of gleaming DC-9 fuselage outside an airport shop. A little blond-haired boy was standing proudly in front of the rotor blades of a jet engine, waving at them. The scene reminded Paul of his own fascination with flying when he was that age. He waved back. He'd give anything to be that little boy waving at passers-by, in the rock-solid belief that the world was one big playground.

'I feel as if I've turned into glass,' Edward said, as they walked on. 'And I don't mean the bulletproof variety. I'm taking blood-thinners, cholesterol-lowering tablets and ACE inhibitors. I'm in charge of a pharmacy instead of an editorial office. And everyone's saying I got lucky. But it's the kind of luck that leaves you with a sour taste.'

They'd reached the escalator to the indoor car park. Edward stood still, turned away from Paul, stretching his back. His posture was reminiscent of a high-jumper about to propel himself backwards across the bar, but Paul knew it had nothing to do with athletics and all the more with a stressed-out mind in a distressed giant's body.

'I sent her there, damn it. I've got that on my conscience.'

'She's safe, Ed.'

'Safety doesn't apply to Farah. How can I ever look her in the eye again?'

'She never once implied that she blames you. That's not who she is.'

Paul heard grumbling and looked over his shoulder. A group of travellers with suitcases and other bags had gathered behind them. 'Let's go – we're holding people up.'

He gave Edward a gentle shove in the back and stepped on to the escalator behind him.

'How's Mum?' he asked, as they glided up.

'She's been jolting awake at night lately, because she hears footsteps.'

'Is that what she thinks, or –'

'No, she's certain of it. She hears them. At one point she even thought it was Raylan.'

'More than thirty years and she still refuses to believe he's dead.'

They arrived upstairs in the hall with the payment terminals, where Edward jumped off the final step with a ridiculous little skip. The two men continued alongside each other.

'A couple of nights ago she heard those footsteps again. That's when the penny dropped and she calmly informed me that Comrade Death was shuffling around the farm.'

'The Grim Reaper. That sounds like an anti-climax.'

'Perhaps dying is one big anti-climax,' Edward said, as he slipped his parking ticket into the payment machine. 'A fiasco, except a grandiose one.'

En route to the *AND* office the Saab's windscreen wipers were working overtime. Edward pressed play on the CD player. As he heard the opening strains of *Tubular Bells*, Paul felt a faint smile appear on his lips for the first time in days. He pictured the sleeve: a triangular steel tube floating above a tempestuous sea. For Paul's seventeenth birthday, Edward had taken him to the Royal Albert Hall, where they attended the performance of Mike Oldfield's opus. Three years later Edward gave him the symphonic version of *Tubular Bells* for his birthday and asked him to come to work at the *AND* as a trainee journalist. With that, *Tubular Bells* became the instrumental consolidation both of their family tie and of their bond as newspaper men.

A north-westerly wind swept the autumn rain in implacable waves across the concrete space in front of the *AND*. Even though Edward had parked as close as he could to the main entrance, they were soaked by the time they made it inside. There they crossed the lobby with the glass walls and took the long escalator all the way up to the fifth floor. Edward flung the door to his work unit wide open.

'Our nerve centre,' he said proudly, as he ushered Paul into a space that, like the rest of the building, was separated from the outside world by enormous glass walls. Part of Edward's office was taken up by three room dividers. Resting on reinforced castors, they were set up like a harmonica and served as movable white boards. One of them bore Farah's name and featured visual and written material she'd gathered before she left for Moscow. Written at the top of the second, otherwise empty, board was Paul's name in capitals. The third one clearly belonged to Edward, who'd devoted himself to Valentin Lavrov's life. He'd managed to condense the Russian's comet-like career into a clear and coherent account.

'Know thy enemy,' he said. 'We can't rehabilitate Farah without going after the bastard himself.'

Paul looked at a photo of a youthful Valentin, smiling stiffly at the photographer, clearly ill at ease, in a suit he probably didn't wear every day.

'He must have been eighteen there,' Edward said. 'An economics student. He'd only just arrived in Moscow.'

Paul knew relatively little about Lavrov. Anya had given him material only about the structure and working practices of AtlasNet, so information about the man behind the scenes was more than welcome.

'This,' Edward said, pointing to another black-and-white photo, 'is our man when he was twenty years of age and a rising star in the Young Communist League, Komsomol.'

Paul saw a different Lavrov. The somewhat shy-looking young man had been replaced by a self-assured guy: comfortable among his Communist peers, a cigarette dangling between his fingers.

Tracing the course of Lavrov's career, Paul soon realized it wasn't just well planned; he'd also been given a leg up by those in political power. Economics and politics were inseparable in Russia. Before too long, Lavrov's economics degree and his connections at Komsomol brought him to the Institute of International Relations in Moscow, an elite school where students were trained for the KGB and government roles. While working at the Ministry of Trade, he and some partners founded the energy company AtlasNet. He was introduced into higher political circles by people who'd later occupy important positions in his company. Lavrov cunningly presented himself as a committed nationalist with a rock-solid faith in the Kremlin's power. Besides, he was young, ambitious and completely in line with the man rising to power, Potanin, whom he'd befriended.

'This is a unique copy,' Edward said. 'I dug it out of the archive of one of our photographers.'

Paul was looking at a private snap of Potanin celebrating his first presidential election victory with his bosom buddy at his *dacha* on the Black Sea coast.

'Less than a week after this photo was taken, Potanin's main rival, oligarch Aleksandr Zyuganov, was locked up in Siberia after a show trial,' Edward said. 'On account of so-called tax fraud. Tax fraud, my arse. Zyuganov was the owner of energy company NovaMost, one of the biggest energy firms in the country, and with an international presence too. And what happens? As a reward for his arse-licking, our friend Lavrov is handed three quarters of all NovaMost shares. Overnight, he becomes what he has now been for years: the filthy rich CEO of a global energy consortium.'

While Paul studied the photos of Lavrov, Edward marched over to his pride and joy, which stood on a sturdy wooden frame in the middle of his office: a handmade bar globe, featuring the continents and oceans in vintage colours.

'I want to be able to prove that AtlasNet is nothing other than a Potanin-led criminal organization that resorts to bribery, intimidation and probably even murder on a worldwide scale,' Edward said, while snapping open the globe.

But Paul was momentarily blind to its attractions. In his mind's eye he was back on the fiftieth floor of the Ponte City tower in Johannesburg, helplessly watching how Lavrov's henchmen had hurled his battered informant over the edge. The man had been on the verge of giving him information about AtlasNet's secret payments to the South African authorities. At that moment he could never have foreseen, not even in his wildest fantasies, that only a little later this same Lavrov would be linked to Farah.

He turned to Edward, who waved his arm like a showman to highlight a collection of American, Japanese and Scottish whiskies, both single malts and blends.

'My phone hasn't stopped ringing,' Edward said. 'Everybody, from the Russian Ambassador in The Hague to the Foreign Secretary, they all want to know why we jobbed out Hafez as a PR lady for a bunch of Chechen terrorists.'

With a confident gesture, he singled out a particular bottle.

'And, since you're going to show them they're all completely wrong, I've purchased this Kilchoman especially for the occasion. A solid young whisky, ripened in bourbon casks with plenty of peat smoke.'

Paul took out his laptop and decrypted the file Anya had sent him. While loading the first photo on to his computer, he heard the generous gurgling sound of Edward filling the glasses. When he looked up, Edward was standing in front of him with a triumphant look on his face.

'Everything, and I mean everything, from growing the barley to the bottling process, is done on one and the same farm. That's pretty unique in this day and age,' Edward said, as he handed him a glass. They toasted with their long-standing credo.

'To you, to me . . .'

'. . . and to us both,' Paul finished his sentence.

As he drank his first sip, Paul could feel this wondrous mixture of peat smoke and herbs flowing over his tongue and down his throat. He knew what would happen next. They'd drink, he and his uncle, until they felt invincible, until the real world had narrowed to the bar globe standing between them, and with each passing hour they'd feel more and more like kings.

'With heartfelt greetings from Rockside Farm,' Edward joked. After his first generous gulp, he leaned over to look at a photo on the laptop showing a large number of people in a posh gallery full of paintings. 'I see you had time to take in some culture too.'

The rain, which was blowing across the River IJ, hammered on the panoramic windows.

'Welcome to the Pushkin Museum,' Paul said. 'To mark the official visit of our Prime Minister, Finance Minister Lombard and a trade delegation, a number of Russian artists showed their interpretations of classic Dutch works such as *The Night Watch* and *The Garden of Earthly Delights*. And look who's there.'

He pointed to Farah, who was standing next to Lavrov in a cocktail dress borrowed from Anya and with a glass of champagne in her right hand. He knew how insecure she'd felt at that moment. She'd told him. But in the photo she looked indomitable, like a woman who was used to rubbing shoulders with the upper classes, politicians, celebrities and oligarchs.

'It was the first time they met after she'd arrived in Moscow. That exhibition was perfect for an opening article in the art supplement. But then all hell broke loose. A dissonant symphony of buzzing mobiles, because everybody had set them to vibrate mode. The news sent shockwaves around the room. A group of Chechens had forced their way into the Mass Media Centre of Moscow State University, where they took some two hundred International Summer School students hostage. It quickly emerged there were Dutch students among the hostages, so the entire opening ceremony fell to pieces. Our Prime Minister and Minister Lombard were ushered out by security agents. Amid that chaos, I saw Farah being whisked away by Lavrov and his bodyguards.'

Paul remembered the panic in her eyes when he caught a final glimpse of her, just before she disappeared from the gallery, shielded by the bodyguards.

'We'd agreed that she'd never just go off somewhere with him. She'd only meet with Lavrov if we were able to shadow her and intervene if necessary. That was the plan. Then we found ourselves in an unforeseen situation. They drove off in two armoured Falcons, but we didn't know for sure where Lavrov was headed. Luckily, Anya is well informed and had a hunch where they were taking her. Ultimately, we were able to track them to the grounds of Lavrov's country estate on the shores of Lake Glubokoe, some thirty kilometres from Moscow.'

With his index finger Paul tapped the silhouette of the man standing next to Farah on the wide balcony of a futuristic-looking glass structure.

'As you can see, Anya's camera has a terrific telephoto lens. I was lying on the other side of the lake. Farah later told me what happened, although not exactly: she was still too confused to string together a coherent story. But what it boiled down to was that Lavrov was aware of her true intentions long before their first meeting.'

Edward's whisky went down the wrong way. 'Damn! How come?'

'Does the name Joshua Calvino mean anything to you?'

'Of course. Around here we called him Catwalk Calvino. I'd never seen a detective who looked so much like a runway model. A day after the hit-and-run, he turned up here in my office. Farah was doing her own investigation into the case. She was a step ahead of him, maybe even two. She'd found an earring in the woods and Calvino came here to claim it. They got involved, Hafez and this guy. She's got rather good taste in men . . . and I have to admit I tend to fall for the same type.'

'What?'

'Never mind.' Edward sighed and drained his glass. 'You're far too slow. With the whisky, I mean.'

'Maybe you're going too fast. This can't be good for that ticker of yours.'

'That's for me to decide, and it's called a heart, by the way. If I'm not mistaken, you've got one too.'

'You're no good to me drunk, Ed. At least, not yet.'

'I'm all ears.'

'Farah told me that when she made contact with the man who claimed to have hit the boy, she took him to Calvino.'

'You mean Lombard's driver?'

'That's the one, yes. On the strength of his statement, a warrant was issued and Lombard's home office in The Hague was searched. Apparently they found incriminating material on his computer. Child pornography. At the time, Lombard was in Moscow with a trade delegation. Calvino travelled after him, hoping to get the Dutch Embassy to use their influence to get the Russian authorities to detain him. During his meeting at the embassy he must have spoken in confidence about Farah's undercover investigation into Lavrov.'

'So Lavrov knows about us.'

'He knows about Farah. He doesn't know I'm involved too.'

'But what did he want from her?'

'He wanted her to work for him.'

'In what capacity?'

'He's involved in a large-scale nuclear-energy project. Farah would play a role in it, he said. Getting fellow investors on board, that sort of thing.'

'Playing the whore, you mean,' Edward muttered.

'*His* whore. Anyway . . . As it turns out, he knew everything about her: her real last name, who her father was. She said no to the bastard.'

'Very brave.'

'Do you know what she said about that? Refusing to be someone's whore isn't brave.'

'Sounds just like Hafez.' Paul picked up on a faint tremor in Edward's voice.

'She thought she was free to leave. That her refusal and everything he'd revealed to her wouldn't have repercussions.'

'Sounds like Hafez too,' Edward said. 'Somehow she manages to be hard as steel and incredibly naive at the same time. There's still no balance.'

Paul took a sip and scrolled down to the photos that showed the three men ambushing her once she'd left the house, and pushing her into the Falcon.

'So this happened the minute she walked out.'

He moved on to another photo. Without a word, Edward looked at Farah, who had a gun held to her head by a bald-headed man, while nearby three men scrambled to their feet.

'She can fight like a tiger, but that counts for nothing when you're coerced with a weapon.' Paul pointed to the man with the face of a condor. 'Arseni Vakurov. Nobody knows whether Arseni is his real name, but his reputation certainly precedes him. A confrontation with Arseni means you're either scarred for life or your life is about to end. For years, he eliminated anyone who got in his boss's way. I saw him throw an informant of mine in Johannesburg off the fiftieth floor. Then he had a go at *me*.'

'I didn't know that.'

'A couple of days before you phoned and told me about this job.'

He showed Edward the photo of Vakurov dumping Farah into the boot of the Falcon, handcuffed and with a bag over her head.

'This is how she was taken to the university where the hostage situation was playing out.'

'How were you able to follow them?'

'Visibility was limited because of the forest fires. Ideal circumstances for a slow car to follow a much faster one.'

Next up, Edward was shown the photo of the Falcon carrying Farah being waved through the cordon.

'You need extremely powerful friends for that,' Edward said. 'How else can Vakurov get through a military cordon without having his armoured car inspected?'

'The hostage-taking was almost certainly staged by the Kremlin. This could support that theory. Either way, we've also discovered that at least one of the so-called black widows walking around with Kalashnikovs and explosive belts wasn't Chechen at all, but Estonian.'

'How the hell did you get into the building?' Edward asked.

'Anya has a whole arsenal of tricks up her sleeve and a network of the strangest bedfellows. Once we were in, it turned out she knew the leader of that merry band of women, Chalim Barchayev. Number one on Russia's list of most-wanted Chechen terrorists. She'd interviewed him once. I passed myself off as her photographer and the bastard actually let me do my thing. So I walked around taking pictures of everything, of all the hostages, and that's how I found Farah in the auditorium.'

He glanced at Edward, who was sitting hunched over with his nose practically up against the screen.

'I suggest you have that second glass now. You're going to need it.'

'Why?'

'Because of what I'm about to show you, the way I found her.'

Edward's voice sounded calm and determined. 'I want to see it first.'

There was something almost aesthetic about the image. The reality, however, had been far grimmer. Farah slouched in a chair, immobile and semi-conscious, with black tape across her mouth and the explosive strapped to her chest.

'The bastards,' Edward muttered and got to his feet. 'You were right. I could use a second dram. Do me a favour, finish yours too. Let's have another one together.'

'Just one?' Paul asked.

'Dickhead,' Edward said. He took Paul's now-empty glass and walked to the bar globe.

The sight of his colossal uncle standing there over his spherical cabinet – the retro-coloured continents reminiscent of yesterday's world – made Paul smile. He walked over to the window to stretch his legs, pressed the palms of his hands against the glass and took a few deep breaths. Beyond the reflection of his tired, unshaven face, some hundred metres away, he could see Het Fort, an old shipyard now occupied by squatters. Supported by the local population, they were protesting against the takeover bid by Armin Lazonder, who wanted to turn it into a business hub.

'I don't get it,' said Edward, who came to stand next to Paul and handed him his refilled glass. 'Lavrov's a global player. Then one day a Dutch journalist crosses his path. He must have known that she posed no threat to him whatsoever at that point. She didn't know nearly enough about him. He could have just played along. Could have made a fine art supplement together. It would have been excellent PR for his company.'

'But he does the exact opposite.'

'Exactly. He dumps her. Why?'

'Because he made a mistake – one he couldn't undo.'

'What kind of mistake?'

'He tried to make a potential opponent his ally.'

'But our girl is not for sale.'

'By then he'd revealed information about himself and his business concerns he should have kept to himself. How do you undo something like that? A woman like Farah can't simply be eliminated. You'd generate the wrong kind of international publicity.'

'I can picture the newspaper headlines: FOREIGN JOURNALIST MISSING IN MOSCOW.'

'So what does he do? He comes up with a plan that's as brilliant as it is deadly. With that jihad statement he not only portrayed her as a terrorist, but also obliterated her credibility as a journalist.'

He took a large sip of his whisky. He felt like downing it in one gulp.

'What happened next?' Edward sounded hoarse.

'I just showed you.'

'You mean the time bomb?'

He looked at Edward and saw how emotional his uncle was.

'That time bomb fitted seamlessly into the manipulation of the facts. She'd have blown herself up as a black widow, had it not been for . . .'

Paul fell silent and thought back to the moment he'd yelled at the leader of the commandos who'd come charging in that Farah was his *colleague*. He'd only just realized there probably hadn't been any need for him to do that. Experienced as they were, they'd no doubt figured out that she couldn't possibly be a terrorist. Someone threatening to detonate a bomb isn't handcuffed to a chair in a ripped cocktail dress with her mouth taped shut. In his quest for as much evidence as possible that Farah was a victim in all this, he'd totally overlooked an important witness: the leader of the Alpha Spetsnaz commando team. He remembered the man's words after he'd removed the explosive from Farah.

You no enemy. You free.

Paul's phone rang. He saw Anya's name on the display. She sounded excited, hysterical almost. For a moment it felt as if they were back in the workshop at the Hammer and Sickle steel factory, from where she was now calling him, among the computer screens, mixing panels and connectors, where Lesha had just managed to hack into the YotaPhone's damaged SD card.

'He performed digital mouth-to-mouth, or whatever you want to call it. He did it,' she shouted. 'He managed to restore parts of the damaged card. Of all the footage our supposed black widow recorded, we've only retrieved three fragments, but it's enough. I'd better warn you, they're shocking. I'll send the material to you shortly, encrypted.'

The connection was broken before he had a chance to

respond. Edward was standing with his back against the glass wall, and Paul could see the surprise on his face.

'Ever heard of a *deus ex machina*?' asked Paul as he pushed his chair back. 'Well, this is one.'

He sat down in front of his laptop, in anticipation of things to come.

6

It was pitch-black on the deserted road. She was surprised at the lack of wind. Warm raindrops fell on her body, the leaves on the trees and the tarmac. She walked in the direction of the moaning, unable to determine whether it was a human or an animal sound.

In the light of the moon, which briefly crept from behind a cloud, she saw a motionless heap in the middle of the road. A dog hit by a car, it flashed through her mind. But dogs don't moan like that. It wasn't until she got closer that she saw it wasn't an animal.

'*Ma peshtet amadam.*' 'I'm coming,' she heard herself say.

She knelt down beside the boy, lifted him up in her arms and carried on walking without really knowing where.

She felt the helpless rigidity of his body. But she was afraid to look at his face, not yet ready to confront the truth. Bathe him, scrub him clean, rub him dry and put him to bed – that's what she wanted to do. Then she'd tell him the story: of the young, blond soldier on a river bank, coming eye to eye with the river goddess, who caused him to drown when he tried to swim to her.

He'd ask why she let the soldier drown. Of course he would. Because he'd be speaking again, moving his lips that were no longer blue. And then she'd explain to him that only in death are lovers together forever. Later, when he was all grown up, he'd understand.

After this thought, she finally looked at him.

He stared at her like the girl at the foot of her hotel bed had done. With eyes devoid of any questions.

Then she cried herself awake and felt two warm hands grabbing hold of her. And Aninda's sleepy voice.

'Valentina?'

She didn't respond. After kicking the sheet away, she crawled out from under the mosquito net, sat on the edge of the bed and wiped the sweat from her body. Aninda flashed past like a ghost before returning with a glass of water in her hand.

'Drink up.'

She heard the crackling of a plastic strip and swallowed a tablet in blind faith. Then Aninda sat down next to her, leaned in and wrapped a comforting arm around her.

'Can you hear them?' she asked. Farah listened to the rustling outside. 'Those are bats. They've just given birth, and now they have to go out hunting every night to feed their young. The courtyard is teeming with insects and butterflies.'

They sat silently and listened.

'My name is Farah.' She could hear herself say it, as if someone else was activating her vocal cords. 'I'm a journalist. And I'm on the run.'

Aninda stared at her.

'On the run from what?'

'It's a long story.'

'We've got time.'

Once Farah started talking, she couldn't stop. She talked about her childhood, which had been as sheltered as the big house with the walled garden in Kabul. A childhood with a mother who worked as a lawyer and a father who, as Interior Minister, had his offices in the presidential palace.

'The palace had a large courtyard and part of it had been laid out as a butterfly garden. I used to go as often as I could. The last time I was there . . . I heard the roaring. It's a sound I'll never forget. At first I thought it was thunder, but I couldn't see any clouds. Then they emerged – the planes. They circled above the palace a couple of times before dropping their bombs . . . I don't remember how I got away but I dream about it to this day. Body parts flying through the air, walls collapsing, debris, dust and blood everywhere, screaming and shouting, and yet I'm flying down the marble corridors as if I've got wings. I fly outside, towards the light.'

She fell silent, rested her head in the hollow of Aninda's left shoulder and blinked back her tears.

'Everybody in the palace, including the President's children, were lined up against the wall and shot dead. So was my father. Their bodies were never recovered. Pencak Silat is the only thing that binds me to him, to that time when I was happy, truly happy. I've long forgotten what it means to be happy. All I feel is pain when I think back on that time. I don't want to look back any more. I want to forget everything. It's what I've been doing for more than thirty years. But one evening not so long ago, I saw this Afghan boy in a hospital. He was lying on a stretcher, seriously injured. He'd been dressed and made up to look like a girl and he was draped in jewellery. He whispered "*Padar*". Father. And in his eyes I saw a mortal fear. It was the same fear I'd felt so often as a child, after those planes dropped their bombs. The boy was a part of me that I'd spent my whole life pushing away. His story was my story.'

She talked about her investigation into the hit-and-run, about the unexpected developments, about Valentin Lavrov's involvement.

'I had a contact in the Dutch police force who told me about a link between Lavrov and a Dutch minister. My boss came up with a plan that enabled us to get close to Lavrov quite easily. The businessman is known the world over as an avid art collector, so we asked him to be the guest editor of a special art supplement. When he agreed, we made an appointment and I flew to Moscow.'

Then she talked about the hostage-taking at the university, about the YouTube clip of her jihad statement.

'Sometimes it's better to be dead . . .'

'What do you mean?'

'What Lavrov did is worse than murder,' Farah explained. 'He let me live, all right, but he violated my identity. The person I was no longer exists. He's turned me into a criminal, someone perceived to be a danger to the state. To the outside world I'm now a jihadi.'

Aninda was silent. 'Maybe it's your karma,' she finally said. 'You're fleeing what's chasing you, but the more you flee, the more it comes after you. And one day . . . one day it will catch up with you. And then you'll have no choice but to turn around and look it straight in the eye.'

'I don't think I can,' Farah whispered.

'That's what you told yourself once upon a time,' Aninda said. 'And you've come to believe it. Do as your heart tells you, not as your fear dictates.'

Her restless, pounding heart. The rustling of the bats among the leaves of the weeping fig. Her finger tracing each line in the palm of Aninda's hand. Everything felt as intense as those childhood nights when she sneaked out of her room and climbed up into the apple tree to watch the stars. Sitting a few metres above the ground, she was closer to them, yet the sight of the universe made her feel as small as a fly. Still, all her childlike worries, all her fears, became irrelevant, because she knew the stars would always be there for her – tiny and remote, yet a constant presence.

'How come you've got such blue eyes?' Aninda asked.

'I'm Afghan. And the north of the country, the Chitral Valley, is home to the Kho. They've got blue eyes; some even have blond hair. Myth has it that they're descendants of Alexander the Great's soldiers. My mother said that her father came from the Chitral Valley, although she herself had brown eyes. It skips generations, she once told me.'

She snuggled up against Aninda. The mosquito net hung like a transparent shield between her and the outside world, while the night kept all danger at bay.

She had no idea how mistaken she was.

7

Newton had provided the proof: white light was the sum total of all colours. If you looked through a prism, you could see what was invisible to the naked eye. Over the course of his career, this was how Radjen had cross-examined many suspects and how he'd observed Ewald Lombard during his interrogation. Behind the white light of his ministerial façade, Radjen had seen a range of dark colours hiding.

Ewald Lombard, concluded Radjen, was a man of two worlds. In one world he was the successful standard-bearer of the Ministry of Economic Affairs. But in another world, in a dark-coloured spectrum of self-hatred and a growing sense of guilt, he was a man enslaved by his own paedophilic urges.

Radjen wanted at all costs to expose this man to the public, but until now he'd been thwarted at every turn. To make matters worse, immediately after he'd returned to headquarters from his confrontation with Lombard, he was told to report to his superior, an anxious-looking Commissioner Kemper.

'I just received the preliminary conclusions of the investigative report from the Security and Integrity Office,' Kemper said, as he looked up from the document he had in front of him. Kemper had the appearance of a stern diplomat. His healthy lifestyle and athletic build made him look younger than he was. He preferred to wear his glasses perched on top of his close-cropped head.

'Are those my walking papers?' Radjen joked.

Kemper grimaced. He was all too familiar with his chief investigator's blunt approach. He yanked the glasses from his head – body language that made Radjen nervous. He'd rather be given the verdict on how he'd failed in the matter of the dead prisoner Kovalev in straight terms. No distracting gestures, no diplomatic bullshit.

'Basically, Detective Diba is being held responsible for the death of the Russian,' Kemper said. 'Traces of DNA on Kovalev's head match Diba's DNA.'

'That isn't one hundred per cent proof that Diba actually smashed Kovalev's head against the table,' Radjen said. 'It could have been an act of desperation on Kovalev's part and perhaps Diba tried to stop him.'

'That's possible,' Kemper said. 'And, of course, there are people who claim we never landed on the moon.'

Radjen couldn't help but smile at Kemper's dry humour.

'Besides,' Kemper continued, 'phone records reveal that Diba had regular contact with Kovalev for almost two years. And then I still haven't mentioned the four-figure sums that were regularly transferred from a Luxembourg bank to Diba's private account. Whether you believe in moon landings or not, Diba was working for Kovalev too.'

'What's the finding on Detective Calvino's involvement?'

'He's being held responsible for restraining Kovalev during his interrogation.'

'Kovalev was armed and dangerous.'

'Once someone is frisked and dumped in a jail cell, they're no longer armed and dangerous. Calvino will get off in this matter. But regarding another matter . . .' Kemper nonchalantly placed his glasses on the desk and frowned at Radjen.

'Did you advise Calvino to go to Moscow to see if he could arrest Lombard there?'

'It was his suggestion,' Radjen replied. 'But I gave him the green light. On the condition that he didn't go as a detective on active duty, but as a private citizen. Calvino paid for his round-trip ticket out of his own pocket. Legally, he's done nothing wrong.'

'For God's sake,' Kemper responded. 'It just proves how far you're prepared to go to get Lombard.'

'Since when is there something wrong with that?'

'Since the polls for the upcoming elections show that at least one third of the Dutch populace will likely vote for Lombard's party, while we're jumping through hoops to put this guy behind bars. What the hell happened at the ministry this morning?'

'What do you mean?'

'Lombard has filed an official complaint against you.'

'On what grounds?'

'Slander and intimidation.'

Kemper grabbed his glasses and balanced them on his nose. He needn't have bothered, because, after leafing through the report for a few seconds, he looked up at Radjen again.

'While this report is somewhat forgiving about your responsibility in the Kovalev case and Calvino's failed attempt to arrest Lombard in Moscow, I know that the Board of Police Commissioners is looking for a scapegoat. Thanks to the tone of this morning's interrogation, you've eliminated all the competition. Congratulations.'

'Listen, Kemper, we've known each other a long time. The night of the raid on Lombard's home office, I saw images on his computer that made my stomach turn. And then there's the boy from the hit-and-run. The chauffeur placed Lombard in the car at the time of the accident, and Kovalev's initial statement placed him at the scene as well. For God's sake, what more do we need to haul this guy in?'

'Proof,' Kemper said.

'Proof that was destroyed last week by a hacker, an explosion and a so-called suicide,' Radjen said.

'I'm aware of that too, damn it,' Kemper sighed. He placed his glasses back on top of his head with a firm but clumsy gesture. He stared, seemingly mindlessly, at the wall behind Radjen. An illustration of despair and powerlessness.

'And why a scapegoat?' Radjen asked.

'I've received an official request to put someone else in charge of your current MIT case,' Kemper finally said.

Radjen stared at Kemper in silence; Kemper returned the look.

'It isn't a request I can ignore.'

'I understand.'

'I'll have to take it into consideration, damn it.'

'Of course.'

'I'll need some time to do this.'

'How long?'

'Three days at least. Is that enough?'

'The world was created in seven days,' Radjen said, as he stood up. 'Why can't we solve a murder in three days?'

'I'll make it five,' said Kemper. 'And do whatever you think is necessary.'

'Better yet,' said Radjen, who'd turned in the doorway, 'I'm going to do something a gentleman should never do.'

'And what's that?'

'Destroy a lady's alibi.'

Fifteen minutes later, Radjen exited the ring and drove on to the A1 motorway in the direction of Amersfoort, while beside him Esther thumbed through Melanie Lombard van Velzen's file.

'We need to hurry,' Radjen said. 'We have to meet with the pathologist in an hour and she hates tardiness.'

'What did Kemper have to say?' Esther asked.

Radjen gave it to her straight. 'We have five days.'

'Five days for what?'

'Until I'm removed from the case.'

She looked at him amazed.

'It's very simple, Esther. Put a minister under pressure to admit his guilt and he'll do his best to push you aside. Yet Lombard's actions have only made him more of a suspect. I'm afraid we won't be getting much sleep for a while; we need to take advantage of every minute we have left. Agreed?'

'Absolutely.'

'All right, then. What do we know about Melanie Lombard van Velzen?'

'Forty-seven. Born in the coastal town of Bergen op Zoom, raised in Eindhoven, eldest of three girls, father was once on Philips' Board of Directors. Sixth Form College, then . . . get a load of this.' She whistled through her teeth.

'Then?'

'The Sorbonne, French Language and Literature. Then Spanish in Salamanca, and, as if that wasn't enough, Italian in Perugia. Then she got a job as an interpreter.'

'Any children?'

'None.'

'Work?'

'Hasn't worked as an interpreter for years.'

'Is that it?' he asked, nodding towards the file on her lap.

'The best is still to come,' she said. 'Melanie Lombard was the first Dutchwoman to sail around the world alone, in ninety-eight days. And to add another twist to the tale, the last few years she's been giving gardening courses. She's even written a book: *The Healing Garden*.'

She closed the file, sighed and looked at him. He sucked in his stomach. 'The healing garden . . . Really. I don't expect that to be of much help to us.'

'She's come in for questioning before. Answered everything. Fully cooperated in the investigation. But now I want to see how she behaves under pressure. Did she discuss all the details with her husband? Do all the aspects of their stories match? Perhaps she'll slip up. The problem with things you invent is that you often forget the small details. And we'll get her on that.'

With a sharp turn, he took Exit 8 in the direction of Blaricum. The urban landscape gave way to lakes, heathland and forests. They drove along a sloping road through an autumn forest filled with gnarled oaks, pines and stately beech. After leaving the centre of town with its restored farmhouses, they ended up on a tree-lined lane, with freestanding villas peeking out from behind tall hedges.

The three-storey detached house they stopped at was probably more than a hundred years old and surrounded by a fence. The electric gate was open. Radjen parked the Corolla near the carport beside a red Mini Cooper. On the driveway closer to the house, he spotted a Porsche, a Range Rover, two Aston Martins, and a Citroën 2CV reminiscent of a 1950s French film. They walked around the house and found themselves in a gardener's paradise, a green utopia where the approaching autumn had barely taken hold and a handful of women in trendy casual clothing were gathered with all kinds of gardening tools.

Radjen looked around and smelled the scent of roses, but there was also something else pungent in the air. It all seemed too idyllic to be true. He sharpened his senses.

'They used to smear arrowheads with it,' he heard Esther say. She pointed to one of the small garden signs. 'Blue monkshood. Contains aconitine. A few milligrams can kill a horse. Really. This isn't an herb garden, it's a killing field.'

Absent-mindedly, Radjen picked some black berries from another bush and was about to pop one into his mouth.

'I wouldn't do that if I were you.'

He turned and looked into the chestnut-brown eyes of a woman who was undoubtedly close to fifty, but still a seasoned beauty. She would have been the kind of girl you did anything for in school just to get a chance to give her a lift to a party on the back of your scooter. Her voice had a sensual, warm, smoky edge, probably the result of too many cigarettes, a lot of drinking, or a combination of the two. She had round amber-coloured sunglasses perched on her head and a scarf almost nonchalantly intertwined with her reddish-brown hair, which was a bit unkempt. Her red-and-black plaid flannel lumberjack shirt was unbuttoned rather low. She wore faded jeans and calf-high Hunter wellies.

'*Atropa belladonna*. Deadly nightshade. Ingest a handful and you'll be writhing in agony and close to death within minutes.'

'Know your enemy,' he said, laughing. He quickly tossed the berries and extended his hand. 'Radjen Tomasoa. Chief Inspector.'

'Melanie Lombard.' She had a firm handshake. 'Nature, Inspector Tomasoa, knows us better than we know ourselves.' She spoke with an air of pretentiousness, with the inborn disdain that characterizes people from the upper classes. Her two bracelets jingled as if they were musical instruments.

'And this is my colleague, Esther van Noordt.'

Melanie Lombard couldn't muster more than a brusque 'good afternoon' for his partner. She immediately directed her attention back to Radjen, as if his presence was all she could manage.

'What I can I do for you?'

Strangely enough, he felt a fatherly impulse to put his arm around her shoulders. Melanie Lombard van Velzen was a woman who carried a quiet sadness deep within her soul. He could hear it in her voice, saw it in her dark, dilated irises, filled with melancholy. But she was too strong-willed, too stubborn, too proud to share this with others, let alone two unknown investigators who'd found their way into her garden unannounced. He tried to shake off the feeling. Any kind of compassion for this woman would only get in the way of why they were there.

'I'm sorry to bother you, Mrs Lombard, but I'd like to ask you a few more questions related to our hit-and-run investigation,' he said.

She threw him a distrustful gaze. 'Shouldn't you be talking to my husband? Or, better yet, my husband and his lawyer?'

Radjen nodded at the group of women by the fountain curiously looking in their direction and ignored her question. 'Is there a place where we can talk quietly?'

'I'm about to give a workshop for these women, Inspector.'

'I understand, but there's still some confusion about the alibi you provided.'

She looked at him suspiciously again. 'I assume you've read my statement?'

'Certainly.'

'In it, I already told the police everything I know.'

'We'd like to go over a few of the details again with you,' Esther said.

For a moment it actually seemed like Melanie Lombard had forgotten there were three people involved in the conversation.

'Details?'

She turned her head ever so slightly, as if distracted by something outside their field of vision. It was a diversionary tactic so she could gain the upper hand. 'I'll give you a few minutes,' she said. 'But then I really need to get back to work as quickly as possible.'

With hasty but controlled steps, she walked over to the group of women. It struck Radjen that there was something about her gait, a charming, hidden shortcoming.

'She's a poseur,' Esther said.

'A what?'

'Someone who's pretending to be something that she isn't.'

'They say that after a time spouses start to resemble each other,' Radjen said.

They watched Melanie Lombard direct the group of women armed with pruning shears, rake, pitchfork and spade towards the back of the garden and walked in her direction.

'You might be wondering what this group is up to,' she said in an unexpectedly light-hearted tone. 'The new moon is almost here. A new moon means a new beginning. High time for us to look back at what is behind us. What have we accomplished, what do we want to keep, and what do we want to let go of? The transition to darker days can leave you with a chaotic feeling. By talking about this and planting another part of the garden, I help them to find a new balance.'

She ended her explanation with a high-pitched laugh, apparently realizing she was wasting her breath on them. Radjen saw Esther struggling not to laugh out loud.

They walked into a conservatory with marble floors, high ceilings and stained-glass windows. Melanie Lombard crossed her arms and scrutinized them. There was something in her attitude that intrigued him.

'I assume you're aware of the death of your husband's chauffeur?' he asked.

She looked at him in disbelief. 'You mean the man who ran down that child?'

Radjen thought about what Esther had just said. Melanie Lombard van Velzen was not just any poseur; she had mastered the art.

'How well did you know Mr Meijer?' Esther asked.

'Barely. My husband has multiple drivers.'

Radjen couldn't tell if she was a woman who took everyone and everything seriously or one who had contempt for the whole world and, right now, especially them.

'You claimed that your husband was brought home by Mr Meijer at ten thirty,' he said.

'That's right.'

'According to your husband, he had two heavy briefcases with him. It's protocol that the driver carries the bags inside. That evening, did you see or hear him doing this?'

'No, I didn't.'

'Where were you at that time?'

'I was in the kitchen.'

'Would you mind showing us the kitchen?' Radjen wanted to take the lead, but saw her frown. 'So we have a visual reference.'

She sighed and led the way past two high panelled doors into a spacious kitchen with an old table the size of a pool table in the middle, almost completely covered with pots full of herbs, dried flowers and a fruit bowl filled to the brim. Through the large stained-glass window that overlooked the backyard, the sun conjured the slowly shifting coloured patterns of red, yellow and blue on the whitewashed walls.

'Did your husband come through the front door that night or from out back?'

'Really, Inspector, is this the reason you've interrupted my workshop?'

'Could you please answer my question?'

'He's always dropped off out front.'

Radjen looked around and pointed to the door that opened into the hallway. 'Was that open or closed?'

'The hallway door was closed; otherwise I would've seen him arriving home.'

'Didn't you hear the car?'

'I was making tea at the time. The kettle was on.'

She sounded impatient. Radjen thought that was a good sign. He nodded at the copper kettle on the Aga cooker.

'Would you mind boiling some water?'

She looked at him in amazement. 'Inspector, you've had your few minutes of my time, and that's more than enough.'

'We're trying to get as precise a picture as possible of the situation when your husband arrived home,' he said calmly. 'I can come back this afternoon with a team and do a detailed reconstruction, or we can do it now, and in a few minutes you'll be rid of us. Up to you.'

She filled the kettle and lit the stove. Then she crossed her arms and stared at him arrogantly.

'Happy now, Inspector?'

'Yes, thank you. So you were here in the kitchen, with the door to the hallway closed, when your husband's chauffeured car arrived. The front door opened, the driver put the brief-cases in the hallway, the door was closed and Mr Meijer drove away. And you didn't hear anything?'

'That's correct – the water was boiling and I –'

'May I have the key to the front door?'

'No, I want you to leave now. This is not a reconstruction; this is harassment, which I'm going to report to your superiors.'

'You have that right, ma'am. But I'm not going to argue with you. Cooperate, or I'll send a team here this afternoon to conduct an extensive investigation.'

Melanie walked over to the large table, pulled open a drawer, removed a bunch of keys, walked towards him and just stood there with the keys in the palm of her open raised hand. Radjen didn't look at the hand or the keys but straight into her eyes, and he saw the deep contempt there.

'Could you tell my colleague which key is for the front door?' he asked.

With her other hand, she grabbed the biggest key and handed it to Esther as if it were a dead rat.

In hushed tones, Radjen instructed Esther to drive the Corolla closer to the front door, to open and close the car doors and to then come back through the hall to the kitchen. Esther disappeared down the hallway. He heard the tapping of her boots as she headed to the front door, which opened and shut again.

'Do you mind if I smoke in my own home while you're finishing up your masterful reconstruction, Inspector?'

Melanie Lombard didn't even wait for his response: she removed a cigarette from a packet lying on the table, lit it and, with a small hop up, sat on the edge of the marble work-top. No matter how he looked at it, Radjen felt a hundred times more intimidated by this woman than by her bully husband. He couldn't figure her out. One minute she seemed helpless like a child, and the next she was an ice queen: cold and unapproachable. Yet perhaps the worst of it all was that he could barely keep his eyes off her. It unsettled him.

He cleared his throat. 'An innocent boy nearly died, Mrs Lombard. And a number of people have placed your husband at the scene of the crime. As it happens, your alibi is the only thing that contradicts those statements.'

'That's what alibis are for, right?' She took a drag of her cigarette. The disdain in her eyes was killing.

'That's the reason we have to double-check your alibi,' Radjen said.

She gave him a long and serious look, inhaled the smoke from her cigarette and exhaled through her nose. 'I have the feeling, Inspector, that people don't think you're the empathetic type. No wonder. You're obsessed with the misery of the world, unable to think of anything besides violent crime. I see it in you. Do you ever take time to visit a museum or listen to a moving piece of music?'

He looked past her at the kettle on the cooker. The water was almost boiling. 'I want to make sure we've correctly understood what you've already told us. Can you tell me what you did after the water boiled?'

'The usual things that a woman does when she makes tea for herself and her husband.'

'Perhaps you could show me exactly what you did?'

'You mean, so you can empathize?'

'Please, Mrs Lombard.'

She hopped off the kitchen worktop and put her cigarette out under the tap. She removed a glass teapot from an antique pharmacy cabinet, plucked mint leaves from a plant on the counter, filled the teapot and put a small glass jar with honey beside it.

'This will make the ladies in the garden happy,' she said with false cheer in her voice. The water in the pot was now almost boiling. Nevertheless, Radjen heard the distinct crunch of the pebbles in the driveway, the opening and closing of the front door and Esther's footsteps in the hallway. At the time the kitchen door swung open, the kettle whistled as if a fire alarm had gone off.

Esther threw the keys on the table. Radjen turned off the cooker.

'You said that you didn't hear your husband arrive home because the kettle was almost boiling.'

'Correct'

'Didn't you just hear the car?'

'No, Inspector.'

She looked at Radjen with a dislike as immense as the Great Wall of China is long. 'I have otosclerosis, an abnormal growth of bone in the middle ear.' She walked to the table, pulled open a drawer and showed him two small hearing aids. 'I never wear them at home. Makes me feel a bit too bionic.'

'Your husband claimed in his statement that you were in the living room,' Esther reminded her. 'But you're saying you were in the kitchen. So you were in two places at the same time. A rather good trick.'

Melanie Lombard looked at her with a mixture of disgust and contempt. 'When my husband came home, I was in the kitchen. I didn't hear that he was already in the hall. I went into the living room with the tray. After a busy day, no matter what time it is, my husband enjoys sharing a quiet moment together. We drink tea and indulge in dark chocolate. Space, silence and chocolate, the essentials of life.'

She smiled as if she had the whole situation under control.

'That leaves us with the third and final riddle,' Radjen said. 'How did you know that your husband would be home at that time?'

'I knew because he told me.'

'When?'

'About ten minutes before he arrived home. He called me from the car.'

'Neither of you mentioned this in your statements.'

'Because nobody asked, Inspector. Is it so strange for a man to call his wife to say he's almost home?'

'Do you realize, Mrs Lombard, if it turns out you've concealed certain things, or that your alibi is a lie, you're complicit in the crime your husband is suspected of committing?'

She sighed. 'All right. You got me.' She looked at him intently. 'I didn't make mint tea that night. It was star anise. Now I think it's time for you to leave.'

They drove on winding country roads for a while in silence, while Radjen racked his brains over the life-sized puzzle Melanie Lombard van Velzen had become for him. He'd seen the pain in her dark eyes. What was she hiding from the outside world?

It was as if Esther could read his thoughts. 'Don't you think it's strange they don't have children?'

He thought about it. 'Lombard isn't exactly the fatherly type.'

'Maybe in a horror film.'

'Okay, but that's not the impression I get from her. And I'm not talking about the Melanie Lombard van Velzen we just met, no, perhaps around twenty years ago. Is there something in her medical records?'

She picked up the folder and began thumbing through it. 'Those kinds of things are usually not listed, unless it's a case of . . . wait . . . she was involved in a serious accident, eighteen years ago. She spent a long time in rehab.'

'Look into it, okay?' He glanced at her. 'Like a ninja.'

'Fine, but what do you hope to find?'

'I don't know. Besides the fact that she's probably lying about her alibi, what surprises me most about this woman is her aggressive nature. There are other things she's hiding as well. Matters, perhaps from the past, things she knows about her husband, but doesn't want to reveal, or can't reveal. Something that will bring us one step closer to Lombard.'

'Are you sure you're not losing it a bit?'

Esther had lit two cigarettes and given him one. This small but meaningful gesture had quickly become a familiar ritual.

'It's almost a new moon, you know?' she said in the same affected tone Melanie Lombard had used. He'd just inhaled, but started laughing. And with this came a billowing of smoke and all his frustration. She laughed along with him.

'When I saw the photos in the hallway,' she said, 'I was immediately reminded of what they say about sailors.'

'What photos?'

'A young Melanie at the helm of an extended Jeanneau Gin Fizz ketch.'

'Do you eat that or drink it?'

'It's a type of sailboat.'

'And what do they say about sailors?'

'That they have a way with rope. Sailors are experts at making a wide variety of knots.'

He threw her a grin. 'Speaking of occupational hazards. Perhaps you're losing it too?'

'More and more, I feel like we're starting to resemble each other,' she said, completely serious.

'Who?'

'The two of us.'

'Come off it.'

He had just enough time to take one more drag. Then the phone rang. He heard the voice of Ellen Mulder, the pathologist.

'Meijer's autopsy waits for no one, not even a chief inspector. How long before you get here, Radjen?'

8

'Julius Caesar was the first to dispatch his messages encrypted,' Edward said. 'He'd developed a simple type of algorithm, a code that was very quickly cracked. Some crazy scientist even claims it was the beginning of the end for mighty Caesar, would you believe it?'

They were sitting side by side, each with another glass of whisky, both with their eyes glued to the screen of the laptop in the middle of the table in front of them.

Paul thought of the explanation he and Farah had received from Anya in Moscow, just before they'd parted ways. They'd be sending one another messages that had been 'locked' by a digital key. A key, Anya explained to them, was an infinite algorithmic series of figures and other characters that made any form of information unreadable to an outsider. Besides, rather than the single key that was used to encrypt and decrypt data in the outdated symmetrical system, they'd be working with asymmetrical cryptography, which used two keys. Anya would be locking the messages and files she sent to Paul with a public key. But as soon as the communications reached Paul, he'd only be able to open them with his own private key.

The moment his email buzzed to indicate he'd received a message, Paul put Anya's lesson into practice for the first time. The 'encrypted' symbol lit up red to indicate that the file received was locked. In accordance with Anya's protocol, he now activated Enigmail, an application in his email program that managed his private key. Then he typed in 'decrypt'.

A window popped up, prompting him to type in a password – an additional security measure. When he did so, the outcome flashed on the screen.

Access denied.

He looked down at his keyboard, noticed the green light of his 'caps lock' key, deactivated it and tried again. He waited.

The media player was activated and three video files were automatically transferred.

'God almighty,' Edward sighed. 'The days of Caesar's basic algorithm are truly over.'

Paul took a hurried gulp of his whisky. The opening image of the first file loaded. A wide shot, blurry and from an angle. Paul saw a camera on a tripod. Sitting some three metres before it, handcuffed to a chair, was Farah. Her hair was loose and her black dress ripped up to her waist. She was barefoot and her head was stretched forward, like that of an eagle about to attack. It must have been her fury, wanting to flee, yet knowing she couldn't move. Beside the camera he saw a second woman. It was the girl he'd seen in the flat – conclusive evidence that it had indeed been her. She was squatting next to the camera, on her knees, with her head down.

Paul looked at Edward. When his uncle nodded to say he was ready, Paul pressed 'play'.

The first thing they saw was a passing shadow. The image was too fleeting for them to tell who or what it was. But Paul had his suspicions. The moment the shadow passed, the picture shook, violently, as if they were watching footage shot from a ship in rough seas. The person filming was doing so on a mobile with an unsteady hand, probably trying to be as unobtrusive as possible. There was something voyeuristic about it all. They were looking at things they weren't supposed to see. They were sharing a secret.

Paul recognized the man in front of the camera, who was now pressing the barrel of his gun against the girl's head.

Arseni Vakurov.

The girl beside the camera was muttering. '*Pozhaluysta*,' 'Please, have mercy.'

Vakurov leaned towards Farah and pointed to the camera lens. Then he yelled at her in an atrocious Slavic accent: 'Look at this!'

She raised her head and stared at the camera.

Vakurov carried on spewing his gibberish. 'Now say what I want you to say, bitch. And do it convincingly.' He produced a piece of paper. 'Repeat after me!'

Paul was almost surprised to discover that old Arseni wasn't illiterate. He barked the lines he wanted Farah to repeat, while keeping the barrel of his gun pressed against the girl's head.

Farah moved her lips in an effort to repeat Vakurov's words. But she appeared to be incapable of producing a sound. Her vocal cords were paralysed.

Not a word, not a sound came out.

Vakurov made a show of cocking the gun and planting its barrel back against the girl's head. The girl flinched, muttering, praying, begging, sobbing.

Vakurov roared, 'I'll kill her if you don't say it right now. I'll kill her, you hear?!'

But nothing came out. Farah appeared to have lost her voice completely. She was on the verge of hyperventilating. Suddenly a flash of lightning crossed the screen, followed by a rain of pixels that rendered everything invisible. Then the screen turned black – right before the moment that the media all over the world had focused on. That one isolated moment when she'd shouted: 'I, Farah Hafez, support the jihad against President Potanin's criminal regime.'

At the start of the second fragment, the girl was lying on the floor, broken, as though Vakurov had shot her in the head. Paul heard Farah swear. In Dari. He understood her words and smiled in spite of himself.

Vakurov stomped over to Farah and swore back, calling her every name under the sun, at which she kicked him in the shins. So hard he buckled forward and landed on top of her.

That's the moment the second pixel storm erupted and the screen went black again.

The sound that the third fragment opened with was bone-chilling. It was Farah shrieking. Vakurov's behaviour was monstrous: in that moment he was less noble than a Neanderthal. He yanked Farah by her hair and dragged her behind him. At that point, the man whose shadow had slid past in the first fragment reappeared on screen. Paul recognized him by his fatigues, the Kalashnikov in his hand, the munition belts slung across his chest and the big gun in his holster.

Chalim Barchayev. Self-styled brigadier general of the Smert-niki suicide squad, one of Moscow's most wanted terrorists.

He yelled something at Vakurov in a mixture of Russian and Chechen. And then the unexpected happened. Vakurov hit back. His Russian words were unequivocal.

'If you start interfering, my boss will have you and the rest of this bunch taken out immediately. This is *our* operation. *I'm* giving the orders around here.'

And off Vakurov marched.

Barchayev stayed put, taken aback. He turned to face the filming mobile, which promptly swerved down and went black.

Paul's heart was pounding like crazy.

For a while they sat there, speechless, staring at the black screen, each deep in thought – astonished and agitated.

It was Edward who spoke first.

'Bloody hell.'

Then they let the silence speak for itself again. Paul's head was full of noise. Thoughts, hypotheses and conclusions criss-crossed his mind, touching, connecting, setting off sparks.

'This doesn't just prove Farah's innocence,' he muttered. 'This shows that the whole hostage-taking was a pretence.'

'The casualties were real.'

'How were they to know? The commandos were ordered to eliminate the terrorists.'

'We need to make this public as quickly as possible,' Edward said.

'Not this film material,' Paul said. 'Not yet. We ought to keep this under wraps for now. These images are our trump card. This matter reaches all the way to the Kremlin. We're not ready for that yet. Farah is our first priority.'

He turned to Edward. 'I'd like you to organize a press conference for me. So I can release the photos I've just shown you. I bet these and the story behind them will be picked up around the world. And their impact will be big enough to convince everyone that Farah is the victim in all this and Lavrov the manipulator.'

'You're right,' Edward said. 'We mustn't overplay our hand. Lavrov is coming to the Netherlands in two days' time. He and Minister Lombard are due to sign the contract for the construction of an underground gas hub in Bergermeer. I think that may be the ideal moment for your press conference.'

The two men fell silent once more. Edward swore a couple of times. 'With this you're finally following in your father's footsteps. You do realize that, don't you?' he said.

Paul felt his uncle's large hand on his shoulder. How often had he felt it there, how often had he heard the older man's encouraging words? Edward had been like a father to him since Raylan's death, had always believed in him. He'd shown him that when you lose a father you're not necessarily left to your own devices, abandoned, unsettled, beside yourself with anger. He'd shown him more affection than his frequently absent father had ever done. Raylan had been primarily interested in himself, in the revelations, the spectacular reports from Vietnam with which he'd surprised friend and foe alike. No, if there was anything Paul didn't want it was to follow in his father's footsteps. Though he'd probably been doing this his whole life, resulting in broken relationships and pointless conflicts with colleagues, editors-in-chief and the big bosses. In fact, more than once it had cost him his job.

He thought of the reproach his most recent girlfriend, Susanne, had hurled at him during their final row, months ago in Johannesburg. 'It's about you,' she'd yelled. 'About your life with those ghosts you're always chasing. Because you want to prove to everyone you're as brilliant a journalist as your father.'

He was jolted from his thoughts by his buzzing mobile. He answered and instantly picked up on the tension in Anya's voice.

'Did you watch it? What do you think?'

'I'm here with Edward,' Paul replied. 'I'm going to put you on speaker phone, okay? Shall we switch to English? Edward's Russian isn't what it used to be.'

'Hello, Anya. I'm very proud of you,' Edward said in broken English and laughed.

'You sound like Sean Connery,' Anya said with a hearty chuckle.

'Why do you think that woman filmed the whole thing?' Paul asked.

'I'm hoping to find out,' Anya replied. 'Maybe she did it to prove what a dirty game my government is playing to justify waging war against breakaway republics. I don't know.'

'I reckon we shouldn't use it until we have more evidence. I want to start with the photos and focus on Farah's story. See what kind of impact it has.'

'How do you aim to do that?'

Paul told her about the plan for a press conference.

'You do realize, don't you,' Anya warned, 'that by doing this you're putting yourself on the radar of the Russian security services and, of course, Lavrov himself? The moment it comes to light that you took those photos you'll have to look over your shoulder day and night.'

'Sure, but what's the alternative?' Paul replied. 'I want to do everything in my power to get Farah out of the hell she's ended up in. I promised her.'

'Do you agree, Edward?'

'I'm one hundred per cent behind this. As a journalist you can't run from the truth, however threatening it might be.'

'Then it's my turn now to be proud of you,' Anya said, laughing again. 'I'm going to find out more about that Estonian woman and what she was doing in the Seven Sisters. Let's keep in touch.'

After she ended the call, Paul stood up and walked trance-like to the window, surprised at the speed with which night had caught up with them. IJkade, which earlier had been full of people strolling up and down and going in and out of the trendy bars and restaurants, was deserted now, save for a handful of night owls tottering towards the ferries.

Edward joined him and wrapped an arm around his shoulder.

'Do you remember that time I carried you through the surf?'

'Of course I do . . .'

Edward chuckled. 'You were squealing like a pig. Must have been sometime in August 1974. You were about –'

'Five. I was five. And on television we saw Richard Nixon mounting the steps to his Army One helicopter, turning around and, with that joker grin of his, waving one last time at the cameras and the White House staff. And that's when you said –'

'An historic day.'

'"Two journalists have forced the most powerful man in the world to resign," you said, and I understood bugger all.'

'You were five.'

'And then you took Mum and me to the beach.'

'"The desert is being eaten by the water!" I can still hear you yelling this.'

'It was the first time I saw the sea. Afghanistan doesn't have any beaches.'

'When I took you by the hand into the water, you tried to pull yourself free.'

'I was five, I'd never seen a sea before and I couldn't swim. You knew that, so you lifted me up and said –'

'The water is your friend.'

'That's what you said, yes, and I flung my arms around your neck and that's how we met the big waves. And when the first wave washed over us, you let go of me, bastard that you were. I remember screaming and thrashing about in a panic, and swallowing what felt like half the North Sea. But you lifted me up, let me soar through the air and shouted, "The water is your friend –"'

'"And the surf your fear!"'

'And then you let go of me again and I thrashed and flailed my arms about and swallowed whole waves, but every time you lifted me up my fear lessened a little.'

He leaned over to Edward and looked him straight in the

eye. 'That's how I'd like us to tackle this. You and me. There's a danger I'll drown, and maybe I will, but . . . I have to do this, Ed.'

'If you go under, I'll pull you up,' Edward said.

Without a word, they looked towards Het Fort, where fires burned on the high, flat roof. Squatters walked around, patrolling the place. The sleeping city and the fires on the roof merged with their silhouettes, reflected in the glass. Paul thought of the old folktale about the dead who came to visit their loved ones in their dreams at night. Farah was alive, but her spirit still roamed around this office.

'What are you waiting for?' Edward asked. 'Jakarta is five hours ahead of us. Phone her. Besides, I need to speak to her as well.'

'About what?'

'About my plan.'

'What plan?' Paul looked at Edward in surprise.

9

She was awakened by excited children's voices, rapid, light footsteps and high-pitched laughter from outside. Still dizzy from getting up too fast, she crossed the room to the wall with the children's drawings. A sun dressed as a clown and stars with funnily distorted children's faces were among the images on display. It filled her with melancholy and reminded her of Sekandar, of the promise she'd made him.

I'm here. I won't leave you.

A promise she'd broken by fleeing to the other side of the world.

She heard the sound of a phone and looked around before realizing it was her RedBerry. She snatched it out of her rucksack.

'Farah?'

His voice – so unexpectedly close. Butterflies scattered, turned into stars on paper. The fleeting kiss on his cheek before she'd boarded the train to Kiev.

'Paul . . . How are you?'

'Fine. Given the circumstances. Are you still in that hotel?'

'No, I checked out.'

'It wasn't safe?'

'I don't know why. But . . . I just had to leave. I'm somewhere else now.'

She wanted to be home. Home. With her window open, looking out over the market stalls of Nieuwmarkt and hearing the church bells ringing. Home. At her desk in the *AND* offices with their view across the water.

'Where are you now?'

'At the Waringin Shelter for Homeless Children.'

'What's the address?'

'I'll send it to you later. I'm . . . It's a long story.'

'Is it safe there? Are *you* safe?'

That's when it hit her. The realization that she was in a completely unfamiliar place. And last night she'd not only slept beside a complete stranger, but even told her everything about herself. What possessed her? She'd broken their pact by opening up their world to someone else. Should she tell him? She looked around in a daze. She heard children running around outside. Then a woman's voice telling them to be quiet. Aninda's voice.

'I'm not sure. Did you locate the girl?'

She heard him clear his throat.

'Yes.'

Another uncomfortable silence. Was it a delay on the line?

'What did she tell you?'

'The FSB was trailing me. You could say I led them to her. I was detained, questioned and then released again. I was strongly advised to leave the country. I don't know what happened to the girl.'

Farah's head began to pound, her legs grew heavier and the heat was suddenly unbearable. She felt as if the walls were closing in.

'What about the terrorist? The one with the mobile?'

'That's why I'm calling you.'

She heard the triumph in his voice and a huge weight lifted off her shoulders, as if an army of children disguised as falling stars had jumped off the paper.

Speechless, she listened to his story – about the fragments on the Estonian woman's damaged SD card. With her heart racing faster and faster, she paced around the room, through the morning light with its tiny dust particles. She wanted to know every single detail: about how Vakurov, and not Barchayev, had been in charge during the final few hours of the hostage-taking.

'Lavrov used the hostage-taking as a cover to get rid of you. They played the worst possible trick on you, worse than you led me to believe.'

'Maybe worse than I can or care to remember.'

'I understand. Listen, I'm at the *AND*, with Edward. And Ed wouldn't be Ed if he didn't have a plan of his own. I'll put him on. Speak soon.'

'Hang on! Paul?'

'Yes?'

'How's Sekandar doing?'

'I only just got here. As soon as I get permission from the police I'll go to visit him.'

'Please do. Promise?'

'I promised you in Moscow. Hang in there.'

She heard stumbling and fumbling sounds, and pictured Paul pressing his mobile into Edward's huge hand. Edward hated mobiles. As far as he was concerned, the old Bakelite phones should never have been decommissioned. As usual, he talked louder than normal, as if he still couldn't quite believe that such a small phone was capable of establishing contact with someone thousands of kilometres away.

'Hafez?'

Hearing his voice, she had to swallow a few times.

'Ed.'

His voice broke.

'I'm so sorry, Hafez.'

She'd grown used to his cantankerous style of communication, which was entirely in keeping with his oversized physique. She'd never heard him speak like this. This helpless stammering was unfamiliar territory to her. Man-of-steel Ed was falling apart a world away.

'It's okay, Ed.'

'God damn it, it's not okay, Hafez.'

She couldn't help but think that this was how teenage boys sounded when they were determined not to cry, yet couldn't help themselves. It evoked in her what could almost be described as maternal feelings.

She summoned her most upbeat voice. 'It's reassuring, don't you think? The idea that you've got a heart, I mean. That you're just like any other human being.'

She heard him chuckle. 'And you've broken that heart, Hafez.'

'Sure. You always manage to twist things so it's my fault.'

'Jesus, I can still picture you sitting opposite me in the old office. With that Rasta hair and those blue eyes of yours. How long ago was that? Ten years?'

'Eleven. But I never had dreads, and Jesus doesn't factor into it at all. Go on, tell me about your plan.'

'All right. I assume you've read Anya's report?'

'I have.'

'*Independen*. Remember that name? The leftist paper that wrote about Gundono feathering his nest illegally.'

'The government has now slapped a publication ban on that paper.'

'It's still being published underground, but it's a hundred times worse off than the *Moskva Gazeta*. I've spoken to the Editor-in-Chief, Saputra. He's an old contact of mine. I had to be extremely cautious about what I told him, because his phone is bound to be tapped. He wants to meet you. He gave me his prepaid number. Paul will text it to you in a minute. Phone him and make an appointment as soon as possible. He's got information for you. For us, that is. Get back in touch once you've spoken to him, all right?'

'Will do. And listen, Ed, look after your ticker, okay?'

'As if you care.'

She heard him break the connection, chuckling. She waited for Saputra's number to appear on her display and keyed it in.

A suspicious-sounding male voice answered, 'Hello?'

'*Bapak* Saputra?'

'Who is this?'

'Edward's contact.'

'Whose contact?'

'Is this Mr Saputra speaking?'

A moment's silence.

'*Ini dengannya.*' 'Yes, speaking.'

'Then you know who I am.'

Another silence.

'Do you know the Jakarta History Museum, on Taman Fatahillah?'

'No, but I'm sure I'll find it.'

'Meet me there in two hours' time. In the room with the deity statues.'

'I'll be there.'

The connection was broken.

She turned towards the bed, remembering the night and, with surprise, her impulsiveness. Why had she told Aninda all about herself? Why had she trusted her so implicitly?

After a quick shower, she got dressed in a hurry. Then she gathered up her things, checked nothing was missing, put it all in her rucksack and slung it over her shoulder. She walked to the door and took a deep breath before pushing it open. As soon as she did she had to squeeze her eyes shut against the bright sunshine. Gone was the muted light cast by the moon over the courtyard and the weeping fig. The grey stone walls, the once whitewashed cornices above the windows, the wooden frames, doors and floors – all were being gradually overtaken by mould. The damp was wreaking its destruction, causing the wood to rot away and the walls to crumble.

Something sharp shot across her feet. Ice-cold water. It splashed up against her legs. A skinny little boy with close-cropped hair in oversized khaki trousers and a faded shirt was washing leaves, dirt and other deposits away with a hosepipe. When he saw her he froze. The hose fell from his hand.

She picked it up and tried to give it back to him. *'Di sini, silakan. Pergi.'* 'Here you are. Carry on.'

The boy made a run for it, but, since he was barefoot, he slipped on the wet tiles and went down hard. He was quiet for a bit, but then he began to bawl. She helped him to his feet, pulled him close and touched his head.

'Saya minta maaf.' 'I'm sorry.'

He stopped crying surprisingly quickly and looked at her wide-eyed. She smiled. He smiled back shyly through his tears.

'Nama saya Farah.' 'My name is Farah. What's your name?'

He pressed his face against her chest.

'His name is Rino.'

Aninda's voice. Farah turned her head and looked into her cheerful face, her confidence-inspiring eyes.

'I frightened him.'

'You seem to frighten everybody.'

Aninda took Rino's face in both hands.

'The hose is gone. Where's the hose?'

As if stung by a wasp, the boy looked around and saw the hosepipe wriggling across the tiles, still spewing water. He squirmed out of her grasp and ran towards the hose. As he grabbed hold of it, he slipped again, as if it were getting the better of him, but he scrambled back up with the hose tightly clutched in both fists. Then he scampered away

229

down the tiled gallery, past the earthy-brown walls covered in Disney characters, which he also gave a quick rinse.

'Rino is a rubbish-dump angel,' Aninda said, as they watched him go. 'Father unknown, mother killed by TB. From the moment he could walk he's been scavenging plastic at Jakarta's biggest landfill. He . . .'

Farah saw her expression darken.

'Tell me.'

'Rino is an abused angel. We brought him here a week ago. Now he has a bed to sleep in, but he doesn't want to go near it. A piece of cardboard on the floor is enough for him. When he sees a bed, he doesn't think of sleeping softly, like most people, but of pain and humiliation. On more than one occasion he's been lured to a hotel by men with sweets or money and then raped.'

She pointed to a large photo of a man Farah recognized: comfort-zone man Baladin Hatta.

'You told me about him last night. You should know that he's the founder of the Waringin Foundation. Years ago, when he was still a budding lawyer.'

Farah heard respect and pride in her voice.

'Boys like Rino are invisible their whole lives. They simply don't exist for the government, because they have no birth certificates. Baladin wants them to be registered and given shelter and schooling. He wants them to get their lives back.'

Only then did Aninda see that Farah had her rucksack on.

'Are you leaving?'

'Yes, I have an urgent appointment.'

'Where?'

Farah hesitated. 'At the Jakarta History Museum. I'm meeting somebody there.'

'Is it to do with what you told me last night?'

'Yes.'

Aninda looked at Farah. 'Will you come back here afterwards?'

'I don't think so. I'm sorry.'

Aninda took Farah's hand in hers. She did it so tenderly it brought tears to Farah's eyes.

'Before you go, I'd like to introduce you to someone, if you don't mind.'

She ushered Farah past a sewing shop where young girls were cutting old batik dresses and trousers into strips. The ancient sewing machines were whirring, and needles whizzed through the fabric. 'The children who are given shelter here quickly grow out of their clothes. We constantly need new ones.'

They stopped by a shaded area in the courtyard where a group of women were busy assembling cardboard boxes and filling each with a bottle of cooking oil, two bags of noodles, rice and sugar.

'The flood we had a couple of weeks ago left many poor families in the *kampongs* all but homeless,' Aninda explained. 'Because the government does so little to help, we're putting together aid packages for them.'

Farah noticed that the eldest woman in the group, whom she estimated to be at least eighty, immediately stopped working when she spotted them. She came towards them. Her long, silvery-grey hair had been tied into a knot and her smile was practically toothless, and yet she looked as radiant as a young woman when she bowed to Farah with her hands pressed together. It was the greeting used by Pencak Silat fighters to show respect.

Farah returned the salutation as respectfully as possible.

'This is Satria,' Aninda said. 'She was keen to meet you.'

'*Kamu sudah datang.* You've come,' the woman said in a trembling voice. Farah saw that she was moved.

'I'm extremely honoured to meet you, ma'am,' Farah said, while holding Satria's hand. 'But how did you know —'

'She's about to leave again, *Ibu*,' Aninda interrupted her.

Tears were streaming down the woman's cheeks.

'I'm sorry, Ibu Satria,' Farah said, and let go of the woman's hand.

'Our ways are often unfathomable, especially to ourselves,' the woman said. '*Pergilah dalam damai anakku.*' 'Go in peace, my child.'

After bowing again, Farah walked off with Aninda.

'It was as if she knew me,' Farah said. She could feel the woman's eyes in her back.

'She probably does,' Aninda replied. 'Ibu Satria is a woman with special gifts. She's Baladin Hatta's grandmother and was the very first person to work for the Waringin Foundation.'

On their way to the exit, they paused one last time. Farah looked at the weeping fig, and at the old woman standing motionless underneath it in a beam of sunlight.

'You need people you can trust. Don't you trust me?' Aninda asked.

'It's better if I go my own way,' Farah said. 'If they find me here, there'll be repercussions, not just for you, but for everybody here.'

She gave Aninda a hug.

Then, without looking back, she walked through the gate, which fell shut behind her with a loud bang.

10

For whatever the reason, Radjen found crimes comforting. Perhaps because they were so absolute and allowed him to compensate for his emotional shortcomings. Thinking rationally gave him something to hold on to in life. The greater the unknowns related to an offence, the more compelled he felt to solve it with reasoning.

He'd already felt close to solving this case a number of times. But he was lost in a labyrinth. Sometimes he thought he'd found his way out, but then fate played a dirty trick on him, hurled him back into dead-end passages. For the first time in a long while, reasoning threatened to let him down. A sense of powerlessness had become a part of his daily routine.

Hopefully Thomas Meijer's autopsy would provide some new leads. Was it really suicide or was it, as Esther had suggested, all a set-up? And even if it was suicide, then he still had some doubt about Meijer's motives. Because a man about to move to another country with his wife to be reunited there with their foster child surely doesn't take his own life.

Given the suspicious circumstances under which Thomas Meijer had hanged himself, or been hanged, it was only logical that a court-ordered autopsy be done. Normally, the Public Prosecutor commissioned the Netherlands Forensic Institute, but the situation was far from normal and Radjen had managed to prevent this. After the débâcle of files disappearing from Lombard's hard drive and the subsequent explosion at Nationwide Forensics, he'd arranged for Meijer's autopsy to be done by a pathologist independent of the police: Ellen Mulder. He'd received little resistance to this choice. Mulder had done another autopsy for this case, namely on the paediatrician Danielle Bernson.

He walked the long corridor with Esther. The sound of a symphony orchestra drifted in their direction. Esther looked at him questioningly.

'Ellen Mulder always has classical music on in her office,' he said. Radjen knew she listened to it even while doing autopsies. She'd once told him it was her salvation. While clinically observing and analysing death in one room, there was this continuous counterbalance in the other room: the sound of life.

It had been some time since Radjen had seen Ellen. She'd returned to work six months earlier after having taken disability leave because she was suffering from depression. Her husband, a criminal lawyer, had abandoned her for a woman twenty years younger. For the fifty-year-old Ellen, who already practised a profession that required the utmost in emotional stability, it had been the final blow. The break-up of her marriage pushed her into a black hole. Radjen had visited her a few times in that period, something she had greatly appreciated. Sitting behind her Steinway grand piano, her favourite spot at home, she told him about the voices in her head, voices that constantly reminded her that she had to be better than everyone else, because otherwise she didn't count for anything. Voices that cried she was too fat, too old and unattractive. She'd managed to silence those voices again.

As they neared Ellen's office and the music was clearly audible, Radjen couldn't help but think of the accusation Melanie Lombard had hurled at him. That he didn't exhibit much empathy and that it might be good for him to listen to a good piece of music on occasion. As it turned out, Ellen Mulder had once invited him to go to a concert with her, and he'd accepted. Afterwards they drank a glass of wine and he brought her home. But finding his own way home was another story. Music, like emotion, was more powerful than he was. Believing that it was raining, he turned on the windscreen wipers. Until he realized he couldn't see the road because of his streaming tears.

When they walked into the room, Ellen Mulder was already waiting for them. She wasn't wearing makeup, and her shoulder-length, ash-blonde hair was elegantly pulled back. She'd lost weight. Her eyes were a clear shade of grey-blue, and her slightly mocking smile was rather engaging. The expression of an intelligent woman who knew the dark side of life through and through and had opted for the light. You saw it in how she dressed: a white cotton blouse trimmed with floral lace underneath a matching dress. Vanity wasn't one of Ellen's character traits. She wore what she felt comfortable in, but always looked stylish.

He saw her hesitate at first, because he was with someone she didn't know, and not follow her impulse to give him a kiss on each cheek instead of an extended hand. But one glance at Esther was apparently more than enough to put her at ease and Radjen was warmly greeted in the usual manner.

'Good to see you again, Radjen, even if you kept a woman waiting,' Ellen said.

Radjen felt the tension that had built up in his body while questioning Melanie Lombard fall away.

'You look good, Ellen.'

'I wish I could say the same for you,' Ellen said. 'You look exhausted.' As charming as she was, she wore her heart on her sleeve. She turned to welcome Esther. 'I'd appreciate it if you kept a close eye on him.'

'I will,' Esther said, and introduced herself. From the way Ellen shook Esther's hand, he saw that she immediately liked her, and apparently the feeling was mutual.

'The last time we saw each other was at a concert,' she told Esther as she looked sideways at Radjen. 'I haven't seen him since. Do you like classical music?'

'It's not really my first choice,' Esther said.

'No matter, it's certainly mine,' Ellen said. 'These are the *Enigma Variations* by Edward Elgar. There's a wonderful story behind this piece. In each variation, Elgar created a musical portrait of a friend. But I'd better stop talking about music or I'll be going on and on about it all night. Because we're late getting started, best we immediately get down to it. Shall we, Radjen?'

Before he could answer, she led them to a room where they donned green surgeons' scrubs. Then she brought them to the DNA-sterile autopsy room. Thomas Meijer's naked body was already laid out on a two-metre-long dissecting table. The exhaust, which absorbed odours and dust through its small holes, hummed softly. Special scalpels, forceps, tweezers and a saw were lying beside the body. Radjen and Esther officially confirmed that it was Thomas Meijer lying there; he could tell from Esther's body language that she felt uncomfortable. He knew only too well that looking at a corpse at a crime scene was not the same as watching a dead body being split open and stripped of most of its organs. No matter who you were, you never really got used to it.

'Do you want to take the pictures?' he asked Esther.

She nodded.

'Do you mind if my colleague takes the photos?' he asked Ellen, who was instructing her assistant.

Ellen looked at him in surprise. She glanced at Esther, understood the problem and asked her assistant to give Esther the camera. The first thing Esther did was to take a full-length photo of what was now only the shell of a man. During their research they'd discovered that Meijer, once an ambitious student, had trained to be a pastry chef and then worked as a kitchen porter in a variety of restaurants. Later he'd opened up his own place by the sea in Scheveningen. It went wrong from there. In every possible way. Meijer wasn't flexible enough; he couldn't handle the competition; he had difficulties supervising his kitchen staff. Eventually he went bankrupt. After training to be a taxi driver, he worked for nearly six years for City Tax in The Hague. With that job his modesty and accommodating nature came in useful for the first time. He was the perfect man behind the wheel, someone with an unobtrusive character. The personification of anonymity. He was lent out to ministries by his company, until he was dispatched to Economic Affairs. There he became one of three chauffeurs who drove Ewald Lombard around the country each day. The job that seemed perfect for him would ultimately land him on a cold metal table, just another body.

Radjen had read the transcript of Meijer's interrogation and listened to the recording countless times, attempting to determine whether he was telling the whole truth. Radjen had no doubts. Meijer wasn't a criminal but rather a coward who'd taken the idea of following orders too far. Similar to subjects in the experimental research carried out by the social psychologist Stanley Milgram in the 1960s at Yale University. The people in that study had been prepared to administer a severe electric shock to co-participants who gave an incorrect answer, simply because it was ordered by a professor.

While Radjen knew there were plenty of people just like Meijer out there, he was happy to have to deal only with the one now lying in front of him, lifeless and naked, ready to be dissected.

*

Ellen Mulder began the autopsy with an extensive examination of Meijer's body. She indicated every finding aloud so it would be recorded via the microphones in the room. The software system saved the information as an interim report, which could be printed out right after the autopsy.

'Red dot-shaped discolorations on the face, in the eyes and to the back of the ears, indicating an accumulation of blood. Multiple abrasions to the skin on the front and sides of the neck.'

Despite the clinical way in which she stated her findings, she was captivating, like someone giving a presentation to a rapt audience. That was because of her warm, clear voice. Radjen recalled the time he was about to knock on her door unannounced, but stopped when he heard singing coming from the house: she was accompanying herself on the piano. He almost reached for the bell, but thought twice about interrupting her, turned and drove away again.

'A slight discoloration of the skin around the throat, extending horizontally along the neck. Possibly as a result of impact from external mechanical compression, strangulation. Inside upper lip: small area with dark-red coloration indicating damaged tissue.'

After she'd extensively inspected the chest, arms, abdomen, pelvis and legs and the abrasions on Meijer's heels, at Ellen Mulder's request, her assistant rolled the body on its stomach. Ellen's first statement got Radjen's immediate attention.

'A small bruise at the base of the neck, possibly caused by a hypodermic needle.'

After Esther had documented this with a photo, Radjen came closer and leaned forward to look through the magnifying glass that Ellen was holding above the neck. He saw a minuscule black hole, which would have likely gone undetected by the naked eye.

'Was he drugged?'

'I don't speculate,' Ellen said with a sigh. 'I only relate what I see.'

She instructed her assistant to roll Meijer on to his back again and then, making a Y-incision, sliced open the front of the body to expose the liver, lungs, heart, pancreas, adrenal gland and spleen, so these could be removed and examined. She took a slice from each organ. Her assistant placed each slice in a separate plastic bag, which was sealed and labelled. Radjen knew the organ tissue would be studied under a microscope and that the toxicologist would look for substances foreign to the body.

Ellen Mulder used a handsaw to open the skull. If given the choice at that moment, Radjen would've rather heard her singing than sawing.

Mulder's first finding when she examined Meijer's skull couldn't have been clearer. 'A bone fragment from the axis shot into the brain, pushed the vertebrae apart and severed all the nerves.'

Ellen Mulder straightened her back and stated for the record. 'Traumatic spondylolisthesis of the axis.'

'A hangman's fracture,' Esther said.

Ellen looked at Esther amused. 'Correct. In a perfect fall, the neck breaks. The spinal cord is severed close to the top, usually between the first and second vertebrae, resulting in immediate paralysis of the entire body including the respiratory muscles. In addition, the body's weight also closes off the carotid arteries, cutting off the blood flow to the brain. The latter causes the victim to lose consciousness within ten seconds.'

'And death?' Radjen asked, who thought of those ten seconds in which your entire life flashes by you.

'About eight minutes later,' she said, as she began to remove the brain for further examination. When she'd finished, the assistant reinserted the organs and the brain into the body. Head and pubic hairs were removed for eventual DNA testing. All the tissue samples were preserved for counter-expertise.

Ellen took off her goggles and dropped her plastic gloves in a bucket.

'I'll send some colleagues to retrieve the corpse,' Radjen said. 'Is there a possibility that you could expedite the toxicology results for me?'

She looked at him, worried, tapped him on the chest with her finger and scolded, 'I know detectives who've let unsolved cases become an obsession. Don't let that happen. Solve this case, however little time you've got. And once you've done that, take a break.'

While Esther had already gone outside to have a much-needed smoke, Radjen lingered behind in Ellen's office, admiring the elegant handwriting with which she added extra notes to the preliminary autopsy report. He wondered why it moved him so, until he realized it was the music she was playing.

'Elgar's Ninth Variation,' she said, as she looked up and saw his expression. '"Nimrod". The only piece that isn't a portrait but an ode. It's dedicated to a dear friend who continued to visit Elgar when he was so depressed that he wanted to stop writing music, and who encouraged him to continue his work despite his problems.'

She handed him the report.

'I'll make sure that you have the preliminary toxicology report by tonight.'

He found Esther outside by the car. She handed him her half-smoked cigarette and lit a new one. A variation on a theme, Radjen thought.

'Thanks so much,' she said.

'For what?'

'The idea of giving me that camera.'

'Looking through a lens helps to distance yourself.'

She gave him a look that he'd never seen before. He was amazed at her show of tenderness.

'That woman,' she said, 'Ellen —'

'What about her?'

'She means a lot to you, right?'

'She's had a rough time,' he said. 'I think how she fought her way back is wonderful.'

'Nice to see how you interact with her. It's a gift few men have.'

The surprise with which he looked at her made her laugh. It was a liberating laugh. 'Hasn't anyone ever told you that?'

'No.'

She took a few long drags and looked at him seriously. 'I want to figure out how Meijer was hanged. Even if he was sedated, and that must have been the story, it's no small task to put a man on a stepladder and hang his head in a noose.'

'It will take quite some time to make a dummy and re-create the setting so the dimensions accurately match.'

'Not what I had in mind. I want to do it ninja style.'

'What do you need?'

'A sturdy beam, and some mountain-climbing gear.'

'The man was strung up in a shed, Esther, not on a climbing wall.'

'Mountain climbers tie themselves to each other using all kinds of knotting techniques. If something happens to one of them, the other can reach him or pull him up. I suspect that Meijer was lifted and then his head was put in the noose. But I want to check if it's possible.'

She stared into space. 'Normally we'd do a reconstruction in the shed.' She turned her head in Radjen's direction. 'But this is a ninja operation, so we need an alternative space and I've got an idea. The only thing I need is a volunteer. Preferably one who can keep a secret.'

She looked at him.

'Interested?'

The words that came to him when he opened his eyes sounded like an ancient text, a forgotten fragment from a dust-covered book, which he must have stored in his subconscious after reading. And now, as he was watching his sleeping mother, they suddenly resurfaced.

Respect for the truth.

Isobel was nearly sixty, and, although life hadn't been easy, she was as beautiful and wonderfully eccentric today as she had been in her younger years, with bindi rhinestones on her heavily made-up face, big fake eyelashes, henna-red hair, a silk blouse and flared Indian skirt. In the former cow shed that Raylan had converted into a studio for her – now a mess of tubes, brushes, unfinished canvases, and all saturated with the smell of linseed oil and paint – she spent her days working on yet more portraits of Raylan. She'd keep painting the love of her life until she dropped.

After the research and other preparations for the press conference, which had taken him and Edward the entire night and the best part of the day, Paul had finally dropped by the studio to visit her.

'I'm planning another exhibition, Paulie,' she'd said. 'A major retrospective, which will showcase my enduring love for him and the city where we were so happy.'

He looked at the panoramic canvases she'd made of Kabul. The everyday scenes from a bygone era were painted in earth colours – ochre, sienna and moss-green. When he was still only a baby, she'd wrapped him in a sling around her waist and taken him on her long rambles through the streets of the Afghan capital together with her sketchbook, pencils and pastels. They'd walk along the banks of the River Kabul, where men washed their clothes and where he, when he was a little older, dived in after the other boys to mess about in the green water. In his mind, he was back meandering with her through the cattle market of Jalalabad, inhaling the aroma of the smoky bread ovens, tasting kebab with coriander. The trees were blossoming again, and he could see the snow-capped mountaintops in the distance.

He ran his hand through Isobel's reddish-blonde hair and thought about the first few weeks following his father's death, when she would sometimes wander around the fields in the middle of the night, half-naked, whining like a wounded animal. On those occasions he'd go out and search for her, and when he found her she'd be confused and unresponsive. Back at the farmhouse, he'd help her into the shower, rub her dry, put her to bed and lie beside her until she was asleep, their faces close together, his hand in hers.

Perhaps it was Isobel who'd got him thinking about the meaning of truth. He didn't know anyone who denied the fact of Raylan's death so categorically. Instead, she created her own truth through her paintings. Each portrait of Raylan reinforced her belief that he was alive and well.

Paul checked his watch. Just under six hours before the start of the press conference. Standing at the kitchen worktop, he looked out over the foggy farmland, drinking a mug of black coffee.

It could be a good opening line for the press conference: *Respect for the truth; a right to the truth.* But he didn't want to think about that now. Not now. He wanted to *do* something. Feeling restless, he went to the old barn, where he paused in front of a contraption hidden under several horsehair blankets.

'A motorbike deserves to be treated like a friend,' his father once said. And Paul could no longer leave their old friend, a BMW R27 with sidecar from 1963, standing there swaddled in blankets. As a little boy he'd often sat in the side-car, next to his father, and, while going up and down the streets of Kabul and far beyond, he'd grown as attached to the motorbike as Raylan was.

It was raining. Thunder could be heard in the distance. An old song popped into his head: 'Riders on the Storm' by The Doors.

He looked at his watch again and came to a decision. He'd breathe new life into the BMW. He'd use it to travel to the three locations where he'd deliver on his promises and carry out his duties today. He was well aware that by doing so he was going against Isobel's wishes. His mother had held on to the motorbike all this time only because she stubbornly believed in a miracle that would defy all laws of physics: her husband's return.

He started by cleaning the engine block, the gear box and the rear-wheel drive. Then he checked the oil level and greased the gear box. He filled up the battery with distilled water, washed the air filter with petrol, took apart the car-burettor and gave the bores and nozzles a good flush-out. He made sure the wheel axles, screws and nuts were properly fastened, adjusted the valve lash and checked the spark plugs.

Girl, ya gotta love your man. Take him by the hand. Make him understand, the world on you depends.

When he rode off an hour later, he did so with the feeling that both Raylan and Isobel watched him go until he'd become a fading dot in the polder landscape and the engine's roar had all but died away.

But he knew it was only an illusion.

Isobel was fast asleep and Raylan had been dead for more than thirty years.

In the ninety minutes it took him to reach the first location, the one where he'd fulfil the promise he'd made to Farah in Moscow, he and the machine under him had become such a tight unit that all of his manoeuvres, including the cornering, avoiding and especially the overtaking, were going more and more smoothly. He was trying to explore the boundaries of controllability by slowing and gearing down as little as possible when taking corners.

Although the ride through wind and rain made him feel elated, he frequently glanced at the empty sidecar in which he'd sat so often as a little boy. Now grown up, he'd assumed his father's place, but the emptiness of the low seat beside him seemed to symbolize that sinking feeling he'd had for years now.

He'd had many relationships, but there'd been no pitter-patter of little feet.

Paul must have been an intimidating sight as he entered the children's hospital in Rotterdam, dressed head to toe in leather and holding Raylan's battered helmet like a relic. The way the trauma surgeon, who introduced herself as Marileen, looked at him when they first shook hands in the lobby made him realize this.

'Tough guys like you are not all that common around here,' Marileen said mockingly before escorting him down a long corridor that connected the main building to the secured pavilion.

There, from the doorway of the last room in the hall, Paul caught his first glimpse of the little boy who'd been left for dead on a deserted woodland road weeks ago and was now staring silently at the ceiling, as if trying to burn a hole in it. The first thing he noticed were Sekandar's hands. They were tied to the bed.

'He tried to undo the screws of his fixator,' Marileen explained. 'We couldn't think of any other way to stop him from trying again.'

Paul slowly leaned over to Sekandar and listened to his breathing, which was becoming shallower. Paul cleared his throat.

'Hello, Sekandar, my name is Paul,' he said in Dari. 'Your friend sent me. You remember, the one with the blue eyes and the black hair. *Fereshteye nejat.*' 'Your guardian angel.'

He saw Sekandar's eyes grow moist and slowly turn towards him. His first words were little more than a hoarse whisper. 'Where . . . is . . . ?'

Paul leaned in closer. 'There were men. They wanted to hurt her. So I helped her escape. To a place where nobody can find her. That's why she can't be here with you. But she's safe and she asked me to look after you while she's away. Is that all right with you?'

'Yes.' After some hesitation.

'Do you know why you're here?'

'I was running, but then the light hit me.'

'It hit you hard, that light. You broke your leg and your pelvis, too. And you had an operation to put everything back together again. The best doctor in the world helped you. She did quite a job, I've heard. Do you mind if I take a look?'

He waited for Sekandar to nod before lifting the sheet a little, so he could see the fixator. He didn't let on how shocked he was but exhaled deeply instead.

'Looking great. It's meant to help everything that's broken inside your belly and legs grow together again. And once it's all grown back together, they'll remove it. And that's going to happen really soon, I hear. Perhaps even in a couple of days' time.'

When he saw that Sekandar's eyes lit up, he lowered the sheet and leaned in as close as possible.

'But it's really important to leave it all in place for now, not to touch it. Do you think you can do that?'

Sekandar nodded solemnly.

'Excellent. If I untie your hands, do you promise not to touch the screws?'

For the first time, Sekandar turned his head all the way to Paul and looked at him. His soft voice sounded firm. *'Wada medaham.'* 'I promise.'

Paul turned to Marileen, who was standing behind him. 'He promises not to touch it again.'

Very gently, he began to untie the restraints around Sekandar's wrists. Then he picked up his leather shoulder bag, opened it and took out a parcel.

'A little surprise,' he said, and held the parcel in front of Sekandar. 'From Farah. For you.'

Speechless, Sekandar looked at the object emerging from the wrapping paper: a butterfly the size of a fist, made from fabric, rope and paper.

'This butterfly,' Paul whispered, 'will bring you good luck.'

Sekandar ran his fingers along the two long antennae on the butterfly's head. Then he looked at Paul with unexpectedly sad eyes.

'Man degar nametoanam.' 'I can't do it any more,' he stammered.

'What is it you can't do any more?'

'Fly . . . I can't fly any more. My wings are gone.'

'Your wings . . . ah . . . but they'll grow back, won't they? A little bit every day. Once the metal's out of your body, it won't be long before you can stand again. And once you can stand, we'll teach you how to walk again. And once you can walk, I'll teach you how to run again. And once you can run . . .' He touched Sekandar's cheek. 'I'll teach you how to fly again.'

For the first time he heard Sekandar giggle, a high-pitched chortle under his breath. He reached for Paul's hands, held them like he'd never let go and looked at him with incredulous eyes.

'And when you're better,' Paul said, 'we'll go and see Farah together. Because she'd love to see you.'

'We'll fly to her,' Sekandar whispered.

'We will,' Paul said, and kissed the boy on the forehead. '*Man ba zudi pas miayam.*' 'I'll be back soon.'

The second he'd made eye contact with Sekandar, he understood Farah's fascination with him. The boy not only brought back memories of their distant childhood, but, more than that, he personified Farah's traumas. Paul too was deeply touched to see a child in this state – so fragile, so uprooted, so desperate to trust someone, someone who understood what he was going through. Someone who could help him.

In the forty-five minutes it took him to reach Westerdoksdijk in Amsterdam, where today's second task awaited him, he'd come up with a new plan. It was a plan that would not only help Sekandar, but also Farah, his own mother and perhaps even Chief Inspector Radjen Tomasoa, who'd arranged for him to see Sekandar today.

He was now meeting the same Tomasoa at the National Police Intelligence Service. As he came towards him in the large lobby, with his bald head and square jaw, he vaguely reminded Paul of the classic Hollywood film star Yul Brynner.

'Good to meet you,' Tomasoa said, after they'd exchanged a sturdy handshake. He accompanied Paul to the fourth floor where, in an empty, windowless room, a well-dressed and sophisticated man was waiting for them. He introduced himself as Detective Joshua Calvino.

Paul smiled in spite of himself. He remembered the paparazzo picture from *De Nederlander* that had been tacked on to Farah's white board among all the other notes and photos. It showed Calvino, wearing three-quarter-length sweatpants and sandals but bare-chested, in a clinch with an equally scantily clad Farah on the deck of his houseboat on a canal somewhere in Amsterdam. The photo was captioned, 'In her leisure time Farah H. does not adhere to the letter of Islamic law.'

'Detective Calvino has been officially relieved of his duties for the duration of the internal inquiry into the death of a witness in the hit-and-run case,' Tomasoa said.

'And by witness presumably you mean that Russian, the freelance muscle from AtlasNet,' Paul replied.

'Correct,' Tomasoa said. 'Detective Calvino is currently working at Interpol, where he's in contact with an old friend of yours from Johannesburg, Detective Elvin Dingane. He asked us to get in touch with you.'

Tomasoa and Calvino exchanged a knowing glance and, after a nod from his former boss, Calvino launched into his story.

'Detective Elvin Dingane is keeping me abreast of the investigation into suspicious financial transactions within South Africa's ruling party, the ANC. We're in contact because the name Valentin Lavrov has cropped up both in this case and in a European matter. Dingane has reason to believe that Lavrov's energy company, AtlasNet, bribed several leading political figures in South Africa in exchange for mining concessions, but so far he's got insufficient evidence.

The reason he wants you to contact him is that you were also involved in the case and were about to receive some crucial information. Dingane told me what happened to you in Ponte City.'

Calvino pointed to the fading bruises on Paul's face. 'I assume those are the legacy of that encounter?'

'Among other things,' Paul said. 'My informant was murdered right before my eyes. He was thrown off the fiftieth floor by the same scum that went on to beat me to a pulp. Dingane visited me in hospital. He explained they were Lavrov's men. I was lucky to be alive and it was best for all concerned if I left South Africa for a while. What does he need from me?'

Calvino looked at Tomasoa, who said, 'It turns out that Zhulongu, your informant, took serious precautions before meeting up with you. Not only had he stored his findings on a USB stick, but he made a good backup as well.'

Paul stared at both men in disbelief. 'Are you telling me the information is still available?'

Tomasoa nodded. 'If anything happened to him, Zhulongu told his wife to pass the information to you. And nobody else. Apparently you were the only person he really trusted.'

Paul looked around. He felt the need to sit down for a moment, but there was no furniture in the windowless room.

'I take it that the main reason I'm talking to you now and not with Dingane is that you want me to share that information. Correct?'

'Much more than a piece of journalism is at stake here. We're neck-deep in a criminal investigation,' Tomasoa said.

'Well, I'm an investigative journalist,' Paul said. 'And if there's one thing we value, it's our independence.'

'Our cooperation doesn't have to get out. This secret is safe with us,' Calvino said.

'That remains to be seen,' said Paul, who realized that Calvino's superior tone, the way he was dressed and, in fact, his whole attitude were beginning to irritate him no end.

'Come again?' Calvino asked.

'I have a problem with your interpretation of "secret". More specifically, the secret with which Farah travelled to Moscow. Officially, our newspaper had asked Valentin Lavrov to be a guest editor and put together an art supplement with Farah. But the real reason for her trip was to find out more about Lavrov himself. Aside from my Editor-in-Chief and me, you were the only one who had this information.'

'That's correct,' Calvino said.

'You shared that confidential information with a fourth party, someone at the Dutch Embassy in Moscow.'

Joshua Calvino looked at him alarmed. 'Where did you hear that –'

'I'm a journalist; I don't reveal my sources,' Paul said. 'But Lavrov had been briefed on Farah's true intentions before she'd even set foot in his villa. It almost cost her her life.'

'Almost,' Calvino said. 'So she's definitely still alive, right?'

'She's missing,' said Paul, aware of his mistake. 'So I assume she's still alive.'

Calvino looked at him closely. 'Do you know where she is?'

'Even if I knew, do you really think I'd reveal that to someone who works for Interpol?'

Calvino was clearly upset. His hands were shaking and he was perspiring. 'To someone who's never doubted her innocence – not for a moment,' he said.

'That makes two of us,' Paul said.

'Three,' Tomasoa said.

'With this difference,' Paul said. 'Of the three of us, I'm the only one who can prove it.'

They looked at him as if he were the new Messiah. He saw

the relief on their faces. This was the critical moment in his decision – a decision informed by the realization that the three of them had the same interests at heart and if they didn't cooperate, none of them would get anywhere.

He agreed to their proposal.

But not before telling them that he had a condition.

He smiled, feeling sure of himself and amused by their growing bewilderment.

And then he added something else.

'In actual fact, it's not a condition. Conditions are negotiable. This is a demand.'

Life could be simple. All you had to do was hop on a motorbike, step on the accelerator and ride away. Solitude could become synonymous with freedom. But Paul knew this freedom wasn't worth anything to him unless he carried out the tasks he'd assigned himself and fulfilled the promises he'd made.

Riding his motorbike from one bank of the IJ to the other, he took little if any notice of the maximum speed limit.

Of the six hours that had initially separated him from his third assignment that day, the press conference, only six minutes remained. Now he was standing on the fifth floor of the *AND* building, in Edward's office, and he was nervous. He hated addressing groups of people. Since it made him feel insecure, he either tended to be incredibly loud or, the opposite, withdraw deep into himself. Unlike Edward, he simply wasn't the kind of eloquent speaker or elegant storyteller who managed to win people over. But he wouldn't, no, he couldn't, run out on this one.

He *had* to do this.

During the course of the day he'd come to realize how much those four words that had popped into his head in the morning really meant to him.

Respect for the truth.

As a journalist you have to respect the truth, since the truth is nothing other than a collection of unquestionable facts. And all citizens have the right to learn about those facts without spin doctors, multinationals and politicians twisting them. Readers have to feel confident that the information they're given squares with the facts. He'd now taken it upon himself to refute something that everybody took to be true and he was certain it would unleash a storm of reaction, as Edward had predicted.

He felt his uncle's hand on his shoulder. 'Ready?'

Together they walked to the escalator.

And as he approached the army of national and international journalists in the downstairs lobby, the opening words popped into his head.

12

Close by the Dutch fortress, which looked out across Sunda Kelapa, Farah crossed the drawbridge to the other side of the Kali Besar, the old canal that linked up with the River Ciliwung. Once upon a time colonial ships laden with goods set sail for the Netherlands from here; now an emaciated old man in an unsteady canoe scooped floating litter out of the murky water.

A television screen high up on a restaurant wall could be heard blaring out the news. Farah paused and watched a correspondent reporting that last night large groups of demonstrators had marched towards the Parliament building, where they clashed with police. She saw footage of cars being torched to serve as fire barricades, armoured vehicles driving into the crowd to break up the demonstration, and the military police firing rubber bullets and tear-gas grenades. The clashes last night had claimed twenty to thirty lives, while hundreds of injured people had been taken to hospitals in vans; even *bajajs* were serving as improvised ambulances. Before going into hiding, opposition leader Baladin Hatta had delivered one final passionate speech, fiercely criticizing Gundono.

'Nuclear energy has no place in a democratic society. We must fight Minister Gundono's political regime. He runs a state within a state, which enacts decisions without our consent. These new energy plans make Minister Gundono an enemy of democracy and an enemy of the people.'

Thousands more demonstrators were expected to march

on Parliament today, this time to protest against the excessive force used by the police.

Farah entered Taman Fatahillah from the spot where she'd got off the bus previously. The square was teeming. A group of Japanese tourists with face masks were mesmerized by a macaque monkey dressed up as a doll, wearing a fake leather jacket and riding around in circles on a wooden miniature Harley Davidson. From a distance, the creature looked like a frightened gnome with dark, hairy legs and a rat's tail.

Clustered around a dry fountain, American tourists were listening to a female guide who needed a small megaphone to be heard above the din. Four hundred years ago, this was the heart of the old walled city of Kota. A majority of the population had been enslaved, controlled by a minority of Chinese and European colonizers. A guillotine where rebellious slaves were publicly beheaded had stood close to the fountain. The guide tried to illustrate this by bending over as deeply as she could while bringing the megaphone down on the back of her neck in simulation of an axe. But the group only had eyes for a skeletal street artist in a shabby circus ringmaster's uniform who was trying to squeeze his wiry body through a wooden barrel.

A small fairground wheel with four pods had been mounted on an acid-green cart. The children who were lifted into the seats by their parents would go around for a while, either crowing with pleasure or crying with fear. Meanwhile, vendors selling *wayang* dolls, *barong* masks and other exotic wood carvings tried to make themselves heard with tired slogans to attract the attention of tourists who had money to burn.

Farah checked her watch: twelve forty-five.

She hurried over to the eastern edge of the Taman Fatahillah, where the former Palace of Justice, now converted into a museum, was located. There she exchanged the square's stifling chaos for the refreshing calm of the entrance hall, which was bathed in a soft, almost orange light. Floating above her head were angels made of bleached wood with cotton wings and red boots. Every single one of them boasted an impressive erection. Their white faces were made up with bright red lipstick and black lines around their wide-open eyes. Attached to their chests were small boxes full of used clock parts and old pieces of electronic equipment. A small speaker near their navels produced shrill birdsong, insect noises and distorted Javanese words.

It was close to one when she bought her ticket.

After stowing her rucksack in one of the lockers, she walked past two towering malevolent demons into a dimly lit gallery crammed full of old statues of Hindu deities. The silence made her realize just how tired and agitated she was. As she walked among the ancient blocks of granite and tufa, with their carved patterns of flowers, butterflies, birds and the heads of demons, she noticed her heart was pounding much too fast. She paused in front of a large, four-headed statue of Brahma, the creator of all life, who was seated on a granite swan. The Hindu gods – among them Shiva, the great destroyer of life, and Vishnu, half bird, half human – had arrived on the Indonesian archipelago around AD 150, in the wake of Indian immigrants and monks. Since then, their images had figured prominently in the Prambanan temples.

From the moment Uncle Parwaiz had taken her by the hand and shown her around Kabul's large National Museum as a child, she'd been fascinated by the history of old statues, paintings and other objects, by the stories they told of how people long ago used to live, fight and love. In Amsterdam, she was a regular visitor to the Tropenmuseum, where she could while away hours among the historical collections from the four corners of the world. Her most impressive experience to date had been a visit to the 'Hidden Afghanistan' exhibition in De Nieuwe Kerk in Amsterdam. This time, she'd been the one to take Parwaiz by the hand. Speechless with admiration, they'd filed past the treasures from Tepe Fullol dating back more than four thousand years: statues crafted by nomadic tribes, jewels from the burial mounds of Tillya Tepe and objects from Begram with their Indian, Greek and Egyptian influences. The two of them had stood in front of the statue of Sharada.

'Do you remember, Uncle,' she'd asked him, 'how you told me the secrets of love at a very young age?'

'But my dear child,' Parwaiz had replied, 'surely you're never too young for the wonder of love?'

Meanwhile, someone had sidled up to her. Glancing sideways, she saw a man in his fifties with a battered face. Tears trickled from his swollen left eye, as if he were crying silently.

'Ibu Hafez?'

He hardly resembled the combative *Independen* editor she'd seen online. Prison, torture and fear had transformed Saputra into a whispering shadow of his former self who kept staring straight ahead while dabbing his weeping eye with a handkerchief. His right cheek was swollen and he wore false teeth.

'I think you're a brave man,' she said.

'That very much depends on your perspective, ma'am.'

He kept a watchful eye on his surroundings. He talked with difficulty, as if every single syllable hurt. And it probably did. One of the consequences of the abuse the police had meted out to him recently.

'I don't have much time. The State Intelligence Agency, the BIN, keeps a constant eye on me. By now they will have discovered that we're trying to continue *Independen* underground. Perhaps we can be of assistance to each other in this regard.'

'You guys are after Gundono; I'm after Lavrov.'

'If you want to expose Lavrov's practices in Indonesia, you'll have to do so via Gundono. As you know . . .'

He fell silent. Mechanically, almost like a radar device, he moved his head to try to pick up the noises that Farah heard too from the entrance lobby. Curt, measured male voices. Although not loud, their tone was alarming and therefore all the more menacing. Saputra began to tell her everything as fast as he could, but did so in a whisper.

'As you know, Gundono is the CEO of Perusahaan Listrik Negara, the state-owned electricity company. As Chairman of the Concession Committee, he has a decisive say in who receives licences for any new nuclear power stations. I'm telling you, Gundono is your direct link to Lavrov.'

'But how do I get to Gundono?'

'We've got a mole at his headquarters, a heavily armed compound on the coast near Tanjung Priok. All the important digital communications take place there. If we could hack into –'

'I'm a journalist. I work on an ancient laptop. I know nothing about zeros and ones.'

'Edward Vallent told me that you're working with an IT expert. If you come up with a way of hacking into Gundono's computer network, our man there can help you on the inside.'

'What kind of help would that be?'

'Our contact is the compound's facilities manager.'

'I don't know what's possible,' Farah said. 'I'll need to discuss it with the others first. Where and when can I meet your man?'

Saputra didn't respond. When she turned to him, she saw him staring across the room, where a man had just walked in slowly but assertively. He wasn't alone. A second man appeared from the lobby, his dark silhouette sharply outlined against the soft, orange light.

They'd stood side by side in the half-light, she and Saputra. They'd barely even looked at each other. It had been brief. It hadn't seemed even remotely like a meeting. Now they had to become casual passers-by. Saputra understood. He was the first to move.

'Tomorrow afternoon at four,' he whispered in passing. 'Jalan Surabaya Market, the record shop. Ask the owner for Foreigner.'

He leaned forward, as if trying to read Vishnu's history, while she walked in the direction of the entrance lobby. She paused in front of the statue of Brahma, turned around and noticed that Saputra was now walking to the entrance of the room called the Hall of the Golden Artefacts. The two men briskly followed him, each from a different direction.

Farah watched them until they were gone. Only then did she see the caption by the entrance to the other room: MONI-TORED BY CCTV. By failing to scan the sculpture gallery for camera surveillance she'd made a schoolgirl error. Any security official with rudimentary lip-reading skills could zoom in on them and figure out what information they'd passed to each other.

She studied the room from her current position, checking all possible corners, all the places where the walls met the ceiling, where cameras that could monitor the space with 90-to-180-degree rotations might be mounted, but she couldn't detect anything in the dimly lit room. Not even a tiny red light that revealed the location of a well-hidden security camera. She drew a relieved conclusion: apparently the gods' golden objects qualified for video surveillance, but the gods themselves did not.

Now she had to try to get away unseen.

The moment she made a move, a third man entered the sculpture gallery from the lobby. He was dressed almost identically to the other two: dark-blue baggy trousers and a loose-fitting jacket in the same colour, a white shirt and a dark tie. A pair of sunglasses dangled from his hand. Only the sculptures in the space separated them from each other. As calmly as possible she walked in his direction. When she got closer, she heard him talking softly with two fingers pressed against his right ear. She paused and tried to pick up what he was saying. No luck. He was issuing orders, that's all she could make out.

From the Hall of the Golden Artefacts she heard the sounds of a brief but intense scuffle. As if someone were trying to get away but had been stopped. Shortly afterwards, she saw Saputra being marched out of the Hall by the two men. He walked with difficulty because one of his sandals had come undone. His undamaged right eye was open wide. It was practically popping out of his head with terror. His left eye was watering heavily. Each of the men pinned one of his arms against his body. The third man turned around and followed them into the lobby.

Her first impulse was to run towards the group and free Saputra. But it was doubtful that she could eliminate three trained security agents, while sacrificing her cover once and for all was probably not a smart move either.

She kept watching as the two men dragged Saputra away through the sliding glass doors.

The third man remained in the lobby, where he issued orders to two museum guards, who then took up positions by the exit. From now on visitors were only allowed to exit the museum after showing identification. Although it wasn't very busy, it didn't take long for a line of grumbling people to form, all eager to leave the museum.

Farah weighed up her chances. So far, her false Russian passport had taken her past two checkpoints at international airports. But she hadn't forgotten the two officials she'd had to eliminate in the Moscow-to-Kiev train. She couldn't take any risks here. She needed an alternative.

That's when she spotted movement by the glass doors. Initially, the sharp backlight stopped her from being able to see exactly what was going on, but, judging by the shrill sounds of gleeful voices echoing through the lobby, she figured it might be a large group of children entering the museum.

One of the guards reached for his walkie-talkie and called for immediate assistance. The other walked towards the children, who'd now noticed the wooden angels above their heads and were jumping up excitedly while raising their arms in the air to try to grab hold of them.

Of the five veiled women accompanying the group, one headed straight for Farah.

As soon as Farah recognized her, she felt just as happy as the children, who were growing giddier by the minute.

'I couldn't just let you go,' Aninda said, and handed her a silk headscarf. 'Put it on. We're all wearing one.'

'My rucksack is in a locker,' Farah said as she wrapped the scarf around her head. 'My passport –'

'Give me the key,' Aninda said. 'Quick.' She beckoned to Rino, who came running over. She issued a few brief orders. 'This key fits that little door. Go over, open it and bring back the rucksack. And please be quick.'

After he finished barking into his walkie-talkie, the guard tried to persuade the women to take the children back outside as quickly as possible. Then some twenty Chinese tourists emerged from another gallery to see what the noise was all about. They squeezed past the children and the guards to get to the lockers, where Rino had just opened the door. He pulled the rucksack out and ran to Farah with a delighted expression on his face.

She took his hand and, on Aninda's sign, the other children all crowded around her as they made their way to the exit.

Against the backlight of the low-hanging sun, all the people on Taman Fatahillah resembled faceless shadows from a big *wayang* show. Cheers could be heard, rallying cries. Before long, Farah saw what was going on. The people on the square parted for a large group of young protesters with white bandannas around their heads, demonstrating against Gundono's nuclear-energy plans. The military police closed in on them from various directions.

The children, who'd been so gleeful only moments earlier, now looked disappointedly at the cart with the fairground wheel, which was hurriedly whisked away by its owner.

'We'll come back soon and then you'll all get to have a spin,' Aninda shouted. 'We're going home now.'

She turned around to Farah.

'And you're coming with us.'

It was already well into the evening when Radjen drove through the IJ Tunnel to Amsterdam-Noord. He reflected on the unexpected demand Paul Chapelle had thrown at him that afternoon in return for cooperation on the international developments surrounding AtlasNet.

His mind wandered back to the injured boy. Once Sekandar had recovered enough, he'd be brought to Chapelle's farm to continue his rehabilitation there. As far as security was concerned, his idea had a large number of obstacles that would need to be worked out, but a quieter, more rural environment might help the boy recover faster, and it could very well improve the communication with him. Chapelle and his mother both spoke Dari. So far, the boy had told Farah only his name. Now, he'd spoken his first words in a long time to Paul. There was a good chance that he'd follow up with the rest of his story. An important step in getting an official statement from him.

He'd just parked his car in front of the middle of three old VOC warehouses when his phone rang.

It was Ellen Mulder with the results of the toxicology tests. She confirmed what he and Esther had already suspected before the autopsy.

'Meijer was drugged. He had traces of alfentanil in his blood. It's often used for short surgical procedures. It takes effect within a minute.'

'How long does it last?'

'Fifteen minutes.'

'Thank you, Ellen. I hope you have a good evening.'
'You too Radjen, bye.'

He had his apprehensions about the night ahead as he entered the refurbished warehouse's main hall, located all the bells and tried to find Esther van Noordt's nameplate.

Her voice sounded as strained as he felt. A buzzer alerted him to the fact that the barred gate had clicked opened. He walked into an area where hundreds of years ago, coffee, tea, tobacco and cocoa from the Dutch colonies were stored. Now the three warehouses had been put to a variety of uses, including a business and innovation centre, a café, and exhibition and studio spaces for artists – all part of a project called Nieuw Amsterdam. It was an initiative of Kars Moonen, a rugged fellow who liked to refer to himself as an artistic entrepreneur. Kars had spent years in Australia living and painting with the Aborigines. Then he retreated to somewhere in the northern Canadian woods and lived like a hermit while sculpting angels from tree trunks. When he returned to the Netherlands, he purchased three abandoned warehouses from the city of Amsterdam, which didn't have a clue what to do with such a run-down industrial area. At the time, he paid next to nothing for the buildings.

Kars brought together a small army of young artists, which at first glance resembled some kind of creative anarchistic society, and he also had apartments built in the old complex.

In the central shared space, an array of colourful characters were mounting an exhibition about Afghanistan. Radjen gazed at a panoramic image of a city that could have been Paris in the 1980s. But the immense white mosque dome and the Venetian balconies with Byzantine arched windows looked out of place. He walked over and read the caption: KABUL 1976.

On the gallery of the first floor, where the apartments were located, Esther was waiting for him in the doorway. She was wearing light, wide-legged joggers and a T-shirt with thin horizontal black-and-white stripes. She looked like a cross between a seaman and an inmate.

'My hangman,' she said to welcome him. He saw that she was nervous. Perhaps just as nervous as he was.

She walked him into a large room, where a grainy blue evening light seeped through the arched windows. 'Pretty special place to live,' Radjen said, ill at ease.

'Hard to imagine that it would all have been demolished,' she said.

As they spoke, menacing clouds massed on the horizon above Amsterdam's old city centre.

'A few hundred years ago people visited this part of town on Sunday for their amusement,' Esther said. 'They came here to see executed prisoners rotting on the gallows. You won't leave me hanging that long, right?'

Radjen didn't respond. By now all his attention was focused on the rope construction that she'd secured around a high wooden beam.

'I gave a lot of thought to whether they used some kind of harness to hoist Meijer into position,' she said. 'But the problem is that you'd have to put both legs through it. That would have been pretty hard if, as I surmise, Meijer was out cold. You'd also have to remove the harness afterwards. That would take a long time and leave traces on the clothing. So it didn't seem like a practicable option.'

She showed him a wide nylon strap with a locking mechanism on the back on to which a 10.5-mm-thick Wall Master Unicore climbing rope could be hooked. That rope ran through a self-locking pulley device she'd attached to the ridge beam. She'd passed the rope through and pulled it tight.

'Okay, we can get started,' she said, with an uncertain look on her face, 'but I need to smoke a joint first. Any objections?'

'I'll have a hit too,' Radjen said.

'It's pretty strong stuff,' she said, as she walked into the kitchen and pulled a small plastic bag out of a biscuit tin. 'Home-grown.'

'Shall I nab you on possession of an illegal substance and then hang you?'

'You might as well make yourself my partner in crime,' she said. 'Ninjas share everything anyway.'

She sat down on a wide sofa, pulled out a pack of Rizla papers, rolled a joint, lit it, inhaled and passed it to Radjen. He held it up in front of him and eyed it the way you do things you distrust.

Esther spread out her arms along the back of the sofa and sunk into the cushions as she stretched her legs. 'It's good stuff, trust me.'

Radjen inhaled deeply and held the smoke in for a bit. Then he exhaled. He felt slightly euphoric.

'It's been ages,' he said, as he returned the joint.

'How long?'

'I'd just become a detective. We backpacked around Europe for two weeks.'

'We?'

'Me and my girlfriend.'

'Did she look like Ellen Mulder?'

'No, she was ... different ... we ended up at Lake Trasimeno.'

It was out before he knew it. He didn't know why he'd told her. His voice faltered. Suddenly he saw the empty tent before his eyes, after he'd unzipped it. He was soaked because he'd been swimming. He felt the bewilderment of the past embrace him. It had been so long ago, but the sensation was still just as strong as then.

Esther didn't seem to notice.

'They say that Trasimeno, the son of the Etruscan King Tyrreno, drowned there,' she said, exhaling a long stream of smoke, 'and that the ghost of his beloved nymph is still searching for him. When the wind blows and you listen closely, you can supposedly hear her crying as she calls his name. "Trasimeno, Trasimeno . . ."'

With a high-pitched voice she imitated a restless spirit.

'Did you hear her, Radjen?'

'Sorry?'

'I asked if you heard her crying?'

'Who?'

'The ghost of Trasimeno's beloved.'

'No . . . No.'

'Are you okay?'

'Yes, sure.'

'You suddenly seem so . . . distant.'

'It must be the weed.'

'Hmm . . .'

She took her time inhaling and kept the smoke in her lungs. Then she exhaled with a cough.

'Was she your childhood sweetheart, the girl who travelled with you?'

He wanted to tell her everything, but it had been so long since he'd talked about it. 'No. Well . . . yes . . . actually. She was . . .'

'She was what? C'mon, spit it out! I mean, was she just one of many, or was she the love of your love?'

'The latter, yes . . .'

'Well, that's beautiful, right? Did you marry her?'

'No. She . . . I ended up marrying someone else.'

'And what happened to your great love?'

He shook his head and gestured that he wanted the joint.

'Sorry,' she said, after sitting up straight and offering him another toke. 'I shouldn't be so nosy.'

'Doesn't matter,' Radjen said. 'But what you said about marriage . . . when we were at Meijer's place, why . . . ?'

'What are you getting at?'

'I'm curious what you have against marriage?'

'You need a man, right?'

'There are men in abundance.'

'It's about the type of guy.'

'What type?'

'Jesus . . . well, he has to be at least as tall as I am.'

'Is that the key criterion, height?'

'I don't like short men.'

'Okay, tall. Age?'

'Irrelevant.'

'Tall, ageless. Profession?'

'Typically male question. Maybe he protects the world from all evil,' she said, grinning. 'But without the giant *S* on his chest and he doesn't fly around in a red cape or the like.' She grabbed the joint out of his hand, took a drag, then giggled and asked, 'Are you actually happy, Radjen?'

The question hit him hard. He acted as if nothing were wrong and heard himself giving her a relaxed answer.

'Seems like everyone is talking about this nowadays: being happy.'

'Life's too short. A bit of happiness goes a long way, right?'

She took a last toke, and then looked at him the same way she had that afternoon when they had stood outside Ellen Mulder's office. She seemed so vulnerable, no longer the indomitable detective who flipped around chairs, tossed her hair over her shoulder, sailed the high seas and crushed out a cigarette with the heel of her boot. Everything seemed crystal clear to Radjen at this moment: the colour of her eyes, the smell of her skin and the tone of her voice, which sounded deeper than usual.

'I'll walk you through it,' she said. 'You drag me back towards the pulley device, you fasten the strap around my hips and hoist me up. Once I'm hanging high enough, you secure the rope.'

She didn't wait for his answer. She removed her trainers, then her socks and went and stood in place.

'C'mon, get up and catch me.'

Radjen went and stood right behind her. He felt a bit dizzy. He caught a whiff of her scent: apples and the sea. She let herself fall backwards. He extended his hands and caught her under her armpits. She tried to remain as limp as possible. He bent through his knees to support her weight and dragged her backwards.

'I trust you,' she whispered in his ear, letting him drag her five metres or so across the floor to the stool.

He sat her on the stool, and, with one arm on her hips, tried to place the nylon strap around her with the other hand. She was still pretending to be as limp as possible. He wanted her to trust him; hoped that she'd keep feeling safe with him. He tightened the nylon hip strap, which was attached to the rope now holding her in place.

'Everything okay?'

She nodded, but the expression on her pale face indicated otherwise.

'Shall we stop?'

She shook her head no.

He grabbed the rope and unfastened it. The first short tug he gave it made the beam creak. The nylon strap tightened around her hips.

With the next tug, her feet left the ground. Her body began to lean forward, so she was hanging at a slight diagonal in the air. But when he pulled the rope again, the resistance exerted by her body weight made her hang more vertically.

After a last firm tug her head was just a few centimetres under the beam. With some difficulty he secured the rope. Only once he'd looked up again did he see that she was making jerking movements in the air.

He quickly lowered her to the ground.

She threw her arms around him and wept silently.

He did his best to console her.

PART FOUR

Prayer

I

For anybody about to be hanged, the sound of a trapdoor opening must be terrifying. It's then that death, disguised as gravity, begins to tug at their feet.

Once Esther was hanging at the highest point on the beam in her apartment, she felt as if somewhere inside her a trapdoor had opened and an unforeseen fear tried to drag her into a bottomless pit.

Radjen saw it in her eyes.

Within seconds he'd lowered the device she was strapped into and freed her from the belt tightly fastened around her hips. In his arms, she soon regained her composure.

'Sorry,' she said, determined to control her tears.

'Why?'

'I lost it there for a minute.'

'Nothing to be ashamed of.'

She looked past his shoulder at the rope hanging from the beam, which was still swaying slightly in the air.

'In any case, we proved it's possible.'

'To ourselves, then,' Radjen said. 'To the outside world, we haven't proven a thing.'

'In fact, it's probably better if nobody hears anything about this,' she said with a slight smile.

'My ninja lips are sealed,' Radjen said.

She wiped the mascara streaks from her face and said, 'I could do with some time alone.'

*

He drove in the direction of the IJ, listening to the soothing cadence of the windscreen wipers. He'd lost track of the time. On the other side of the river he saw the lights of the old city, the coming and going around Centraal Station, and the brightly lit modern flats of KNSM and Java islands resembling a giant Mondrian mosaic.

Passing the village of Schellingwoude, he then crossed a wide bridge and drove on to Panamalaan, into the night-time heart of Amsterdam, along the illuminated canals, until he reached Westermarkt, where during the day there was always a queue of visitors hundreds of metres long waiting to get into the Anne Frank House. Further down, he saw men stumbling out of cafés with women on their arms and zig-zagging away on their bikes, back to apartments where they'd fall into unfamiliar beds and barely sleep.

Esther's scent was still with him. His shirt was slightly damp with her tears. He kept driving until he'd left the city centre, reached Hobbemakade, and the East Indies Monument appeared in front of him.

Then he knew what he had to do.

He stopped in front of Efrya and Thomas Meijer's house and peered inside. It looked dark and deserted.

As he pulled out a skeleton key, he knew he was breaking just about every existing police rule. Yet that didn't stop him.

His mind wandered back to his childhood. Every evening before he went to bed, his grandmother would tell him a differ-ent story about a clever dwarf deer named Kantjil, but she would always leave it to Radjen to make up an ending. 'You got your gift for fantasy from me,' she'd say, grinning. And every evening, once she'd said good night and left his room, in the light cast by an oil lamp, Radjen would re-enact the entire story as a shadow play on the whitewashed wall of his bedroom.

Only when he became a detective did he realize what a unique skill he'd developed. Unlike others, he could reconstruct loose fragments into a cohesive whole. This skill went much further than just putting together the pieces of a puzzle, which is what most of his colleagues did. He had the ability to re-create events in his mind's eye: his very own shadow play. After he'd gathered enough information about a wrongdoing, he could place himself in the middle of a crime scene and, as a spectator, imagine the course of events in front of his eyes. Of course, not everything he saw was equally clear, but he often discovered those last details he needed to solve the case.

After putting their hanging theory to the test in Esther's apartment, Radjen believed he was ready to let the story of Meijer's death play out in front of him. But he needed to be alone to do this, much like every reconstruction he'd done in the past. Not even Esther was allowed to be present.

Motionless, he stood on the spot where he'd shaken Efrya Meijer's hand and expressed his condolences over the loss of her husband that first night.

Now he was there alone, in the pale moonlight, beside her stripped bed, in the curtainless room with its emptied linen closets.

A smell permeated the air. The scent of two people who'd spent years sleeping next to each other in the same bed.

He heard them breathing, as if they were lying there.

Thomas Meijer moved restlessly, woke up and leaned over Efrya to see if she was still asleep. Then he quietly slipped out of bed, pulled the curtain slightly aside and gazed into the garden. Although there was not a breath of wind in the empty room, Radjen could hear the stormy weather kicking up, the intermittent rain hitting the window. He realized there wasn't any banging. The gate at the rear of the garden was apparently shut tight.

Thomas Meijer removed his pyjamas, donned some lounge-wear, shoved his feet into his slippers and, barely making a sound, left the bedroom. Radjen looked at Efrya, who didn't stir. He wanted to wake her; ask her to go after Thomas and drag him back to bed. But the scenes he saw were merely images in his head.

Radjen left the bedroom. He paused on the small landing, where he and Esther had wormed their way out of their forensics gear, surprised at the unspoken feeling of intimacy: a closeness they'd shared from that moment on.

The pounding of his heart accelerated as he descended the stairs. He went and stood in the middle of the living room, closed his eyes, and deeply inhaled and exhaled for a few minutes.

When he opened his eyes again, he was staring into the dim light of a floor lamp. The doors leading to the garden were open wide. The sheer curtains were moving in the wind.

At the rear of the garden he discovered Thomas Meijer's hunched silhouette, bent over the garden gate while holding an umbrella above his head.

It took a while before Meijer turned and walked back towards the house. Halfway, the wind got hold of his umbrella, causing the thin metal stretchers to break and partly collapse. Meijer couldn't manage to close the thing and left it beside the shed door. Radjen knew that forensics would find the umbrella in the garden later that night.

Meijer shut the French windows to the garden, but didn't lock them, and returned to the kitchen where he poured a glass of milk and made a sandwich with white bread, butter and chocolate sprinkles. He took the plate and glass into the living room, turned on the computer and entered a search term. He arrived on the homepage of a Ghanaian estate agent, where he clicked through a series of beach houses in bright shades of green, yellow and orange.

Radjen felt a gust of wind from behind, turned and saw the sheer curtains flapping fitfully, as if they were fighting off the rain. When he looked back in Meijer's direction, he was facing the screen, but the weight of his body was slumped backwards in his chair. A figure as fleeting as a shadow was standing over him.

Radjen knew it had been quick. The sudden injection Meijer received in his neck was administered silently. He was gagged and his mouth sealed shut with tape.

To lift his weight, hands were slipped under his armpits and clasped behind his neck. Now being dragged into the garden, Meijer had lost all control over his muscles. His body seemed to be made of rubber. His head hung like a weight and his arms trailed alongside his body.

The series of events that unfolded before him in the garden shed were as he and Esther had re-enacted. A belt was fastened around Meijer's hips. The rope that ran along his back up over the beam was given a few forceful tugs. Radjen couldn't tell if Meijer tried to offer any resistance. His body was undoubtedly too numb to heed the distress signals sent by his brain.

As he was being hoisted with a final tug, Meijer's head brushed along the rope. The noose felt rough as it slid past his face. He was hanging motionless in the neon-blue glow of his fish tanks.

The noose was quickly thrown over his head and secured. The stepladder was pulled out from under him and positioned in such a way that it looked like he'd kicked it over.

Meijer dropped vertically. You could hear the taut rope crack his neck. His limp tongue hung from his mouth.

Radjen observed him hanging there, exactly how they'd found him, while the images of that night slowly faded from view.

He was now alone in the neon-blue light of the aquarium tanks, where the fish were fitfully darting about among the plastic ruins in murkier water. They probably hadn't been fed in days. Radjen opened one of the food containers and sprinkled a handful of small pellets into the water. The fish followed their primal instincts and swam towards the food, fighting for every morsel.

Suddenly, above the hum of the water pumps, he heard the hinges of the garden gate creak.

As quietly as he could, he went and stood beside the closed door. Without thinking he grabbed for his weapon, which, having been sat at a desk most of the time, he hadn't carried in years. He waited apprehensively.

The handle slowly turned downwards. The door opened a crack. Radjen braced himself.

At first he thought the sound was in his head. That it was his body releasing built-up tension. But it was the buzzing of his mobile. He was paralysed for a split second, looking down at his pocket. Then he quickly turned back to the door just as it was forcefully slammed in his face.

Radjen lost his balance and fell backwards on to the hard floor.

The sound he heard after his head hit the cold tiles resembled a buzzing phone.

2

Along with the children and the other women, Farah and Aninda were squeezed into the bed of the pickup taking them back to the Waringin Shelter. The sky had turned ashen-grey. A rain storm was brewing.

'What made you follow me?' Farah asked.

'I had a feeling you were in danger,' Aninda replied. 'So I gathered the children together and told them I'd show them Fatahillah Square today and promised them a spin on the wheel afterwards. As we passed the museum, I saw two men shoving a third into a car. I instantly knew it had something to do with you.'

It started to rain. The women picked up a large sheet of blue tarpaulin and held it up over their heads, so they and the children could shelter underneath. In no time at all, over-flowing drains were spewing dark-brown jets of water into the streets.

'But I'd have come anyway, even if you hadn't told me anything last night.'

Farah gave her a puzzled look.

'Weeks ago, Satria declared that one of us would meet an unknown woman. She'd look oriental, like Indonesians with a Hindu background, but she'd be a foreigner with blue eyes.'

Farah shook her head in disbelief.

Satria, the old woman who'd been so delighted to see her this morning, who'd greeted her like a Pencak Silat warrior without knowing that she too was a practitioner . . . But then again, she must have realized, otherwise she wouldn't have saluted her the way she had.

'A woman I don't know predicted I'd come here before I knew it myself. I can't get my head around that,' she said. 'Besides, how did *you* know it was me?'

'I didn't,' Aninda said. 'You looked nothing like Satria's description, but when I spotted you during the demonstration I knew I had to help you. It was only because of the tear gas that I discovered you were wearing lenses and that your eyes were actually blue. Then, once you'd told me your story, I knew for certain.'

The tarpaulin flapped fiercely in the wind and the rain beat down hard, but the children were crowing with delight. All of a sudden they were in an artificial underwater world, pretending to swim and puckering up their mouths and gulping like deep-sea fish. They roared with laughter. Then one of the women began to sing. The children joined in.

'Their favourite song,' Aninda said with a smile. 'It's about dancing and shining brightly, like stars in the sky.'

When they arrived back at the Waringin Shelter an hour later, the rain had moved inland and the sun was beginning to peep out from behind the clouds. The children jumped out of the pickup and ran shrieking into the courtyard, where the plants and trees looked even greener than before.

She was back in a place she thought she'd never see again – a place where, as soon as she saw the large weeping fig last night, she'd immediately felt at home, as if by some strange geographical detour she'd returned to the garden of her childhood. For the second time in less than twenty-hour hours, she'd been rescued from a seemingly impossible situation by a woman she didn't know, but to whom she'd revealed the most personal things; a woman who seemed to share her own determination and with whom she felt an emotional bond.

As she looked around, inhaling the musk of wet earth and trying to get her bearings again, she saw a group of scruffy men and women, some clasping small children by the hand, accepting packages of food from the Waringin volunteers. She spotted Satria with her silvery-grey hair among them.

The old woman observed her from a distance with that reassuring look in her eyes, as if to say, 'Don't worry, you're meant to be here.' This was the woman who'd foretold her arrival.

She greeted Satria the way Pencak Silat practitioners do, and the old woman bowed in response before calmly continuing to distribute food.

Aninda came and stood beside her with a warm smile on her face.

'You're someone with good karma,' she said. 'You've got guardian angels looking after you wherever you go.'

'I guess I'm someone who needs a lot of looking after,' Farah replied.

She took the young woman's hand, realizing that without her she'd probably be in a BIN cell by now, and together they walked further into the courtyard.

3

As he knocked back his second gin cocktail in the Dutch Bar on Holland Boulevard at Schiphol Airport, Paul watched a special edition of *The Headlines Show* on one of the big plasma screens.

Exactly two hours earlier he'd stood in the huge *AND* atrium, explaining to an army of international journalists that the hostage-taking in the Seven Sisters and Farah's alleged involvement had all been a ruse of the Kremlin's.

Now Cathy Marant, with a condescending look and her eye-popping breasts in a low-cut ready-to-wear suit, was presenting her take on things.

'According to Chapelle, his former colleague Hafez is the victim of what he calls "media manipulation". But who exactly is Paul Chapelle and how reliable a journalist is he?'

Paul ordered a third cocktail and saw some old pictures of himself flash across the screen.

'Chapelle, a former foreign correspondent at the *AND*, has left a trail of work-related conflicts at the various places he's been posted – in London, Paris, Istanbul and, more recently, Johannesburg. As a result of his inflammatory articles on members of the South African government, he's now on the official media blacklist there.'

A photo from the Johannesburg police archives appeared on screen.

'Not all that long ago, Chapelle was arrested in Johannesburg for assault and public intoxication.'

Paul stared at the photo with horror. It had been taken after his last girlfriend, Susanne, was killed during a burglary at her home and the police blocked him from entering the crime scene. Yes, he'd been drunk, and yes, he'd knocked down the policeman who'd tried to stop him, and yes, five of them had then roughed him up and thrown him into a cell. But what was the point of including this in a news item on the press briefing he'd given this afternoon?

'At his chaotic press conference, Chapelle really had it in for the CEO of AtlasNet, Valentin Lavrov, holding him directly responsible for what he described as "victimizing Farah Hafez". Chapelle backed up his story with a handful of photos whose authenticity has since been questioned by a Russian government spokesperson. Should Paul Chapelle be taken seriously or is he a news manipulator himself? Find out in our main broadcast this evening. This was Cathy Marant with a special edition of *The Headlines Show*.'

By now Paul had turned away from the screen and was dialling Farah.

The first thing he noticed when she answered was how upbeat she sounded. It had been a long time since he'd heard her so determined and positive. Even now that sultry quality of her voice, which he loved so much, resonated with exuberance. Trying to remain as calm and collected as possible, he gave her a quick update on the press conference. It earned him a rich laugh. He heard raucous children in the background – the sound of cheerful chaos.

'Where are you?'

'At the Waringin Shelter, surrounded by guardian angels. I spoke with Saputra, Edward's contact. He's arranged for me to meet a mole in Gundono's organization tomorrow.'

'Can this Saputra figure be trusted?'

'Edward knows him. He's kept under surveillance, though. Shortly after our meeting he was picked up, probably by Indonesian State Intelligence.'

'Jesus, Farah. That meeting tomorrow is either a set-up, or Saputra will crack when they interrogate him and you'll end up walking straight into a trap.'

'There's only one way to find out, right?'

Paul didn't know which he found more challenging: her apparent naivety or her unyielding obstinance.

'You'd love to put me on a leash, wouldn't you?' she said, laughing.

'No. I'd like to help you out.'

'You can help by listening to me.'

'I'm all ears.'

'According to Saputra, the best way to expose Lavrov's practices in Indonesia is through the man who introduced him to government officials.'

'Gundono?'

'Exactly. Gundono is not just the Finance Minister, he's also the Chairman of the commission that granted the concessions for the new nuclear power stations. Through Gundono, we'll find out how Lavrov pulled this off.'

'How do we get to Gundono?'

'Saputra says the facilities manager can smuggle me into Gundono's headquarters and give me access to the computer network, but I've no idea how we'll do it once we're in.'

'Sorry I can't help you. It sounds awfully complicated. And I'm headed to Jo'burg shortly.'

'Jo'burg? What are you going to do there?'

'The evidence I was looking for – about the connection between Lavrov and the South African government – I can get my hands on it after all.'

'That's good news.'

'It turns out that the South African crime squad I've had contact with, the Scorpion Unit that investigates corruption cases, is working closely with Interpol. By the way, we know someone there.'

'We do?'

'That's to say, you do. Joshua Calvino.'

He instantly regretted mentioning the name given the awkward silence that followed.

'What's Calvino –'

'It's a long story. The contact who was going to pass me information about Lavrov's shady deals with the future President, Jacob Nkoane, was tortured and murdered at the meeting we'd arranged. But he'd backed up his findings . . . For me, and me alone. A kind of exclusivity clause. The South African crime squad has now approached me via Calvino and asked if I'm prepared to share that information with them.'

'And are you?'

'If it's the only way to get hold of it, then yes.'

'Jesus, Paul, this is always a tough call as a journalist. I know how much maintaining your independence means to you.'

'It's a lofty ideal I'm happy to sacrifice in order to build a watertight case against Lavrov. That's what you want, right?'

'So you're doing this for me?'

'No, I'm doing it for us.'

There was a brief silence on the other end. The children's noises had died down. He could even hear her breathing – or was he imagining this?

'Paul?'

'Yes?'

'Do you think we're going to be okay?'

'No, I don't think so.'

'You don't?'

'I'm certain we will.'

'You're really rather annoying, you know that?'

'I've been told before.'

'We'll see each other again soon, right?'

'Yes, we will, Farah, yes.'

'*Saya cinta kamu*, Paul.'

'Take care,' he said awkwardly and ended the call.

During his flight to Johannesburg, Paul tried to catch up on the TV coverage of his press conference on the small screen in front of him. CNN had an initial response from Valentin Lavrov. He was at the Ministry of Economic Affairs in The Hague, where he and Minister Lombard had signed the contract committing Russia and the Netherlands to realizing Europe's biggest gas-distribution hub. It was set to be built in the province of Noord Holland.

'I don't usually react to libel,' a relaxed Lavrov said, looking directly into the camera. 'But let me tell you this: a so-called journalist who bandies about these kinds of allegations can be described only as an outrageous fantasist. I'd like to advise Mr Chapelle to leave journalism to people who are actually qualified and to apply for an acting job in Hollywood instead.'

Via a satellite link with the Kremlin, a government spokesperson announced, ironically enough, that Paul had doctored the photos when it was exactly the opposite. Paul saw that same photo he'd taken of Lavrov and Farah on the balcony, looking out over Lake Glubokoe together, but the image on screen showed Lavrov on his own. In the second picture, it wasn't Farah being bundled into the boot of the Falcon but a large suitcase. And the third showed a military vehicle being waved through the Seven Sisters cordon – not the Falcon with Arseni Vakurov inside.

Paul resisted the impulse to grab the backrest of the seat in front and give it a good shake. But Edward had anticipated this reaction from the Russians. He'd already phoned the NFI and asked them to thoroughly examine Paul's photos to corroborate their authenticity.

All they had to do now was wait. He took another swig of his whisky, inserted his earphones and put on his favourite song, 'Yer Blues' off *The White Album*.

4

Radjen reached for the alarm button, just like he always did from bed. But his head wasn't lying on his comfortable goose-down pillow and no familiar streak of pale morning sun was visible between the narrow opening of the curtains. His face was pressed against a cold floor, and the light penetrating his half-open eyes was harsh and blue.

Still groping with his hand, he realized the sound had nothing to do with his alarm clock but everything to do with his phone. When he finally pulled it from his inside jacket pocket, it had stopped ringing.

He saw the same number listed four times on the screen. Without thinking, he pressed the redial button, turned on his side and made an unsuccessful attempt to get up from the ground. In his dizzy state, he heard a woman's voice.

'Radjen?'

'Yes?'

'Did I wake you?'

'What?'

'Where are you? Are you at home?'

'Who is this?'

There was a pause on the other end of the line.

'Are you drunk?'

'No.'

He was trying as hard as he could to connect the voice to a face, to give that face a name.

'Then what's going on?'

'Who is this?'

'Stop kidding around, please.'

'No, I . . .'

He felt his heartbeat accelerate.

The woman on the other end was silent.

'Monique? Is that you?'

He heard the sobbing tone of his own voice as he spoke. 'Everyone thinks you're dead.'

'What on earth are you talking about?'

A different face emerged for the voice, a different name.

'Esther . . . Damn . . . Sorry.'

'Jesus, man. What's wrong with you?'

'I . . .'

He looked around. He still didn't know where he was. He grabbed on to a leg of one of the tables holding the fish tanks and pulled himself up. He heard the water splash. He hung over the tank, nauseated, until he fully realized it was Esther's voice.

She asked, 'Where are you?'

He took a hurried breath and tried to concentrate.

'Atlantis.'

Her voice was strained. 'Look around you. Tell me what you see.'

He turned around with difficulty. In a flash he saw Thomas Meijer hanging there again, in the blue light, his tongue limp.

'Meijer . . . I'm in the shed . . . in his garden.'

'What are you doing there?'

He looked at the wide-open door and once again felt the blow that had knocked him to the ground. Struggling to breathe, he staggered to the doorway and deeply inhaled the crisp night air. Lights were being switched on in the surrounding houses; windows were being opened. In the distance he heard Esther call his name several times. Questioningly first, then with urgency, followed by a command.

He brought the phone close to his ear and asked, 'Could you come here?'

There was apparently something in the way he'd asked, because she not only sounded calmer, but her voice had a caring tone.

'I'm on my way, but first I'm going to call it in to Central Dispatch, to cover our bases.'

'Esther . . .'

'Yes?'

He stared straight ahead; his thoughts swallowed up in a void.

'What is it, Radjen?'

'Central Dispatch . . . Tell them it's not a burglary, that it's just me. In case the neighbours have already called the police.'

'Okay, I will.'

'And send the forensics guys. As soon as possible. To collect and secure any trace evidence from the garden.'

'But what happened?'

'Please, just do what I say and come.'

'First say you're okay?'

Just as she was asking, he got the feeling he'd been stabbed in the head with a knife. He couldn't catch his breath. Once he'd inhaled deeply, he said in a raspy voice, 'I'm fine.'

'You're not fine. I can hear it.'

'I got whacked in the head. But I'll be okay.'

'I'll send medical assistance. Stay put.'

He pressed his back against the wall and let his body sink to the ground, until his legs were stretched out in front of him on the wet patio tiles. The phone slipped out of his hand.

He hung his head and listened to the sound of the rustling leaves. It reminded him of water lapping the shores of a lake.

Dogs barking in panic were the most dangerous. The voice ordering him to stand up sounded the same. He lifted his head, opened his eyes and looked straight into a blinding torch beam.

'Police. Stand up!'

He muttered, 'Just stay off the grass.'

The second voice sounded a lot calmer. 'This guy is drunk, man.'

A hand was rested on his shoulder. A face came close to his. A nose sniffed. The hand was removed from his shoulder. The face withdrew.

'No alcohol.'

Radjen reached for his inside jacket pocket.

'Keep your hands where we can see them!'

'My ID . . .' he whispered.

This time the hand grabbed him by the shoulder. The other hand slid inside his jacket and pulled out his wallet. There was a hushed consultation. Central Dispatch was contacted via mobile radio.

The subdued voice of the face right in front of him now sounded calmer.

'Sorry, Inspector. Suspicious activity was reported by a neighbour. We'll ask Central Dispatch to send an ambulance.'

But Radjen had other priorities.

'This is a crime scene. Stay off the grass for God's sake!'

Less than an hour later, the bump on his forehead was the size of a golf ball. The worried paramedic had checked Radjen's pupils with a light and asked him how long he'd been unconscious. Based on the time that had elapsed between the first and last time Esther had phoned him, Radjen figured about three and a half minutes. The dry heaving had stopped and the nausea too. The paracetamol he'd been given seemed to be helping.

He stood looking out of the bedroom window together

with Esther. They silently stared into the garden, where forensics were going through the motions of collecting any fingerprints or footprints left behind.

'It's no use,' Radjen mumbled, still holding the bag of frozen peas against his forehead. 'Laurel and Hardy have contaminated any evidence there might have been.'

She turned her head in his direction. 'Shouldn't you go to hospital?'

'The paramedic only told me to take it easy.'

'Did you tell him about the explosion in The Hague? About the crackling and whistling sounds you've been hearing since then?'

He shook his head. Esther stared into the garden again.

'I thought we agreed to do everything together,' she said.

'Isn't that what we're doing?'

'You go snooping around here in the middle of the night on your own, without official authorization, without permission. So, no, that's not what we're doing. And when Kemper finds out you were here without a search warrant, you can flush this entire case down the drain.'

'I'll talk my way out of it.'

'Like you did with the policemen who arrived on the scene. Bullshit.'

'That went okay.'

'Sure.'

He removed the bag of peas from his forehead and turned towards her with some difficulty.

'When I went . . . and left you . . .'

She looked at him cynically. 'Man, sounds like the beginning of a schmaltzy André Hazes song.'

'This isn't the first time I've gone back to a crime scene on my own, because . . . Jesus, I've never told anyone about this before.'

'So maybe it's something I don't want to know?'

'I think you need to know.'

'Because?'

'Otherwise, you'll think *I've* lost it completely.'

She pulled out a packet of Gauloises, lit two and passed him one.

'Well, I already think that, so don't be shy.'

Strangely enough, it wasn't hard for him to tell her how he could replay a crime in his mind, discover new insights this way – that details were literally revealed to him. She listened without interrupting. Then she drew her conclusion.

'Thomas Meijer must have had an appointment with whoever killed him.'

'Only he had no idea it was his murderer.'

She blew smoke against the windowpane and seemed to enjoy the foggy effect created on the glass.

'Why do you think they were meeting?'

'Perhaps to arrange something or to exchange information or money.'

Esther turned her back to the window and gazed around the room.

'What I still don't understand is: why meet in the middle of the night? And why at home, while your wife is upstairs in bed sleeping?'

Radjen stared into the garden. The two white shapes in search of footprints beside the shed looked like they were engaged in a slow *pas de deux*. He spoke methodically, carefully weighing his every word.

'His execution had to take place in this setting. That was the express intention: a murder made to look like suicide. So the appointment had to be here, not somewhere else. And that's why it was in the middle of the night and not during the day.'

He heard a faint squeaking. Esther had taken a seat on the edge of the bed.

'I wonder how they arranged to meet up,' she said. 'We've checked all of Meijer's emails and his phone. No trace of an appointment.'

Radjen sat down beside her, with the cigarette pressed between his lips, and held the sack of frozen peas against his forehead again.

'In any case, the person responsible for your injuries was neither a burglar nor a tropical fish enthusiast.'

'Oh no?'

'No. It was his killer. He also came here to find something.'

He looked at her.

'I want that shed stripped. Everything inside needs to go to police central storage. We're missing something and I'm going to find out what it is.'

Esther stood up and took a last puff. 'I'll take care of it,' she said. 'You need to lie down. I'll drive you home.'

Radjen shook his head. 'Over my dead body.'

Esther drove Radjen to her place in Amsterdam-Noord instead. She turned the sofa in her apartment into a bed and made him lie down, still fully dressed. Then she started to untie his shoes. He was feeling a lot less queasy.

'Why did you call me in the first place?' he asked.

She stopped loosening his shoelaces and looked at him.

'I didn't want you to get any crazy ideas about me in your head.'

'What kind of ideas?'

'That there's . . . something wrong with me.'

'You're . . . I mean . . . there's nothing wrong with you.'

She pulled off his shoes.

'In any case, you don't have to worry about me.'

'I don't.'

She draped a blanket over him.

'But by now someone else should be worried about you? Have you called your wife?'

He shook his head. She pulled out her phone.

'What's her number?'

'What are you going say?' he asked. 'Mrs Tomasoa, your husband is sleeping at my place tonight?'

'Yes, exactly. And that perhaps she should take better care of her husband.'

'Don't. She's sleeping.'

'Jesus, Radjen –'

'I'll talk to her tomorrow, I promise.'

She was now standing very close to him.

'Your wife, her name's Monique?'

'No.'

'Then who's Monique?'

He sighed deeply as if to say something along the lines of 'It's a long story' and didn't reply.

'All right, then,' Esther said, as she started to turn off all the lights in the room. Before she pressed the button on the lamp beside the sofa, she hesitated.

'So how do ninjas say good night to each other?'

'I don't know . . . just good night, I suppose.'

'Okay, then. Good night.'

She switched off the light and walked towards the door.

'Good night.'

Radjen silently stared at the ceiling. The night sky in the arched windows was the colour of copper tarnished black. He saw volatile electric streaks of light shooting across the darkness. This continued for a bit behind his closed eyelids, until a black veil of sleep blotted out everything.

5

A hand on his shoulder woke him. The plane was shaking like a wet dog. The hostess pointed to his unfastened seatbelt. Paul was still too sleepy to start panicking. But just in case, he swallowed an oxazepam with a few gulps of whisky. For what felt like an endless bumpy descent, he was as calm as a Zen master who'd just raked together all the gravel in his garden in cosmic harmony.

With a relaxed smile of recognition, Detective Elvin Dingane was waiting for him in the arrivals hall. Standing there in his cream-coloured suit, he was the spitting image of the young Miles Davis on the 1950s album cover *Live at Newport*: handsome, hip and a force to be reckoned with.

'From where I'm standing, it would've been better if they'd kept you in hospital a while longer,' Dingane said, giving Paul a firm handshake. 'Or is a smashed-up face a badge of honour in your profession?'

Dingane's smile was warm and engaging. For someone who fought serious crime, he was remarkably civilized. Perhaps his refined nature was how he shielded himself from all the cruelty and ugliness that came with his line of work. He was the type of guy you could spend an entire night with shooting pool and propping up the bar philosophizing about how to avoid the dark side of life, but also how attractive it might be on occasion to give in to its temptations.

Dingane drove Paul into Johannesburg in his Toyota Cressida. Every available square centimetre of the city was plastered with election posters. From the Mandela Bridge,

Paul spotted an immense banner on the COSATU building of the equally immense and despicable face of Jacob Nkoane. The slogan underneath proclaimed A BETTER LIFE FOR ALL.

'Some people call him the man with roubles up his arse,' Dingane said. 'According to the polls, he's going to win by a landslide. Apparently a hundred million rand was dumped into his campaign and that's not just South African money. You really have to ask yourself where the ANC gets the nerve to keep waving the struggle-for-freedom flag when a man like Nkoane is undoubtedly going to be President. If our beloved Madiba had ever imagined the country's ruling party indulging in this kind of conduct, he might have stayed on Robben Island forever.'

Paul took a long hard look at Dingane. He noticed the wrinkles around his eyes, the touch of grey at his temples. Dingane was, as always, smartly dressed, and was undoubtedly just as decent in his dealings with others, but Paul could tell that in only a few weeks' time he'd become a different man. More cynical, older.

'Where's the man who claimed a few weeks ago that the majority of the ANC's people could be trusted?' Paul asked.

'He'll soon be out of a job,' Dingane said. 'Once Nkoane becomes President – and that will be the case in just three days – he'll declare our investigation illegal and dissolve the Scorpion Unit. Mark my words.'

'So the ANC is even prepared to undermine the constitution to protect its own interests and people?'

Dingane threw Paul an emphatic look. 'That's why it's so important you're willing to share your information with us.'

'Says the man who not so long ago insisted I leave the country.'

'That was for your own safety.'

'What about your safety, then? Damn, you're a state official poking around in your government's shit.'

'I was appointed to take a closer look at all aspects of the ANC. That's my job. That was my assignment. And, as long as I'm still a Scorpion, I plan to keep doing just that. I know I'm being watched by agents from the PIU, the Presidential Intelligence Unit. They ripped apart Zhulongu's computer and office, and when that offered up nothing concrete, they turned his house upside down. They didn't find the backup. So then they interrogated Zhulongu's widow, Miriam, for hours. They even threatened to take her children away from her if they later discovered she was withholding information. She didn't give an inch.'

'She sounds like a strong woman,' Paul said.

'She is,' Dingane replied.

They drove to Ferreira Town, the heart of Johannesburg, where Dingane parked his car directly opposite the oldest building in the city, the Hut, a former dynamite warehouse from the era when the city was known as Egoli, 'the place where gold was found'. Not so long ago, it was a bleak neighbourhood better to avoid, even during the day, but the tide had turned. Young entrepreneurs, who took the slogan 'rainbow nation' seriously and applied it in practice, had breathed new life into these districts.

Dingane ordered two kudu pies and two large mugs of organic beer, and they sat down at one of the big tables right outside the Hut, to keep an eye on the Cressida.

'What should we toast?' Paul asked.

'The wisdom of *Ubuntu*,' Dingane said.

'Here's to *Ubuntu*,' Paul replied. 'Humanity towards others.'

After a few welcome gulps of beer, Dingane gave him a serious look. 'You never told me how you originally got involved in the Nkoane case.'

'That's because you've never asked me.'

'I'm asking now.'

'My father spent years researching how the Soviet Union tried to spread its Communist ideology around the world. I can assure you that there would not have been an armed black struggle in South Africa without an enormous amount of Russian weapons and money. In other words, without the former Soviet Union, there may not have been an ANC, and without Khrushchev, Mandela might never have become the President of the country decades later. The arms trade between Russia and South Africa is as old as the ANC itself. In that respect, nothing new under the sun. But when President Potanin announced during an official three-day visit to South Africa several months ago that the cooperation between the two countries would be strengthened, I knew there was more to this. In fact, it's about the exchange of nuclear fuel and technology for large-scale energy projects. As the most important presidential candidate, Jacob Nkoane might someday come in handy for future deals with Russia. There were rumours about secret deliveries of weapons. I've spoken to sources behind the scenes who have confirmed that Lavrov lined Nkoane's pockets with bribes. The *Citizen* dared to publish the story.'

'And that led Thaba Zhulongu to contact you.'

'He didn't reveal on the phone who he was or that he worked for the South African Ministry of Defence; only that he'd seen my piece and had important additional information.'

Paul saw Thaba Zhulongu before his eyes, tied to a pillar in Ponte City. His face beaten to a pulp by Lavrov's thugs . . . unrecognizable.

'How is his wife doing now?'

'Miriam was moved to a safe house, together with her three children. They're being well taken care of.'

Dingane had been scanning the street the entire time they were eating and talking. Paul could tell he was anxious.

'What is it?'

'See that white Toyota Land Cruiser that just passed us?'

Paul caught a glimpse of the vehicle just as it turned the corner.

'That's no coincidence. They followed us.'

'PIU guys?'

Dingane gave him a telling nod. 'They were probably just establishing where we were the first time they went by. Driving by a second time means they're keeping a close eye on us. It doesn't seem wise to wait until a third drive-by, unless you want to take your last bite of kudu pie riddled with bullets.'

Dingane stood up, threw some money on the table and walked away from the restaurant with Paul.

'Market on Main is a few kilometres away, in the middle of the Maboneng district,' Dingane said. 'As much as you can, stick to the quiet side streets and make sure you're not being followed. Gallery Arts on Main: I'll pick you up there in thirty minutes.'

Dingane crossed the street and, before Paul knew it, was swallowed up by the chaos of pedestrians, traffic and illegal street vendors who cluttered the already narrow streets with their carts and stalls.

Paul ducked into the first side street, then turned left and arrived in a place where vacant blocks of housing alternated with run-down office towers, now full of illegal workers and their families from Zimbabwe, Mozambique and Malawi.

He didn't recognize the neighbourhood. He wasn't sure in which direction to walk and looked over his shoulder more times than he cared to. The matter-of-fact way Dingane had behaved had thrown him. If Dingane knew he was being watched, why had he met him out in the open, in the middle of airport arrivals? And why didn't they go directly to Miriam Zhulongu's safe house? Why did he choose a table at the Hut right on the street? Was it Dingane's plan all along to abandon him in this neighbourhood?

In a doorway of a neglected block of flats – owned by speculators waiting for a good offer and in the meantime appropriated by junkies, illegal immigrants and criminals – he saw young boys lying on mattresses on the floor. *Skadukinders*, 'twilight children' of ten, eleven, twelve years of age at the most, unconscious because of glue they'd been sniffing from half-litre milk cartons.

He glanced at his watch. He hadn't even been walking for ten minutes and already he was completely lost in a concrete wasteland of tower blocks wedged between up-and-coming districts. On each and every corner he passed, Nigerian drug dealers clicked their tongues and hissed at him, 'Coke, ecstasy.'

At that moment, he became aware of an unkempt pair coming up right behind him. From their silence, he knew that this was anything but a coincidence. He could literally feel the man closest to him breathing down his neck.

Just before Paul took action, his mind registered the image of young white woman about ten metres away running towards him. She had snow-white hair and was wearing a dark-grey jogging outfit.

This image stuck in his mind as his right fist hit the man behind him in the solar plexus. Paul spun around and planted the second punch right between the guy's eyes. With the flat of his left hand he rammed the Adam's apple of the second guy. He got him in a headlock and then kicked his calf and right leg out from under him. Paul retreated a bit, pulled the guy towards him in a stranglehold and let him fall backwards on his buddy like the piece of shit he was.

The woman was now eye to eye with Paul. For a split second he thought she looked familiar, but he couldn't place her. She smiled oddly and addressed him calmly, not in Afrikaans or in English, but in Russian.

'Hello, Paul.'

This was followed by a painful electric shock to his chest, which knocked him unconscious.

6

The Jalan Surabaya Antiques Market, which was tucked away in Menteng's leafy embassy district, came in for a lot of criticism – most of the goods were fake and customers mightily ripped off – but two things more than made up for this: it got you out of the scorching heat and the vendors left you in peace.

That said, Farah's planned meeting with Saputra's contact was a risky endeavour. Not least because of Saputra himself. Or, rather, because of his vanishing act.

Edward had phoned his old friend from his office in Amsterdam, only to discover that his mobile number was no longer in service. He reckoned it meant Indonesian State Intelligence had cut him off from the outside world. And this led Edward to assume they'd analysed Saputra's call history. If that was the case, they would have noticed he'd been in touch with the Editor-in-Chief of the *AND*, the newspaper that had dispatched a supposed terrorist to Moscow.

All possible alarm bells would be ringing by now.

And then there was the very real chance Saputra would crack during his interrogation.

It could also mean plainclothes policemen had been planted among the vendors at Surabaya Market and Farah's contact replaced by a BIN agent. Put differently: she could be walking straight into a trap, which was precisely what Paul and Anya had warned her about.

Did that mean she shouldn't do it? Standing still equalled going backwards. Taking risks was an inextricable part of the attack. It was her father's number one rule.

She glanced over her shoulder. Within a radius of around fifteen metres, five other women, including Aninda, were keeping a close eye on her. They were the same Waringin Shelter women who'd escorted the children to the museum. As it turned out, all of them had been trained in basic self-defence skills by Satria. Born Satria Wanengpati, the old woman used to be one of the country's most renowned Pencak Silat masters. She'd managed to weave diverse combat techniques together in such a formidable way that she was unbeatable, even for most men.

Five years ago she'd called it a day. Now she only trained the female Waringin workers. And not without reason. The way in which the street kids were being resocialized at the various commune-style Waringin shelters in Jakarta had attracted a great deal of opposition. There had even been attacks. Because of this, founder Baladin Hatta had made it compulsory for all female workers to practise self-defence techniques. And Satria Wanengpati's training sessions had provided an exceptionally strong basis.

Farah slowed her pace.

She'd reached the location Saputra had mentioned to her: Andy's Record Shop. The Valhalla of vinyl fanatics who didn't mind digging around in crates for musical gems, bootlegs and obscure live recordings by forgotten artists.

She looked around and saw the other women unobtrusively scanning the market. There was nothing to suggest they were being shadowed.

Aninda came and stood beside her. On Farah's nod, she entered the record shop first. Aninda had insisted on doing it this way. If there were any BIN agents inside, she'd recognize them at once. Farah wouldn't be in any danger.

Through the glass door Farah watched Aninda wander around and engage in animated conversation with a handful of older men. Before long, she received the all-clear signal.

She was still wary, though. It all seemed a bit too easy. That said, contact had yet to be established.

When she stepped inside, she was met by cool, air-conditioned air. There were a total of seven men in the small shop, all over forty, all rummaging in crates in which nothing was arranged in alphabetical order or by genre. It was a total hotchpotch, an impenetrable jungle of vinyl.

'That's Andy, the owner, over there,' Aninda whispered. She pointed to an ageing rocker with a fuzzy goatee and long grey hair tied into a ponytail that was dangling through the rear opening in his baseball cap. 'Back in the day, he used to be pretty famous.'

Farah approached Andy just as he lit a *kretek*. She caught a whiff of clove.

'I'm looking for a record by Foreigner,' she said in Bahasa.

Andy looked at her with barely disguised contempt. 'And you'd like me to help you with that.'

'Yes, please.'

'Women always need help in here,' he said, before walking over to one of the many crates and flicking through it like a seasoned pro. In no time at all, he dug out a record with a young woman's face on it. He pressed it into her hands and sauntered back to the till.

Farah looked down at the sepia sleeve. She didn't know what to do next.

'A Foreigner fan, I see?'

She looked up. The man who'd addressed her in impeccable English was Chinese Indonesian. He wore the kind of branded casual wear you'd normally put on for lunch in an expensive restaurant, not for finding records in obscure vinyl stores. He was the type of man who could get away with a Clark Gable moustache without looking ludicrously old-fashioned. Farah hadn't seen him come in.

'An acquaintance told me to ask for this album,' she offered.

'May I, please?' He took the sleeve from her and studied it like some kind of rare find.

'This is the sixth album they released,' he said. 'Not their best, if you ask me. But in those days the masses went crazy for the dullest ballads. The kind you know before you've even heard them. So saccharine they make battle-hardened generals wave white flags.'

He gave her a winning smile. 'But I don't know if this is the kind of information you're after.'

She considered her options. The man seemed to be too friendly, too jovial for a BIN agent. Then again, maybe that's exactly what he was: an intelligent charmer with a sense of humour, a trained master in establishing contact.

She decided to take her chances.

'I'm more interested in this,' she said, pointing to the album title: *Inside Information*.

His gaze grew sombre. He lowered his voice. 'What is it you'd like to know?'

Anya had explained to her how they could gain access to Gundono's computer network. It would need to be done via the router, the device that channels processor requests to the internet. A router was a digital gateway with its own internal logic. And in that system, Anya reckoned, lay their best chance. Fierce competition was forcing manufacturers to rush their devices on to the market, leaving them with less time for exhaustive testing. As a consequence, most router operating systems contained a few unidentified weaknesses. Once she'd found and analysed those, Anya reckoned they effectively had a way into Gundono's digital network. But before she could do that, she needed to know the router's model and serial number.

'I need a good look at the router used in Gundono's compound beforehand,' Farah whispered.

'You mean you need a photo of it?' the man asked.

'A photo, yes,' Farah explained, 'that clearly shows the make and model.'

He nodded. 'When do you need it?'

'As soon as possible. Preferably today.'

'Is this evening all right?' he asked.

'Fine.'

With a smile, he slipped the record back in its sleeve.

'Why don't you leave this here? It's middle-of-the-road dross from the eighties. I'm more of a Stan Getz man myself. This evening, when you return, I'll make sure Andy has a Getz album for you. It was nice meeting you.'

He was about to leave, but she stopped him.

'The person who told me to ask for this record . . . How is he?'

His face fell. 'I can't tell you that.'

'Do you know where he is?'

'I have my suspicions.'

'The BIN?'

He leaned towards her. 'That's an acronym you'd better not mention again. Certainly not in public.'

'What are the chances he'll crack?'

'Negligible, ma'am.'

'How can you be so sure?'

'Because I know my friend.'

And with that he turned and walked out of the shop.

7

Radjen had taken a long, hot, morning shower. When he came into the kitchen in the oversized sweater and much too short, ragged joggers that Esther had lent him, she was sitting at the kitchen breakfast bar behind her laptop, with a large mug of black coffee and her usual packet of Gauloises within reach. She was barefoot and wearing only a black T-shirt that was so big on her it looked like a dress. Her long hair was in disarray, but her eyes were clear.

She looked up at him with an amused smile. 'I hope you feel better than you look?'

'Doing great,' he said, touching the bump on his forehead. 'But I guess I only learn the hard way.'

She poured him a mug of coffee and placed a croissant on a plate in front of him. 'You know,' she said, 'I've been thinking about that comparison you made to different levels of a computer game. Well, we're after the guy at the highest level now . . .'

'That's the idea, yes.'

'But perhaps we've overlooked the help available to us at lower levels.'

He responded with a question mark on his face, his coffee mug in limbo somewhere between the counter and his mouth.

'Last night I took another look at all the case files related to our investigation.'

'All the files?' he said. 'Must have been one hell of a night.'

'It was worth it.'

She clicked open a file and directed the laptop towards

Radjen. He saw the file of the woman who'd called the emergency number after Sekandar was found on the road, Angela Faber.

'Why was so little done with her statement?' Esther asked.

Radjen washed down a last bite of croissant with a swig of coffee. 'All in all, an unfortunate affair. Initially, she denied having anything to do with the hit-and-run; said she wasn't even in the Amsterdamse Bos that night. But the telephone number she used to report the accident was in her name. After the interrogation, we just released her. She was no longer a suspect. The forensics investigation confirmed the boy was run down from the other direction. Detectives Diba and Calvino handled the matter.'

'Handled? More like botched it.'

She indicated some sentences from Angela Faber's statement that were highlighted in yellow.

'She first says she was blinded by an oncoming light as she neared the spot where the boy was lying. But what happened after that?'

'What do you mean after that?'

'After the headlights blinded her.'

'Somehow, she avoided hitting the kid who was lying in the middle of the road.'

Esther quickly lit a cigarette.

'I meant in that brief interval. What happened in between the moment she couldn't see anything and the moment she saw the boy? Calvino and Diba didn't give this any attention.'

She clicked open another file. The one belonging to Thomas Meijer.

'I have his first statement here. Try following my logic.'

She started to read aloud. '"She appeared unexpectedly. Out of nowhere. As if she had wings. I still see her face in front of me. Her eyes when she hit the glass."'

'He thought Sekandar was a girl,' Radjen said. 'Because of how the child was dressed.'

'Yes, clearly,' Esther said, as she took a quick sip of coffee and continued reading. '"I slammed on the brakes, but it was too late. She bounced off the car, as if she were a rubber doll. But that blow, the blow was so hard. It's stuck in my head. I can't sleep any more. Whenever I close my eyes, I hear it over and over again. And I see her eyes, staring back at me."'

'He slammed on his brakes,' Esther repeated. 'Thick oily skid marks on the road. So that vehicle practically came to a standstill. But "Lombard yelled to keep driving. He kept shouting. So, I gave it gas."

'The bastard takes off. Switches gears, speeds ahead. But less than two hundred metres later there's an approaching car: Angela Faber's Citroën.'

She took a quick puff of her cigarette.

'Now from Angela Faber's point-of-view. Hello?' She waved her hand. 'Are you still with me, Chief Bulging Brow?'

Radjen nodded.

'Angela Faber was awfully upset that night. She'd walked in on her husband shagging someone else. A guy, for that matter. She'd been drinking and drove into the woods without thinking. She saw the approaching lights coming straight at her and hit her brakes. Meaning both cars crossed each other's path that night at relatively slow speeds. So that brings us back to the question that was never asked: what did Angela Faber see?'

'You know what I think?'

'Enlighten me, my guru in drag.'

'Angela Faber didn't see anything. Even if she managed to glance inside the passing car, she still couldn't have recognized anyone. It was a split second, and, besides, it was too dark in the woods to see anything.'

He saw that amused smile reappear on her face. 'Okay, Es, let me have it,' he said.

'It's right here,' she said. 'In Meijer's statement. When he's talking about Lombard's back-seat antics over the years.'

She scrolled down and read aloud. '"Maybe if it had happened in the dark, it wouldn't have been so bad; I don't know. He was afraid of his shadow, at least that's what I think, a grown man afraid of the dark. The light in the car always had to be on at night. Even if there was nobody with him."'

She looked up and stubbed out her cigarette. 'So what we have is two vehicles passing each other at a slow speed. Angela Faber is in one and our minster is in the other with the inside light on.'

She removed two cigarettes from her packet of Gauloises, placed them between her lips and lit them both.

'I like how that sounds,' she said as she handed him a cigarette.

'How what sounds?'

'Es.'

'Did I call you that?'

'Yes, you did.'

'Jesus.'

'No, you didn't say that. You said Es.'

He felt the smoke tingle on his tongue.

'So we need to interrogate her again?'

'No. She's going to volunteer the information. It's a gamble, but if it works, we'll have the most reliable witness statement you can imagine.'

She'd spelled out her plan. He'd listened and hoped that she'd keep talking the entire morning, that she'd then do the same the whole afternoon, sitting at the kitchen breakfast bar drinking mug after mug of coffee and smoking cigarettes.

He wanted this to continue late into the evening, if necessary until the next morning, until the morning after.

Of course he'd nodded when she'd asked if she could get to work on her plan for Angela Faber. And of course he'd put on his smelly clothes again while she was taking a shower. Of course – that's how life goes.

All good things come to an end.

When she entered the room again, she'd swept up her hair. Her blouse, corduroy trousers, fitted jacket and boots were all in shades of black.

'Meijer is being buried today,' she'd explained as he stared at her in surprise. 'And I think we need to go. To see who else shows up.'

'I never go to funerals.'

'You don't know what you're missing.'

She first drove him back to his car, which was still across town on Olympiaplein, and then went directly to the station to set the plan they'd discussed in motion.

Driving home at a snail's pace, Radjen thought hard about what he'd say when he got there. But he also knew it wouldn't matter. She'd see it on him. How something deep inside had changed.

Before he'd put the key in the lock, she'd already opened the door. When she saw him standing there, with a forehead the size of Frankenstein's, she was so startled she didn't say a word.

'Probably a mild concussion,' was all he said. 'We worked through the night because we're about to break an important case. I only came to change my clothes.'

Although over the years she'd grown accustomed to the irregular, hectic pace of his job, he saw in her eyes that she couldn't muster the energy to believe him. She also showed no sign of protest. She only looked at him with a dull sort of acceptance. As if she'd always known that a day like this would come. A time when a stranger would arrive on her doorstep: no longer the man who lay on his back beside her in bed and, as part of their trusted ritual, stared at the crack in the ceiling.

Radjen would have preferred to throw his arms around her, to tell her any way he could that it wasn't as bad as she thought. Yet what often happened when he wanted to react spontaneously happened here again: he shut down. He mumbled something about his black suit: was it still hanging in the same place? And what about those shoes that were too tight: the only ones he had that looked good with a suit?

He said to her, 'I'm going to a funeral.'

'You never go to funerals,' she replied.

Even her response didn't sound like a protest – more a clear-cut observation. She was an expert at this. Observations that were so matter-of-fact they were practically clinical.

'Well, today is different.'

Fifteen minutes later he was standing by the front door again wearing his suit and uncomfortable shoes.

'When will I see you again?' she asked.

'Soon.'

The tone of his response was one used to reassure children. Only she wasn't a child. She was his wife.

8

There were more comfortable ways to take in the Johannesburg sunset. But this time it wasn't up to Paul. Somewhere in a tower block, which had been stripped bare, he was hanging fifteen centimetres above the floor with his hands tied high above his head to a frayed rope attached to a pulley. A few metres from him was that woman: hazel eyes, alabaster skin, snow-white hair pulled tightly back in a ponytail. Her tightly fitting jogging outfit complemented her athletic figure.

She was having an agitated discussion with a black man wearing a run-of-the-mill blue suit, whose head was covered in tiny grey curls. Standing right behind them was a strapping white guy in blue jeans with a clean-shaven head. He was cradling a Kalashnikov in his arms.

When she caught Paul watching them, the woman ended her conversation with the man in blue and smiled benignly. 'You've got some technique. A bit rough around the edges, but I can appreciate that,' she said to Paul in Russian.

'English, please,' said the man standing beside her.

She pretended not to hear.

'Under other circumstances we could go a round or two. But it's all about setting priorities.'

She held up Paul's phone. 'The passcode. It would be wise for you to give it to me.'

'I don't understand what you're saying, speak English,' the man in blue repeated.

She threw her strongman a glance. A single nod was enough.

The barrel of the Kalashnikov was rammed into the back of his blue suit.

'This wasn't the deal,' griped the suited fellow. 'You get us the information first. Then he's yours. Only then. We've got fuck all now!'

The woman remained composed and turned to Paul. 'Are you familiar with the concept of pain tolerance, Paul? The point at which pain is no longer bearable? If you don't give me that passcode, we're going to explore your tolerance threshold.'

'Is it Lavrov?' Paul asked. 'Are you his errand girl?'

'You have a lot of questions for someone who should only be volunteering answers,' she said.

'Occupational hazard. Journalists never stop asking questions.'

'Have it your way.'

She put the phone in her pocket, grabbed him by the hips and gave him a forceful shove.

The rope tightened around his wrists.

She grabbed him by the hips again and pushed him even harder. She did this repeatedly until he was swinging back and forth with considerable speed. He saw her estimating the distance to the front-most point, where he hung weightless in the air for a split second, or so it seemed.

Then it struck him, what he'd become.

A human punchbag.

He kicked his feet back and forth in an attempt to touch the floor and slow down his movement, but he couldn't reach the ground. As he swung forward, she turned and lunged from the hip. The tip of her shoe shot into his stomach like a spear. He couldn't breathe. His body swung backwards, and the pain ripped through him like an electric shock. His body wanted to cower, roll up in a ball, somehow to alleviate the worst of the agony, but he could only hang there, stretched in mid-air. He felt like there was a large crater where his stomach had once been that an arm could easily reach through.

She let him sway to and fro until he'd almost come to a standstill, and then she came and stood right in front of him.

'Any idea what they use to stuff punchbags? Scraps of fabric, remnants of cloth, unimaginable volumes, and it all goes into the bag until it's sturdy enough. That's what your insides are going to look like when I'm done with you. On the outside, intact, okay, black and blue, but, for all appearances, fine. On the inside, it's a different story: catastrophic. What now passes for your intestines, liver, kidneys and your stomach will be bits and pieces bobbing around in blood. You know what you can do to prevent that, right?'

She pulled out the phone again.

At that moment muffled shots rang out. They came from a lower storey.

The man in blue drew a pistol and descended the stairs. Snow White in her designer wear didn't seem the least bit fazed. She looked at him like a beast of prey and simply said, 'The passcode.'

Paul shook his head. Even this slight movement hurt.

'You can beat the shit out of me, but you can't touch Farah.'

'There's no way you can win this,' she said.

A second volley of gunfire sounded from below.

She grabbed Paul firmly, started pushing him back and forth again, and took up position. He tried to anticipate how she was going to hit him this time around. Judging from her footwork – she was jumping about like a boxer – he suspected she was going to go after him with her bare fists. He felt the rope cut deeper into his wrists. Taking advantage of the backward momentum, he tilted his pelvis and pulled in both his legs. With all his strength, he gave her a good hard kick and hit her chin.

As she fell backwards, the Kalashnikov started clattering and the brawny bald guy hit the ground for cover.

The Russian scrambled to her feet, face contorted in rage. But, to her astonishment, seconds later she felt the barrel of a gun pressed against the back of her head: Dingane's 9-mm Glock.

Her astonishment lasted no more than a split second.

She didn't need longer than that to spin around, duck under the barrel of the gun and give Dingane a sharp kick to the right kidney. She grabbed his wrist with her left hand, and with the right shoved the gun out of his hand. It all happened so quickly that Dingane had no idea her elbow was about to bash his nose.

It took a few seconds for her to catch her breath, evaluate the new situation and draw her conclusions. There were at least two bodies one storey below. The third was behind her, in his blue jeans, bleeding out.

Before her was the man who was responsible for this, lying on top of his Glock.

She didn't need a weapon to finish off Dingane.

A few hard kicks to the skull and larynx would be enough.

Paul saw that she was about to make her move. At that exact moment Dingane raised himself up on his left arm and pulled the trigger three times with his right hand.

The bullet that hit her in the gut must have worked its way through her body and then exited her right shoulder. At the same time, the second bullet pierced her sternum. The third got her right between the eyes.

But she kept standing, her mouth gaping and her eyes filled with a cloudy sort of disbelief, and, while the hail of lead raced through her body, she put one foot before the other, and then again, as if she'd decided to defy the laws of nature and just keep walking.

She sank to her knees and remained motionless beside Dingane. She looked right through him while thin rivulets of dark blood began to flow from her ears. The life drained from her bulging eyes.

As she fell forward she didn't utter a sound.

Dingane rose, moaning, his smashed-up nose bleeding. A red stain started to appear on the right side of his jacket.

'No wonder you have a face like a second-rate boxer,' he said, after he'd used the last bit of his strength to cut down the rope that held Paul suspended in the air. 'Somehow you manage to fight with everyone.'

9

Farah had no idea how long she'd have to stay here. But it was the only option. On a dark and deserted section of the seafront promenade, where cats and dogs prowled around waste containers, he'd opened the boot of the car so she could climb in.

She trusted him. Not that she had any choice. Her contact, who went by the name of Oka Haryanto, possessed not only charm in abundance but also the necessary authority to convince her of the need to take this measure.

She'd smiled when she saw he'd put a blanket and a pillow in the boot. But that smile was short-lived. Nothing could dispel the claustrophobia that had gripped her the second she was shut in. And compared to what awaited her later that evening, this was just a comfortable warm-up.

In her mind, she ran through the most important phases of the plan. As agreed, Haryanto had given her an image of the router. It was tucked into the inner sleeve of the promised Stan Getz album. It was a TP-Link, model TL-WDR3500. She'd taken a picture of it on her mobile and sent it encrypted to Anya.

First thing the following morning, she'd received an email from Moscow containing firmware with a fully adapted Linux operating system, which she was supposed to install on Gundono's router. If she managed to pull it off, from then on all outbound digital traffic from Gundono's compound would automatically be split into two streams: the regular one would go unhindered to the IP addresses, as usual, while a second stream would be forwarded to the central server

Anya was connected to in Moscow. This would allow her to intercept all of Gundono's email traffic.

But to get to that point, Farah had to overwrite the firmware currently on the TP-Link router with what she'd downloaded to her laptop. 'Patching' is what Anya called it. And that patching could only be done in person, with a LAN cable. She had to break into Gundono's compound and get to the router on the fifth floor.

Gundono's gated and heavily secured office was surrounded by tropical gardens that stretched all the way down to the Bay of Jakarta. It was a seven-storey round tower with its stairwells, piping and mechanical ventilation shafts on the exterior. The steel frame made the building look like a futuristic stronghold, especially at night. To reach the fifth floor without being seen either by a patrolling guard or one of the security cameras, she'd have to make her way through the ventilation system. The shafts would be even narrower and darker than the boot of the car.

It was her only option.

Aninda had wanted to come along in the pickup taking her to the promenade where she had transferred to Haryanto's car. But Farah needed that time to prepare mentally for what was ahead. She wanted to concentrate the way she did for a fight: turn completely inward, to focus on the rock-solid core inside herself. And that left no room for anyone else or for sentimentality. Only for willpower and conviction.

'I need to do this alone,' she'd said. 'I don't want you to come along.'

Aninda had quietly held her hands and looked at her as if this might be the last time they'd see each other.

Now, in the dark boot of the car, recalling the sadness in Aninda's eyes and her anxious grip as she pulled her hands away, Farah regretted the flat tone in which she'd told her not to worry, that she'd be back. Then she'd turned and walked to the waiting pickup without so much as a backward glance. Why couldn't she be as candid and spontaneous as Aninda? Why did tears and fear not go together in her mind? Why compartmentalize everything?

The car slowed down before coming to a complete standstill. The engine was kept running. One of the voices she heard was Haryanto's. He sounded just as civilized in Bahasa as he did in English.

'I've forgotten an important report.'

Entering the compound would be the least difficult part of the operation, he'd said in his last conversation with her. His car was rarely inspected.

She heard metal scraping across metal – it was the electric fence opening. The car slowly drove over a bump and stopped soon afterwards. She held her breath.

Haryanto's voice was soft, muffled as it was by the thick leather upholstery of the back seat. He was talking to her.

'Don't worry. Everything's going well, my dear.'

Why would he say that? Why were they standing still? Why didn't he open the boot?

Next, she heard what sounded like a large sliding door opening. Then the car started to descend. She began to worry – not about the plan, but about her own state of mind. Because of nerves, she'd forgotten they'd be going into an underground car park, where he'd place the car in the security camera's blindspot, right by a ventilation panel.

The car stopped. The door on the driver's side was opened, and footsteps could be heard. She braced herself.

As Haryanto opened the lid, he didn't look at Farah, but instead scanned every nook and cranny of the concrete space. They were alone in a deserted, brightly lit garage. This time around there were no Waringin women to protect her, and there was no bustling square where she could disappear into the crowd.

Her legs were trembling when she clambered out of the boot. Then she donned her headlamp. It was small, but its beam was wide. She pulled her rucksack with the laptop and the LAN cable closer to her body. The trainers she was wearing would hopefully provide her with a decent grip on the ridged interior of the metal ventilation system. Finally, she put on her rubber gloves.

Haryanto climbed on to the roof of the car, lifted a panel off its hinges and lowered it cautiously. Then he surveyed the surroundings. Farah joined him on the roof of the car. She somehow had to get into the shaft with a standing jump. Breathing fast and fully focused on the opening, she flexed her knees a few times, and, with her arms extended, swung up and pushed off.

The edges were sharper than she'd expected and she had less of a grip than she'd hoped. She had to hoist herself up fast to make the most of her momentum, but in a controlled way, since the shaft was narrow. Ideally, her head would end up just past the bend in the shaft, so she could squeeze inside without ending up flat on the bottom.

She only partially managed this. She pulled her arms in and continued to hoist herself up until she was completely inside. When she lifted her head, she saw the contours of the narrow tube ahead of her. She heard Haryanto closing the panel behind her. Her heart was racing now and her breathing shallow and ragged. She was locked inside a dark shaft in which every move she made was painful. But there was no way back. Literally. The only way was forward, upward, sideways and then forward again.

*

When she reached the first vertical ascent, she ran into trouble. The angle was so sharp, she could barely worm her way through. The laptop in her rucksack made it particularly tricky. It was a bulky model, not designed for crawling through narrow ventilation systems.

She tried to get as good a grip as possible as she clambered the first three metres up before manoeuvring around a wide bend and proceeding horizontally again along the tower's façade. She became increasingly aware that if she lost her grip and slid, it would not only produce a terrible racket, but also leave her with fractures and severe bruising. Unlike those big slides you see in swimming pools, there was no water here to break her fall – only metal. Aside from what a possible slip-up might do to her body, she also worried about the impact on her laptop – and especially the software she had to download on to the router.

The first climb left her panting for quite a while. She was pleased to have made it out of the underground level, but also acutely aware that each new climb would prove more and more exhausting.

Five more levels to go.

Her movements grew slower, and took on something mechanical in their doggedness. Like a robot made of rusty components, she mindlessly inched her way forward. Despite her headlamp, the fatigue and the darkness seemed to blur her vision, robbing her of any sense of orientation. Her clothes were soaked with sweat.

The secret was in the countdown, in the elimination, she thought to herself, as she slithered up the second vertical shaft. Each metre climbed could be crossed off. Each metre ascended took a metre off the height she had to conquer. Going forward meant leaving more and more distance behind.

She began to keep track. Panting, she counted each metre

she'd crawled. But soon the temporary euphoria began to feel forced. Fear had already taken control of her body, had burrowed its way into her blood vessels and her head, proliferated and spread. She could hear it in her breathing; it had clawed itself into every movement, and despair swept through her mind. She knew she was able to carry on, but with each metre covered she'd be less well equipped to deal with any kind of setback. By the time she reached the panel on the fifth level she was at the end of her tether.

All she had to do was push, Haryanto had said.

The panel was shut tight.

The scream, which she could feel rising up from her toes, was soundless. She froze. All that remained was an emptiness, a sense of futility bordering on insanity. She didn't want to feel anything. She wanted to disappear, be flushed out of this suffocating ventilation system, far, far into a darkness from which she'd never have to wake again.

But she kept breathing, kept thinking. And the thought came to her that perhaps she'd miscalculated. She'd started in the underground garage. She was only on the fourth level. If she wanted to get to the fifth, she'd have to climb another shaft.

She didn't know where she found the energy, the motivation and the strength to start moving again. Not that it mattered. However much further she had to go had become irrelevant. *Keep going* was all she could think now. *Keep going.*

Climbing those final three metres seemed to take as long as all the other vertical shafts put together. And throughout she had to fight the growing urge to let go, simply to let herself fall.

As she crawled through the horizontal section, she could feel salty tears streaming down her sweaty face. She'd lost all faith in a positive outcome. She no longer cared what they'd do to her when she was discovered. If she failed to make it out of the shaft again, she'd yell her lungs out.

At her wits' end, she pushed against the panel.

It gave way and swung open.

The round space in which she was crouched down had walls made of thick glass. The lift shaft was also made of glass, providing a 360-degree view across nocturnal Jakarta, across a coast line full of polluting industries and a sea in which nuclear reactors would be floating in the near future.

She looked up and saw small, flickering LED lights in three locations: the security cameras had been activated. They covered the entire space, Haryanto had told her. But, instead of sweeping the room at cross-angles, they swerved synchronously across the floor, each time giving her ninety seconds to move on a specific path, unseen by the cameras.

Enough to reach the router undetected, patch in the LAN cable and wait underneath a steel desk until all the software had been installed on the router.

The download time was an estimated seven minutes.

Five of those had passed when she heard a loud whirring in the distance. Two razor-sharp light beams cut through the night: the searchlights of a helicopter heading straight towards the tower's landing platform.

The room was bathed in white light. She withdrew deeper underneath the desk and checked her timer.

One minute and thirty seconds remaining.

The whirring became louder. The helicopter slowed down and flew around the tower. She could hear the walls vibrate when the aircraft landed on the platform.

One minute.

The helicopter's rotors were stopped and the engines switched off.

Fifty seconds.

She could hear the lift being activated.

Her mind was racing. There were two options: stop the transfer and get the hell out of there, or – against her better judgement – carry on.

She opted for the latter.

Thirty seconds.

The lift whizzed up, passing her floor.

She looked at the cameras. They began to swerve in her direction.

Twenty seconds.

Gauging the distance between the floor and the opening of the shaft, she figured it was too far to jump. It would take too much momentum to pull herself up and squeeze inside. A chair, that's what she needed. She looked around and spotted one on castors. That'll do, she thought.

Ten seconds.

The cameras swept over the desk she was lying under.

Three seconds.

The lift stopped two floors above her.

Done!

She reset the router, configured the Wi-Fi password to the one at the back of the router, pulled the LAN cable out, rolled it up and put it back in her rucksack with the laptop. Then she crawled to the edge of the room until she was right underneath the open panel, grabbed the chair, stepped on to it, nearly losing her balance because she'd forgotten to lock the wheels.

After she pushed off, the desk chair rolled away against the glass wall and toppled over. She grabbed the edge of the shaft with both hands and hoisted herself up.

The lift whizzed down.

With her head facing the direction she'd come from, she

wriggled into the ventilation system. Then she repositioned her body in the opening, reached for the panel, stuck her fingers through the grille and pulled it towards her.

At that moment the lift doors slid open and the light came on.

Someone entered the room. She lay motionless inside the shaft, trying to ignore the searing pain in her cramped fingers that were holding the panel in place; trying not to think of the chair, which got flung against the glass wall when she jumped.

She saw a man standing beneath her, looking at the chair. She held her breath and her heart skipped a beat when she recognized him.

Gundono.

He picked up the chair and straightened it. Then he moved away from the panel. If he'd waited a second longer a bead of sweat from her neck would have dropped on to his head instead of the floor.

Not long after, she heard the ring of an incoming Skype call. Gundono greeted the caller in English.

The very first reaction of the caller made it clear who he was talking to.

Valentin Lavrov.

His voice sounded tinny and distorted through the computer's small speakers, but no less menacing.

'Everything going according to plan?'

'I don't think there'll be any problems during the vote,' Gundono replied. But she detected a note of doubt in his voice. So did Lavrov.

'Is that what you think, or are you sure?'

'There are a few sceptics in my party, but they can be persuaded.'

'Listen, Gundono, there's no room for doubt. Or risks. I

want you to pull out all the stops to make this work. All the stops, do you get my drift?'

'That sounds like a threat.'

'I don't care what it sounds like. I've got an interesting dossier on you, a long list of shady dealings you've had a hand in. You won't be able to undo the damage as easily as you did with the *Independen*. If I take my information to the *Jakarta Post*, you won't be sitting in that ivory tower of yours for much longer. So you tell me how you're going to fix this.'

Gundono's response sounded measured. And this time around he seemed certain of himself.

'Don't worry. You're talking to a former general, let's not forget that. We're not just talking about your project, but the future of this country. The Army has always determined the course of events here. This will prove no exception to the rule.'

'Arrange it, one way or another.'

'I'll take care of it. Come to Jakarta. We'll celebrate Sharada's triumph, and that of the whole of Indonesia.'

Indonesia's triumph. What did he mean by that? He wanted Lavrov to come to Jakarta. What was he up to?

When she heard Lavrov say that he would arrive in two days' time, she felt the adrenalin surge through her body. She kept very still. Her head was throbbing by the time Gundono broke the connection, got up and headed to the lift.

The lights went out. The lift descended.

She realized that she had to get going, but her body simply refused to comply. The fingers on her right hand were numb. She was holding the panel without any feeling in them. She had to use her other hand to prise her fingers out of the grille, which then swung down with a bang.

She rummaged for the mobile in the breast pocket of her nylon jacket and sent a one-word message to Haryanto: DONE.

The security cameras would have recorded the open panel. The message told Haryanto she'd accomplished her mission and would be on her way back to the garage. He'd carry out a routine check of the building before reporting a loose ventilation panel on the fifth floor.

This time she inched backwards, so she wouldn't be descending the vertical shafts head first.

While navigating the initial shaft she reflected on her good luck so far. Probably the luck of the ignorant. Still luck, whichever way you looked at it. Or karma, as Aninda would say.

By now she'd moved down a floor and crept across the panel she'd mistakenly earmarked earlier as her endpoint. Five more levels to go. Her whole body hurt, but she'd completed the key component of her task. She was determined to see this through to the end, at all costs.

Between the third and second floors the inevitable happened. She slipped and fell. She managed to break her fall by making herself as large as she could, meaning the landing in the bend of the shaft was less painful than she'd anticipated. The only thing she worried about was the noise.

Even though the shafts were on the outside of the tower, the walls were practically soundproof, and the building's air-conditioning was on, she kept as quiet as possible for a while. She'd do the subsequent descents less rigidly by sliding down instead of constantly resting her hands and feet on the ridges.

It got easier with each new vertical descent.

The panel inside the underground garage was open. Haryanto was waiting for her. He was tense. He said it'd been forty minutes since she'd crawled inside the ventilation system, and that he hadn't expected Gundono to come back to the office. But she'd done it, she'd completed the mission.

*

She lowered herself back into the boot. Compared to being stuck in a shaft, it felt luxurious. Haryanto closed the lid, started the engine and drove off. He stopped briefly to wait for the car-park door to open.

When he halted in front of the security fence, her heart was racing. She could hardly believe they'd done it.

The humming of the engine as the car drove across the speed bump, the squeaking of the fence mechanism, the traffic noises outside the compound – it all sounded like a feast to her ears.

The Java Sea spewed white foam across the promenade as she clambered out of the boot on the same spot where she originally got in. Afterwards, Haryanto crisscrossed Jakarta, until they ended up in the heart of the Golden Triangle, where glass banking towers and other business giants competed in silence to be the tallest structure in the rust-coloured evening sky.

Haryanto stopped only when he was absolutely certain they weren't being followed. In front of the immense Plaza Indonesia shopping centre, he looked at her properly for the first time, revealing the intense emotion behind his stoic-looking Chinese–Indonesian mask.

'I didn't want to tell you earlier,' he began, 'but Saputra didn't survive the torture.'

For a moment, the clamour outside appeared to subside. Haryanto took a deep breath. 'But you've ensured that he didn't die for nothing. *Terimah kasih*. Thank you.'

Before she had a chance to react, he got out, walked around to her side and – like a true gentleman – held the door open for her.

'I couldn't have done it without you,' Farah said, after she got out of the car.

'All the best,' he said, and before she knew it he'd disappeared in a nocturnal haze of exhaust fumes.

She looked around. Young men and women in trendy casual wear sauntered up and down the gleaming pavement, on their way to nightclubs, bars and restaurants, which were all brightly illuminated like funfair attractions. The sounds of pumping bass, shrill dance music and plaintive Indonesian ballads poured out through open doors.

She flagged down a motorized taxi, which came to a halt in the middle of the road. When she ran for it, she had to dodge several cars, whose drivers honked their horns and called down hell and damnation on her.

You made it, said the voice inside her head.

You made it.

She still couldn't believe it.

IO

When Radjen arrived at the station, Esther was already waiting for him. She had a file in her hand and motioned for him to step out from behind the wheel. As he did so, she whistled like a construction worker at a female passer-by.

'That suit looks good on you.'

'Is that why I had to get out of the car?'

'No, for this.' She shoved the file at him and got in behind the wheel. 'You read. I'll drive.'

She raced out of the car park and took the roundabout too fast, hurling Radjen, who hadn't buckled his seatbelt yet, against the window.

'I've spoken to Angela Faber. She's agreed to be hypnotized, how about that? But before the first session she wants to get her hair done. Because she's left her husband, the quiz show host. You know, the guy with the orange glow? She wants a new look that goes with her new life. Good God.'

She reached for the file on Radjen's lap with her right hand and turned the front page.

'Now read!'

Radjen saw that it was the case file of Sasha Kovalev, the Russian suspect who'd tried to hijack the MICU transporting Sekandar to another hospital. It was a transcript of the first seven minutes of his interrogation. After that, Detective Joshua Calvino had stopped the recorder and gone to Radjen to tell him the Russian had so much incriminating information he wanted to be placed in witness protection in exchange for his testimony. And, while Calvino was discussing this possibility with Radjen, Marouan Diba smashed Kovalev's head against a table so hard that he'd never be able to give anyone info again.

'What am I supposed to do with this?' he grumbled. 'Because of that guy's death, I'm going to be out on my arse soon.'

'That may well be, but Kovalev is also someone on the lower level of the game we're involved in. He can help us tie some of the loose ends together.'

She turned on to the A10 and glanced at him with an almost triumphant look.

'You once told me about anthills that are all connected to one another, or some such comparison you were going on about? Well, Kovalev is the connecting factor.'

'And how did you reach that conclusion? Female intuition?'

'Go to hell with your female intuition,' she said. 'It's simply called ace detective work. Kovalev was supposed to arrange the meeting between Sekandar and Lombard the night the boy was run down. But he broke all the rules and agreements and did the opposite. I think I understand why, but I need your help with this.'

'What kind of help?'

'I want to see that top-secret skill of yours in action.'

'What do you mean – where are we going, then?' asked Radjen, who saw she was headed in the direction of the Amsterdamse Bos instead of the cemetery on Amsteldijk where the funeral would take place.

'I'll tell you more when we get there – just keep reading.'

Radjen was already familiar with Kovalev's testimony, but, to prepare for what was to come, he gave it another good look. He had to crawl into Kovalev's head – retrieve the images of that fateful night when Kovalev saw the boy for the first time.

Once he'd gone through the file twice, he looked up. They were approaching the driveway of the abandoned villa in the woods.

'I've never done this before,' he admitted as they were getting out of the car, 'with someone else present.'

'Ninjas share everything,' she said with a grin. 'So you'd best get used to it.'

He felt pressured and walked back and forth a few times. Esther hung back and gave him the space he'd asked for.

After a time, he heard the crunching of gravel under car tyres and the sound of the villa's large old door opening. When he looked up, it was dark. There were hardly any lights on in the building. Kovalev was about ten metres away from him wearing a white shirt, black trousers and boots. His long hair was pulled back in a ponytail. He stood motionless in the headlight beams of a fast-approaching vehicle, which came to an abrupt stop a few centimetres from him.

The two front car doors were swung open at the same time. The driver, clad in a black leather jacket and half hanging over the roof of the car, stared at Kovalev, while his mate opened the rear door.

'Two men,' Radjen said. 'One stays beside the car. The other grabs the boy from inside the vehicle.'

'How does Kovalev react to the boy?' Esther asks.

Radjen could see Kovalev freeze.

'As if he's transfixed.'

'What happens next?'

'The first man forces the boy into the villa. Kovalev follows them. After that . . .'

'After that?'

The images became blurry. It was almost impossible to pull them up in his mind and report on them at the same time.

From the villa, a crisp muffled bang sounded and another followed shortly afterwards.

'Two shots with a silencer, from somewhere in the hallway.'

Radjen saw how the driver immediately grabbed for his weapon, walked around the car and fired twice when Kovalev came outside with the boy. The first bullet grazed Kovalev's upper arm and chest. Without thinking, Kovalev pressed the boy against his body in an attempt to protect him.

The second bullet, judging from the sound, lodged in the top of the doorpost. Kovalev took hold of the boy, kissed him, shouted something in Russian and gave him a shove in the direction of the woods. The boy ran towards the trees, while Kovalev tried to cover him.

In the brief silence between the shots, the shrill screech of car brakes sounded.

Followed by a distant and dull thump.

It wasn't much more than that.

But to Kovalev's ears it must have sounded horrifying. Because it came from the direction in which the boy had fled.

In a fit of powerless rage, forgetting the need to take cover, he ran towards the vehicle screaming, while emptying his weapon into the driver, who had nowhere to go.

By the time Kovalev reached the vehicle, the driver was on the ground. He was still moving a bit and mumbled something in Russian. Kovalev leaned over and shot him twice through the head.

From the road came the sound of brakes again. This time higher pitched and more drawn out than the first time.

Kovalev ran into the woods.

Radjen was exhausted and let go of the images. Esther approached him.

'It was a fucking rescue mission,' he said.

Esther gave him a burning cigarette, which tasted like her lips.

'That's why I wanted you to do this,' she said.

On the way to Zorgvlied Cemetery, she told Radjen why she'd sprung the surprise visit to the villa on him.

'It was Kovalev who arranged the encounter, but, from the way he talked about Sekandar during his interrogation, it was as if something broke down inside him the first time he saw the boy. Kovalev must have known what was in store for Sekandar and made a rash decision on the spot. He wanted to save him. But he had to improvise. Kovalev let him get away, and that's why Sekandar was hit by a car. And ironic-ally enough, by the very person Sekandar was meant for.'

'Tragic,' Radjen said. 'But I still don't understand why that makes Kovalev an important link here.'

'Between that night at the villa and the evening Diba bashed in his brains, a MICU was hijacked and, in a separate incident, a doctor killed. Kovalev was involved in both attacks and could be the link to Lombard too. That's all being looked into at this very moment.'

'By whom?'

She threw him a stern gaze.

'Laurens Kramer.'

He felt his temples throb. 'On whose orders?'

'On my orders.'

'So now, without consulting me, you got the cavalry involved.'

'Hold on. Laurens is the only one who can help us here. I asked him to put everything aside today so that we —'

He didn't let her finish. 'You went behind my back.'

'You were passed out on my sofa.'

'Ah, I get it. You spared me the trouble.'

'No, I was just doing my job. Like we agreed.'

'And what did we agree on? I just heard someone whining that ninjas share everything.'

'The pot calling the kettle black. You go poking around a crime scene in the middle of the night, without informing me. And then you have the audacity to criticize me for bringing on board one of the best digital detectives the department has. Give me a break.'

'I'm still your boss and you should have asked for my authorization.'

'You don't want to use that tone with me.'

'It's the tone of your superior.'

She drove off the road on to the verge, slammed on the brakes, flung the door open, stepped out and slammed the driver's side door. Above the noise and occasional honking of the other cars on the motorway, he could hear her swearing as she continued through the high grass alongside the road in the direction of the woods.

Radjen watched her walk away, all in black, her hair tousled by the wind. He thought about getting behind the wheel, putting his foot down on the accelerator and leaving without saying a word. Getting away from everything he couldn't come to terms with. Anything was better than getting out of the car, running after her and saying he didn't mean what he'd just said.

But that's exactly what he did.

She rubbed her face, ran her hands through her hair a few times and took a few deep breaths.

'You're an ungrateful mongrel, really. It's true what they say.'

'What do "they" say?'

'You push the people who work for you to the brink, but once the case is closed, you quickly forget what they did for you. Because then you're already up to your neck in the next case. You don't give a damn about people. As long as you're working on something and you can be the boss.'

'That's nonsense.'

'Oh, yeah? Isn't that exactly what's happening now? I do something you don't like and . . .'

'No! It's different with you. It's . . .'

'What?'

'I mean . . . I really enjoy working with you.'

'Well, it doesn't show.'

'It takes some getting used to, this.'

'What do you mean by "this"?'

'How you . . .'

'Try finishing a sentence, man.'

'How you . . . how I . . . well . . . Damn. I'm sorry, Es. Really.'

He'd never felt so exasperated. And apparently it showed. Her angry eyes softened.

'C'mon,' she said, as she gave him a gentle shove towards the car. 'It would certainly be a shame not to put that fine suit you're wearing to good use.'

A few kilometres outside Johannesburg, the rain clattered on the roof of the Toyota Cressida. The ash-grey clouds hung so low around the mountains of mining debris that Paul felt like he was driving through an endless tunnel. No matter how firmly he clutched the wheel, his hands wouldn't stop shaking. As quickly as possible, he tried to pass all the taxi vans, four-wheel drives and lorries crammed full of goods, but the bad weather on the busy four-lane motorway made these kinds of manoeuvres perilous.

He glanced at Dingane, who was slouched in the seat beside him, heavily perspiring and wheezing. He had the blank look of someone who was half in another dimension. The dark-red stain on the right side of his shirt continued to grow in size.

'I should take you to a hospital,' Paul said.

'I killed three men and a woman,' Dingane muttered. 'Two of them were probably PIU agents. I'd never leave a hospital alive.'

After finding their way out of the high-rise flat via the stairs, Paul had needed to support Dingane, who'd barely been able to walk as they'd stepped over the lifeless bodies of the blue-suited man and his companion. Dingane had given Paul a quick recap of what had happened to him when they'd parted ways at the Hut. He'd waited for the Land Cruiser. When it passed him for the third time, he decided to follow it on foot. This was possible only because the traffic had come to something of standstill. The man in the blue suit and his mate had finally parked the Land Cruiser in front of the building where Dingane had rescued Paul at gunpoint.

The painted cooling towers of the coal power station in the South-Western Townships loomed in the distance.

Paul drove across the bridge at the corner of Klipspruit Valley and Khumalo Street. They passed the stone statue of a little boy in an old-fashioned school uniform with a raised arm, smiling at everybody who came by. The statue had been erected as a memorial to the children who had died there in a 1976 massacre carried out by the apartheid regime's riot police.

Following Dingane's instructions, Paul drove on from Khumalo Street, past the small houses – some made of stone, some of corrugated metal and discarded wooden pallets – and along the *shebeens*, those local pubs with their colourful façades, arriving finally at one of Soweto's most famous spots, Vilakazi Street. The vendors, who usually had their overabundance of handcrafted souvenirs displayed for the many tourists who visited Soweto, had thrown large pieces of plastic over their wares. They were huddled under makeshift awnings, shivering and smoking cigarettes together. The tourists had found shelter in the many restaurants along the street or taken refuge in one of the museums, such as the former home of Nelson Mandela.

At the corner of Moema Street and Vilakazi Street, Dingane indicated that Paul should stop.

'You drive like an old woman,' he said. 'But at least you got us here.'

Paul saw a house painted pink, surrounded by a white latticed fence, and noticed some movement behind the windows. Soweto's busiest street didn't seem like the most obvious choice for a safe house, but he knew Miriam Zhulongu had powerful friends. As a high government official, her husband had worked for the Ministry of Defence, and Miriam herself had worked for years as a doctor for the Tutu Foundation. It was Leah Tutu, the wife of the renowned Archbishop, who had taken Miriam under her wing after the violent death of her husband, which Paul had recently witnessed. It had been a deliberate choice not to send Miriam and her children off to some secluded hiding place, but to keep them right here in the public eye, under the protection of round-the-clock bodyguards. The idea was that the PIU wouldn't dare to harass her again while she was living here, at least not for the time being.

Two men came out of the house and approached the Cressida.

'Are you going to be okay?' Paul asked.

'Don't worry, they'll arrange someone to patch me up,' Dingane mumbled.

Paul put his hand on Dingane's left shoulder. 'You saved my life. I don't know how to thank you.'

'A matter of *Ubuntu*,' Dingane said. 'You would have done the same for me, right?'

'Well, I don't know about that,' Paul said with a wink. Then he addressed Dingane seriously. 'Take care of yourself.'

One of Miriam's bodyguards opened the door on Paul's side. The other was already bent over Dingane, checking how badly he'd been wounded.

Paul got out. He watched the car with Dingane and the guard until it was out of sight. Only then did he turn towards the house, where a woman was waiting for him in the doorway.

Miriam Zhulongu was a tall, slender, attractive woman with high cheekbones, a sensual mouth and dark-brown eyes that radiated both strength and compassion. She had a natural grace about her, but her affable smile struck him as merely polite – maybe because he found her striking beauty rather intimidating. Her handshake was as firm as her gaze.

The house was sparsely furnished. The table in the living room was covered with sheets of drawing paper, markers and crayons. Miriam showed him a drawing of a man, a woman and three small children. A family portrait of colourful stick figures with faces as round as pumpkins. He was struck by the large sun hovering over their heads.

'They've made hundreds of drawings like this,' Miriam said. 'One after the other, with that sun overhead. It's their way of coming to terms with their father's death.'

'I greatly appreciate that you want to do this,' Paul said.

'It was his express wish,' Miriam Zhulongu said. She lovingly glanced at the drawing. 'Colleagues and friends often remarked that Thaba was so serious, but when you saw him with our children . . . He was the funniest father in the world. And he was caring, so caring. I used to say, "You're too kind for the world," and then he'd laugh. "I'm not so kind," he'd say, "it's just that the rest of the world is basically unkind."'

She gestured to the table, where they awkwardly sat down facing each other. She frowned.

'I want to ask you something, Mr Chapelle, and I want you to answer me honestly.'

'Of course, I will.'

'You were there, for the last moments of his life.'

Paul nodded.

'What I want to know is . . . Was he already dead? Before they . . .'

He looked at her in surprise, and for a moment didn't know what to say. 'Why do you want to know this?'

'My husband was not a fighter, but he had his principles. He stood up for what he believed in. It cost him his life. Thaba was my hero. I want to know how my hero died.'

Paul looked at her long and hard. In these kinds of circumstances he'd normally lie through his teeth. But this wasn't a woman you lied to. Not telling her the truth would be tantamount to not taking her seriously.

'They tortured him,' he said hesitantly.

'How did they do that?'

He paused and tried to hide how ill at ease he felt. 'They tied him to a pillar,' he finally said. 'They beat him repeatedly until he passed out.'

'Did he say anything?'

'You mean did he tell them things?'

'Yes.'

'I can't imagine. Otherwise –'

'Otherwise what?'

'They needn't have kept beating him.'

The silence that followed made them both uneasy; it lasted for an unbearably long time.

'The government first tried to convince me it was suicide,' she said.

'That's a lie.'

She looked at him questioningly. Paul thought about how to give her a truthful version of what had happened that would be more bearable than what he'd witnessed in person. 'They . . . pushed him,' he said finally.

She lowered her head and covered her face with her hands. Even now she looked elegant, but he realized it was a gesture of quiet desperation.

'I'm so sorry that I had to tell you all this,' he said, when she looked up again.

'No, no, don't be sorry.' She placed her hand on his. 'I wanted to know the truth and now someone has told me. I'm thankful to you.'

'You must have loved him very much,' Paul stammered.

She smiled. 'I still do. And I'll continue to do so for the rest of my life. Alongside of grieving for him. If I no longer grieved for this great loss, then with Thaba's death I would have also lost the capacity to love. It makes no sense to continue fighting what you cannot change. Contrary to what people think, I harbour no resentment against those who killed my husband. I just want the truth to come out.'

No anger, no revenge. Somehow, Paul wasn't even surprised by the fact that she felt this way. In her eyes, perhaps forgiveness was the most dignified form of self-preservation. Without forgiveness she would also fall victim to those who had killed her husband – and that would deprive her and her family of a future.

'I want to raise my children as proud South Africans,' she said, as she stood up.

'That's my mission. Yours is reveal to the public what my husband wanted to give you.'

She went over to a cabinet and pulled out a jewellery box, from which she removed a USB stick and handed it to him.

'Thaba gave me love, happy years and three beautiful children. I want them to grow up with what he taught them and showed them of the world. I want them to grow up in a country that still holds the promises of equality that Mandela believed in. I want to make sure that my husband didn't die in vain.'

Paul stood there with the USB stick in his hands, feeling a bit anxious.

Exposing the corruption of the soon-to-be South African President was no longer Paul's priority. His objective was to expose the global criminal network Valentin Lavrov had masterminded. Thaba Zhulongu hadn't died in vain, no. But he didn't have it in his heart to tell Miriam Zhulongu that the main reason he'd come to see her was because he needed this new information to help a woman who was still tainted by suspicions of being a terrorist.

A woman who meant more to him than he cared to admit.

After he'd said goodbye to Miriam Zhulongu, one of her bodyguards took Paul to the trusted neighbourhood clinic where Dingane had been admitted. South Africa never ceased to surprise Paul. Thanks to widespread idealism, what had once been a local GP's office had developed into a huge health centre with an HIV outpatient clinic, a radiology department and nutrition centres with vegetable gardens and a plant market.

The bullet had gone straight through Dingane's shoulder, said the nurse who escorted Paul to the room where Dingane was recovering from emergency surgery. Even though he'd lost a lot of blood, there was no irreparable damage to the bone or muscles.

'You didn't have to come visit so soon,' muttered a pale Dingane, who was trying to use his laptop with one hand.

'You didn't have to save me,' Paul replied.

'Of course I did,' Dingane said. 'Matter of self-interest.'

'So nothing to do with *Ubuntu*?' Paul asked.

'I suppose a bit of both,' Dingane replied. 'I got word on the identity of the woman I killed in the flat in Johannesburg. Natalya Yegorova. She was head of Lavrov's security for a time. Expert in martial arts and Russian Pencak Silat champion.'

Now Paul knew why this woman had looked so familiar to him. On Farah's white board in Edward's office hung a poster of the Pencak Silat Gala that had been held at the Carré Theatre; Natalya's photo had featured prominently.

'Did you get what I dragged you back to South Africa for?' Dingane asked.

Paul showed him the USB stick on which Thaba Zhulongu, according to his widow, had painstakingly gathered all sorts of documents. These proved without a shadow of a doubt that AtlasNet had bribed the future President of South Africa with weapons and money to the tune of at least one hundred million dollars in exchange for mining concessions of uranium and thorium, without restrictions.

'You know,' said Dingane, 'not so long ago the ANC informed us that there was not enough money to provide medicine for the six million HIV and AIDS patients in this country. Now that I know how much money Nkoane pocketed, I hold him personally responsible for the deaths of three hundred thousand people to whom he denied anti-retroviral treatment.'

'Why don't you worry about getting back on your feet first?' Paul said.

'Deal,' Dingane said. 'If you get the hell out of here with that USB stick!'

'I know when I've worn out my welcome,' Paul said, as he grabbed Dingane's left hand and gave it a firm squeeze to say goodbye.

He then took a taxi to Lanseria Airport, just north-west of Johannesburg. After the incident that afternoon in the high-rise flat, it seemed a lot safer to make his way back from a small private airport.

He chose a flight to Gaborone, the capital of Botswana, where he would change planes for Amsterdam.

Through the airplane window, he saw the last lights in the night-time landscape being extinguished. Myth would have it that death was always good for one thing: it freed the soul from the body. And that soul went to a world where flowers bloomed in an abundance of beautiful shapes and colours, and where friends, family and the ancestors who had gone before you were waiting to lovingly receive you in their arms. Paul still had this inner longing to believe in these comforting stories.

But they were invented by the living, those who'd never experienced death from the other side.

12

The exhaustion that had almost proved fatal in the ventilation system of Gundono's compound seemed to disappear when she saw Aninda standing at the entrance to the Waringin Shelter. Farah hugged her, and held her for a long time.

'I so wanted to help you,' the young woman muttered.

'I know,' Farah whispered, and wiped the tears from Aninda's face.

'Satria is waiting for you,' Aninda said. 'She'd like to see you right away.'

'I'll go to her,' Farah said with a reassuring smile. 'Why don't you get some sleep?'

When she entered the courtyard, the old woman, barefoot and dressed in black, was standing under the weeping fig in the light of a dented oil lamp. Old as she was, when she moved she looked like an ageless dancer who seemed to shrug off gravity with slow, yet nimble moves. She concluded her sequence with a lengthy, static pose, which bore a strong resemblance to a flower opening.

She greeted Farah with the Pesilat salutation.

'*Kamu sudah berhasil*,' she said. 'You did it.' 'Sometimes it takes an outsider to do something that nobody else is capable of. Breaking into the compound was just the beginning. I've waited up for you to prepare you for the next battle.'

'But how did you know I –'

'Some things you just know,' the woman replied. 'You don't have to understand. Knowing is enough.'

'But what's the next challenge?'

'An impossible challenge. At first sight anyway. Appearances can be deceiving. But show me what your father taught you.'

'How do you know my father –'

'My dear child, if you insist on asking all these questions, we won't get anywhere.'

'My father taught me to be hard.'

'Hard?'

'Like a rock. "Take up your position," he'd say. And then I'd take up my position. Sometimes with my arm held out, at other times with my leg put forward. And then I had to block his kicks and punches. It was incredibly painful, but I didn't want to disappoint him.'

'What techniques did he teach you?'

'All kinds of kicks and punches, and he taught me keep moving forward, intercepting, attacking. Never stop attacking. Retreat equals surrender.'

'Show me how you attack,' Satria said.

Farah assumed her starting pose, took a deep breath, stepped forward and lashed out with her right arm. Satria effortlessly grabbed her fist and took a step back, using Farah's momentum to pull her along. At the same time, she pinned down her arm.

'Let's try that again,' the old woman said, as she let go of Farah's arm.

Farah attacked even more forcefully this time, but again Satria managed to block her with seemingly great ease.

'Again.'

With an even sharper punch, followed immediately by a fierce kick, she initiated her third attack. She used her fists and elbows, her knees, legs and shins. She kicked and punched while always observing her father's golden rule: one step, one blow. Each step accompanied by a blow, and each blow intended to hurt the other as much as possible.

But Satria simply let her approach before stepping forward and intercepting each kick or punch with her open hand. She brushed them aside, one after the other, the way you swat away annoying flies. She seemed to intuit each and every move before Farah even made it. She was at least eighty, yet she fought like a twenty-year-old. She drove Farah back, little by little, and then locked her in a stranglehold.

'You've got many skills, my girl,' she said. 'But you practise them from the wrong conviction.'

'What do you mean?'

'Your father trained you like a man. And that's how you've been fighting your whole life. You've specialized in *serak*, one of the most powerful attack-oriented forms of Pencak Silat. But a true Pesilat is someone with both a noble mind and a noble character. A warrior with inner peace and mental balance.'

She gave Farah a penetrating look. 'If you want to become such a warrior, you'll have to forget what your father taught you.'

'Impossible.'

'In that case, you'll soon be dead.'

Satria's words took Farah's breath away. She averted her head and looked towards a motionless silhouette under the weeping fig. He must have been there all along, in the camel-coloured linen suit he'd worn the last day she saw him. He was still wearing it after all these years, and probably always would in her memories. Now he took off his jacket and hung it on one of the tree's branches, just as he did every morning in the walled garden of their house in Kabul.

She thought about everything he'd taught her. Morning after morning.

'*Satu, dua, tiga . . .*'

It had occurred to her before that he'd chosen the spot on

purpose, because she could see him quite clearly from her window. He knew how curious she was, how much she looked up to him, how many excuses she invented just to be near him. He must have known that one day she'd join him there, under the old apple tree. And when she was finally ready to show him what she'd learned by watching him from afar every day, he'd bowed to her.

That bow seemed to say that he'd been right all along. From that moment on, father and daughter were forever bound by an unspoken agreement, by secret rituals. Now she'd have to forget that bond to save her life.

He was still standing there. She looked at him. Normally she bowed to him. Not now. This time she just stood there, watching him silently.

He lifted his suit jacket off the branch and put it back on. Then he slowly turned and walked away. His silhouette faded against the dark courtyard wall.

She turned back to Satria.

'I don't want to die,' she said. 'Teach me.'

13

Thomas Meijer was buried in a coffin made to look like a shiny black Mercedes. Six men, who were almost dancing carried it on their shoulders to his grave. A line of high-spirited grieving Ghanaian women and men followed them, all dressed in black, brown and red. Radjen and Esther watched the exuberant procession pass by on Zorgvlied Cemetery's winding main path.

To Ghanaians, the number of people who come to mourn for you indicates how important your life has been. In the case of the unassuming Meijer, Radjen estimated that there were as many as a hundred people present. Probably no more than a handful had actually known Meijer. It was Efrya's circle of friends and acquaintances who'd gathered here today in the festive mood of mourning.

Apparently nobody outside her circle wanted to be associated with a man who'd run down a child while driving one of the ministry's vehicles.

An exception to this was an indomitable-looking middle-aged white woman in a classic black suit at the end of the line. Radjen first thought she was from the funeral home, but she nodded to him and Esther the moment they joined her in the line. She seemed rather relieved to be flanked by two other white individuals, even if they were strangers.

Radjen saw the look in Esther's eyes and now understood why she'd been so set on attending this funeral. The woman, who obviously knew Meijer, hadn't come to light during the investigation into his suspicious death.

The procession came to a halt. Everyone made a semi-circle around the grave. The bearers sunk to their knees, placed ropes through the handles of the coffin and slowly lowered it into the three-metre-deep grave. A group of women sang a song. Though Radjen couldn't understand the words, he still found it deeply moving. As if he were listening to the rhythm of his own life, which raised its voice in lament and momentarily lifted his spirit out of its everyday grind.

When the coffin bearers pulled up the ropes again, Efrya Meijer stepped forward and spoke some calm words of farewell to her husband. For a moment, it felt like the world held its breath. It was so quiet that in the pauses between Efrya's words, Radjen imagined he could hear his blood rushing through his veins.

As a farewell Efrya threw a handful of earth on the coffin. Then the sound of crying and wailing from the crowd swelled, and the others took turns throwing handfuls of earth on to the roof of the Mercedes as well.

Crying, singing and sometimes dancing, the mourners slowly streamed away from the grave until only Efrya remained. She stood there so motionless that Radjen thought she might never move again. He walked up to her and shook her hand. It was different from the way he'd done this in her bedroom. That night, her hand had been helpless and warm. But now it felt cool to the touch and strong.

'I'm very sorry about what happened, Efrya, and I wish you all the best,' he said.

She was standing right in front of him, but he was looking into the eyes of a woman who was somewhere else entirely. She gave him an understanding smile.

'I've released his soul to the spirit world,' she said. 'Maybe you should do the same?'

She let go of his hand and walked away from him. She was

soon encircled by a group of women who escorted her along the tree-lined path in the direction of the exit.

Radjen glanced into the grave and then looked at the leaden-grey sky, as a flock of geese flew past. He thought about what he'd read in Meijer's case file: 'Obedience is your greatest virtue. I always believed people got their just desserts if they'd been obedient.'

Obedience as the greatest virtue. You spend your whole life being humble and compliant, and you end up in a coffin with fake wheels that takes you on a last ride to the hereafter, Radjen thought.

The phone in his pocket started to vibrate.

Laurens Kramer didn't ask if he was disturbing him. He never did. If Kramer rang, you'd be better off picking up. Kramer never left a message nor did he call back again.

'I've had a good look at Lombard's telephone calls the evening of the hit-and-run, as you requested, Chief.'

'And?'

'He didn't call home that night. At least not from his apartment phone in The Hague, and not with his mobile phone.'

'Any other ideas?

'Perhaps using a talking drum or smoke signals, but not through any other channels I can check.'

'So?'

'What more can I say? I'm a digital detective, not a fortune teller who reads tea leaves.'

'Okay, Kramer, thanks.' He hung up and went over to Esther, who was now speaking to the woman in the suit. She introduced her to Radjen as Astrid van Woerkom.

'I'm the coordinator of Haaglanden Facility Management, the governmental organization that dispatches all of the ministry's drivers,' said the woman, as she shook Radjen's hand. 'Please call me Astrid.'

'Nice to meet you, Astrid,' Radjen said. 'I think you're the only representative from The Hague here.'

'We were actually advised not to attend,' Astrid said. 'But I originally hired Thomas, and he was one of my most reliable drivers. Even if he did what the authorities have claimed, it didn't seem right to let him leave our midst without paying my respects.'

Radjen remembered how he'd stayed away from Marouan Diba's farewell ceremony and said, 'That's kind of you.'

Esther gave him a pointed look.

'Astrid here was just telling me how she was immediately suspicious when Meijer informed her about the damage to his car.'

'Usually I don't make a fuss about damage claims,' Astrid explained. 'But I instantly knew something was wrong. Thomas was a very careful man, and throughout his time with us he never damaged any of our cars. I was completely confident that if he ever did, he'd report all the details at once. Now he tried to convince me that he'd taken a turn too widely and he'd hit something. He claimed he didn't know where it had happened. It was one of the few times I've slammed my fist on the table, and the only time I've ever got angry at him. I told him he shouldn't lie to me.'

'And then?' Esther asked.

'Then he told me what had happened.'

'Also that Lombard was in the car at the time?'

Astrid van Woerkom nodded.

'What did you do then?' Esther asked.

'I conferred with my boss, the Secretary-General.'

'Why didn't you go to the police?' Radjen wanted to know.

'There was the possibility that a minister was involved. I

357

felt that I first had to report this internally to the person ultimately in charge.'

'How did the Secretary-General respond?' Esther asked.

'He said he'd look into it, and, due to the seriousness of the matter and the possible involvement of a minister, he suggested I keep it to myself.'

'Didn't you think of your civic duty at the time?' Radjen asked.

Astrid peered at him. 'Of course,' she said. 'But you must understand that I . . .' She looked the other way as if she were ashamed of what she was about to say. 'There's a strict hierarchy at Haaglanden. My drivers and I, we're at the very bottom of the ladder. All of our drivers are supposed to keep their mouths shut about what happens in the back seat of their vehicles. WikiLeaks would be considered child's play if the chauffeurs working for us revealed what they knew. See no evil, hear no evil, speak no evil. That's what we advise our drivers. Ultimately, I'm the person responsible for them. I don't want to be a whistle-blower.'

Radjen was silent. He felt as if his heart had turned to glass, and Astrid van Woerkom had shattered it with her honesty. He'd been successfully fighting crime for years now, but in his private life he'd long buried the most basic of feelings, pretending certain things hadn't happened, in the same way that the ministers' drivers habitually turned a blind eye.

'How was contact between Meijer and Lombard?' Esther asked.

'In general, Lombard wasn't particularly friendly to his drivers.' Astrid said. 'And Thomas wasn't exactly the life of the party.'

With a slight head movement in Esther's direction, Radjen indicated that he wanted to leave. He noticed that his chest was beginning to fill with a sickening kind of heaviness. He craved a cigarette.

With a subtle arm gesture, Esther invited Astrid to accompany them to the exit.

'How many drivers does Lombard use?' she inquired.

'I usually schedule three.' Astrid said. 'But I'd say that Meijer drove the most shifts over the past year and a half.'

'How is it possible that the contact between Lombard and Meijer was so distant that even Lombard's wife didn't really know who Meijer was?' Esther asked.

Astrid van Woerkom's answer was almost casual, but Radjen felt as though a slight shockwave went through his body.

'What makes you think that? I saw them together not that long ago.' In the ensuing silence, the gravel crunched under their feet.

Then Radjen asked, 'When was that?'

'About ten days ago.'

'And where exactly?'

'Downstairs, at Economic Affairs, I mean. In the car park used by the drivers. They didn't notice me. They were talking to each other. She pulled something out of her bag and gave it to him.'

'Did you see what it was?' Esther asked.

'No. My view was obscured by one of the vehicles. Then Thomas got into his car. He was supposed to pick up Lombard from Parliament and drive him to Groningen.'

'And you're absolutely sure they didn't see you?' Esther asked emphatically.

'Absolutely,' Astrid said with complete resolve.

They'd reached the arch by the cemetery entrance, where Astrid removed her business card from her handbag and handed it to Esther. 'I'm late and I have to hightail it back to

The Hague. If you have any more questions, you know where to find me.'

She shook hands with them, wished them success with their investigation and strode back to her car.

Outside the cemetery, there was an enormous chaos of double-parked and honking cars filled with exuberant Ghanaians. The next funeral procession was already approaching from a distance. The dreariness of the day was reflected in the jet-black hearse in the lead.

'What kind of coffin would you want to be buried in?' Esther asked, as they walked back to their car, smoking cigarettes.

'Forget a coffin, I want to leave this earthly realm in a rocket,' Radjen said. 'Be launched, up through the clouds into the stratosphere. And you?'

'I want a boat: to go the way the Vikings did long ago. Float out to sea on a bed of branches. And then a fiery arrow is shot from the shore and in open water I go up in flames. I can't think of a more beautiful ending.'

She flicked her cigarette away, opened the door on the driver's side, got in and punched Lombard's address in Blaricum into the car-navigation system.

To each his own, Radjen thought, as he collapsed into the seat beside her. He couldn't shake off the despondency he felt in his chest. It was like all his energy had seeped from his body.

This was exactly the reason why he never went to funerals.

Dead bodies at a crime scene were never a problem. But as soon as they were laid out in a coffin and lowered into the ground somewhere, it became a totally different story. The same anxiety he had whenever he completed a case would come into play. Then he needed a new crime, a new violent death.

Because any new case was better than facing the realization that he might actually need to stop and reflect on his own life, which had reached as much of a dead end as Thomas Meijer's wooden Mercedes.

14

On the plane from South Africa to Botswana, Paul copied all the data from the USB stick to his laptop. Then he got to work on what would be his feature story in the *AND*'s international edition about AtlasNet's illegal practices worldwide.

The exposé would focus on Valentin Lavrov's secret involvement in years of extensive research on thorium, a very profitable raw material. The name of the soft, silver-white metal was derived from Thor, the Norse god of thunder, and it was found in abundance in South African mines. Lavrov had acquired the patent for the latest thorium technology. He'd used bribes and blackmail to influence South African politicians. The objective: to acquire mining concessions for the thorium.

But this wasn't only about mining. The material was going to be used in floating nuclear power stations being planned off the coast of the Indonesian archipelago. If this succeeded, it would be the first step in building new facilities using this technology all over the world. A well-conceived and extremely lucrative plan.

Paul realized that publicly exposing Lavrov's bribery practices could well cause an international uproar, but the effect would undoubtedly be offset by the hype around this ground-breaking technology.

Moreover, AtlasNet was a state-run company, and Lavrov enjoyed the personal protection of the Russian President. Whatever Paul or any other journalist had to report about Lavrov and AtlasNet, it would all too easily be dismissed by the Kremlin as slander from the West. Lavrov wouldn't be hurt in the least. He would keep travelling the world unimpeded, victorious with his new technology.

And as long as that was still going on, Farah had to stay under the radar. Even if it could be proven without a doubt that she'd had nothing to do with the hostage-taking at the Seven Sisters, she was still in danger.

And that danger wouldn't be over until Lavrov was gone. Not a moment sooner.

Paul looked out of the window as the lights of Gaborone came closer and closer. He wondered if it was at all possible to eliminate Lavrov once and for all with the power of the pen.

The answer presented itself sooner than he'd expected.

Just before he entered the gate to catch his connecting KLM flight, he received a phone call from Anya. She'd never sounded as elated as this.

'She did it. That star of yours has managed the impossible. She broke into the stronghold of one of Indonesia's most powerful men. And got away with it. Thanks to Farah, we can now hack into Lavrov's network via Gundono's server.'

'His personal network? Does that mean you can access his financial records as well?'

'Should be possible, yes. Why?'

'If certain cash flows within AtlasNet are not managed the way Moscow would like them to be –'

'So you're saying that Lavrov is doing what so many other oligarchs before him have done: stashing his funds in foreign accounts. Is that what you're hinting at?'

'Yep. Imagine if we could prove that – what would to happen to our friend then?'

Anya burst out laughing. 'He'd be hanged, drawn and quartered. Not publicly on Red Square – somewhere in a subterranean tomb. But his number will be up, that's for sure.'

Paul felt the adrenalin rushing through his body. 'Find the evidence. Follow the money, honey.'

'What was that you said?'

'Follow the money.'

'No, not that Tom Cruise shit. After that!'

'Uh?'

'You said "honey".'

'Yes, you are. If you pull it off, that is.'

'I'm going to chase down that bastard's money, even if it's the last thing I do,' she said, laughing. 'And if I can prove that he has indeed been double-dealing –'

'Then what?'

'Then I want you to come to me and say it again, but this time to my face. "Honey."'

He didn't get the chance to react. She'd already ended the call. But he knew he'd have to keep his word. He owed it to her.

15

The sun must have been high in the sky. It was bursting through the tiniest cracks in the door and the chinks in the closed shutters. It drew sharp lines across the mosquito net suspended over the bed.

It was early morning by the time Farah went to bed. All night, Satria had made her perform the techniques she'd been taught by her father: no longer with physical strength, but with inner conviction.

She had to learn to fight out of compassion instead of anger.

At sunrise, they concluded their session by praying together. It reminded Farah of her first morning in the hotel in the old port of Sunda Kelapa, when she'd opened the shutters and the muezzin at the mosque had sung his call to prayer. She'd only turned to God once in all her adult life, and that was the day Uncle Parwaiz had died in her arms. At the time, she'd knelt down in his apartment and, despite her lack of faith, she'd asked Allah to accept her favourite uncle into His house. It never crossed her mind that one day she'd kneel down and engage in genuine prayer. But now, more than thirty years after her flight from Afghanistan as a ten-year-old, she'd joined an old Indonesian Pencak Silat master underneath a weeping fig. She and Satria faced Mecca, in *sajdah* position, then stood, raised both their hands and together recited Allahu Akbar.

The shrill voices of children rattling off verbs could be heard in the classrooms, and mixed in with this was the monotonous whirr of sewing machines that came from the workshop, where the eldest girls were making new clothes from old remnants of fabric. In the carpentry workshop, meanwhile, the boys were hammering away like players in a marching band.

Her laptop produced a Skype signal. She quickly wrapped a sheet around her body and jumped out of bed. Paul appeared on screen.

'I was really worried about you,' he said. 'And, looking at you now, I'm even more so. You've not joined some cult, have you? You look like a young Indira Gandhi.'

'I'll take that as a compliment.'

'You should, you have her courage,' he replied. 'I spoke to Anya. She told me what you did. Jesus, Farah. I'm speechless. What a risk.'

'What else could I do after Moscow?' she said.

'Well, then, I've got some news for you. Want to hear it?'

'Sooner or later you're going to tell me anyway,' she said. 'So go ahead.'

'The Netherlands Forensic Institute has analysed all the photos I took in Moscow and passed its conclusions to the police. The Public Prosecutor is convinced they're authentic and have not been doctored. Interpol, Scotland Yard and the FBI have since confirmed the authenticity of the photos as well.'

He looked at her expectantly. 'Do you realize what this means?' he asked. 'It proves your innocence.'

It was too much. She could barely take it all in.

'Right, then,' he said, 'let me take it up a notch. The Dutch Foreign Minister has asked the Russian Ambassador for clarification and demanded that his government do every-thing within its power to remove you from the international list of wanted terrorists as soon as possible. All Western nations have already done so.'

'What's the likelihood of the Kremlin complying?' she asked.

Paul looked doubtful. 'Potanin isn't very receptive to appeals from the West. But we've got something that could exert extra pressure on him. Anya found another video file in the phone belonging to our so-called black widow – you remember, the one who filmed you on her mobile. In it, she talks about the hostage-taking in the Seven Sisters being a set-up, staged by the Kremlin as a justification for the military interventions Potanin is planning to consolidate his power. The hostage-taking was intended first and foremost to show the Russian people what can happen when homeland security isn't up to scratch.'

'The same strategy that was behind the explosives planted in Roman Jankovski's building?'

'Exactly. If Anya and I hadn't found those bags with RDX the building would have been blown to pieces, and of course the Chechens would have been blamed. But, anyway, thanks to our material, the whole hostage-taking has become rather an embarrassment for the guys in the Kremlin. No doubt they'll be trying to spin it massively in their favour again, but I have a hunch it might work out favourably for you as well. What you need to do now is to report to the Dutch Embassy in Jakarta. Whatever happens next, you'll be safe there.'

Paul's hands disappeared from view. 'But I've got more. Are you ready?'

'What do you mean?'

He brought a little boy into view. As soon as she saw the look of wonder and the pleasantly surprised smile on his face, her eyes filled with tears.

Sekandar brushed his hand across the screen as if he hoped to touch her face.

'I can fly like an eagle,' he said in Dari. 'Every night, I fly to you. And then I protect you.'

'It helped, Sekandar. *Tashakor.*' 'Thank you.'

'Why are you crying?'

'They're tears of joy.'

'I have no more tears.'

'I promised to stay with you. But I'm somewhere else now.'

'When are you coming back?'

She looked at him, slightly flustered. 'Can you keep a secret?'

He nodded.

'You can't tell anyone that you've seen me. Okay?'

'Okay.'

She smiled through her tears.

'*Tu ba khatar dega nesti.*' 'You're safe now. And I'll always be with you.'

'I made Sekandar's transfer to the farmhouse a condition for sharing the information from Jo'burg with the police,' Paul said.

'Why didn't you tell me earlier?'

'I didn't want to disappoint you, in case it fell through . . .'

'What will happen to him now?'

'He'll be given a temporary residence permit based on his medical condition, but then we'll have to find out whether he has any relatives left in Afghanistan and, if so, whether they're prepared to take him in.'

'What if we can't locate his relatives, or if there aren't any?'

'Who knows . . . maybe he'll be eligible for a residence permit on humanitarian grounds.'

An image flashed across her mind – as sudden as it was joyous: Paul, Sekandar and herself, gazing out over the Dutch landscape together.

'So you got your information in Jo'burg?' she asked.

He nodded.

'And?'

'Our Russian friend has a pretty firm hold over the man

who looks set to be South Africa's next President. Lavrov started corrupting Nkoane years ago through secret arms deliveries. That's his method. He homes in on a politician in a key position who can give him access and a leg up in a country where AtlasNet sees a potential for profit or where it can extract raw materials. He makes sure that the official becomes vulnerable enough to blackmail. In Nkoane's case, it was done through money, lots and lots of it, which ended up in Nkoane's Swiss bank accounts via all kinds of clandestine channels. And to put the squeeze on him, Lavrov fed info about how Nkoane came by that money to certain bodies. In this specific instance, the information didn't go to the press, but to the Scorpion Unit, a special crime squad that's investigating Nkoane's cash flows.'

'Now I understand what Lavrov was talking about,' Farah said.

'What do you mean?'

'When I was in Gundono's office, I heard him Skype with Lavrov, who threatened to send information about him to the *Jakarta Post* if he failed to take the necessary action to push the Sharada Project through Parliament.'

'Same strategy, same methods, different country,' Paul said.

'Gundono also said that the Army has always determined the course of events here. And that the implementation of the Sharada Project would prove no exception.'

'Sounds like he's planning a coup,' Paul said. 'It would be a bold move. Imagine if the Army were to step in and declare a state of emergency now, with all the unrest and anti-government demonstrations. All they'd have to do is to dismiss Parliament and there wouldn't be any need for a vote.'

'A win–win situation,' Farah reacted. 'Lavrov gets what he wants, but so does Gundono. He'd declare himself President. It's a horror scenario.'

'But listen, Farah, your job is done. You did what you had to do. It's time for you to go to the embassy.'

'No, Paul. There's more for me to do here. Time will reveal what it is . . .'

'Leave it to Anya and me. We're really close. Let me tell you what Anya and Lesha have been up to. Via Gundono's router, they were able to carry out a digital raid on AtlasNet's central server and install spyware on Lavrov's network. It's only a matter of time now. You mustn't take any more risks, especially not after that break-in.'

'When it's all done, Paul. Only then will I be safe.'

At that point the door was flung open and Aninda came flying into the room like a whirlwind.

'I'm going to take you to someone,' she exclaimed.

'Who?'

Aninda's smile became broader still.

'I can't tell you that. Please, no more questions. Satria has arranged it. Come with me.'

Less than fifteen minutes later, Farah threw her right leg over the crossbar of an old Batavus bicycle, plumped down on the saddle and followed Aninda into the street, which was now full of *warungs* and street vendors, mostly women, preparing food. Everybody was sitting crouched down by the side of the road, laughing and talking to each other. In the dense smoke of cooking oil and frying fat, people were eating off plastic plates and out of small bowls.

She cycled after Aninda, who skilfully dodged lorries, pickup trucks, buses and SUVs, and weaved in and out of the spaces between cars.

They rode past a market where live frogs and birds were tied together like garlic bulbs. And everywhere you looked were tanks with all kinds of fish, cages full of birds, wildcats and tree shrews, as well as crates filled with poultry. They were all more dead than alive. In and among the thundering traffic, sinewy men pulled their carts laden with fruit, fabrics, boxes and sometimes even more caged animals. At each traffic light, barefoot street urchins thrust bottles of water, small bags of roasted peanuts, newspapers and cigarettes at Farah and Aninda.

Through a thick haze of exhaust fumes, they cycled past skyscrapers, through slums, along wide boulevards, and over bridges and viaducts under which entire families lived, right beside open sewers full of floating debris.

At first she'd wondered why they were doing this by bike, but, as traffic became increasingly gridlocked they, the motorbikes and the scooters were able to swerve past the stationary vehicles. Meanwhile, sweat gushed out of each and every pore, and her shirt was nothing but a large wet rag flapping shapelessly about her body.

They carried on cycling through a gently sloping landscape with *kampongs* that went on for miles, until they ended up in a long line of idling, stinking lorries.

Then a dark mountain loomed up ahead of them.

It was at least twenty metres high and made of waste that was being pulled apart by big fluorescent-yellow cranes. Hundreds of masked men, women and children were crouched down on its edges. With iron sticks they prised the plastic loose, which they then deposited in baskets on their backs.

'Welcome to Bantar Gebang,' Aninda said. 'Indonesia's largest landfill. You've told me your story; now I'll show you part of mine.'

They cycled around the mountain. A black fluid seeped out of it, bubbling and emitting fumes. Walking among the stray pigs, chickens and rats, which she'd initially mistaken for small dogs, were mothers carrying babies and men also lugging large baskets with debris on their backs. Metres-high piles of sorted rubbish were stacked up in front of shacks made of sheets of corrugated iron, tin and cardboard.

When a wooden cart full of plastic got stuck in the mud, the women dismounted, rolled up their trousers and, together with a few men, tried to pull it out. The stench was almost unbearable. By the time Farah got back on her bike, her eyes were burning and her nose was running.

'How do people live like this, in this terrible stench, among the filth and the flies?' she asked.

'I was born here,' Aninda said. 'I thought the whole world looked like this. When you grow up here, you picture the world as one big rubbish dump. I didn't know any better. Besides, I hardly had any time to think. I spent all day collecting plastic. Everybody you see here, working on this mountain, will do the same for the rest of their lives.'

Farah braked. Her eyes were burning so badly she was seeing everything in a blur.

'What's wrong?' Aninda asked.

'I feel so ashamed.'

'Why?'

'I always thought I had it tough. But I had a happy childhood. I practically lived in a palace. And to think you were born here . . . it almost makes me weep with shame.'

'Nonsense,' Aninda said. 'I got away. I'm happy now.'

'How did you get away, then?'

'It was Satria's doing. She set up the first school here and taught both boys and girls Pencak Silat. Come, or else we'll be late.'

They cycled a bit further and stopped in front of a small wooden building, which turned out to be a shelter and a school for the children of Bantar Gebang. They walked through a narrow, muddy passageway to a shack, where a man stood watch outside. His size, suit and earpiece all suggested he was a bodyguard. Aninda exchanged a few brief words with him before he checked them both for weapons. Then he allowed them to step through a badly fitted door into the dim half-light of the shack, which was crisscrossed by slender beams of sunlight that looked like lasers.

In the centre of the room she made out the silhouette of a slight, bald man.

Aninda respectfully greeted him: '*Selamat siang, Bapak Hatta*.' 'Good afternoon, Mr Hatta.'

His voice had the sensitive quality of someone who can break iron with his hands through willpower alone.

'I've got the greatest possible respect for my grandmother, Satria, so when she told me to listen to your story I couldn't refuse,' Hatta said. 'Then again, why would I want to meet a woman who, if the media are to be believed, is an internationally wanted terrorist? Please convince me otherwise, Ms Hafez.'

This caught her completely off guard. 'So you know who I am?' she stuttered.

'I can't take any risks. Naivety is fatal in my position.' He said it in a mischievous way. 'But your secret is safe with me. I've got a sneaking suspicion that, like me, you're on the run from the authorities for entirely different reasons than the media would have us believe.'

'That's correct,' she said. 'Together with two colleagues, I'm investigating the Russian industrialist Valentin Lavrov and the illegal strategies he uses to realize his international projects. I came to Jakarta because of the Sharada Project. We suspect that Lavrov bribed Gundono to get it off the ground.'

'Tell me something new,' Hatta replied. 'Here in Indonesia it's become something of a tradition for politicians to strike backroom deals with industrialists who are out for their own greater good rather than the country's. Corruption may well be the most insidious of all wrongdoings in our country. It's a practice that ought to be eradicated, but in most cases there's no evidence whatsoever. And, even if there *is*, the investigators are either bribed, in the best-case scenario, or simply murdered. I'm afraid the Sharada Project is no different, especially after Saputra's death.'

Farah had no intention of giving up so easily. 'The Sharada Project is lethal, Bapak Hatta. AtlasNet has sunk its tentacles into lots of Russian military projects. As early as the 1960s, the company was developing installations for use on board nuclear submarines, like the *Kursk*. And we all know what happened there. It exploded. The entire crew perished. The wreck was eventually raised, but not before nuclear waste leaked into the Barents Sea. If Parliament votes in favour of the Sharada Project, there'll be several small reactors off your coast in a year's time. If something were to happen to one of those reactors, it will spread to another, triggering a chain reaction with devastating consequences.'

'You know I'm an outspoken opponent of the government's nuclear-energy plans. It's why we're meeting here and not at my office downtown. The only way I may be able to delay or even block the project altogether is rock-solid evidence. Can you deliver that?'

'Within the foreseeable future.'

'That assurance doesn't get us very far, Ibu Hafez. If you don't come up with some evidence within the next twenty-four hours, I'm afraid it will be too late. Once Parliament has voted, it will be virtually impossible to block the implementation of Sharada.'

'Gundono has something drastic up his sleeve to protect the project,' she said in another attempt to convince him. 'And, as far as I can tell, it's not just related to the project. He's talking about Indonesia's future.'

Hatta looked at her in shock. 'How do you know?'

'I can't tell you that, but I can assure you my source is extremely reliable.'

Judging by the anxious look on Hatta's face, she knew he took her remarks seriously.

'Could Gundono be considering a coup?' she asked.

'I doubt that a nuclear-energy project alone would be the motivation for that,' Hatta replied. But he didn't sound convinced. It offered her another chance. Probably her last one.

'My colleague Paul Chapelle has proof of Lavrov's practices in South Africa. His modus operandi is to corrupt prominent politicians so he can control them. It's likely that he applied this same strategy to Gundono. Gundono's in a tight spot now. He's got to do something.'

But Hatta appeared to have run out of patience. She could tell from his reaction.

'Ibu Hafez, this evening I have a meeting at an as yet unknown location with fellow party members and the leaders of some smaller political factions to see if there's anything we can do to at least postpone the vote. But we have little hope. It's true that the moderate Islamic movement, the Muhammadiyah, which normally backs the government, has spoken out against the Sharada Project, but it won't be enough. We'll need hard evidence of bribery, so I can get the others on board. I'm afraid you've come here for nothing. I'm sorry.'

In a last-ditch attempt, she grabbed hold of his arm. 'Please tell me where that meeting will take place, Bapak Hatta. I'll make sure I've got enough evidence by tonight for you to convince the others.'

'You're an indomitable woman,' he said. 'I understand why my grandmother sent you to me.' He extricated himself from her grip and shook her hand. 'As soon as the location is known, I'll send you word.'

'*Terima kasih, Bapak Hatta,*' she said.

He left the shack, accompanied by the bodyguard, who'd stood discreetly in the corner the whole time.

She felt her spirits sinking. Paul's response to her question about whether they'd make it still echoed in her head: *I'm sure.* That certainty was rooted in a naive idealism, in the romantic notion that if only you believed in something strongly enough, you'd be able to achieve your ambitions. What on earth had made her think she could go up against a multinational, here or anywhere else in the world?

Her promise to come up with evidence was just as empty and shadowy as the interior of the shack in which they were standing.

16

A broadcast vehicle topped by a large satellite dish was stationed outside Lombard's Blaricum villa. The logo of IRIS TV was clearly displayed on both sides of the mobile television unit. Radjen and Esther parked their car right beside it and entered through the wide-open front door, following the bulky cables running from the van into the hallway.

All the windows in the living room were covered with blackout cloth. Spotlights on heavy tripods created a circle of light in the middle of the room, where three armchairs were positioned. A mannequin had been placed in each chair. The middle figure was bent slightly forward, as if it were about to say something; the left one had its legs crossed and looked like it was waiting to respond; while the right one seemed to just be listening. Men wearing one-eared headsets operated three heavy cameras on castors. Two men with smaller cameras on their shoulders swiftly moved from place to place. Radjen was about to enter the room when a man with the IRIS logo prominently displayed on his cap stopped him.

'Where do you think you're going?'

'Police,' Radjen said, waving his ID. 'Where can I find Mrs Lombard?'

'Nowhere,' the man retorted. 'Mission impossible, mate. This interview begins in fifteen minutes.'

'Listen, friend,' Esther interjected, positioning herself right between them. 'How'd you like to take a ride with me? And I'll show you a good time at the station for obstructing a criminal investigation. Where is she?'

The man rolled his eyes and flexed his jaw in a weird way, as if he needed to swallow something before he could talk. 'In makeup.'

'And whereabouts is that?'

'Upstairs.'

'Thank you, champ.'

Radjen was the first to turn to head back to the hallway. The man sped past them and raced up the stairs. When they reached the landing, they saw him anxiously gesticulating in a large bedroom, where Lombard and his wife were each sitting in front of a mirror having their faces made up with an array of brushes, pencils and small sponges.

Lombard went ballistic when he saw them enter, and rose so unexpectedly that he sent a powder box flying through the air.

'The nerve of you charlatans is astounding!' he shouted as a beige cloud of powder encircled him. Lombard looked like he hadn't slept in days. Rivulets of sweat ran down his forehead, and his eyes were bulging in their sockets. Perhaps a case of tightly wound nerves, but if there was one thing Radjen didn't give a rat's arse about, it was Lombard's present state of mind.

'We have a few pressing questions for your wife,' he said, turning towards Melanie Lombard. She met his gaze with a condescending smile.

'I'll sue you for trespassing,' he heard Lombard say, while the way Melanie Lombard rose from her seat and walked towards him made every sound, every other movement in the room, seem of less importance. In a form-fitting burgundy dress with long sleeves which accentuated her figure, she looked like a woman who could bring a man to his knees. And, even though it was the last thing Radjen wanted, he couldn't deny that he found Melanie Lombard van Velzen quite intriguing.

And, as it so happens, he had a weakness for intrigue.

'Inspector,' she said, with the sensuality of a French chanteuse, 'my husband is under an immense amount of pressure. You of all people should understand this. I suggest we continue our conversation elsewhere. Then my husband can prepare for this television interview in peace and quiet.'

Radjen nodded, and before he knew it she had calmed Lombard down and coaxed him back into his chair, and they were standing in what appeared to be a guest room, also used as a kind of storage space. Opposite a folded ironing board and a blanket box stood a wall unit filled with sailing trophies.

'You told us you didn't know Thomas Meijer,' Radjen said.

'That's right.'

'Then what were you discussing with him ten days ago?'

Melanie Lombard could also have pursued a glittering career as an actress, he thought. In any case, the amazement that appeared on her face seemed genuine.

'And where did this happen?'

'In the car park of Economic Affairs,' Esther said.

Melanie Lombard also looked at her in surprise as if she'd just realized she wasn't alone in the room with Radjen.

'I don't recall, unfortunately.'

'And what you gave to him, you don't remember that either?' Radjen asked.

'Gave? No, I . . .'

Something seemed to dawn on her. She glanced at Radjen with an amused twinkle in her eye. 'So that was Meijer?'

Radjen sighed. 'What did you discuss with him?'

'Nothing.'

'Mrs Lombard, please.'

'I gave him instructions.'

'Instructions?'

379

'He had to give an injection set to my husband. Ewald is diabetic. He was going to be away from home a day or two, and he'd forgotten his insulin syringes. My husband didn't want it splashed across the news that he's been diabetic for about a year and a half. So it didn't seem wise to call a courier. I decided to take what he needed to The Hague myself.'

'Then why did you give the set to Meijer and not directly to your husband?'

'Ewald was in Parliament for an emergency debate. His driver was going to fetch him and take him to Groningen afterwards. I know how discreet and reliable Haaglanden's drivers are. I gave the insulin set to the man who was going to be his driver that day. I didn't know he was Meijer.'

Radjen looked at her in disbelief. She met his gaze with a contemptuous smile and said, 'My husband can corroborate my story.'

'Why doesn't that surprise me?' Radjen said. 'I'm not sure that will be necessary.'

One of Melanie Lombard's eyebrows rose.

'The issue is, you tell us things that at first sight seem clear as day, but as soon as we take a closer look, there are suddenly all kinds of discrepancies.'

'Such as?'

'You told us that your husband called you on the evening of the accident to tell you when to expect him home.'

'That's right, yes.'

'But your husband didn't call you. Not with his mobile phone and not from the phone in his apartment.'

'Correct.'

'So you told us something not in accordance with the truth?'

'You mean I lied?'

'That's another way of putting it, yes.'

'The problem in our communication, Inspector, is that you think we're on opposing sides. You're convinced I'm not telling you the truth. But I'm not your enemy. And if that's how my husband and I come across, it's because of the pressure we're under right now.'

'Then maybe you could improve on that communication by explaining how in God's name you knew what time your husband would be home?'

'Well, God wasn't really involved, Inspector. Ewald and I have a private line: via a prepaid phone. To keep our business and our personal lives separate.'

'Why didn't you say anything about this in either of your earlier statements?' Esther asked.

Melanie Lombard kept staring at Radjen.

'Nobody asked me anything about it. And it didn't occur to me to mention it. Sorry.'

'We'll need to take those prepaids with us,' Radjen said. 'So they can be examined.'

'Certainly.'

Melanie Lombard now looked at him with a gentleness he'd not seen in her and that hardly seemed to fit her personality.

'I'm totally convinced that we got off to a bad start, you and I,' she said, glancing at her watch. 'The interview will start in about five minutes. It's time for me to support my husband. I propose that immediately after the interview I give you the prepaids and you can question my husband about this and the matter of the injection set. Can we agree on that?'

Radjen's eyes sought Esther's approval. Then he nodded.

'I greatly appreciate this, Inspector.'

She glanced at him as if they now shared a huge secret. But there was a discordant tone in the way she exited the room. Radjen noticed that she was very slightly dragging her right leg. A motion in stark contrast with her almost aristo-cratic bearing.

'I didn't have time to tell you,' Esther said, once she'd installed herself next to Radjen in front of the wall of monitors in the soundproofed broadcasting vehicle. 'Your girlfriend Melanie had an accident during one of her sailing trips. Crashed on a reef near Tuvalu, an island in the Pacific. She was seriously injured and spent a few days there wander-ing about until they found her. Her gait is probably related to that.'

He looked at her and said, 'I have a very different idea about who I have a crush on.'

She smiled and said, 'I know.'

On the wall of monitors, Radjen watched Ewald Lombard and his wife take their seats in the left and right armchairs. A tiny microphone was pinned on each of them.

Esther said, 'Good decision of yours, to stick around.'

The director — a stocky, unshaven man, who, with his enormous head of curls and forlorn look, could have just stepped out of an Italian arthouse film — gave hasty instruc-tions to his crew.

Radjen asked, 'What makes you say that?'

The director counted down. 'Five, four, three . . .'

'Just one of my hunches . . .'

'. . . two, one, action!'

'Good evening and welcome to this special edition of *The Headlines Show*,' said Cathy Marant, who, right after 'action', immediately turned to the camera. 'We're here with the cou-ple who've been the talk of the town for the last few weeks.

'Tonight we're going to have a heart-to-heart with them about one of the most turbulent periods in their lives. We'd like to welcome you, Minister Lombard, and your wife to the show.'

Melanie and her husband nodded pleasantly.

'I'd like to start with you, sir,' Marant continued. 'You've put the Netherlands back on the map economically throughout the world, but now you're having to defend yourself at home against the most bizarre allegations from a totally unexpected source.'

The director snapped his fingers and cried, 'Three.' Radjen watched as Lombard appeared on the screen in a medium shot.

'It was like a bolt from the blue,' Lombard said.

The director snapped his fingers and said, 'Two.'

Melanie Lombard appeared on screen.

'At first we didn't know what to say, so we didn't say anything,' she added.

'And camera one!'

'Can you tell me the reason for these outlandish accusations?' Cathy Marant asked.

'To this very day it's still a mystery to me,' Lombard replied. Esther gave Radjen a mocking look.

'It seems,' continued Lombard, 'to have started right after that terrible accident in which a boy was run down by a driver who worked for Haaglanden Facility Management, the organization that provides the chauffeurs that ministers use. The driver concerned brought me home the night of the accident. The collision took place after that.'

'What is even more tragic,' Melanie Lombard added, 'is that the driver left the scene of the accident and eventually took his own life.'

'But why have you been implicated in this accident, sir?'

'Three, zoom in!'

Lombard had undoubtedly been instructed by his spin doctor to act like he was above this all. He had to give the viewer the feeling he was virtually untouchable as a suspect.

But what Radjen saw on the screen was a man with a tense face beaded with sweat. There was no trace of his usual confident smile.

'The driver involved gave a statement to the police in which he claimed that I was with him in the car at the time of the accident.' Lombard said.

'In actual fact, we were here, enjoying a quiet evening in each other's company.' Melanie Lombard continued. 'I testified to this. Is the word of a minister's wife not enough? People often talk about class justice, but here you're seeing exactly the opposite happening. The chauffeur who admitted his guilt was set free and my husband is the one who . . .'

Here Melanie Lombard seemed momentarily overcome by emotions, which she managed to graciously control. With a look of intense compassion, Cathy Marant handed her a tissue, but the minister's wife modestly waved it aside.

Cathy Marant said, 'It must be hell –'

'It's unbelievable,' Melanie Lombard sighed, 'when you know for certain that it never happened. My husband was here with me. However, this hasn't stopped the Amsterdam police from conducting a witch hunt against him. They even raided his apartment in The Hague where he often is for work.'

The director shouted, 'Handheld two on Lombard, stand by.'

Cathy Marant turned to Lombard and asked, 'What was the reason for this raid, sir?'

'And two!'

'Completely without my knowledge,' Lombard said, in an unsteady medium shot this time. 'While I was in Moscow attending an economics summit. According to the police, there were incriminating images on my computer.'

'Go to camera one!'

'But what does that have to do with the accident?'

'Three!'

'Nothing. As my wife already explained. A witch hunt against me is under way.'

'And what kind of images are we talking about?'

'Photos taken by a female artist that are hanging in my office at the ministry. Not only in my office but in the conference room where I meet with top officials from all over the world.'

The director shouted, 'Stand by for stock shot.'

The same photo that had thrown Radjen the first time he'd seen it now filled the screen. The blonde girl with her half-open mouth, swinging back and forth, hanging on a dark rope that was tautly clasped between her legs. And while Lombard talked calmly about how any rational person would find it a complete mystery that, based on such artistic images, he was being accused of possession of pornographic material, Radjen realized that this media offensive had been put together ingeniously. He felt overwhelmed by a sense of powerlessness.

'And one!'

Cathy Marant asked, 'Is it a coincidence that these accusations come on the eve of the parliamentary elections?'

'Three!'

With a trembling hand Lombard sipped some water from a glass. He then took his sweet time dabbing his sweaty face with a handkerchief.

'He doesn't look well,' Esther whispered in Radjen's ear.

'It's an orchestrated plot,' Lombard stammered. Then he looked into the camera as if he were paralysed with disgust.

Melanie Lombard took over.

'Two, zoom in to a medium shot.'

'There is now an official police inquiry into the actions of the Amsterdam investigation team going after my husband,' she said. 'Not so long ago, members of that same team beat a handcuffed suspect to death during an interrogation.'

Meanwhile, Radjen saw that Lombard was writhing in pain.

The director shouted, 'Handheld one and two on Lombard!'

Melanie Lombard seemed to be ignoring what was happening to her husband for the time being and was concerned only with her charm offensive for the media. 'We have been so heartened in the past weeks by the incredible expressions of support we have received. From people who've said, "We believe in you, we have always believed in you." That has helped us through this difficult period.'

Lombard seemed to be gasping for air. He desperately held out his arms, as if he'd gone blind and was grabbing for something to hold on to.

'The guy can't breathe,' Esther cried, and she jumped out of the broadcasting van.

Cathy Marant started to scream as Lombard tried to stand up. Melanie Lombard remained frozen in her chair.

Lombard dropped to his knees in front of his chair and started to vomit.

On one of the monitors, Radjen saw Esther enter the image. She wiped Lombard's mouth with a cloth, quickly laid him on his side in a stable position, shoved her hand into his throat, pulled out the phlegm that was impeding his breathing and indicated with a sweeping motion of her arm that nobody should come near them.

Like a madman, the director kept shouting commands to change the camera angles.

Radjen was interested only in the screen showing Melanie Lombard.

A shadow descended over her face as she observed her

husband's suffering with chilly detachment. She looked like a queen who'd thought she'd found her perfect match in the future Prime Minister of the Netherlands. Now, however, after he'd puked up his guts on the carpet, covered nationwide by five cameras, she couldn't suppress her disgust for him. Was he even refusing to respond to the life-saving lips of a female detective?

Because of the wooded area surrounding the Lombard villa and all the vehicles on the driveway, it was impossible for a trauma helicopter to land anywhere close by. After seven endless minutes, Esther had Lombard breathing on his own, but he hadn't regained consciousness. All that time Melanie Lombard had watched, seemingly unmoved, from a few metres away. Radjen didn't see a trace of fear or despair on her face, not even a sign of gloom or acceptance in what fate had in wait for them. He actually thought he caught a hint of satisfaction in her expression. In any event, her response was not what you'd expect from a woman who'd shouted from the rooftops that she lovingly poured her husband a cup of sleepytime tea while statements from others indicated that at the time he was in a government vehicle that had run down a child.

Only once the paramedics arrived and fastened an oxygen mask to her husband's face did Melanie Lombard finally stir into action. Two handheld cameras followed the stretcher with Lombard's body being lifted into the ambulance. She got in uninvited and sat down beside her husband. She demonstratively took his limp hand and gave it a squeeze.

Cathy Marant took up position in front of one of the handheld cameras, and, as the ambulance raced down the lane with its blue lights flashing and the siren wailing, she flung her unparalleled conclusion at the world.

'And thus the life and perhaps career of our future Prime Minister takes a new tragic turn. This is Cathy Marant for *The Headlines Show*.'

Euphoric cheers sounded from the broadcasting vehicle, followed by the doors being swung open and the director emerging, pumping his fists.

The media world had yet another scoop.

Radjen walked with Esther into the garden.

'You okay?'

She just nodded, pulled a cigarette from her packet and lit it. He saw her hand shaking.

'Well done, quick thinking,' he said.

She inhaled deeply.

'I just hope he makes it, the bastard,' she said. 'We want him in a prison cell, not in a coffin, right?'

Radjen reached for the cigarette packet she was holding in her hand.

'Sorry,' she said, handing him her cigarette instead, and then lit another one for herself.

Radjen walked away from her for a moment and dialled the number of the Public Prosecutor. In brief, he told him that there were still valid reasons to question the alibi Melanie Lombard had provided for her husband. The timing and numbers on the prepaid phones, which had to be somewhere in the house, might be crucial in that regard and he wanted a search warrant.

But the ambitious young prosecutor wanted to do it according to the book.

'But didn't you say that Mrs Lombard had already indicated she would hand over the phones voluntarily?' he replied.

'Given the state her husband was in when he left here, I think Mrs Lombard will be occupied for the next few hours,' Radjen said. 'And because there's a complete television crew wandering around the villa at this moment, the risk of things disappearing is not one I'm willing to take.'

'Given the suspect's influential position, I'll have to discuss this with the Examining Magistrate,' the Public Prosecutor said. 'He'll probably want to be brought up to speed on the matter first. You'll have to be patient.'

Radjen hung up and returned to Esther, who had just stamped out her cigarette on the garden path and blew out a thin line of smoke.

'I'm not waiting for anyone any more,' he said as he brushed past her.

He'd been searching the first floor of the villa for half an hour before he discovered one of the prepaids. It was in the nightstand of a bedroom, which, judging from how it was furnished, belonged to Melanie Lombard. So the Lombards slept separately. Yet another home with two separate worlds, where very little was shared except the same roof.

He wrapped the prepaid in a handkerchief and went back downstairs, where Esther was on the phone in the kitchen.

He heard it in her voice right away. She'd asked Kramer to help them again.

'We can be there in half an hour,' she told him, and quickly hung up.

'Am I invited?' he asked.

'You can come along for the ride, arsehole,' she teased, grinning.

Radjen placed Melanie Lombard's prepaid on the table. 'It was in her nightstand.'

Esther pulled out the prepaid phone she'd found in the drawer of the antique kitchen table and placed it next to the device Radjen had found. They were different colours and different brands.

'Perhaps this means that somewhere in the big bad world partners of these two are floating around somewhere,' Esther speculated.

At that moment, Radjen's phone rang; it was the Public Prosecutor.

'In view of the situation you indicated to me earlier, the Examining Magistrate has approved the search warrant, provided it's limited to the two devices you mentioned.'

'Fine,' Radjen said. 'We'll get to work.' He hung up and looked at Esther.

'Time for a cigarette, then?'

'Not now, Sherlock, time to report to the cavalry.'

17

It was later than Farah would have liked. Much later. The sun had already sunk behind the weeping fig's dense crown of branches.

She checked her watch. It was more than three hours since she'd last spoken to Anya. She'd begged her to use whatever means necessary to come up with something. Anything at all to present during this evening's meeting between Hatta and the other members of Parliament.

But Anya had warned her. 'I'm not a magician; I can't pull a rabbit out of a hat.'

She and Lesha had been frantically trying to access Atlas-Net's financial files. Now, especially for Farah, Lesha was using spyware to get into Gundono's network via the router in his compound. Once he was in, decoding the files could be a slow and laborious process. It looked as if she'd turn up empty-handed this evening.

She walked into the courtyard.

There was a sense of foreboding in the air that she'd experienced before, long ago, in the garden of the presidential palace in Kabul. At that time she'd been too young to recognize the threat. It wasn't until the planes appeared overhead that she realized what was happening.

She looked up. The sky was empty. The sounds in the courtyard were familiar. The weeping fig stood perfectly still in the sweltering heat – like it always had, and always would. Children walked over to the canteen in small groups. Sounds and actions, everyday rituals that would normally be reassuring.

But today they felt like a lie, as if impending doom was sneering at her from behind a mask of familiarity.

Her mobile rang. It was Anya. Lesha had managed to access Gundono's financial files. In exchange for his 'advice' to AtlasNet on the installation of the nuclear power stations, Gundono had cashed slush money worth a cool 3.8 million dollars. The payments from AtlasNet were made via a shell company in Singapore, Mohana Consulting Ltd. Gundono had transferred the money to two different offshore bank accounts in Hong Kong.

Farah was sent screenshots of the bank statements on her mobile.

The road to Hatta lay open.

The youngster behind the wheel of the pickup drove into the labyrinth of Glodok, Jakarta's old Chinese district, as fast as he could. The narrow streets were crammed full of stalls selling traditional medicine, alongside grey concrete shops filled with cheap electronics and small Mazu temples, half shrouded in clouds of incense. The whole scene was illuminated by a blinding spectrum of screaming neon. Through the chaos of hooting cars, cycle rickshaws, impatient pedestrians and pedlars trying to sell their wares, he tried to make his way to the old trading centre, where, as Satria had informed them, Hatta and the other members of Parliament were gathering tonight.

In the rear-view mirror, Farah saw a military jeep approaching at great speed. Its driver sounded his horn and furiously gesticulated for the pickup to move aside, but there was nowhere for the vehicle to go.

'*Lanjut!*' 'Keep driving!' Aninda shouted to the youngster.

They were approaching a junction. The traffic light changed to green, and he floored the accelerator.

The jeep behind them came to an abrupt stop in the middle of the junction. Armed soldiers jumped out, stopped traffic and directed a second jeep followed by an Army truck across the junction and into the street that the pickup had just entered. An Army helicopter whizzed over low in the direction of the trade centre.

Farah knew this couldn't be a coincidence. The helicopter was part of a coordinated attack. Hatta and his close colleagues had been betrayed.

In a flurry of gravel and sand, the pickup came to a halt in front of the old building. The helicopter was hovering overhead. Farah shouted at the young man, telling him to drive around to the back of the building, and then she ran inside.

In the stairwell, she saw Hatta coming down the stairs flanked by two bodyguards. Behind them were about ten other men, presumably members of Parliament. She heard the screeching brakes of the jeep and the shouts of the soldiers outside the front entrance.

'The rear exit,' she yelled.

A strident voice shouting through a megaphone out front ordered everybody to vacate the premises.

'One at a time. With your hands on your head.'

Don't think now – act, run!

Head for the light flooding through the door at the rear.

The pickup was parked at the end of an alleyway. Aninda was leaning out of the driver's cab, telling them to hurry up. Hatta was hoisted into the bed of the pickup by his bodyguards, who jumped in after him. Farah followed suit, and grabbed hold of the edge of the truck to pull herself up. She'd just managed to place her left foot on the towing hook when the young man stepped on the accelerator and drove out of the alleyway. As the pickup swerved into the street, the rubber sole of her trainer lost its grip on the towing hook's ball and she started to fall.

For a split second she hovered in mid-air. Then someone grabbed hold of her.

Hatta.

The second arm that grabbed her belonged to one of his bodyguards.

She flung her right leg over the edge of the tailboard and rolled on to the truck bed, where she lay down, gasping for breath.

The Army helicopter hung right above them. The pickup's engine growled. Then she heard shots and the pickup swerved to the left and clipped a moped with a crate full of chickens on either side. One of the crates came loose and flew through the air amid a furious cackling and a cloud of swirling feathers.

Then there was a second burst of gunfire. Instinctively, she ducked. The rear window of the driver's cab shattered. The pickup skidded to a halt crossways in the street.

All was silent for what seemed like eternity. Then came Aninda's screams. Along with the bodyguards and Hatta, Farah jumped out of the pickup. A gleaming black SUV screeched to a halt beside the vehicle. The doors were flung open. Hatta and his guards jumped into the car, which then tore off again.

Farah yanked open the pickup's passenger door. Aninda was covered in the blood of the youngster, now lying lifeless in her lap. The SUV had already reached the end of the street when they heard the rattle of machine guns. She pulled Aninda out of the cab and dragged her into a nearby alley.

'*Lari!*' she shouted. 'Run! Run as fast as you can.'

As if it were all they'd ever done and would continue to do for the rest of their lives, they ran through the narrow alleys of the *kampongs*. Until they paused for breath in a muddy passageway and Aninda started to vomit.

Sirens could be heard in the distance. An Army helicopter searchlight swept over the rickety corrugated-sheet roofs.

'He was only seventeen,' Aninda said. 'He came from Bantar Gebang, like me.'

Farah put her arm around her as she watched the helicopter fly off in the direction of the city centre. Paul's voice echoed in her head.

Your job is done. You mustn't take any more risks.

'We'd better get back,' she said.

The usually teeming streets were now deserted. Restaurants and shops had rolled down their shutters. Army jeeps patrolled the area.

They flagged down a motorized taxi. The guy at the wheel managed to skirt the checkpoints at the major junctions, all the while keeping an old-fashioned transistor radio clasped to his ear.

'The Army is occupying the Parliament building, Medan Merdeka and the television studios,' he shouted as if providing live news coverage.

In another part of the city, where there was little or no sign of police or soldiers, the nightlife was still in full swing. They stopped outside a restaurant where on several television screens they saw Gundono against the backdrop of the Indonesian flag declaring a state of emergency.

'After weeks of street protests, demonstrations and violence, Indonesia is balancing on the precipice. The arson attacks, vandalism and other disturbances of the peace in our capital are part of a Communist conspiracy. The conspirators are thought to have congregated within the PDI, the Indonesian Democratic Party, led by Baladin Hatta. Since the current government has proved incapable of maintaining order, henceforth the National Council to Restore Order will govern the country and issue new laws. Parliament will be dissolved.'

The horror scenario she'd discussed with Paul: it had become reality.

Half an hour later, they arrived in front of the gate of the Waringin Shelter. It was unusually dark and quiet. As they walked through the passageway to the courtyard, they caught a smothered sob. They stopped dead in their tracks. It was so quiet Farah's own heartbeat sounded like heavy footsteps, her breathing like a man's wheezing and the chirp of a cricket like the click of a revolver.

But when she felt the cold metal of a gun barrel against her temple, she knew that all those sounds had been real.

PART FIVE
Betrayal

I

With the two prepaids they'd found now safely sealed in plastic bags, Radjen and Esther drove from the Lombards' Blaricum villa directly to the station in Amsterdam.

In Laurens Kramer's digital workspace they sat down in front of a computer screen displaying the homepage of an Indian hospital that specialized in complex bone fractures.

'One of Kovalev's last searches on his home computer,' Kramer said.

'I understood that Kovalev erased all of his files?' Radjen asked.

Laurens Kramer laughed. 'When someone erases their hard drive, only the data in the index is removed. The rest of that information actually remains. Compare it to ripping the table of contents out of a book and believing that you've rid the book of all the chapters as well.'

'In any case,' said Radjen, who'd developed a strong dislike for the know-it-all Kramer, 'enlighten me: what's so interesting about the webpage of an Indian hospital?'

Kramer pointed to flight information for an Indian air-ambulance that had landed at Schiphol Airport less than an hour before Sasha Kovalev hijacked the MICU transporting Sekandar to a safer location.

Radjen didn't need to know more than that.

The air-ambulance had apparently been booked to fly Sekandar to Goa, where he would have received further treatment in a specialized hospital.

'This man ordered that jet,' Kramer said, pointing to the

photo of a good-looking Indian man you'd implicitly trust to borrow your car. 'Bikram Shaw, until fairly recently Armin Lazonder's financial adviser. He disappeared right before Lazonder hit rock bottom financially.'

Esther leaned towards Radjen. 'We suspect that Kovalev, together with Shaw, had elaborate plans in India to enjoy all the money he'd undoubtedly accumulated defrauding Lazonder.'

'I see,' Radjen said. 'But that Kovalev wanted to play happy families with Sekandar is what finally cost him his head.'

'Spot on,' Kramer said. 'But there's more, Chief.'

Kramer's fingers flew across the keys of the laptop in front of him.

Radjen saw some of Kovalev's financial transactions whizz by. Kramer pointed to a transfer of twelve hundred dollars for a one-way business-class airline ticket to Haiti. In the name of D. Bernson.

Danielle Bernson. The doctor who had saved Sekandar's life. She'd been richly rewarded by Kovalev, who, on top of that, donated twenty thousand dollars to a children's hospital in Port-au-Prince, where she could have anonymously picked up her life again. However, Bernson never made it to the airport in Amsterdam. She was raped and murdered only a few kilometres from where Sekandar had been found in the woods. There was a sign of tyre marks made by a four-wheel drive at the crime scene. But the rain storm that night had washed away just about everything else.

There'd been a mega pile-up on the A9 the night Bernson was murdered. A four-wheel drive was apparently the initial cause of that accident. A black Touareg had sailed over the railing, plunged into oncoming traffic, only to land on top of a taxi and explode. In what was left of that wreck forensics discovered a Zastava M57 – and the bullets that killed Bernson had come from a Zastava M57.

The face of the man driving the Touareg was burned beyond recognition. What was left of his passport was undoubtedly false. The man was wearing a locket. With a photo of three men. One was identified as Arseni Vakurov, another as Valentin Lavrov. There had to be a much larger organization behind Bernson's murder.

Radjen was still absorbing all the new information he'd just received when his phone rang.

It was Kemper. His boss sounded like he'd just choked on an expensive steak dinner.

'I heard you went back to Lombard's place this afternoon,' he said reproachfully.

'You heard correctly,' Radjen said.

'I've just had word: he's dead!'

2

The gun was pressed against her temple, while a blinding light was shone in her face. A man shouted that it was her, 'the terrorist'.

She heard children crying as she was handcuffed, blindfolded and forcefully shoved into the back of the jeep. One man sat down on each side of her. She caught a whiff of their pungent sweat through the fabric of their khaki uniforms. Her skin was tingling. Before she had a chance to react to Aninda's screams, she was jolted back against the seat, as the vehicle suddenly drove off.

During the drive, she couldn't stop thinking about what Satria had said. *You're on a mission. And you'll have to complete it, however impossible it may seem.* It was something to hold on to. The only thing.

The jeep slowed only to take sharp corners. The men beside her barely moved. Helicopters flew overhead, their noise mingling with that of breaking waves. They came to a halt in front of what must have been a gate in the process of opening electronically. The sound was vaguely familiar to her. When they drove down a ramp, she knew for sure.

She was back in Gundono's compound.

One of the men snarled that she had to get out. A lift door opened and closed, followed by electric whirring. Her breathing was ragged. She tried to keep calm.

The space they pushed her into smelled musty and damp. The relief of having the cuffs removed lasted mere seconds. Almost immediately men grabbed hold of her and placed her on a wooden board. She tried to resist, but it was no use. They strapped down her upper body and hips and then tilted her, board and all, backwards into a diagonal position.

Before he ripped the blindfold from her face, she'd already smelled his musky body odour with hints of mint, lavender and bergamot. The scarcely lit space they were in had a low, vaulted ceiling and was crammed full of dusty Hindu–Javanese statues. Valentin Lavrov's grey-green eyes betrayed a cold-hearted kind of pity.

'The boy in the pickup was easy to trace to you, *moya milochka*. Too easy, really. And a bit insulting, my dear.'

He grasped the bottom of the wooden board and tilted it so Farah toppled backwards at a downward angle, and her head ended up in a wooden container filled with water.

She tried to raise it, to gasp for air, but all she took in was water. Adrenalin surged through her body. She wanted to flail her arms and kick her legs, hoping to free herself with those reflexes. Impossible. What followed was blind panic. A desperate struggle to survive. And as she thrashed about, caught in her own spasms, she saw his figure looming over her, monstrously distorted by the splashing water above her.

The moment she thought she might suffocate the board was forcefully raised from the water, back to its original diagonal position.

She tried to gasp for air again, but threw up water instead.

'Being dead is easy enough,' he said calmly. 'But dying, that's quite a challenge. Dying can be hell. Seriously, it will get worse every time you're down there. You never get used to it. Who knows how long you can keep it up . . . spare yourself that hell.'

He slowly leaned towards her. 'Journalists usually refuse to reveal their sources. But I'd advise you to give me the names of your contacts, the names of those you worked with. Then I'll make this easy on you.'

She could hear herself stammer. She seemed to have no control over it.

'You've got . . . You've got . . .'

'I've got what?'

She heard Satria's voice in her ear. *Never let on, never reveal a thing. Be as elusive as water.*

She was shivering all over, shivering with fear, yet she looked him straight in the eye and kept her mouth shut.

'You're too predictable,' he taunted, and tilted her back into the water.

Her fear of dying was even more intense this time. As were her reflexes. It was an instinctive physical reaction. It was her body fighting to survive. It took over. She lost all control and felt her bladder emptying itself. She kicked, lashed out, swallowed water, thought she'd go insane with panic and was about to lose consciousness when she was unexpectedly tilted back out of the water yet again.

Gasp for air. She needed air. Spit out the water. Her laboured breathing was coupled with heart palpitations. And then there was the fury. Raging fury.

But she wasn't dead yet.

'You and me. We're so similar. And yet . . . We'd be so much more effective if we cooperated. Why you stubbornly persist in refusing to talk is a mystery to me. I don't get it. Enlighten me.'

She shook her head.

'You're more afraid than you look. More afraid than you care to admit. You're afraid to do great things. It's your fear. It holds you back. The world is a scary place. Has been since your childhood. And still is. There are no more walls to protect you, Farah.'

He slid his hands over her wet body. 'Names, names, names . . .'

How long would she be able to stand this? She didn't know. Paul and Anya's work mustn't be in vain. She had to sacrifice herself. The thought filled her with despair. She started to cry. She wanted to remain silent. It would spell her death. But she had to do it. Remain silent.

'You're nothing but a scared child,' he said. 'With so much to lose.'

He produced a mobile phone and said casually, 'That girl who was with you. What's her role?'

This came as a shock. 'Leave her out of this.'

'Impossible. We've got her as well.'

He pressed a key. 'Is she there? Hand her to me.'

He brought the mobile to Farah's ear. When she heard sobbing, she said Aninda's name.

'Farah?'

She tried not to let on that she was crying.

Aninda sounded just as fearful as Farah felt, but she could tell her friend was trying to control her emotions.

'Do you remember what I told you, that night? About how to act?'

'Do as your heart tells you, not as your fear dictates.'

'Do that.'

Lavrov pulled the phone away. 'I can make her howl in pain as she's raped over and over again. I can also be merciful and have her killed quickly. It's up to you.'

'No,' she exclaimed. 'Let her live. Kill me, but let her live.'

She was screaming now, cursing him in Dari through her tears. But he just stood there and smiled, waiting for her to finish.

'Anya Kozlova. What's her role in all this?'

'How do you know –'

He flew into a rage. 'What's Kozlova's role?'

'She . . . She hacked Gundono's computer . . . She knows how you concluded the deal.'

He seemed beside himself with fury. He yelled into the receiver.

'Shoot the girl!'

She begged, screamed, cried out. She'd tell him everything, she'd . . . Then came the tinny sound of gunfire and she froze. She couldn't believe it. Lavrov kept barking into the speaker, but when no response was forthcoming he hurled the phone across the room.

Life had lost all meaning. She wanted to be dead.

Dead like Aninda.

He came and stood in front of her. In his raised hand she recognized a *golok*, a large, razor-sharp knife.

All she felt was a gust of wind when his arm came down like the sail of a windmill.

With surgical precision, he slit the blade through the straps that bound her upper body. Then he cut loose those around her hips and thighs.

'I can't stand it when defenceless people are executed. You ought to die feeling you had a chance to fight for your life.'

After wriggling free from the straps she stood before him, still reeling. She was acutely aware of the urge to flee, but a voice inside told her to keep an eye on the knife.

It will seem like an impossible challenge. You'll need to be well prepared if you want to survive.

She opened the palms of her hands, as she'd practised with Satria. Not fists, but open hands.

She'd die without fear.

Aninda was with her again, lying beside her like before, and reassuring her.

You're fleeing what's chasing you, but the more you flee, the more it comes after you. And one day . . . one day it will catch up with you. And then you'll have no choice but to turn around and look it straight in the eye.

And with Aninda's voice came the realization that she mustn't die. Not now. Not yet. He had to die first. The man in front of her. The man with the knife.

He was well trained. She stood little chance. In fact, she didn't even want a chance. All she wanted was revenge. His death for that of Aninda. It was the least she could do. With the anger surging through her body, she failed to heed Satria's warning: *Anger is an energy, but feed it too much and it will destroy you.*

Her first task was to fend off any attack. By moving around him in circles, she could catch her breath and recover her strength.

But he was already charging at her.

She managed to duck, surprised at the speed of her reaction. Aninda was giving her strength. Satria was giving her good council. There were three of them present now. He was alone.

As she continued to move around him, she realized it intimidated him. He must have anticipated her fear, not the apparent calm with which she fixated on him and tried to second-guess his every move. She'd wait for a moment of inattentiveness. She kept circling him, ducked, avoided another blow and noticed that his moves were now driven by anger, whereas she'd recovered her composure.

With the voices of Satria and Aninda in her head, she began to create her own reality. It wasn't Lavrov who'd gone looking for her so he could eliminate her here. No, she'd sought *him* out so she could fight – and defeat – him right on this spot.

She could tell his concentration was waning. His movements were now driven by a growing lack of confidence. He tried to camouflage it, but she could tell by the look in his eyes and his breathing, which he now did through the mouth rather than through the nose.

She began to anticipate what was coming, to predict his lunges, to estimate the speed and dwindling force with which he lashed out. And each time she took a step closer.

She lured him into an imaginary circle.

Quite unexpectedly, she countered the sideways chopping motion he made by grabbing his wrist and aiming an elbow punch at his sternum, which he managed to block.

He pushed her elbow away and lashed out again, this time from above.

She met his blow with her arms crossed and grabbed the wrist of his slashing arm with her left hand before ducking underneath it in a *hapkido* motion, yanking the limb towards her and pinning it behind his back. With her right fist she punched him hard in the gut. She heard him groan in pain.

He dropped the knife.

It wasn't enough.

She put him in a headlock and, by kicking his lower calf, swept his right leg from under him. Then she stepped back, pulled him towards her in a stranglehold and felt all resistance fade.

She let go and stood before him. The look she gave him seemed to signal goodbye.

His eyes were turned inward. He looked like a broken man, as defenceless as a child.

She hesitated.

But it wouldn't be over until his life was over.

She had to finish it.

She had to finish *him*.

Then came the sound of rapid, heavy footsteps on concrete stairs.

Do it.

The entrance was being battered down.

Do it. Now!

She rotated her hips so she could deliver the fatal blow.

They emerged from the half-light: figures with laser-guided guns. A male voice shouted: *'Jangan!'* 'Don't!'

But she was already halfway through her rotation.

Red laser beams skimmed her body.

She pulled in her right leg to launch the deadly kick.

The laser dots hovered over her heart and her forehead.

'Don't do it!'

3

The low country by the North Sea was once again in the international news – and for all the wrong reasons. First, because of the Dutch journalist of Afghan origin who had become a celebrity terrorist with her jihad statement on YouTube; and now, because of the way the Dutch minister under investigation, Ewald Lombard, had very publicly met his demise.

In particular the modus operandi of the Amsterdam MIT was questioned. Why were these detectives rigorously investigating a government minster when there wasn't a shred of evidence to prove him guilty? And why did this same team of detectives back Lombard so far into a corner that they were possibly complicit in his death? A number of striking examples were used to illustrate just how disastrous the work of the Amsterdam police had been.

There was the unparalleled way Detective Marouan Diba had disrupted a popular live TV show by barging into the studio, grabbing the host, Dennis Faber, by his collar and dragging him away like a serious criminal, all in front of the cameras.

Then there was the fanaticism that drove his partner, Detective Joshua Calvino, in a break with police protocol, to travel to Moscow and, behind closed doors, attempt to have Minister Lombard arrested during his stay in the Russian capital.

But perhaps worst of all was the exceedingly violent death suffered by the suspect Sasha Kovalev when he was being interrogated in custody. Especially as the crime committed by Kovalev – who was known in daily life for his extravagant interior designs for AtlasNet's offices worldwide – had been nothing more than the hijacking of an ambulance. The Russian government had lodged an official complaint related to this incident. But, despite an internal investigation into the circumstances surrounding Kovalev's death, up until now it seemed like the team of detectives hadn't learned a thing from the whole sorry business.

This was the state of affairs when Radjen took a seat opposite Commissioner Kemper to bring him up to speed on the results of their ongoing investigation.

'So, you think this whole Lombard matter,' Kemper concluded after Radjen had explained the background of Kovalev's involvement in the Sekandar case and the murder of Danielle Bernson, 'is a lot bigger than we first assumed.'

'It's huge,' Radjen replied. 'Vakurov instantly makes it an international matter. And the person ultimately responsible for all this anguish is probably not Ewald Lombard but Valentin Lavrov.'

'Do I understand correctly,' Kemper asked sarcastically after an awkward silence, 'that you've based your sweeping conclusion on a small photo in a locket?'

'Perhaps small, but awfully valuable as evidence. Lavrov's right-hand man, who recently died during that staged hostage crisis in Moscow, had close ties with the hitman who came here to kill the injured boy and his doctor, perhaps because they knew too much. That needs to be investigated.'

'I get it,' said Kemper, 'but before you go labelling an oligarch like Lavrov a criminal, you'd better come up with some watertight evidence, don't you think?'

'I've passed information on to Interpol for their support,' Radjen said, 'but it remains my case, so my responsibility. Besides, you gave me five days.'

'And you've used up four. The main suspect is dead, so what more is there to investigate?'

'Lombard's involvement in the hit-and-run,' Radjen replied. 'We may have a new witness who can destroy the alibi Melanie Lombard gave for her husband.'

He told Kemper about the time-regression method, which, using hypnosis, would return Angela Faber to the night of the accident in the Amsterdamse Bos.

'Therefore, we still have a chance she can place Lombard at the scene of the crime,' Radjen continued. 'And we've still not finished with our investigation into Meijer's murder.'

Kemper straightened his back, puffed out his chest and leaned in a bit. 'First of all, apart from the doubts the pathologist expressed in her preliminary report, I still haven't seen any conclusive evidence to suggest Meijer was murdered. And, as far as Lombard's involvement in the hit-and-run is concerned, the man is dead. We can't prosecute a corpse. And even if Angela Faber could remember anything that could be damaging to Lombard, her statement would be inadmissible in court because the Dutch judicial system still considers an account given under hypnosis unreliable.'

'I don't agree,' Radjen said. 'But there's more.'

'There's always more with you,' Kemper sighed.

'Lombard's official cause of death.'

'A perforated bowel and a ruptured aorta.' Kemper said.

'Lombard was checked by his doctor a month ago. He was in good health.'

'So?'

'So perhaps it was something else. Shouldn't we err on the side of caution?'

'And what would that entail?'

'A second autopsy needs to be carried out.'

During their entire conversation, an extremely stressed

Kemper looked like he was about to throw a tantrum unbe-fitting a man in his position. And what Radjen had been dreading now happened. The Police Commissioner grabbed a handful of international newspapers from his desk and waved them in Radjen's face as if he were trying to swat a fly.

'Have you seen the papers recently!' he shouted. 'The only thing our department hasn't been accused of is necrophilia. What's wrong with you? I've been patient, Tomasoa. I've done everything in my power to control the damage done by your team. And this is what I have to show for it. You have to stop abusing the goodwill you've built up here.'

Kemper's face was as red as a beet. He slumped back in his chair. The newspapers were now strewn across his desk.

Radjen didn't challenge Kemper's torrent of criticism. He'd never really liked his boss and now he knew why.

'You're finished, Tomasoa. And that's that,' Kemper said after a few minutes. 'With Lombard's death, your position in the force has become untenable. From this moment on, you're not to take any further action. So no hocus-pocus hypnosis, no additional cutting into corpses, nothing that might damage the image of the police even further. As of tomorrow, you're officially suspended. And, if I were you, I'd choose the honourable way. The Board of Police Commis-sioners has promised a substantial payout in exchange for your resignation.'

Radjen didn't respond. He just stared at Kemper.

'Damn it, Tomasoa, you knew the situation,' Kemper said, in a half-hearted attempt to gloss over his outburst. But it was too late for that. Much too late.

'I wasn't entirely aware of *your* situation,' Radjen said, as he slowly got up from his chair. 'And, by the looks of it, you're not in a good place.'

With a calm gait, Radjen left the room, quietly closing the

door behind him, and returned to Esther, who was just down the hall waiting for him.

'What a jerk,' she said. 'His tirade was bouncing off the walls.'

'C'mon,' Radjen said, 'we've got a bunch of things to take care of and we don't have much time left.' They headed for the Forensics Department. On the way Radjen said, 'I heard you had a chat with Kemper too. What did he want from you?'

'What do you think? He advised me to say yes to all the interview requests I got. "It'll be good for you," he said. And I said, "You mean, good for *you*?"'

Radjen smiled. He knew what she was talking about. In the news items on CNN, Al Jazeera, Fox News and all the other international media that covered Lombard's death, the spotlight was on the female detective, completely clad in black, who'd appeared out of nowhere and gave Lombard mouth-to-mouth in an attempt to save his life.

As a result of this, Esther had become something of a sought-after celebrity.

'Kemper even said there might be a trip to America in it for me, to do an interview with CNN,' she said mockingly. 'But I don't need to go to America. I told him he could go to America by himself. And could stay there for all I cared.'

'You didn't really say that last bit?' Radjen replied with a chuckle.

'I would have if I'd known he was going to flip out on you.'

At the Forensics Department, Radjen and Esther inquired about the examination of the evidence found in Meijer's garden. The first news wasn't promising. The two policemen who thought they'd caught a burglar in the act at Meijer's place that night had basically contaminated any evidence there might have been, which was exactly what Radjen had feared. But, fortunately, there was one clue that hadn't been compromised. They were busy making a cast of a footprint, which would then be examined further.

'If necessary,' Radjen said, 'I'll pay your overtime myself, so long as that cast we're talking about provides us with some kind of clarity by the end of the evening. Otherwise, it'll be too late. As far as the big boss is concerned, this investigation ends tomorrow.'

Afterwards they headed to the police storage depot where, at Radjen's request, everything from Meijer's shed had been catalogued and stored. A still life consisting of empty fish tanks, dented containers of fish food, do-it-yourself kits for creating underwater ruins, cleaning materials, pumps, strainers and an array of hobby items. Radjen was handed a printed form listing everything in alphabetical order. He skimmed the page. Pointless waste of time and money, he thought to himself. Until his eye fell on the words 'mobile phone'. The device was found in one of the aquariums and had already been passed on to Laurens Kramer.

'It's in bad shape,' the depot worker warned. 'And that's putting it mildly. I don't know if Kramer will manage to pull anything off of it.'

Esther was already on the phone with Kramer to implore him to find out by tonight the origin of that phone, and to determine the contacts on the two prepaid phones found in Lombard's villa.

Meanwhile, Radjen dialled the number of pathologist Ellen Mulder.

Barely five minutes later they were back in the car.

'Lately, for some reason, we're always off to some place that is a surprise to one of us,' Esther needled him as she sped out of the car park.

'We're going to see Ellen Mulder,' Radjen said.

'Why?'

'There's a quote by Che Guevara, "Be realistic, demand the impossible." I'm going to ask for the impossible.'

They walked down the long corridor, where they were met by the sounds of a symphony orchestra and the lingering lament of a woman singing.

Mulder was engrossed in her work. She was writing a report using a fountain pen. She didn't care much for computers and put stock in handwritten texts. Ellen Mulder belonged to a dying race that still wrote letters. Radjen had once received a letter from her, which he had actually never opened but filed away for safekeeping.

He noticed she was wearing makeup. Very subtle. Eyeliner, a touch of rouge on her cheeks and more colour on her lips than usual. Her shoulder-length, ash-blonde hair was pinned up. The low-cut blue dress she was wearing was a bold statement for her.

She was a bit startled when she looked up. Recognition followed, and then she gave them a tender, ironic smile. 'Well, that was quick for a change.'

When she kissed him on both cheeks, Radjen detected a delicate hint of perfume.

'You sounded worried,' she said. 'And that's how you look, even worse than the last time we saw each other.'

'He won't allow me to take better care of him,' Esther said, extending her hand. 'But I manage to keep track of him.'

'That's reassuring to hear,' Ellen said.

'What's the name of this piece you're playing?' Esther asked.

'Radjen should recognize it,' Ellen said. 'This is "*Song to the Moon*" from Antonín Dvořák's opera *Rusalka*. We saw it performed in the Concertgebouw together.'

The two women exchanged a glance that made it seem like they'd been friends for years, Radjen thought to himself. He looked at Ellen seriously.

'The last time, you said to me that no matter what happens, or how little time I have, I must solve this case. I have less than twenty-four hours and I feel like I'm close to a breakthrough. But I really need your help.'

'Only if you take some time off to rest when you're done, as I suggested last time,' Ellen said.

'I promise,' Radjen responded.

Ellen closed the door. 'Tell me.'

'I suspect,' Radjen began, 'that Lombard's perforated bowel and ruptured aorta were not natural causes of death. He'd recently had a full medical check-up. There was nothing to indicate any kind of condition that would kill him so quickly.'

'A check-up is a single moment in time, 'Ellen said. 'People then often think, "I'm healthy." They are, but only then. The next day it might be different. Our body is a sound, but not always infallible, system.'

'At times you feel that something is true, even if it barely seems logical. But it actually is and it's up to you to prove it, to convince the sceptics.'

'I understand completely,' Ellen replied. 'You want to force a court-ordered autopsy to confirm your suspicions of foul play.'

Radjen nodded silently.

'Over the years, when you've had this feeling about unnatural causes, you've usually been right on the money,' Ellen said. 'But now you're really asking me to go out on a limb. We're talking about a minister who, at least according to public opinion, has been hounded by a ruthless investigation team. And then a day before his funeral we lay claim to his body. How far are you willing to go? What about the ethical considerations?'

'I know,' Radjen said. 'And I'll respect your decision if you don't want to get involved. You have your reputation to protect.'

'Getting to the truth is more important than my reputation,' Ellen said. 'I'm thinking more about your reputation, Radjen.'

'My part in this ends tomorrow,' Radjen said. 'I don't have much to lose, so there's no need for melodrama.'

'All right,' Ellen said. 'I'll call the Examining Magistrate and say that, in close consultation with the Chief Inspector of Amsterdam's MIT, doubts have arisen about the primary autopsy performed on Lombard, and we object to the determination that the cause of death was natural. Another autopsy must be carried out this evening because the burial is planned for tomorrow.'

She stared at him with her bright eyes. That unopened letter came to mind.

'I don't know how to thank you,' he stammered.

Ellen glanced at Esther. 'By letting her take care of you. You're not Atlas. You can't shoulder the weight of the world all alone. We're glad to be of help.'

A half-hour later he was standing outside the Forensic Hypnosis practice, smoking a long-cherished cigarette with Esther, awaiting the arrival of Angela Faber.

'She was going on a date,' Esther said. 'Ellen Mulder. That's why she looked so nice.'

'I'm happy for her,' said Radjen, who with each inhalation felt how nervous he was.

Esther looked at him with something of an ironic expression. 'How come the two of you never became an item?' she asked.

'Where'd you come up with that one?'

'Oh, please . . .'

She smiled at him with an air of superiority. It was a look that conveyed she saw things in him that he reckoned he'd managed to hide. He thought about the story of the aria playing when they'd arrived at Ellen's office. She'd explained it to him when they'd heard the piece at the concert. It was the tale of the beautiful water nymph Rusalka, who fell in love with a man, a prince for that matter. To be by his side for the rest of her life, she was prepared to sacrifice her voice in exchange for a human body.

Rusalka sang that song on the shores of the lake at night, right before she lost her voice forever. Radjen thought of the sacrifice he'd made after the love of his life had disappeared without a trace by Lake Trasimeno. He'd felt her take his hand that evening in the Concertgebouw, as if she'd never vanished from his life. With this, she'd made it clear that as long as he lived he'd never lose her again. A relationship with Ellen, no matter how much he might have wanted this, was out of the question.

'I get it,' Esther said, interrupting his thoughts. 'I mean, apart from the fact that you're married and all.'

'What do you get?'

'Why there's a click between you and Ellen, and yet you never acted on it.'

'Oh?'

'She's too cultured for you.'

Pleased with this realization, she exhaled the smoke from her cigarette.

At that moment, a car pulled up outside the building with Angela Faber inside.

Angela Faber was wearing sunglasses with lenses big enough to be used as side-view mirrors on a lorry. It was the same pair she'd worn when she came down the steps of police headquarters with her husband Dennis – after giving her first statement as a suspect in the hit-and-run – and was bathed in the flashing camera lights of the media gathered en masse for her release.

Though this time she wasn't wearing a wedding ring.

The hit-and-run scandal was immediately followed by the extramarital affair of her TV-host husband. It was the hottest celebrity news when Angela had all her precious belongings removed from the family home: wardrobes full of clothing and suitcases filled with makeup.

Esther shook her hand and said, 'Thank you so much for coming, Angela.'

Angela Faber's answer was as short as it was memorable, 'Thank you. What do you think of my hair?'

'Very Audrey Hepburn,' Esther said.

Inside, the certified hypnotherapist explained what to expect. The image of what happened the night she drove through the Amsterdamse Bos and saw the injured Sekandar lying on the road was stored somewhere deep in her unconscious. That was the fragment they'd find and single out, so each detail was visible. This would allow Angela Faber to call up what she thought she'd forgotten.

Angela said, 'I've learned a lot recently. Also, that it isn't possible to build a new life by just forgetting your old life: you have to work through it. That's the reason I agreed to do this.'

Radjen and Esther were then escorted to a separate room with a sound system and a tape recorder hooked up to it. Via headphones, Radjen and Esther could follow the session.

Angela Faber was first reassured by the therapist and then given some breathing exercises to put her into the early stages of a trance. The therapist spoke in a low, slow, soothing voice.

'Everything here is safe, quiet and peaceful. Relax and breathe deeply, in and out. Listen to my voice and just give yourself over . . .'

Together they walked the imaginary ten steps of the 'hypnotic staircase' to reach a deeper trance state.

'Take the first step down and feel yourself relaxing more and more. Every step is a step further into your unconscious. Now step off the second step and feel that you're becoming calmer and calmer. When you get to the third step, your body will be so relaxed, you'll feel like you're floating.'

Slowly Angela descended the staircase.

'You're now at the bottom of the stairs,' the therapist said. 'You open the door in front of you. You're outside. It's dark. You get into your car and drive away. Don't be afraid. I'm right here with you.'

Angela Faber described what she was seeing: trees, curves in the road, sometimes the distant lights of airplanes coming in to land. There were no other cars on the road. It was deserted, dimly lit and surrounded by trees.

She spoke with a calm voice. 'I see the headlights of an oncoming vehicle.'

'Good, let it come closer, slowly. You can do it; you're in control of the time.'

'It's getting nearer.'

'Good, Angela, when you can clearly make out the vehicle, take your foot off the accelerator.'

'It's close now.'

'Both of you are practically standing still. You have a camera in your hand. Just take a photo. Use the flash, so you can see everything.'

Angela Faber did exactly what was asked of her. She meticulously described what she saw. Then she drove home, got out of the car and went back up the stairs.

'I'm going to count from one to five,' the therapist said next, 'and when I get to five, you'll be fully awake again, alert, and you'll feel refreshed.'

By then Radjen and Esther had already removed their headphones.

Angela Faber had given a detailed description of the man who'd been frozen like a wax figure behind the wheel: Thomas Meijer.

But this was primarily about the person she'd seen in the back seat.

His mouth was open wide, as if letting out a primal scream, his eyes bulged, and he was waving his arms in a panic, just as Radjen had seen him do in front of the cameras during the interview at his villa, before he crash-landed on the carpet.

4

The slums of Cengkareng in West Jakarta, Serpong to the south-west of the city and Ciawi to the south were the first places where it began that evening. As if tacitly agreed, they emerged from the alleyways and streets of their *kampongs* to gather on street corners and junctions. Some wore white shirts; others had tied a simple strip of white cotton around their heads. There were both men and women, and, although they ranged widely in age, they all had the same look of grim determination in their eyes. Together they marched downtown.

By the time they'd converged on the first Army blockade in the city centre from all directions, they were in their thousands. They walked closely together, holding hands, afraid of what might happen, but they kept going until they were right in front of the barricades. These were manned by uniformed young men of barely eighteen or nineteen, who'd been ordered to aim their weapons at the protesters.

They'd stood facing each other in silence for some time. Until somewhere, at one of the barricades, a soldier lowered his gun. Others followed his example. And in the ensuing commotion, barbed-wire barriers were pushed aside. Not a single shot was fired.

News of the advancing demonstrators spread like wildfire. The wide boulevards of Jakarta Pusat filled with tens of thousands of sympathizers. Soldiers joined the protesters. And then it became clear that only a minority of the armed forces actually sided with Gundono.

Eventually they all congregated on Merdeka Square, an estimated three hundred thousand by now. A man climbed on to the roof of a black SUV and brought a megaphone to his mouth. Even before he had a chance to say something, his name was being chanted.

'Hatta! Hatta!'

Meanwhile, Army units that had remained loyal to the President had regained control of the Parliament building and television studios. Special commandos had stormed Gundono's compound. After a brief exchange of gunfire, they'd arrested him, along with the members of the military who'd backed him. Then the commandos searched every floor of the compound. Reliable sources had informed them that somewhere in the building a foreign journalist was being held hostage.

They'd managed to locate her in the subterranean vaults, among dusty temple statues, soaking wet and leaning on her left leg, her upper body tilted back a bit, ready to deliver a death-blow to her Russian nemesis.

The order given by the SWAT team commander hadn't stopped her from doing it.

Nor had the laser-guided red dots on her head and heart.

It'd been the voice inside her head.

Satria's voice.

A true Pesilat is someone with both a noble mind and a noble character.

She'd stopped in mid-air without extending her right leg. Her foot hadn't hit Lavrov between the eyes.

The commander had stood right in front of her. He flipped up the bulletproof visor of his helmet and scrutinized her.

'*Sudah selesai.*' 'It's over,' he said. 'It's over.'

She knew that it wasn't true.

It would never be over.

Her voice trembled as she spoke.

'*Nama saya adalah Farah Hafez.*' 'My name is Farah Hafez. I'm a Dutch national, I'm a journalist.'

She uttered these words with the last bit of energy she could muster.

Then she slumped forward against his chest.

A stinging wind had got up – stinging because sand was mixed in with it, fine sand that found its way into her eyes, mouth and nostrils and shrouded everything in a gritty mist. Everywhere she looked was murky and grey.

A procession of gleaming Bentleys appeared out of the mist.

Sitting in the first car was her father. He was staring straight ahead, with a glassy look in his eyes, as if he didn't want to see her. Her mother, in the second one, did meet Farah's gaze, but with helpless despondency etched on her face.

'Why aren't you in the same car as Papa?' she cried out in a halting, little girl's voice.

Her mother may well have given her an answer, but she couldn't hear it. The next vehicle glided past without a sound. Behind the window, she recognized dear Uncle Parwaiz, looking much better than he had when he died in her arms. She waved and blew him kisses. He smiled faintly at her before vanishing in the sandy haze.

The final Bentley glided by right in front of her. In the back seat was Aninda, in a panic, yelling and banging her fists against the window. Farah wanted to open the door, but just then the car accelerated. She ran after it, screaming, but couldn't keep up. Then it disappeared from sight.

'Calm down now.'

She opened her eyes and saw the face of an unfamiliar blonde woman sitting by her bedside in a large room with high, whitewashed walls. Rain beat against the windows.

The woman gave her a glass of water and a tablet.

'You're safe. Here, drink up.'

'What is it?'

'A tranquillizer.'

Farah took only the water and gulped it back. She looked around the room and saw the official portrait of the Dutch royal couple.

'Where am I?'

'In our guest residence,' the woman said. She took back the glass. 'I'm Sabine. I work for the Dutch Embassy's Economics Section. We've had contact with your Editor-in-Chief in the Netherlands.'

'Edward . . .'

'Mr Vallent informed us about the investigation and your status. And Mr Hatta was prepared to mediate between us and the Indonesian authorities. Everything has been taken care of now. We consulted our staff doctor, who has given you a clean bill of health and declared you fit to travel. A special flight has been arranged for you, and this is scheduled to leave in the afternoon. Are you hungry?'

Farah shook her head and wiped away her tears.

Half an hour later she was sitting on the embassy's covered veranda, which overlooked a large walled garden full of exotic flowers and palm trees. It was raining harder now. She'd been given new clothes – exactly the right size, though not quite her style. In front of her stood an untouched plate of sandwiches, a cup of coffee and a glass of fruit juice. Next to it lay a copy of the *Jakarta Post*. Its front page had a picture of Baladin Hatta addressing the Indonesian Parliament, which had met for an extraordinary session.

A substantial majority of MPs had decided to postpone the vote on the Sharada Project until a special Parliamentary

Commission led by Hatta had reviewed its financing. Minister Gundono had been detained on suspicion of orchestrating a coup. Valentin Lavrov was being treated in a private hospital for what an AtlasNet spokesperson had described as 'cardiac arrhythmia'.

Edward had tried to phone her several times. She hadn't answered. At this point, she had nothing to say to anyone, not even to him. The only person she wanted to talk to was the woman who could no longer respond.

Aninda's death hadn't been a twist of fate, she realized, but the outcome of a choice she'd made that morning when the children came into the museum, when Aninda had saved her for the second time in twenty-four hours. By returning to the Waringin Shelter with her again, she'd not only implicated Aninda in her mission, but also marked her out as a potential target. It had been an impulsive choice, the umpteenth she'd made. And this time it had actually claimed a life.

She was suddenly startled by the young embassy woman, who'd sidled up to her and put a plastic folder on the table.

'Your ticket and your new passport,' she said. 'The authorities wanted to keep the old one. It was fake.'

She looked at the woman in surprise. 'The passport . . . how did you get it?'

'The woman who was also held hostage in the compound –'

'Aninda.' This was the first time since the incident that she said her name out loud.

'She was the one who led us to the Waringin Shelter.'

'She was my friend,' Farah said. 'Could you take me to her? I'd like to say goodbye.'

'We don't think that's a good idea,' the woman said guardedly. 'For your own safety, you understand?'

'My own safety,' echoed Farah, who'd risen to her feet and

clasped the woman's arm, 'means nothing to me. Please take me to her.'

The woman hid her confusion behind a neutral expression. Without taking her eyes off Farah, she freed herself from her grip. 'We don't want anything to happen to you while you're still in Indonesia . . . Your friend will be brought here.'

'I beg your pardon. I don't know what you mean.'

'What I mean is –'

But Farah no longer heard a word the woman was saying. She was looking over the embassy worker's shoulder, and what she saw made her gasp.

The rain wasn't letting up, and in the hallway adjacent to the veranda a door had opened and closed. Three people had entered. What must have been another embassy employee escorted a young woman holding a child by the hand on to the veranda. When an unexpected gust of wind blew a large white curtain to and fro, the man took hold of it to clear the way for the woman and the little boy.

Standing there, Aninda and Rino looked at Farah as if they'd arrived on another planet and she was their sole landmark.

All Farah could do was to wrap her arms around Aninda and pull her close to her chest. They'd stood there for a long time, until Aninda told her what had really happened the night of the coup. She too had been taken blindfolded to the compound. On the commander's orders, she'd been placed against an outside wall. At that point she'd been convinced they were going to shoot her. The man had paced around nervously with his phone in his hand. The soldiers had been even more nervous. The five young men had been told to release the safety catches on their weapons and to form a firing line. But when the order to shoot had come, they'd emptied their rifles into the air. Seconds later, the commandos had stormed into the courtyard.

The embassy woman interrupted Aninda. The car taking Farah to the airport was waiting outside. It was time to go.

'From now on, I'll carry you with me wherever I go,' Farah had said to Aninda, pointing to her heart.

On the plane, she unfolded the drawing Rino had given her. The piece of paper was full of brightly coloured stars with children's faces.

5

Ewald Lombard had been cremated in the morning with only family and close friends present and the last guests had now left the Blaricum villa. In her black dress, Melanie Lombard was sitting beside the fountain in the middle of her garden. Radjen watched her from a distance. She was so lost in thought she didn't seem to notice him. Yet he was sure that she was aware of his presence. Only once, when he'd approached her and was standing very close by, did she look at him.

'My condolences on the loss of your husband,' he said. He was getting rather adept at these kinds of platitudes.

She responded with a melancholy smile. 'It's strange,' she said, 'what the sudden absence of someone with whom you've spent the most important part of your life does to you.'

She gestured to the bench opposite her. Radjen sat down.

'When I felt you watching me, for a split second I thought it was him. My husband often did that – watch me from a distance. It made me uncomfortable. But as you stood there, I realized for the first time that I'm even going to miss that.'

She stared at him. Somewhere behind those dark-brown eyes he suspected there was a vulnerable woman. But she still had that protective layer around her, a second skin, like impenetrable armour.

'I take it you haven't come here to talk about the loss of my husband.'

'No,' Radjen said, 'that's correct.'

'I see it in your face.'

'Really?'

'A different man is sitting across from me. The last time you were a bundle of nerves. Probing, probing. But not now. You have . . . some kind of clarity. You're finally completely grounded.'

She looked around.

'And where's your sidekick? I don't see her, but I imagine she's somewhere close by.'

'She's waiting in the car.'

'Thoughtful of you.'

He neglected to mention that Esther was in the car wearing an earpiece, coupled with the wireless mini-recorder given to him by Laurens, which was in the inside pocket of the sports jacket he was wearing. The end justified the means. He wanted to have a heart-to-heart with Melanie, and Esther's presence would have made that conversation virtually impossible.

Actually, he didn't like this kind of deception. He was old school, accustomed to following protocol: arrest, transport to the bureau, lock up, a phone call to the lawyer, recite the required warning ('You have the right to remain silent'), followed by an interrogation that usually lasts hours. This was how things generally went. But today he'd fashioned his own reality. A ninja reality. Still, with every second that passed, he began to feel more and more uncomfortable. He rubbed his forehead. The bump had already shrunk.

'Does it hurt a lot?' she asked.

'The painkillers seem to work,' he said. 'Kind of you to ask.'

He couldn't keep himself from looking at her. She was like a fire you kept staring at, yet slowly but surely you grew sadder and sadder.

'You know how I got this,' Radjen said.

'Frankly, I'm not very good at guessing,' she replied.

'You don't have to guess,' Radjen said. 'You already know.'

A bit of everything that was once contained in Pandora's box was in the look she now gave him.

'You were on the other side of the door,' Radjen said.

She ran her hand through her hair and looked up at a group of migratory birds, after which she looked back at Radjen. This time a bit agitated.

'You're quite the philosopher, Inspector Tomasoa. At any rate, I trust you mean "door" figuratively.'

She leaned towards him, with that same melancholy smile, and placed her hand on his knee.

'My dear inspector with your impenetrable gaze, I have tried to make it clear to you that we're not on opposite sides of that door. Look at us now, both with our own lives, our own sorrows. Somehow we're connected, you and I.'

He felt the warmth of her hand through the fabric of his trousers, and the strange thing was that for a fleeting second he was inclined to believe her. And for that second he was even able to convince himself he'd come here in a personal capacity. To express his condolences, to apologize for having given her such a hard time the last few days. Then he'd bid Melanie Lombard goodbye, leave her behind in the garden, get into the car and make it very clear to Esther that this was to stay between them, and finally they'd drive away with the intention of never returning to this place again.

'I'm sorry,' he said. 'But I meant it quite literally. You and I were both at the same place at the same time. On either side of a door that you slammed in my face.'

She pulled her hand from his knee and sat straight-backed.

He looked at her the way he'd looked at so many others at moments like this. Through the eyes of a detective. And he used the detective jargon that was appropriate for these kinds of circumstances. Business-like, without any further ado.

'Melanie Lombard van Velzen, I'm arresting you on suspicion of murdering Thomas Meijer.'

Her eyes had a cold-hearted glare, but her answer sounded gentle, even vulnerable.

'Arrest me based on what evidence, my dear? A door slammed in your face?'

'A footprint,' Radjen replied. 'One that was a major headache for our forensics people. Not only because it was very difficult to make a clear cast of the print, but because they then had to get access to the client lists of orthopaedic shoemakers in order to find a match.'

He paused to see her reaction to what he'd just said and then continued. 'Since your sailing accident you've had prescription shoes made by the same firm.'

Her smile remained, despite her dark gaze.

'And that's not the only evidence,' Radjen said. 'As you know, we searched your home for the prepaid phones you promised to give us. We came across two in the villa. But it didn't look like they matched each other. You used one for contacting your husband, as you stated earlier. But the other, which I found in your nightstand, was interesting too. A corresponding device was discovered by our forensics team amid all the stuff in Thomas Meijer's shed. I don't know how it got there, but it was lying at the bottom of one of the aquarium tanks. Of course it was important for you to get your hands on that device, because it was the only evidence that could lead us to you. It was your misfortune that I was on the other side of the door that evening.'

He paused and looked at her. She returned his gaze. He knew she was going to talk. They always did eventually. It was their ultimate attempt to come to terms with themselves and to justify what they'd done to the other. Melanie Lombard's words were calm and deliberate.

'That night, when I realized there was someone behind that door, was the only time I panicked,' she said. 'I never thought it would happen to me. As someone used to sailing, you encounter all kinds of situations where you have to keep your wits about you because it's a prerequisite to making it through alive. Giving in to panic means you won't make it. As you can imagine, I never expected to have a panic attack in a garden in Amsterdam.'

'We have some idea of how you did it,' Radjen said. 'Meijer's murder. But I'd like to hear it from you.'

'Lots of preparation,' Melanie Lombard said, and he could hear the relief in her voice. 'Before you cross an ocean in a sailboat you must be well prepared. More than that: everything has to be just right. Checked and double-checked. Planned down to the smallest detail. I came up with the perfect murder for Meijer. Not a strangulation made to look like he'd hanged himself. Instead a hanging beyond all reasonable doubt.'

'Then why a hangman's fracture?'

'Practical reasons. People who are suffocating, even when they're drugged, tend to wildly kick and flail their arms in the air. I didn't want to take that risk.'

The same self-satisfied smile he'd seen on her face once before appeared – at the moment Lombard collapsed on the carpet in front of the camera.

She was now completely absorbed in her own story.

'Scientists in Argentina came up with a stress-free way to kill cattle. They're guided through a long, padded corridor with subdued lighting. Engulfed by the sound of a Mozart symphony, their bodies are massaged by the padding. As they reach the end of that corridor in utter relaxation, a steel bolt is shot through their foreheads. I applied the same approach to Meijer. I let him believe that everything would turn out fine as long as he trusted me. I would lead him to a new life in Ghana. The night I came to kill him, he believed I was bringing him airline tickets. Of course we had to do this in the utmost secrecy. I'd already given him a prepaid phone when I met him in the car park at Economic Affairs. I would let him know when I'd hand over the tickets. All he had to do was to open the back gate to the garden. I won't bore you with all the rest . . . well, the technical details: an injection to sedate him, just to be sure, and then a few pulleys and some sturdy rope – a system that could be quickly removed.'

'But why Meijer? He'd already pleaded guilty. He would have been convicted.'

'There's no real punishment in a system that makes the guilty into victims. Thomas Meijer was a stupid, naive man. And they're the most dangerous: blindly following a leader so they don't have to ask themselves where they're going. They fall in line because it makes them feel protected, not responsible for what they do. But collaborators must be held accountable for their actions. Meijer was complicit, not just when he ran down the boy, but many times.'

'What do you mean?'

'Let's not play games with each other, Inspector. You and I both know that my husband was guilty. And his abhorrent behaviour was facilitated by Meijer, who drove him places for years without a word of protest and . . .'

She broke off her sentence and looked at him. Although she'd sounded calm while she was speaking, he now understood how truly upset she was. He saw the turmoil in her eyes, the need she had to articulate everything she'd bottled up inside.

'Do you mind if I tell you the rest while we take a stroll in the garden? I need to stretch my legs.'

She'd risen before he could respond and was out in front of him, while he still had to stand up. She spoke before he even got to the question of what had happened to her husband.

'Ewald called me that night. Terribly upset, on the verge of hysteria. He said he was on his way home and that I shouldn't answer the phone if it rang. And I had to draw all the curtains. When he was finally in the room, he was shaking all over. I'd never seen him in such a state. He was in shock. They'd had an accident, he said. And if asked, I'd have to swear that I was at home with him that night. I wanted to know what had happened, why I had to lie. But I didn't really need an answer. I'd actually known for years what was going on. You see, it's like alcoholics. My father was one. Deep down you know without being told. When you stumble across a liquor bottle somewhere it doesn't belong, you can no longer deny it. In Ewald's case I found a DVD in a desk drawer that should have been locked. The images I saw . . . He was also on camera, together with other men. Three men with one boy.'

She was silent as they walked to the other side of the garden together.

'I knew all along,' she said. 'And the whole time I did nothing. If the death penalty still existed, he would have deserved it. But it no longer exists. So *I* condemned my husband to death.'

She seemed relieved to finally be able to let down her guard. He felt strangely sorry for her.

'I admire your persistence, Inspector. You were right to have your suspicions. My husband loved meat. An hour before the interview, I made him a club sandwich of braised lamb and I spiked the dressing with oleander root. He thought it was delicious.'

436

'The interview was the perfect alibi,' Radjen said. 'You were sitting right beside him when he died. But I saw in your eyes something other than love.'

'Am I such an open book to you?' she asked.

'On the contrary.'

'I'll take that as a compliment,' she said.

'I'm afraid you have to bid your garden farewell,' Radjen said.

'May I ask you a favour?' she said. 'I'd like to do that alone, if it's okay with you?'

He hesitated. But she looked so small and vulnerable standing there beside him, he couldn't bear to say no.

'I'll give you a few minutes,' he said, and he walked around to the front of the house, where Esther stepped out of the car and approached him with an irritated expression on her face.

'You didn't leave that woman alone?' Esther asked. 'She's totally unpredictable now that she's cornered.'

'She confessed everything,' Radjen replied. 'She has nothing left to lose.'

He left Esther standing there. At the gate to the grounds he signalled to the men waiting in two unmarked vehicles that it was time to search the entire villa.

Only then did it hit Radjen: he'd left Melanie Lombard on the exact spot where he'd spoken to her during their first visit.

Between the deadly nightshade and the blue monkshood.

She has nothing left to lose.

He raced back around the house to the garden.

To his immense relief, Melanie Lombard was standing somewhere else – in the late-afternoon sunshine unhampered by the high trees, a dark silhouette in a ray of golden light.

'Have you ever sailed?' she asked when he was right behind her, still staring straight ahead. 'I mean actually on the high seas?'

'No,' Radjen said. 'But now I'd like you to come with me.' She seemed not to hear.

'Navigating by the stars. That was my favourite part. The stars guide you. You feel insignificant and at the same time immensely powerful. You're at the mercy of immeasurable forces taking you where you need to go. That feeling you get when you sail into a harbour . . . a feeling of mainly . . . gratitude.'

Radjen gently took Melanie Lombard by the elbow as a sign that it was time for her to go with him.

'Stay with me for a moment, Inspector. I don't want to be alone,' she said as she turned to look at him.

Blood was running from her nose. She was breathing heavily and struggling to keep her eyes open.

He picked her up and carried her through the garden. He knew he must have screamed for help, because he felt his mouth moving, but he didn't hear anything. All the while she kept staring at him, but there was barely a sign of life in her eyes. All the colour had drained from her face.

When he laid her down in the grass to give her mouth-to-mouth resuscitation, someone pulled him away. It was Esther. Her mouth also moved, but he didn't understand the words. She felt the carotid artery and shook her head. She stared at him and, besides an accusatory look, he saw something of pity in her eyes. What good did it do him? He didn't want pity or compassion; he just wanted Melanie Lombard to live.

But from the dismay on the faces of the men passively standing around her, he now saw it was too late.

6

A gigantic cruise ship sailed past on the leaden-grey water of the IJ. The gleaming metal vessel consisted of seven storeys, illuminated by an immense lattice of LED lights. From behind the window of Edward's office on the top floor of the *AND* building, Paul took note of the name of the ship: *Magnifica*.

A fitting name for the phase they were now in. Appropriate for the sense of triumph he and Edward had felt the moment they heard that Farah was safe and about to be repatriated to the Netherlands.

With that same feeling, they were reviewing the layout of the international *AND* edition dedicated to AtlasNet on Edward's large computer screen. They'd now arrived at the lengthy concluding report Anya had written about the company's finances.

She'd managed to get a near-impossible job done in no time at all. Not only had she produced rock-solid evidence that, as a phantom shareholder, Potanin owned more than forty-five per cent of AtlasNet, but she'd also convincingly documented that during his tenure as CEO Lavrov had funnelled a substantial part of the pre-tax profits, which should have been transferred in their entirety to Moscow headquarters, to a private bank account in Bermuda. The amount in question was a cool two billion dollars.

'This will be his downfall,' Edward said, handing Paul a glass of whisky. 'Amsterdam, Jakarta and Johannesburg. The Lavrov triangle. Only a tiny group of insiders were in on it. As soon as we release this, the whole world will know.'

Edward moved his finger to the 'send' button, where it hovered a short while before he withdrew it again.

'I'd like you to do it, my boy,' he muttered. 'You pulled it off, the three of you. The other two aren't here. You are.'

Paul teasingly clapped his arm around Edward's shoulder.

'After all these years your sentimentality is outmatched only by your size.'

'So, go on, do it.'

Paul pressed hard on the 'send' button and then tapped his glass against Edward's by way of a toast.

They silently watched the cruise ship float past.

'Would you believe that I've been thinking of taking such a trip?' Edward said.

'I'd rather kill myself,' Paul replied.

'How about another one?'

Paul handed him the empty glass just as Edward's desk phone rang. His uncle grumbled, but answered it anyway.

'Roman!' he enthusiastically exclaimed while gesturing for Paul to pour the whisky himself. 'What a surprise. We've just . . .'

His voice faltered. The smile slipped from his face as he listened to what Roman Jankovski had to say.

'It's Anya . . .' he finally said with a sigh, his face ashen. 'She . . . she's . . .'

Paul snatched the receiver. 'Roman, what happened?'

Haltingly, with a broken voice, the Russian newspaper man repeated his story.

Early that morning, Anya had left her flat to go to work. Outside the entrance, a man had been waiting for her. He had a bunch of flowers in his hand. That's what it looked like anyway. But the flowers camouflaged a lead pipe, which the man used to bash her on the head, arms and hands. She lost consciousness and was found in a pool of blood.

'She's being kept in an artificial coma,' Roman said. 'Her jaw is shattered and she could lose several fingers.'

Head and hands, Paul thought to himself, a journalist's main weapons.

His mind was immediately cast back to his meeting with Alexander Arlazarov, the Director of the counter-terror unit in Moscow. The seemingly casual way in which he'd retrieved a photo from a dossier before putting it aside again. The ironic tone of his words, 'Let's not talk about your former colleagues here in Moscow, however interesting they may be . . .' The picture had been of Anya. The message was clear. We, the FSB, know everything there is to know about her.

Hacking AtlasNet's server had been a step too far.

'The Russian police are treating the assault on Anya as attempted murder,' Roman resumed. 'Our President has told the press that the attackers will be found and brought to justice. But you and I both know what those statements are worth.'

'Will you keep me posted?' Paul asked.

'I'll call you as soon as I know more.'

The connection was broken. Edward had already taken a seat and was breathing heavily. Feeling dizzy, Paul reached for his uncle's shoulder to support himself.

Anya. *Kamikaze Anya*, as Paul had called her with equal measures of love and ridicule. He'd fallen head over heels in love with her. That had been during his Moscow years. He'd moved in with her, but Anya had driven him mad. She was single-minded and confrontational, pretty much twenty-four seven, and that left no space for anyone else. That was the tragedy of her life in a nutshell. Kamikaze Anya was lonely – in her work, in her few friendships and in her infrequent love affairs.

He thought back to the morning, eighteen months ago,

when he'd closed the door of her apartment behind him as quietly as possible, with hardly any luggage in his hands and a single ticket to Johannesburg in his pocket. He'd just returned. For a brief time. And not even for her, but to help Farah. Anya had picked up on the chemistry between him and Farah and yet she'd helped both of them, in what was for her an unusually altruistic way. And by doing so she'd shown him how much he still meant to her.

He knew it. He was important to her.

He thought of their most recent telephone conversation in Gaborone, just before he'd boarded the plane. 'I'm going to chase down that bastard's money, even if it's the last thing I do,' she'd said.

What remained was the memory of their goodbye kiss in Moscow. Afterwards, she'd walked away from him, vanishing in the low-hanging mist of Kolomenskoye Park.

Paul looked out over the water of the IJ again.

The *Magnifica* was now only a tiny dot on the horizon.

7

She was floating above a web of lights as small as pinheads, stretched out for miles and miles. But soon Jakarta was hidden from view by passing clouds. The Boeing 777, having taken off from Soekarno–Hatta Airport, was headed for Amsterdam. She was on her way home, but strangely enough it didn't feel that way.

In what now felt like the distant past, she'd stood in front of the open window of her Amsterdam apartment, looking out over Nieuwmarkt. That had been on the eve of her trip to Moscow, and she'd had a premonition back then that once she'd closed the door behind her there'd be no way back.

She thought of what Satria had said the night of her training under the weeping fig. Sometimes struggle is just what we need in our lives. Without setbacks, we're condemned to arrogance and complacency and our lust for life peters out. Unless we spread our wings, vulnerable like a butterfly crawling out of its cocoon, life isn't worth living.

The Netherlands, her life in Amsterdam, her job as a regional news journalist: they'd been her cocoon for years. She'd finally crawled out the night she'd seen Sekandar on that stretcher in the Emergency Department.

Since then everything had changed.

She had changed

And now she was flying back to the Netherlands. Back home. But when the KLM Boeing touched down at Schiphol Airport, she was more convinced than ever.

There was no way back.

This was no longer her home.

She'd known even before she'd hugged Paul in the arrivals hall. It was the way he looked at her; the few words with which he described what had just happened to Anya in Moscow. It put the outcome of her actions in Jakarta in a totally different light. In her effort to protect Aninda from Gundono's thugs, she'd put Anya in harm's way.

Edward had grabbed hold of her in a way that combined an embrace and a reprimand.

'You're not to blame, you hear me? The FSB had been on Anya's case for years; they had a detailed file on her. It's got nothing to do with what you told Lavrov. They'd known for ages. All they needed was an excuse.'

While it may have mitigated her pain and guilt, it didn't make the truth any less horrifying.

In the Saab on their way to the farmhouse, where Sekandar was waiting for her, Edward received a phone call from Moscow.

He put Roman Jankovski on speaker phone.

'Anya is still being kept in an artificial coma,' he reported. 'She's stable. We won't know for another couple of days how bad the neurological damage is. But I'm calling about something else. The Director of the FSB's counter-terror unit, Alexander Arlazarov, has just announced in a press conference that Lavrov will be tried on suspicion of conspiracy against the state.'

The ensuing silence in the Saab was deafening.

Jankovski seemed to sense the atmosphere perfectly.

'You're right, my friends, there's little cause for rejoicing.'

'I don't get it,' Farah said. 'They're talking about conspiracy. What about the funnelling of money to offshore bank accounts?'

Roman sounded very firm. 'They won't go that far. If the Kremlin were to arrest Lavrov on the strength of our publications, they'd lose all credibility. Instead, they're putting an absurd spin on things. Lavrov is said to be the leader of a select group of politicians, business people and members of the Politburo, intent on destabilizing the country. By staging the hostage-taking at the Seven Sisters, they wanted to show how weak Potanin really is. That's the official version now. The Kremlin is using these fake revelations to twist the story to its own advantage. All the work we did is now coming back at us like a boomerang. This morning, special FSB units carried out house searches and arrested a number of prominent politicians and business people as well as some journalists.'

'Have we achieved anything at all?' Farah exclaimed.

'We proved we won't be intimidated,' Roman insisted, but it didn't sound very convincing.

'Thanks for bringing us up to speed, Roman,' Edward said. 'Talk to you soon.'

After breaking the connection, he looked at Farah with that gaze she knew only too well. It was a look that hinted at an imminent storm.

'Call me a dinosaur, a journalistic mastodon, who should have been extinct long ago,' he growled. 'But I can assure you that we eliminated at least one villain. Although, having said that, we're dealing with a worldwide network of crooks.'

'A network that keeps renewing itself,' Paul added from the back seat. 'And as long as that network's in place, it's our moral duty to continue our efforts.'

'Please, a standing ovation for my nephew,' Edward said. 'And don't stop clapping just yet, because the European Competition Commissioner has filed charges against Atlas-Net for allegedly violating European regulations. Plans for

Armin Lazonder's New Golden Age Project have been shelved by the Amsterdam City Council because of his dodgy connection to Lavrov. And in Indonesia, Baladin Hatta will be chairing the Parliamentary Commission investigating the financial background of the Sharada Project.'

From the back, Paul stuck his head between the two front seats and chimed in.

'And even in South Africa, where President Nkoane has declared the Scorpion Unit unconstitutional with immediate effect, there was one official who helped us reveal that the new head of state has blood on his hands. Zhulongu is dead, Dingane has been booted out of his job, and Anya is fighting for her life, but each one of them stood up for an ideal we continue to believe in.'

'And however ingenious the Kremlin's spin on the Lavrov case,' Edward resumed, 'the man is damn well going to be sent on a one-way trip to Siberia. So stop feeling sorry for yourself, Hafez, and behave like a proper journalist. I didn't train you for nothing.'

'Stop the car,' she said.

'What, why?'

'Stop the car, damn it!'

Edward swerved on to the verge. She leaped out of the car, her eyes welling up. She wanted to scream, but didn't have the energy.

When she turned around, they were right behind her – two men bewildered by the situation, and by her.

She wrapped her arms around them, pulled them close and cried. She cried like a baby.

'I wanted to kill him . . . But I didn't do it. *Bebakhshen mara.* Forgive me. Please forgive me.'

8

At the moment he saw the hearse with Melanie Lombard's body drive away, Radjen Tomasoa knew he could no longer continue solving crimes. He desperately needed a break from death.

The search of Lombard's villa revealed what he'd already suspected. The minister was part of an exclusive child pornography network, featuring a restricted internet platform where visitors could sign in at different levels by first uploading child pornography themselves. The more frequently members logged in and the more violent the photos and films they posted, the more access they were given to higher levels on the site. This accounted for the increasingly extreme child pornography displayed. Lombard had access to the so-called VIP zone.

Laurens Kramer had managed to track down most of the IP addresses of the members. One of the addresses apparently belonged to a project manager affiliated with Radjen's Murder Investigation Team. The site's administrator was a senior official at the Ministry of the Interior, ultimately responsible for the Department of Implementation, Strategy and Advice for asylum centres nationwide.

These centres, where an estimated eight thousand or more children temporarily lived, turned out to be hotbeds of abuse. Laurens Kramer, together with several refugee organizations, was helping to set up a special website for children in asylum centres that informed them about what they could do if they were being abused.

A unit of experienced child sex-crime detectives was put together especially for the investigation. But even they were regularly repulsed by the images they had to look at to identify victims as well as perpetrators.

Radjen was not responsible for the investigation that followed. Melanie Lombard's recorded confession and Angela Faber's new testimony were enough to prove Lombard's involvement in the hit-and-run.

Paul Chapelle's feature article about AtlasNet, which appeared in the international edition of the *AND*, revealed that for years Lombard had done the bidding of the Russian oligarch Valentin Lavrov. All related to the plans for a large gas hub in the Netherlands, which was of vital importance to AtlasNet. The construction would allow the Russian conglomerate to continue to play a major role in European gas distribution. Lombard had become Lavrov's linchpin, lobbying to get the Dutch government to cooperate with AtlasNet to get the project off the ground. And with success – despite the fact that the European Parliament, municipalities in Noord-Holland as well as the Commissioner of the Queen there, Dutch nature conservationists and the Council of State had categorically rejected the permit request. Over eight hundred and fifty million euro had already been invested in the realization of the project. Most of that money had come from the Dutch government. Without Lombard's intensive lobbying campaign, it would have never happened.

Yet it was still unclear how Lombard had been rewarded for his part in the realization of the gas hub. A special inquiry into his finances would be needed. Radjen requested that such an investigation be initiated, but added that someone else would have to be in charge.

He was not only intent on eliminating death from his life at this moment, but also any kind of professional responsibility.

He'd shut the last file piled on his desk, walked into Kemper's office without knocking, placed his resignation letter on his boss's desk without uttering a word and walked out again.

When he returned home later that day, he also knew his domestic life was over.

He found the envelope she'd left him beside their wedding photo on the mantelpiece. He didn't even need to read the note inside to know what it said. Her story was also his story.

The tent was the only item he took with him. After that summer disappearance, he'd intended to get rid of it, but something had stopped him. Holding it now, he noticed the canvas smelled like the past, as if time had crawled inside to hibernate for thirty-odd years.

And now he was standing on the shores of Lake Trasimeno. A gentle wind caressed his body. Clouds crept along the flanks of the distant mountains, occasionally illuminated by barely audible lightning.

It wasn't the safest moment to go into the water, but he did it anyway.

He struggled to keep his balance. It was easy to slip on the pebbles at the bottom of the lake. He spread his arms like a tightrope walker and waded into the water to waist height. Then he dived under, the way a swan does with its head, and he started to swim.

He was a slave to the rhythm of his strokes, keeping his head under water, only turning it to the right for air after seven strokes, and he swam until he reached the middle of the lake.

Then he looked back at the shore.

He saw the glowing light of the oil lamp, which he'd lit as a beacon in the darkness.

He turned over on his back and floated with the night sky above him, the clouds lingering between the mountains and the sound of thunder resembling muffled machine-gun fire.

He thought of the last time he'd lain here like this. The sight of the empty tent when he'd returned from his swim. Disbelief, panic and later the numbness. It wasn't clear whether she'd chosen to leave or been forced. There was no trace of violence. Still, everyone thought a crime has been committed.

The only crime he'd never been able to solve.

Monique. He'd devoted years to looking for her. Getting more obsessed as time passed, consumed by powerlessness and a feeling of guilt that grew and grew.

As he lay on his back in the water and saw the stars appearing from behind the clouds, he knew that whatever had happened on the shores of the lake couldn't continue to be a part of his life. He'd carried it around with him for much too long, as if it were an original sin. Here, back on this spot, he'd leave it behind.

He swam back to shore with a slow breaststroke. He dried himself in the light thrown by the oil lamp.

Then he carefully unzipped the tent.

A storm burst loose above him. The rain drummed on the canvas. Lightning lit up the top of the tent, which quickly began to show signs of leakage. He didn't give a damn. He lay on his back and deeply inhaled the burning Gauloise between his lips.

Chaos reigned outside. He lay safely inside, in the eye of the storm, presiding over the stillness there.

Master of a life that would soon be forgotten.

9

The reunion with Sekandar had been awkward. In contrast to their recent Skype session, he seemed rather withdrawn in person.

Without a word, she'd accompanied him to the fenced-off meadow beside the farmhouse, where a curious white Arabian horse trotted towards them. The mare moved her wet snout across Sekandar's cheek and then gave the boy a playful little shove, which momentarily threw him off balance. He burst out laughing and couldn't stop. That's how unexpectedly his sparkle could reappear from behind his armour of silence.

'There are times you wish you could simply forget everything you've been through,' Farah said, while trying to make eye contact with him.

He looked away and ran his hand through the horse's mane. He rested it on the spot where he could feel the animal's pulse most strongly.

'But,' she resumed, 'if everything were to disappear, you'd no longer be able to think of the old days, of the time when you were happy, when you were at home and everything was the way it's meant to be . . .'

He put his head against the mare's neck and cried without a sound.

After she'd put him to bed, she gave him Rino's drawing.

He'd looked at it closely and gave her a guarded smile. 'I can fly too, just like those stars.'

Then she'd sung him to sleep.

Now she was standing in front of the window of her apartment, looking out over Nieuwmarkt, which was illuminated with strands of small lights.

You're home, she told herself. But her heart was still wandering around Jakarta.

She thought of a song her mother had taught her, and took a deep breath. The melody came easily, having been embedded in her memory for more than thirty years. And the whispered words followed as if she'd sung them only yesterday.

'*Taqat nadara dilam be tu. Be tu chi konam?*' 'My heart is restless without you. What am I supposed to do without you? My heart tells me: "Go, go." And then it whispers: "Stay, stay."'

She ran a bath and sprinkled a few drops of almond oil into the warm water. The familiar scent had a relaxing effect. She sank down in the tub, became weightless and drifted off.

She thought of Uncle Parwaiz's words on the piece of paper she found in the bundle of love letters from Raylan to her mother.

The past sneaks up on us like a shadow.

Memories and images of all that had happened crowded her mind. They all led to a single man.

Valentin Lavrov.

For the first time in her life she'd felt the urge to kill.

The mere idea of it made her feel agitated. She got out of the bath. As she dried herself, the phone rang in the living room.

The display showed an unknown number, but she didn't hesitate to answer.

'Hello?'

'Ms Hafez?' said an unfamiliar male voice. 'My name is

Enayatullah Alirezaei. I'm the Ambassador of the Islamic Republic of Afghanistan in the Netherlands. I'm sorry to bother you at this hour, but I have important news for you. Is this a good time to talk?'

'What is it?'

'It concerns, how shall I put it, a matter that dates back more than thirty years that's never been satisfactorily resolved. I'm talking about the Saur Revolution of 1978. Prominent victims, including the then President, his entire family and ministerial team, have not been located until now . . .'

'Until now . . .' Farah echoed. She could feel her heart beating faster and faster.

The man was silent for a moment.

'A mass grave has been discovered a few kilometres outside Kabul,' he cautiously resumed. 'One of the bodies identified is that of the former President . . . Another . . .'

'You found my father . . .' she whispered.

'Indeed, Ms Hafez. Dental records have shown that the person in question must be former Interior Affairs Minister Aadel Gailani. It took some effort, but we've finally managed to find you, his daughter. On behalf of the government in Kabul I have the very sad task of inviting you to attend the official ceremony to rebury your father. It will take place in five days' time. As our guest, your travel and accommodation expenses will of course be covered by the Afghan government.'

'I . . . I wasn't expecting this,' she stammered.

'My apologies, ma'am. I've caught you off guard. Please call me back on this number once you've reached a decision.'

After hanging up the phone, she couldn't tell if the tears she brushed from her face were tears of joy or of haunting sorrow.

Acknowledgements

Humility is essential for a writer. Because writing a book isn't feasible without the support and inspiration of others.

So many people shared their knowledge and inspired me with their ideas while I was writing the second part of *The Heartland Trilogy*. I would like to extend my personal thanks to each and every one of them.

First of all, my love, my muse: my wife, Nicole, who every day again nurtures and encourages the passion I have for writing.

My agent and close friend, Marianne Schönbach, for her steadfast faith in me and the *Heartland* project.

My publisher and editor, Tom Harmsen, who, thanks to his keen analysis, lifted this second book to a higher plane. Diana Sno for her inspiring feedback and unique take on the characters. And Baukje Brugman and Leo Boekraad, who pointed me in the right direction when I embarked on this second book.

Thanks also to all the experts who assisted me in word and deed. Leo Erken, who showed me amazing corners of Moscow. Martin Kayser, who encouraged me to send Farah crawling through the ventilation system in Jakarta. Merijn van Vliet for her insights into Sekandar's world. Annet van Woerden, who introduced me to the world of VIP chauffeurs. Frank Schoute, Ronald van Wijk and Vincent Sneek for sharing the enjoyment they experience working as drivers. Vincent Schouten for the efficient and patient way he explained digital technology to me. Jeannet Noordijk and

Rene Bergwerff for their forensics expertise, and Ton de Haan for his detailed assistance with all the other facets of police work that appear in this book.

Thanks to Piet Hein Peute for the safe descent of a Boeing on a stormy night. Jan Willem Zwart for sharing his fascinating knowledge of botany with me. Julian Langitan and Shenaaz Asruf for all their insights and demonstrations of the Pencak Silat techniques described in this book. Nico Plasier and Rolf Jan Wilms for all their efforts as intermediaries. My music-loving brother Arnold for the stories behind the classical compositions mentioned in this book. Celeste Neelen Artisa for her hospitality, and Marcia Karlas for giving me a second home at Mi Casa Su Casa.

And thank you, dear reader, for taking the journey that is this book.

Walter Lucius